HEALING HANNAH'S HEART

PRESLAYSA WILLIAMS

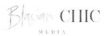

Blasian CHIC
MEDIA

ALSO BY PRESLAYSA WILLIAMS

A Lowcountry Bride

Touched by Fate (a short story)

Blasian Chic Media books may be purchased in bulk quantities for educational, business, or sales promotional use. For information, please email blasianchicmedia@gmail.com

Cover Design by Design Honey, LLC

Edited by Lindsay Clyde Flanagan

Second Edition.

ISBN 978-0-578-80180-3 (paperback)

ISBN 978-0-578-80179-7 (e-book)

This story is dedicated to my parents, Laysander and Presentacion.

Thank you for not only giving me life, but for showing me how to reach beyond the cracks in the concrete.

CHAPTER 1

*T*here was no way I was getting burned again. No. Way. Why was this man texting me—at five a.m., at any time of the day, really. We were separated. Se-pa-ra-ted.

I pulled into the parking lot of the New Brunswick Community Center and turned off the ignition. I shifted my gaze to the text alert on my cell phone.

We need to talk, Hannah. Hit me up when you get the chance.

I didn't want to have anything to do with Jake's sorry self, but whatevs. He wasn't getting no text from me. Should've learned a thing or two from his past mess-ups. Now he wanted to "talk."

I was out here trying to live my best life as an about-to-be-divorced woman. Driving to the gym at five o'clock in the morning wasn't my idea of a fun time, but at least I had some peace and quiet before I faced a day of nonstop photo shoots and go-sees and meetings with the fashion folks. That text from Jake had interrupted my moment of tranquility. He was still hanging on to me like a deer tick. Like for reals, he needed to let us go.

I already had.

I grabbed my workout bag from the trunk of the car and slung it over my shoulder, then headed to the side entrance, which led directly into the fitness area. The dawn's nascent light colored the morning sky a brilliant amber-yellow. The early morning exercisers trickled through the front doors. Like me, a lot of people were gonna work out early in the morning. I wasn't the only one out here. I fixed my eyes on the entrance to the gym, urging my body to catch up with my will that was already weakening.

On any other day, I would've slept in and relished my down comforter and empty, California-king-size bed. As much as I wanted to play the lazy bum, the workout beckoned. Getting into an exercise routine proved to be a beautifully disciplined step in my otherwise out-of-order life.

I wasn't about to allow myself no slack today because this session was very necessary. I needed to lose about five more pounds before my major photo shoot next week. In a matter of days, I'd be standing before some hot lights and posing for a feature in one of the biggest fashion magazines in the nation.

If I nailed this photo shoot, I'd make a huge step forward in the modeling world, but I was scared to death of screwing it up. I really needed to nail this assignment and secure my rising career. Answering text messages from Jake wasn't gonna help with my mission.

If I did well in this gig, it would lead to being seen by the top designers in Milan. If I nailed a runway show in Milan, I could get on Vogue. If I got in Vogue then… swoon. That was gonna be a dream come true.

I was getting ahead of myself. I had a tendency to do that when it came to my career, especially when it seemed like my peers were already miles ahead of me. For reasons.

I rubbed the back of my hand and smiled at my smooth

skin. The makeup artists said I had the most perfect skin they'd ever seen. I didn't believe them until I saw the other models' faces pre-makeup. My skin had saved me many times when a photographer had to decide between me and another model for a job, and I made sure it would always stay perfect. If I ever reached supermodel status, I wouldn't have to compete for modeling assignments anymore. I'd be hand selected because of my status. I smiled at the possibility.

Once inside the locker room, I dressed on autopilot, my thoughts fixed on that text from Jake, the man I wanted out of my life. After we had separated, I realized that I didn't miss him a bit. I was ready to give him back my wedding ring yesterday. Today I needed to stay focused. I headed to the main gym but quickly did an about-face. "Almost forgot my water bottle," I said to the crowded hallway. "Need to stay hydrated for this workout. Paco don't play."

I hooked a right down the narrow hallway leading to the women's locker area and bumped into some kid. "Hey, watch where you're going!" I said.

The teen quickly tilted his baseball hat so that it covered his face. "Sorry, ma'am".

I shrugged past him and continued to the locker to get my water bottle. After I swiped it from my gym bag, I left to meet Paco, my personal trainer.

Paco was fine, like GQ model-fine with his smooth, olive skin, dark, wavy hair, and Spanish accent.

Not that I was looking. Okay, I was looking at Paco a little bit—or a lot. Since my separation, I hadn't been looking at men at all. Paco was a different story, but I kept my emotions in check. Last thing I needed was another man to mess up my life.

Paco was fine though. "Hola, Hannah. How are you?"

"Tired and distracted but here." I pulled my hair back into a ponytail. "Ready to rock this session."

3

"Good. Today, we're gonna spend thirty minutes on the elliptical. Then we'll work on your poochy abs."

I cringed, and my self-consciousness took over. "What you mean my 'poochy abs?'" I looked down at my stomach, knowing he was right. For a model, my abs were too soft. Soft abs didn't land the swimsuit gigs.

"Don't you wanna be the best cover girl on the East Coast?" Paco reached over and grabbed a pair of five-pound weights.

"More like the best cover girl in the world." I sucked in my stomach, but that was a temporary fix.

"As do I. If you ask me, I think you're gorgeous just the way you are." He looked me up and down like I was a snack, and I wasn't having it.

"What?" I snapped.

"Nothing." His lips turned up into a half-smile. "Just appreciating your beauty… and your poochy stomach."

My spine tingled, but as I said, I wasn't interested. "I'll be at the elliptical."

He paused as if he wanted to say something else, and so I cleared my throat and said nothing. I just left.

I liked starting off with the elliptical. Gave me time to think about how exercise had become not just a way for me to get a non-poochy stomach, but also how it was a lifeline. I couldn't imagine not having a healthy outlet to process the aftereffects of Jake's betrayal. Exercise was it.

After tucking my earbuds in my ear, I started up the elliptical. Five minutes into my workout, the faint smell of smoke rose to my nostrils. Who was smoking up in here?

I looked around, but the other exercisers were doing their thing. No smoking. Whatevs. Maybe I was imagining things. I kept elliptical-ing and turned up the music on my player.

Man, it was stinking up in here. I tried ignoring it for a little while longer, but the smell was unimaginably horrible.

Smoking. I turned off the elliptical and made my way toward out the door to the locker, but the gym was locked.

"It's locked?" a gym attendee asked.

I nodded. Strange. Why would Paco lock the door?

"It can't be locked. It stinks up in here," the attendee continued.

I jimmied it, but the door wouldn't open. The room became really, really warm super fast. A flicker of light shone in my periphery.

Fire.

The word singed me and my insides tensed. No way was that a fire. Yet the heat blazed behind me and my skin tightened in a manner of seconds. I did a three-sixty and a huge orange-yellow flame was licking the treadmill that I had just been on, and the flame made a beeline for the rows and rows of exercise machines surrounding me.

What in the world? I jimmied the door again.

People screamed. Panic filled the room.

The flames spread hungry and furious, and I saw a light sheen on the ground—gasoline or oil or something.

This couldn't be happening. Not here. Not now. The warmth of the flame was like a too-hot blanket on an already warm night, smothering me and making me sweat. The flames danced around, sending me into a semi-mesmerized trance.

A flame skimmed my ankle, and I flinched. "Open this door!" I smacked the door with my palms, and my hand stung. Nothing.

My pulse skittered and my upper lip turned slick with fear. I searched for another exit. The only way out was through the window, and I was on the third floor. Dammit. It was either jump or die. I was gonna jump.

Another flame licked the edges of my shoelaces. All of my muscles seized. "Help!" I ran to the window and lifted the

5

jamb, but it was sealed shut. The smoke stung my eyes. I tried to blink away the feeling. The air grew tight, and I hacked out a breath. It stifled me even more. My vision blurred. A light-headedness overwhelmed me.

The flame singed my elbow, and I shook out of my haze. The fire was a bright reddish-orange, angry and unrelenting. A wave of terror engulfed me. I choked on it and tried to eke out a prayer for grace. No words came this time.

Another flame singed my calf. I jumped away. I pressed my body against the concrete white walls. I wasn't a praying person, but I was gonna pray now, especially since I was floating into this smoky, fiery abyss. "God, help!"

Nothing. No one was coming to help. No one. My husband filled my thoughts, along with sorrow and a tinge of regret. The last thing I saw was the thick, dark smoke curling its fingers into my hair. I stepped away, but the flame singed my midnight black ponytail and snapped my Nefertiti neck into place. Too bad I wasn't the kind of woman who kept her place.

I fought against the fire and tried to find an exit. There was no exit, at least not one I could see through the smoke. My resolve weakened. I shut my eyes against the searing flames and the terror that choked me.

I was out.

CHAPTER 2

*D*ead. I must be dead.

I *should* be dead. A weight pressed against my skin, restraining me, strangling me. Needles pricked me into a million little pieces. I inhaled the scent of my fried flesh and choked. Yeah, I should be dead. *Humph*.

The taste of gray-black smoke from that fire scraped down my windpipe and ballooned inside my scorched lungs. I couldn't breathe. Not enough air. I swallowed, and the ashen taste lingered and mixed with the bile in my inflamed throat.

That weight tightened and I panicked. I should've never tried to rebel against the fire to escape the gym. I should've stayed put.

Rebellion had its price. Today's price made me hot and blistering all over. Even now, the more I moved around, the more I hurt. That was too high of a price.

I want... I want... I want...

Escape.

My pain-buzz tapered off and my surroundings came into clearer focus. A sharp pain sizzled my skin from top to

7

bottom. I bore down against it. Shuffling feet, beeping, and more shuffling sounds filled my eardrums.

"Non-rebreather mask for the victim?" a soft-pitched voice asked.

"Right here, nurse," came a deeper-sounding reply.

Someone placed something stretchy and tight around my head. I didn't need any more tight. My skin was already overheated. It was like plastic wrap on the verge of melting.

"Give her humidified high oxygen flow at fifteen liters. One hundred percent."

"On it."

Cool air filled the mask and touched my nose and mouth. I inhaled and my lungs loosened, my airways opened. No more smoky smells. No more suffocating. No more strangling. I opened my singed lashes. Fuzzy figures in light blue scrubs who donned surgical masks moved around me swiftly. Hospital people.

"Patient is awake."

"I'll get Dr. Hutchinson." Footsteps shuffled.

"Good thing we gave her the catheter when she was unconscious. Must've not felt a thing. The other victims won't be so fortunate."

"I'll get an IV and a bag of L.R.," a baritone voice called.

"Get two large-bore IVs. And two bags of L.R. Standard for all burn victims."

I tried rubbing my stinging eyes, but my hands were weighed down by bricks. I blinked, and a nurse in teddy bear scrubs stood over me. She was mahogany and round. Soft.

"Check morphine levels. She'll need two milligrams every three minutes. Titrate to effect."

There was a grandmotherly note in her voice, all honey-coated and feminine and warm. Not clinical. My jaw relaxed, and I exhaled. My breath steamed up the plastic mask.

"You're doing well, Hannah Hart." She stretched out a

thin tube. "You're alive and almost kicking. Thank the good Lord. You're very lucky."

"Lucky 'bout what?" My voice muffled through the mask.

"What'd you say, hon?" She leaned close, and the cap on her head grazed my cheek.

My tongue was lead and iron, all mixed into one. "Lucky 'bout what?"

"First, you have a urinary catheter. Didn't feel that. You may need a nasogastric tube to make sure your stomach isn't dilating. You'll feel that." The nurse placed her hand over mine. "Then I'll do a comprehensive observation. You'll be okay. You're here. It may be that not everyone will survive that terrible, terrible fire."

Sadness mingled with relief followed by more sadness settled within. So, my instincts were right about death. I simply missed the Upper Room. Or maybe not so simply missed it. "I remember exercising, and then all of a sudden there were flames. How'd the fire start?"

"We don't know. For now, focus on getting better." She stretched out the long tube and clucked her teeth like I was some misguided school kid. "Everyone here'll take good care of you."

I didn't need the condescending attitude. What I needed was someone to tell me what was going on. Now. Wasn't gonna be stuck in a nasty hospital. I had a photo shoot on Monday. I had to get outta there.

I pushed myself upright and a thousand knives stabbed my skin. "Ack!"

"Take it easy, Ms. Hart. Those bandages are wrapped mighty tight. The doctor ain't gonna let you go nowhere."

She sounded like Jake—that cheating, soon-to-be ex-husband. He loved smothering me in blankety, suffocating restrictions. Now that I was alive, I wasn't feeling regret about him anymore. We were good as we were—separated.

"Whaddya mean I can't go anywhere?" My breath steamed through the oxygen mask. "I can go anywhere I please."

"Not in this condition. We're keeping you under strict observation. You have a long road ahead."

Someone else in blue scrubs stood over me, peered at me like I was a lab specimen. "Patient anxious?" he asked the nurse.

"Yes. It'll be all right. It gets like this." The nurse's round, liquid pupils cornered me. A prison guard.

Another blue-scrubby person returned with the IVs. "Ready to begin circulation."

"We'll need intravenous access." The nurse rolled up my sleeves. "This may pinch a bit, hon. Won't feel too good on top of what you feel now, but it'll go away."

The other person attached the tube to the IV bag, and my skin prickled. I bit my lip. "Nurse?"

The lady leaned close again.

"You don't understand," I said. "I can't be stuck here. I've got a photo shoot to—"

"Gal, you could've died. A photo shoot is the least of your worries."

I grunted and shifted my weight, a shoddy attempt to loosen the bandages, but they stuck to me like glue. They could've wrapped my bones and marrow too.

"There are victims still back at the community center. Some of the staff members working the early shift. They should be transported here shortly," she said.

Was Paco still there? Worry set in. "Where's Paco?"

"Who?"

"Paco. He was my personal trainer. Is he all right?"

The nurse was silent. "We don't know yet. Best thing to do is heal," she continued.

"I don't have time to heal. You don't understand. I… " I stopped. Why'd I have to sound so weak?

"You what?" She curled her fingers into a soft fist and placed it on her hip.

"Nothing." My voice broke.

"I know, honey." The nurse released her fist and wrapped a Velcro blood pressure strap around my arm. "I know."

Her eyes. They were soul-seeing eyes. I preferred that folks were blind to my pain. I preferred blindness myself, and so I focused on the popcorn ceiling, defeated. A shock of my flesh peeked out from underneath the white blanket. Charred and blistering flesh. Yellow-white and reddened. Fire-scarred.

Soul-scarred.

A memory bubbled to the surface. Metallic smoke filtered through my lungs. I choked and swallowed back the strangling sensation, but more images barreled through: flames, heat.

The heat.

The fire had singed the edges of my curls and threatened to touch my scalp. I had swatted at the flame and my hand crisped. The flesh smell had wrapped around me tighter than those bandages. My vision turned watery and blurry.

The nurse reached for a Kleenex on my bedside table and dabbed my cheek.

Even my teeth burned. "I hurt."

"I can't imagine. You're safe now. I'm disappointed that it's all over the news. Could've given you all privacy for at least a day."

My head snapped at her casual little commentary. "The news?"

"Yep." The nurse swiped away another tear.

What if Greta found out? She'd scratch me off the

modeling agency's roster in a minute. "I can't have people knowing I was in a fire."

"Why?"

Long story. "It's complicated."

"Ain't it always?" The nurse's mouth curved upward. "That's the way life goes sometimes. Complicated. The hospital staff found your ID in your back pocket, but we didn't see any emergency contacts. Is there anyone you'd like us to call? Someone you'd like to have here with you? Family?"

Jake? Or my controlling mama? "No."

Silence lingered for one minute. Then two minutes. Three minutes. She didn't believe me, and I didn't care.

"Let us know if you have family," she said. "You don't want to be alone."

"More people in my life means more drama. I've had my fill of surprises for the day… or the decade."

She released a belly-warming laugh and checked the monitor. "Your pulse is stable."

"So, I'm going to be okay?"

"Can't say for certain—depends on you doing what the doctor orders." She scribbled something on the clipboard. "Anything else I can get for you before I make my rounds?"

"Yes, when will the doctor arrive?"

"Someone left to get her, but Dr. Hutchinson must be busy assessing the other fire victims. She did your initial assessment while you were unconscious." The nurse cocked her head to the side, perhaps an attempt to make me comfortable with that sorry answer. "Lots of victims came in from the community center. Like I said, I don't know if your trainer was one of them. There was a group of elderly women who exercised early in the morning over there too."

How horrible. "I need to get out of here."

"Patience. We'll take care of you now. Rest assured the

doctor will return." She carefully unwrapped the bandage around my forearm and cool air hit the area. I winced.

"Sorry 'bout that cold air." She gestured to one of the men in scrubs. "What's the temperature in here? It's too cold."

"Warm and ambient temps, ma'am," a voice said. "We'll make it warmer."

"Yes, please. Burns and cold air don't mix." She wrapped my body in the loose blankets. "Here you go, darling. These are fresh from the hospital laundry. Nice and warm."

"When will the doctor release me?"

"Release? Oh hon, not anytime soon. Dr. Hutchinson has to do more observations. We won't know the full effect the fire had on your system right away. You may be transported to the burn unit based on her assessment."

"Burn unit. It can't be that serious."

"Like I said. Best be thankful." The nurse adjusted my IV.

I was silent. In a way, I should be thankful, but I also wanted out of here. I had my photo shoot. "How long do people stay in a burn unit?"

"Can't tell. Depends on the severity." She set a clean towel next to my bed. "Sometimes we don't know the severity until days afterward. Don't know all the answers."

Be calm. Be calm. Not like I can go anywhere anyways. "You really don't know?"

"No, ma'am. I'm not the doctor, but even the doctor will have to see how you develop."

"That's not good enough. I need answers!" My voice scratched against my vocal cords and shrilled through my eardrums.

"You know better than to yell at the people taking care of you." The nurse placed more warm blankets on my legs and stomach. "All you need to do is focus on recovering."

My insides hollowed. She didn't understand. She couldn't understand. I was approaching my retirement years in modeling. At thirty-seven years old, I couldn't afford to skip modeling assignments. I needed every single dollar, especially now that I was separated from Jake. Modeling was my only option.

Greta had been hinting that I "transition" to something else, but to what? Modeling was the only thing… the only…

Stop it, Hannah. I was still a model. I would be in front of a camera in no time. This fire was a minor incident. That was all. "You said my doctor's name is Dr. Hutchinson?"

"That's right." She squinted at the heart rate monitor. "You're still stable."

Agitation needled and pricked. All my worries bubbled to the surface. "I'm far from stable. I. Have. To. Work. On. Monday."

"We can call your employer. Tell 'em what happened. They'd understand."

"Doesn't work that way," I said. "I have to get out of here. I'm already being offered fewer modeling assignments… I'm afraid… "

"'Fraid of what?"

My breath collapsed. "That I'm not wanted anymore."

"Ooh, girl. If that makes you afraid, then you gotta whole lotta living to do."

That was the problem. Didn't feel like living. Not like that. "I need to talk to Dr. Hutchinson." I exhaled. "I need to know when I will be released. A doctor's the only one with the authority to give me this answer."

The muscle in the nurse's jawline pulsed. Okay, what I said was a tad snarky, but why make this so hard? Still, I shouldn't have said that. Now I had to worry about her poisoning my IV while I was asleep.

"You right. I'm only the nurse. I can't make a diagnosis or decide on your treatment. You'll wait on the doctor for all that. But you're alive. Alive is good."

No, alive was hard. Especially since I was lying here help-less. Maybe if I made a wish, all this would disappear: the career worries, the Jake worries, the fire worries. Maybe if I made a wish, I could take all the stress, crumple it into a tiny little ball, and light a match.

Okay, that was a bad analogy. Best to keep things to wishes. Not matches.

I squeezed my eyes shut and wished. Wished all would be well. That nothing would've changed. I wanted to still be the "It Girl" everyone gawked at whenever I pounded the pave-ment or took a corner table at my fave coffee shop. I wanted to still be the woman Jake gazed at with honey love in his eyes, even if he wasn't going to be my husband anymore. I wanted to still be everyone's darling. I wanted to be loved.

"Why are you squeezing your eyes? You in pain?"

I opened my eyes. Still bandaged and stuck. *Blech.* "No reason."

She fished her cell from the front pocket of her faded scrubs and checked the time. "You want to sit upright?"

"My skin feels tight. It's like I'm trapped. I don't think I can."

"Course you can. I'll help you." The nurse rearranged my sheets. She tapped a button near my bedrail, and the bed whirred upright, taking me with it. It was like one of those slow-moving kiddie rides at a carnival—except I was in an emergency room.

"There you go." She lowered the bed rails and adjusted the over-the-bed table pushing up against my tummy. "You're set for success."

"Not quite."

She chuckled. "Almost set up for success then. Here's two remotes. One for the TV and one for the table." She placed them both in front of me. "Gonna make my rounds."

"Wait a sec… do you have a mirror?"

"You want a mirror?"

The question hovered, made me second-guess myself. I nodded, afraid if I spoke, I'd renege. "Yes."

"Uh… okay. What you see may surprise you. Lots of red, blistering skin. Be prepared." The nurse opened all the drawers, searched beneath the bedside table.

She was stalling. My gut told me so.

"Aah, here you go. Knew we had 'em here somewhere." She hesitated a millisecond before placing the mirror in my palm. "When you look at yourself, be kind."

She made it sound like I was about to go in for a root canal with no anesthesia. After she left, I rotated my wrist against the bandages, flipped over the mirror, and caught a glimpse. The sight scalded my vision.

My gosh. I was so ugly. My entire head was bandaged except for a snatch of singed hair that stuck out next to my left ear. From the looks of it, my hair resembled frizzed-out electrical wires. Wonderful.

My gaze blurred but nothing soothed the scorching inside. My skin was raw and red. No more golden-brown. The color of heaven's dusk, they used to say.

Used to say. My future was over. I was done. Done and helpless. Couldn't get an answer. Couldn't get my freedom. Couldn't get nothing but a bunch of scalding burns and potential unemployment.

A snatch of my hot skin peeked from underneath the bandage around my neck.

Definite unemployment.

CHAPTER 3

JAKE

*H*annah kicked me out for wanting to take care of Tim, my son.

Yeah, I know. I had a one-night stand during our marriage. That one-night stand created my only child. I'd admitted it to Hannah three years after the fact, back when she was dealing with even more issues. After my admission, I'd ended all contact with Tim and his mother, Melinda. Hannah needed my full attention, and my relationship with her had been crumbling.

I'd have done anything to save our marriage, but no contact with Melinda and Tim was only a bandage to the problem. When Melinda went into drug rehab this past summer, I did what I had to. I agreed to take Tim in—the first time in eleven years when I'd ever had contact with him. So Hannah kicked me out for it.

I looked at my son, hunched over, wearing a black hoodie, black jeans, and white sneakers. He shifted in the seat next to mine in Principal Grant's office. His high-top fade sported the letter *Z* on the side of his head. I didn't understand the whole *Z* thing. He went by the last name Ramirez. Tim didn't even have my last name. If only I could remove the years, the regrets. My mistakes.

"Tim was fighting during gym class." Principal Grant glanced at my son like he was a sack of trash waiting for the town dump. "Aggression is a serious issue here at Rockview High. We don't take it lightly. I'm putting your son on a nine-day, out-of-school suspension starting on Monday."

My jaw tightened. "Nine-day suspension? He'll miss almost two weeks of school."

"Tim has the right to receive educational services during his suspension. He can communicate with his teachers via email and send them his assignments for grading."

I took in the principal's cluttered office: stacks of papers scattered across what would've been a large desk; diplomas and degrees and certificates lined the four walls, some of them tilted a hair too crooked; yellowed staff pictures from the eighties, old and out of touch.

The muffled sound of the school bell rang, and the sudden chatter of students outside the doorway broke my focus. Distractions or not, I'd convince this man not to suspend my son. Tim deserved a fresh start. It was my fault he'd had a bad one.

If I'd been around earlier, Tim wouldn't have gotten into this mess at school. I should've been in his life earlier. I should've been a father. "It was his first altercation," I said. "Give him some leeway."

"Leeway? We have no tolerance for bullies."

"He's not a bully." My voice dialed up two notches, ready for a fight.

"You don't call giving a kid a nosebleed a bully?"

My son could've been defending himself, but the principal's challenge pounded me to a pulp. I forced a nod, fully aware that arguing would get me nowhere.

"Tim's grades are declining. He's habitually skipping classes. And he doesn't seem to give a... look here."

Grant—the man didn't deserve the title of principal—tilted his computer screen and double-clicked a folder on the desktop. "Here are the incidents. They go back to junior high."

I focused on the scribbled-up desk calendar before me. Not on the computer screen. Not on Tim's failures. At my failures.

"They're all listed here, Jake." The man tried to catch my gaze. I wasn't having it.

"I received your email describing today's incident." I shifted my line of sight to just above Grant's balding, greasy head. "What else is there to see?"

"The extent of his mess-ups. It's hardwired into the kid."

Hardwired into the kid? If I wasn't civil, I might've punched him myself. "There's no need to insult my son. Stick to the facts."

"The facts are that Tim has a long pattern of behavior problems. The facts are that I'll recommend a formal hearing with the school board for possible long-term suspension, especially since the other kid's parents are filing criminal assault charges."

"What?"

"The other student has that right," Principal Grant continued. "Tim will have an assault case and a possible long-term suspension on his hands, but that depends on the results of the school board's formal hearing."

"This is a mess."

"This is standard school policy. If Tim gets a long-term suspension, he's at risk for no longer receiving public education services, but the school board makes that decision. I'm only making the recommendation."

"Why are you making that recommendation? We can solve things at this level. No need to take it higher."

"Your son's record speaks for itself, Jake. Don't you want to see him get off this train wreck waiting to happen? It's what any reasonable parent would want for their child."

I bristled. What kind of passive-aggressive guilt trip was he trying to pull me into? I could show him unreasonable. My fist on his face would be unreasonable. I forced myself to calm down.

Principal Grant pointed to the computer screen. "If you were reasonable, you'd look at his record."

Oh yeah, he was asking for a fresh one. "Where's the other student who was in the fight? Why's Tim getting nailed to the cross?"

"The other student is nursing a black eye, and he's getting a nine-day suspension too since there's no telling who started the fight."

"But the kid's parents are filing criminal charges against my son. The nerve." I faced Tim. "Who started the fight?"

"The other kid did." Tim shoved his hands in the pockets of his hoodie. "I wasn't gonna be a chump and let him talk trash."

I knew my son wouldn't have started a fight.

"The other child's parents should be here, Mr. Grant. I'm here."

"They requested a separate meeting with me." Grant cracked his beefy knuckles. "I don't blame them."

This man was biased beyond belief. "Don't blame them? What are you trying to say?"

"I don't have to say a thing. Tim created his own problems."

I could've been there to stop them. The thought pressed my conscience. Tim had caused a nose bleed. Tim had bad grades. Tim had been truant. One talk with this principal wasn't going to erase my son's past—or my parenting failures. "Give him another chance."

I wanted another chance too, a chance to do right by my son. I held my breath and hoped.

"We've given your son a fourth and a fifth chance." He pointed to that computer monitor again. "This year alone, he's been written up twenty-four times. We'd tried contacting his mother, but that got us nowhere."

Melinda was probably too hooked on heroin to care about Tim's schooling, and I hadn't been in his life to fill in the gaps or get familiar with his issues. Despite my marriage struggles, I should've never cut Tim out of my world. Look at where it had gotten my son.

"I could've gotten Tim for vandalizing school property with graffiti before this incident," Grant continued. "Should've done so. It would've saved a kid a nosebleed."

I clenched my fist and tried to stay calm. This man was trying to crucify my son. "Tim needs support, not more reprimands. Don't do it."

"I will. The district policy is unequivocal here. Tim's behavior gives me no choice." He handed me a pink slip. "Tim's suspension is effective Monday and it'll go on his record. I'm also including the vandalism incident with my recommendation to the school board. They have the authority to summon law enforcement, and this will be more than enough reason for them to do so. Good luck with that one."

An invisible punch struck my gut. "You're out to ruin his life."

"I'm out to protect my students' safety and welfare. Hopefully, these blights on his record won't hinder his chances at college. I have a funny feeling they will."

I shot out of the chair and it squeaked behind me. "You trying to limit my son? On purpose?"

21

"I didn't punch the kid in the nose. Tim did."

Tim's cheek twitched ever so slightly, like a tick-tick-ticking bomb.

"This is some B.S. Pure B.S." I ground my teeth together.

Grant tossed his hands up as if to say *I-told-you-so. Your son's a screw-up.*

We were going nowhere fast. Better try another tactic. "Do you have anything else to say in your defense, Tim?"

His sledgehammer expression told me I wouldn't like his answer.

"Like I said earlier," Grant went on. "Tim's still responsible for his school work while on suspension. Is he capable of working independently? Of concentrating on one thing for extended periods of time?"

My skin glazed and the muscles around my neck spasmed. What was this? Veiled racism? The nerve of this guy.

"Anyway." Grant's forearm dropped to a stack of papers on his left, and a shadow crossed his stubbled cheek. "He needs to stay out of trouble. His grades are atrocious, especially algebra. Perhaps this time off will give him a chance to actually do school work instead of causing everyone trouble."

"Whatever, man. You gonna fail me no matter how hard I try. Can't do anything right with you people," Tim said, his voice stripped of fight.

"Not true. Get rid of the bad attitude." Grant's lips thinned. "This is your chance to be redeemed."

Redeemed. Time was short. In four years, Tim would be eighteen. Four years. Four years to get him on track. I may not get four years.

His mother could get out of rehab and petition the court to receive custody of her son—of my son. She'd be justified since I hadn't exactly been Father of The Year.

Could I be redeemed? I'd try. "We'll get on it," I said. "Ain't that right, Tim?"

No answer. Yep, my own son couldn't stand me. Though I guess who could blame him? I'd done nothing but abandon him and now I was trying to swoop in and pretend like what I'd done hadn't mattered so much? "I'll even find Tim some work," I added. "He needs a part-time job to keep him busy."

"You will? This is Tim's battle, not yours. Your son needs to show some initiative. You won't be around forever."

"I haven't been around… ever. Let's leave the 'for' part out of this. Nothing will stop me from helping my son. Not your vandalism report. Not your unwillingness to help. Not your annoying vendetta."

Grant sat taller and he had a presence now. A spark of barely concealed anger. If we were in a boxing ring, he'd throw some heavy blows. Then he'd attempt the brutal: the beat-you-till-you're-unconscious, banged up, and bloody kind of brutal.

Yet it'd only be an attempt. I was a fighter too. "Let's go, Tim." I extended my hand to Grant, the embittered school principal. His handshake was a touch too hard, but I squeezed back, unflinching. I left his office with my son, frustrated with the strength of Grant's grip—and his power over Tim's future.

We made a beeline to my gray pickup. Once inside, I started the ignition, blasted the air conditioner. "You said the other kid was talking trash. What'd he say?"

Tim's shoulders sagged and his mouth was like blood, angry and red. "Don't matter what he said."

I was getting nowhere with him. This was beyond frustrating. "We have a lot of work to do, you and I."

"I don't prove myself to jerks like that principal," Tim said.

"You will if those jerks decide whether you'll graduate

from high school." I locked the doors. "Think of your future, Tim."

"Why? You never did."

My skin prickled and my fingers went dead cold. It wasn't true though I couldn't say he was exactly wrong either. "I always cared," I said. I left the second half unsaid—I always cared, I just cared more about Hannah, which seemed pointless given how my marriage turned out.

"Whatever." Tim scratched his high-top fade, leaving the dark strands spiky on one end.

Fine. Don't talk to me then. I turned on the radio and the local news blared through my speakers. Not the most mature response on my part, maybe, but I needed distraction. And yeah, maybe I wanted to use something besides words to show Tim how frustrated I was feeling.

"A fire broke out at New Brunswick Community Center today. Most of the building is burned to the ground. Many are now at Robert Wood Johnson Hospital recovering from burns, at least three in critical condition."

"My goodness." I slid on my shades. "That's terrible. Good thing no one died." I glanced at Tim. "See? Things could be worse. You could be in the hospital instead of stuck at home with your lame Pop."

Tim looked away.

Poor kid. "I know this suspension is a lot to take in." I gestured to the radio. "I guess I shouldn't make light, but our problems… your problems… aren't as bad as other people's. I mean, being suspended is bad and all. Make no mistake about it."

More quiet. A stranger quiet. I didn't like this quiet. "You okay, man?"

Nothing.

Tim's chin came down, his cheeks puffed slightly. Was he crying? I didn't know what to say, what would make him feel

better. Wasn't even sure I wanted him to feel better. All I
knew was that I wanted to cry too. Cry for my son's future.
Cry that I could've helped him earlier. I could've shown him
that life wasn't about fighting and failing. I could've shown
him he didn't have to be a statistic, another Black boy who
went down the wrong path, but why would he listen to me? I
was the stranger stepping into his life to play Daddy. "We'll
get through this together," I added.

"Just leave me alone," Tim said.

I drove in silence. As soon as I pulled into the driveway
and turned off the ignition, Tim hopped out of the car and
rushed inside. My inhale caught in my throat, didn't make it
down my lungs. I'd do everything to make people see he was
a good kid: help him with homework, get him a job, whatever it took. I plunked my head against the steering wheel.

After an eternity, I walked across my crooked driveway,
still in a helpless haze. I opened the mailbox. Bills. Junk mail.
More junk mail. A cream envelope from The Law Office of
Kimball, Marks, and Graham.

What'd I do?

I tore the envelope open, because hey, why postpone
more bad news on an already awful day? I skimmed the
letter.

An ache settled in my bones. The pressure rose from my
marrow and pushed back down with a lead weight. My
knees buckled.

Hannah wanted a legal separation.

I'd been thinking she just needed a little time to get used
to the idea of Tim being in my life—our lives—and that she'd
come around. I'd been thinking that any day now, she'd be
calling, saying she missed me—missed us. Yeah, I'd resented
her years ago for suggesting I stay away from Tim when I'd
first admitted to the one-night stand.

I told Hannah that the one-night stand was out of anger

and frustration, a stupid, emotional decision. I promised Hannah that I wouldn't have another one-night stand, and I kept my promise to my wife.

But a legal separation? I wasn't expecting this one.

The letter hung from my fingertips, and the cold breeze rustled and curled its corners. I held my breath against the regret knocking in my chest. Why couldn't I get anything right?

I squelched the last question and shoved it into a dark closet. Somehow, I'd have to make this right. I'd have to make everything right.

CHAPTER 4

HANNAH

*I*t felt like a thousand years had passed with all the
hours I waited. I mean, really. I could've turned to
fried toast, all burned up and overly well-done.

Scratch that. I was fried toast and beyond well-done, but I
could've had an acute infection. An infection that seeped past
my skin, my blood, my organs, and attacked all my secrets,
those invisible black strings that triple-knotted themselves
around my heart and punctured holes with bulldog teeth.

What would all these fancy doctors in this fancy hospital
do with my knotted-up holey heart? Nothing.

Good thing I had a kryptonite heart that powered
through pain 'cuz no one else would do it for me. I'd learned
that long, long ago when I was a wee little one and Lola, my
grandma, had died on my watch. I quickly learned that no
one—*no one*—in the world would ever, ever care about me
like Lola had. No one. I'd have to depend on my self-reliance
to get through this too.

A tiny woman in a knee-length white lab coat and black
pants stepped into my room. A surgical mask was tied

loosely around her neck. She must've been about a decade older than me.

Scratch that. *I* must've looked a decade older than her with my burned body and all. Her lapel read Dr. Hutchinson. Goody, goody. I needed to get discharged so I could work again—okay, so I could *try* to work again. The way the hospital staff was talking, I was a lost cause.

Nope. I wasn't a lost cause. If I left the hospital, I could take care of myself and heal on my own.

Dr. Hutchinson was my golden ticket. So far, no one had given me a golden ticket. All I'd gotten was a trauma-inducing mirror (which I'd requested, but still) and some bandages. I was sick of being awakened and poked and prodded by nurses every few hours. I wanted to go home and process this alone. To go home, I had to show Dr. Hutchinson that I was capable.

"When will I be discharged?" I asked.

"Anxious, are we?"

"Of course, I'm anxious. They said you checked me out earlier today, but I was unconscious. I feel right as rain and ready to leave."

(Side note: I really felt like someone tossed me in the dryer and pushed the "tumble dry on high heat" button, but that was beside the point. I wasn't going to tell the doctor that.)

She gave me one of those clinical, I-have-an-M.D.-behind-my-name-and-you-don't stares. My calves cramped but trying to flex my feet to stretch them out wasn't happening. Not with those mummy wrappings.

"We took some X-rays. No broken bones or major brain damage or concussions. Your injuries are at the epidermal level. Second-degree burns."

Dr. Hutchinson let those three words hang around like an unwelcome spritz of Lysol in an overly disinfected room. I wanted to open a window, let some fresh air and better news into my room, but I was bedridden.

"You're lucky," she added. "Could've been third-degree burns. Could've been worse."

I knew this already. I could've died, but would death have been worse?

My question swirled up into the air with the rest of her words, annoying me.

"I saw my skin earlier today." I added a smile to my statement, but that smile was hard-won because of the burns. It made my teeth hurt so I stopped. "Will I look like this forever?"

She shifted and brushed her bangs away from her eyes as if that would give her more time to respond.

"Don't try protecting me with a professional answer. I need the truth." I tried sounding confident, but my syllables were all shaky.

"The burns will leave their mark." The light hit her skin just so. Ivory concealer covered her gray-rimmed eyelids. "Given that it's only your first day here, we don't know the full effects of the fire. There's a strong chance smoke inhalation could lead to lung damage. I haven't seen any signs of that yet, which is why you've only had a rebreather mask, but now I'm getting you a nasogastric tube to keep your air passages open."

"What's that?"

"A tube that goes through your nasal passages and down your esophagus."

Sounded like a death sentence. "Can I talk with that thing?"

"You'll speak with some discomfort. I'll have you start off wearing it in small doses so you'll get used to it."

All my plans for go-sees and photo shoots flushed down the toilet. "I won't be discharged soon?"

"No. In fact, we're transferring you to the burn unit first thing in the morning. The specialists there will get you through all phases of recovery."

"The burn unit?" The words stuttered out my mouth.

"Yes. That's what you need. After we've staved off the possibility of infection and lung damage, we'll start restoration. That'll involve surgery. That'll involve skin grafting. That'll involve a lot."

"Skin grafting? Isn't that where you take skin from one part of my body and put it on another?" I asked.

"Correct."

"If I'm burned all over, where will you take this from?"

Dr. Hutchinson tapped her back. "Your back. Part of your forearms."

"Then I'll be normal?"

"Skin grafting won't cover everything, unfortunately."

The air ripped out of me. "I'll look like a diced Christmas ham… forever."

"You won't. Your burns aren't as deep as they could've been." She tilted her head to the side. "You can be fixed."

My shoulders rounded, a reflex response to her comment. "Fixed? You make it sound like I'm a stray animal."

"I apologize. Didn't mean it to come across that way. We'll want to get the surgery scheduled soon."

"How soon?" I glanced down at the white blankets covering my burned, broken body.

"After the blistering and sores are healed. With second-degree burns, that could be a while. I'd give three weeks as your earliest discharge date. Depends on how you heal."

"Three weeks? I can't stay here for three whole weeks! I don't know if the insurance will fully cover the medical bill. And I have a life. Who's going to check on my house? Pay my bills? Three weeks is too long."

"That's only my earliest estimate of when your hospital

stay will end. You'll also have to return for follow-up treatment and recovery, and that could take a long time. Even when you're discharged from here, it won't be over. You have a long road ahead. We'll be monitoring you, and I can give a better estimate as time goes on."

My body went numb. "As time goes on? You're suggesting a complete life change."

She stopped fiddling with the medical chart and gave me an empathetic gaze. "The process takes time, Hannah, especially with the extent of your burns. We've already removed some of the superficial skin to prevent major infection and lessen the extent of your future scars."

Scars. Those were inevitable, and they'd inevitably impede my ability to ever pose in front of a camera again.

"This is a lot to digest," she said. "We'll take it one day at a time. No need to think ahead."

"I have to think ahead. Someone needs to handle my affairs."

"If you give the staff your family's contact information they can—" Dr. Hutchinson reached for a prescription pad as if she might take dictation from me, write down whatever number I said to call.

"Don't wanna contact my family!"

Okay, okay I was being a tad unreasonable, but staying in the hospital for so long was downright ridiculous. Was there something else that could go numb besides my whole body? 'Cuz right now I was about to take my mummified body and leap off a cliff. "How long will it take till I'm fully recovered?"

"Four months at the earliest for a full recovery."

Three weeks at the earliest. Four months at the earliest. What else was "at the earliest?" My jaw clenched as I tried to control my panic. The fashion industry was very fickle. Everything revolved around the latest new trend and the hottest new model. "I'll be a has-been in four months."

"I'm sorry." Dr. Hutchinson's expression switched from professional to pitiful.

That's what I was: pitiful.

"My profession is dependent on perfection. Physical perfection." Like that time when I lost a major runway gig because I'd gained ten pounds, and I didn't quite fit into the designer's clothes.

"We need to give your body time to heal. That's more important than perfection. Then you can check into ways to work with your new appearance. That'll be toward the end of your recovery process as you transition to fully living with scars."

I wanted to squeeze my hands into fists and punch something. Living with scars? I wasn't gonna live with no scars. My situation was beyond complicated. It was crazy.

My appearance wasn't some afterthought. It wasn't some appetizer or side dish. It was the main course. Steak and potatoes, baby.

"Look, Dr. Hutchinson," I said, sitting up as best I could and leveling a gaze at her. "Modeling's my only way of life. I have no other skills. I dropped out of college because… " I wouldn't tell her the real reason. "Because my modeling career was taking off, and I wanted to make the most of modeling before I got too old. Never thought I'd have to worry about being too burned."

The thought hung heavy as a weighted noose. I blew out a breath and inhaled the faint smell of incinerated expectations.

Dr. Hutchinson dropped her gaze, looked at her clipboard. She went too long without speaking, so I prodded her. "Modeling is my only way of life."

Finally, she looked up. Her lips pressed together like she didn't want to let the words out that she was about to say.

"I'm sorry, Hannah, but modeling… may not be in your future for a while."

I pushed back the urge to ugly-cry—to smother my body in grief and send myself spinning. As soon as I'd woken in the hospital, as soon as the memory of the fire came raging over me, I'd known this fire would send my career to the edge. But hearing Dr. Hutchinson made it all too official. Stupid doctors and their fancy-pants knowledge. "Don't say that. I need my job."

"You need to get better first."

Her face looked kind. Her eyes looked kind. Even her clipboard looked kind, but I wasn't buying her brand of kind. I wanted the drive-thru window type, not the slow cooker type. I wanted a speedy release from this hospital. I tried turning away, but I couldn't even do that. Blasted bandages.

"I've seen your pictures in a magazine," she continued. "You're a beautiful woman."

She might as well have doused me with gasoline and lit a match. Could she make me feel any worse?

"You are," the doctor continued.

Her comment made a part of me grow small and covered up and hopeless. I tried swallowing, but my throat muscles weren't working properly. I wasn't working properly. Not anymore.

The self-loathing I'd carried when Lola died way back when, the self-loathing when I'd tried to be accepted by my peers as a teenager, the self-loathing I'd smothered with praise and model-level perfections, spilled. Spilled all over my bed. Too messy to mop up. "Will all this medical stuff that's gonna take the next decade of my life to get through—will it be covered by my insurance?"

"Your insurance company should cover your hospital stay and care one hundred percent. I'd double check, however. You never know if their policies change."

Call the health insurance company. I pressed the power button on my mental calculator. Hopefully, they'd cover me one hundred percent. Surgeries. Hospital stays. Medications. That'd all be in the hundreds of thousands. The care I'd already received was probably getting up there already.

I'd already paid the lawyer to send those separation papers to Jake. That cost eight hundred bucks. If—no, *when*—I got a divorce, I'd have to pay more money. Another grand?

I'd dipped into my savings to get the attorney in the first place and now, I had two months of savings left. Except now, instead of a busy career, I was looking at at least four months of recovery, and with no modeling… How could I earn enough money to support myself, to pay my regular bills, not to mention my medical ones, if the insurance company decided not to pay up?

The doctor interrupted my cracked-out calculations.

"Don't do anything strenuous during this recovery period. And start thinking about assistance for when you are released."

When I was released in eight thousand years.

Dr. Hutchinson leaned forward and caught my eye. "You have any family nearby?"

Anxiety welled up within me. Anxiety with a pinch of terror. Okay—it was a gallon of terror. The family question —again. My mother and Jake would block all my attempts at independence once they found out. "Not any family I want to talk to."

"You'll need someone to assist you when you transition to life at home. We can't release you until there's someone willing to take on this role. We'll also have to give that person basic knowledge of changing your bandages, cleansing your wounds. Things of that nature."

"I'm not helpless." I touched the bandage wrapped around my hand.

"Never said you were. But you're vulnerable."

"Not vulnerable either." I glanced at the bandage. "Guess what I was doing before this fire?"

Dr. Hutchinson's face went blank.

"Training to run a full marathon and modeling full time."

Dr. Hutchinson's face remained blank.

I continued, "Why should I slow down because of a freak fire? Not fair."

"I know. But you'll live on."

If I slowed down, I'd never gain momentum again. "How?"

She didn't answer.

Why'd I think a medical doctor could solve my emotional problems? My tears made blinking hard. My cheeks turned wet too. Could one thing be made easy for me today?

"The nurse should be changing your bandages within the hour. You'll get through this," she continued. "I'm going to give you the contact information of a support group for burn victims. You should consider attending. They meet here once a week. It's free of charge, and you can continue with the group even after you're discharged from the hospital. It's not the end of the world. Promise."

She didn't have to live with the repercussions of this event. Dr. Hutchinson left and the door clicked behind her.

This sucked cotton balls. I had stuff to do like check and make sure those separation papers were served to Jake. Perhaps the hospital staff could call the lawyer's office for me. I scrunched up my face and reached for the call button, but my skin hurt.

"Come on, Hannah. You can do this." I lifted my left arm again, and then Negative Nelly popped in my head: *Are you suuure you can do that? Like are you really suuure?*

"Shut up." I slowly lifted my left arm, careful not rip

anything off, but that alone was hard. Way, way hard. Was I really this helpless now?

Yes.

After a couple more tries, I pressed the call button on the bed rail. Got it! Success. Someone out there could get the phone sitting on the other side of the room and help me out or something.

Seconds later, a nurse's aide came, and I told her my situation. Not my entire situation—like the part about how I was desperately in need of some girl talk with Liza, my bestie who was a plus-sized model. Used-to-be bestie anyhow. Liza hadn't spoken to me since I snarked about the plus-sized modeling industry last month. Now I missed her presence. I should've never said that stuff.

I didn't tell the nurse the part about how I'd felt like I was about to break down and cry at any moment either. Or the part about how I simply needed someone kind to hold my hand, tell me it'd be all peaches and strawberries.

Didn't tell her those parts.

Instead, I spouted off the number to the lawyer. After Jake moved out this past summer, I'd memorized the lawyer's number. The lady smiled and dialed it for me, handed me the phone. The receptionist answered.

"Hi, this is Hannah Hart. I was calling to double check and see if the separation papers were delivered to my husband, Jake Hart." I wanted to know that at least one of the things I'd planned was still going to happen, just like it was supposed to.

"I'll check," the receptionist said.

Seconds later, the person confirmed the papers had been served and should be in his mailbox today.

"Good. Thank you." I hung up and handed the phone to the nurse's aide. She set it aside and left.

Next on the list-of-stuff to do: explain my hospital situation to Greta.

A hard knot gathered in my throat, pressing and restraining my breath. How would I explain? She wasn't exactly a patient woman, and she had a steady stream of pretty hopefuls knocking on her door, looking for representation. I was pretty sure Greta didn't need me half as much as I needed her. Once I told Greta the truth, then what? Retire from modeling, that's what.

Greta was a shrewd businesswoman who had plucked me from despondency all those years ago. She had shown me I was something better than what I was. Something better than what I am now. I rehearsed a million different conversations. A million different ways to convey my predicament to Greta, but my thoughts gave me a stress headache.

There was no good way of explaining this one.

CHAPTER 5

JAKE

I never figured I'd utilize my childhood friend's expertise on divorce law, but here I was in John's office needing answers. When we'd attended Wilberforce Prep School as kids, he'd always asked me all the questions, and I'd always doled out all the wisdom, even though most of the stuff I'd told him was half-fable, half-street knowledge.

He used to think I had some kind of mystical insight because I was one of the few Black kids in a mostly White school. That had made me magical… I guess.

Today, I felt more mixed up than magical. I needed answers.

"What does this mean, John?" I set the letter on the oak conference table at Green and Winters Law Firm.

"The letter looks clear to me." John's JFK, Jr. drawl reflected the disbelief in his statement. He hadn't changed. John always reminded me of a Bostonian intellectual, athletic with WASP features and boring brown hair. All the kids at Wilberforce looked the same—except me. He pushed his rimless glasses up the bony bridge of his nose. "Means she's ready to end it."

The blunt truth of his words hurt. Why'd he have to be so matter-of-fact?

The annoying ticking of the grandfather clock blended with the sound of beeping horns and traffic outside of the downtown New Brunswick office. I wanted to push a mute button on the noise. Noise that taunted and interrupted what would probably be the most important conversation of my life. A conversation that would determine the fate of my marriage.

Or had I already determined my fate? Had I already turned into my father, the philandering jerk?

"How can I stop this? I agreed to a trial separation in the hopes that we'd go to counseling and iron out our issues. If our separation becomes legal, going to counseling would be even harder. Separation is also one step away from divorce. I want to save my marriage."

"I can't tell you how to save a marriage," John said, swiping his hand through his receding hair. "What I can tell you is how to dissolve a marriage." John pressed up a smile. He liked challenging me ever since we were kids playing t-ball in gym class, but this wasn't child's play.

"Hannah and I never discussed a legal separation." My leg bounced underneath the maple conference table, and I tapped my pen against the desk. "After I tried to convince her that having Tim around while Melinda was in rehab wouldn't affect our relationship, she kicked me out. To see how things would fare, she'd said."

"I'm going to guess things aren't faring well."

"Obviously," I said. "Can I stop this?"

"Course you can." His tone mocked.

The light from the vanilla candle traveled through John's water glass and cast a severe shadow across his face. His features turned razor sharp, and it wasn't a stretch to imagine him standing behind a judge's bench with a gavel in hand, pronouncing failure on my marriage.

Then again, he wasn't just my childhood friend anymore. He was a divorce lawyer who needed to turn a profit. What else could I expect? The reality of another ruined relationship hit. I wasn't doing too well with this family thing.

As if sensing my discontent, he added, "These things are messy. That's the way it is."

I exhaled, aggravated with his *c'est-la-vie* stance. Of all the people I knew, he should be the most understanding. We were friends, and he'd gone through a divorce himself.

I sipped my ice water and focused on the left side of John's office where his desk was located. It displayed his pen blotter, his laptop, his notepad, as well as a picture of his two children: Helen, a blonde girl of about six years, and Kevin, his four-year-old son. Good kids.

When John and his ex-wife, Maria, had been in the thick of their baby-making years, he'd tell me all these funny stories. Kevin peeing on John while he changed diapers. Helen eating an entire apple, including the core, without a second thought. I'd laugh at his quips, but I always left the conversation empty. Empty because in all my scrambling to be the perfect husband, to maintain this perfect image, I'd missed those moments with Tim.

I'd figured that Hannah and I would spend whatever we could on fertility treatments and, one day, we'd have a child of our own and I'd forget about Tim. Well, we never had a child, and I never forgot Tim, my son.

I had let him go—for Hannah—because I'd feared what would happen if I didn't.

One day shortly after I'd admitted my affair to Hannah, I'd returned home and found Hannah asleep in the bathtub, greenish-brown vomit pooled around her head. I freaked out and called 911. Didn't know what had happened.

Later on, I'd learned she almost died from purging. The dehydration had caused her system to purge. I'd asked her about it later, and she said that earlier that day, she was on a photo shoot for a lipstick ad. The photographer, a man from Italy with a thick accent, had said her stomach was too big, and that "big Negro lips sold lipstick—not big Negro bellies." She wanted a flat belly, and so she'd tried purging for the first and last time.

She was crushed—so crushed that she almost crushed herself to death. I didn't want to crush her again by taking in Tim when he was little. It was better for Tim to stay with his mama. Children needed their mothers, I'd reasoned. I couldn't lose Hannah. I loved her too much.

When I had a one-night stand with Melinda, it was after days of endless fighting with Hannah. She had accused me of cheating on her. At the time, I hadn't. After a while, I got fed up with Hannah's accusations and did the deed out of anger. I should've kept my emotions in check.

"Everything's negotiable," John continued, breaking my musings. "Even love."

John had a messy divorce. I knew it was messy because whenever I'd brought up Maria during his separation, he'd get tight-lipped and brusque.

"That what you did with Maria? Negotiate?"

"Maria's off-topic."

Yeah, so I made a low blow, but he wasn't helping me out here. "I'm trying to get some advice."

"I gave it to you. Talk to the woman. Negotiate."

I'd negotiated with Hannah for too long. Always toeing the lines of our relationship, making sure I didn't do something else wrong for fear she'd revert to another bathtub incident. I didn't want to negotiate anymore. I wanted us whole and happy. The way we were as college students at Rutgers.

"Do you have any bargaining points with Hannah?" John added. "Is there anything she really values?"

Being skinny enough for a camera. "Don't know. When I agreed to take Tim in over the summer, everything went downhill. Hannah and I ended roughly. Not even talking by the end." Regret swept over me and drew my shoulders down. "She must've felt so betrayed, but I had no choice. I had to take him in. No way would I let Social Services become a father to my son."

"I understand," John said.

"Hannah didn't understand. I'd thought she'd gotten used to the idea of Tim because so many years passed with her knowing of him while we were still married. I figured she held some semblance of forgiveness toward me. I assumed wrong. She was still angry. Married to me and angry at me."

"Don't I know it." John drained his water glass.

I imagined John and me at McIrish's Bar, drowning our marriage woes in Jack Daniels. Maybe that's what I needed, a drink. Not a consult with my embittered buddy-slash-divorce lawyer.

Then again, I was pretty embittered myself.

"I have to communicate with Maria through the kids now," John said. "She can't stand me."

Outside the floor-to-ceiling windows, the sky changed from a pale blue to a doomsday gray. Those clouds pressed down their darkness. I refocused on the cream letter in front of me. "Got any other recommendations for me?"

"Get me on retainer." He winked. "I'll get her talking."

"You haven't changed. Always trying to profit off someone else's pain, huh?" I was joking but then I wasn't. "How much?"

"A two thousand dollar deposit. I cost two hundred fifty dollars an hour, which will be credited against your deposit."

42

I had to get furniture for Tim's new room. New clothes and shoes too. "That's a hefty price."

"Marriage is costly. Main reason I'm not married anymore." He rubbed his empty ring finger. "Freedom is beautiful."

Not if freedom meant you'd be alone and filled with regret. "Is that what you tell yourself?"

John's composure withered. Thoughts appeared to swim in a stream beneath his tired brown eyes.

I shouldn't have probed. "Look," I said as I folded the letter in half. "I'm also transitioning. You know how it is. And I'm a friend. Don't you have a discount or something?"

"Don't you get money from the military?"

I heard the challenge in his voice. Profiteers always had to justify their actions, especially if their actions involved friends. "A disability check, yes… that's not enough to cover what you're asking."

John paused. His mind must've been working on a cost-benefit analysis. "Standard rates. You won't find any different in town," he said.

"Come on, man. We're buddies."

"Yeah, yeah, but I'm in a partnership here. I don't make decisions alone and business has been slow so—"

"So, figure it out is what you're saying. I'm the potential client. Whose side are you on?"

"Yours."

"If you're on my side, then why—"

"You have to figure some things out for yourself, and I'm not in a position to figure them out for you. Your wife wants a separation, which also means she wants to maintain the financial benefits of marriage without the hassle."

"The hassle?"

"Yeah, the hassle. Having to come home every day to the

same person. The burden of paying bills. After a while, you become more like roommates than lovers."

John may not have liked that aspect of marriage, but that's what I loved most about Hannah: our casual comfort, our friendship. We didn't have to deal with all those dating issues. She'd even forgiven me for the one-night stand (or so I'd thought), and we'd settled into what I'd assumed would last forever: reading in bed together on Saturday mornings, finishing each other's sentences, snuggling on the couch and watching a movie. Guess I assumed wrong.

We must've been sliding into late afternoon because the grandfather clock ding-donged at the top of the hour, pointing to what little time I had left.

"This is what I'll do," John said. "If you convince Hannah to keep a trial separation for, let's say three months, I'll be on standby to answer questions for two-hundred fifty dollars an hour. I'd need a five-hundred-dollar retainer. We've done that in the past with other clients so you're not getting a special break. If you can save your marriage within that time, then you won't need to sign on to the legal separation. Everyone will be happy."

"And if it doesn't work out with Hannah?"

"Then the next step would be drafting divorce papers."

I pondered any other alternatives. Apart from letting my marriage crash, there were none.

John glanced at the picture of his kids. "Tim's with you now?"

"Yeah."

"Good luck with that one."

"What's that supposed to mean?" I asked.

"That kid… I've seen him hanging out downtown with a bunch of other kids his age. Up to trouble probably. It's good you're in his life though. He needs his father."

The notion burned in my ears, and its heat stretched down my neck. I needed to be a father.

I could've attended his birthday parties when his mother sent me invitations.

I could've attended his kindergarten graduation and his eighth-grade graduation and all of his spelling bees.

I could've done better, but I didn't.

"Why didn't you tell me you saw Tim?" I asked, scrambling to keep my fiery emotions intact.

"You wouldn't have been too interested since you haven't seen him in a long time." John's expression flickered. "You know how they are."

A chill brushed against my skin. "They? Who's 'they?'"

"Kids like… Tim." He cleared his throat, a vain attempt to mask discomfort, yet after my meeting with Grant, I wasn't into playing niceties.

"You mean Black kids?" I didn't hide the offense in my voice. Why should I? He was the cad.

John squinted and the skin around his eyes crinkled. "Aw, come on. We've been friends forever. Don't bring that up." His tone was dismissive, superior.

Why was I talking to him? Perhaps our friendship wasn't as strong as I had imagined. Perhaps he only saw me as his magical Black friend, an accessory to his apathy.

"For an extra hourly rate, we could set up mediation with Hannah," he added.

Yep. John and I weren't as tight as I had imagined. It was all business to him, but I couldn't focus on that today. Flustered, I answered with the one thing I knew I wanted. "I'll try and work it out with Hannah. No mediation. Mediation leads to divorce. Don't want to go there with my wife."

My wife. I still called her my wife despite having screwed up our marriage. I'd promised her I wouldn't cheat again, and I hadn't. I'd also promised her I'd never bring Tim into

45

our lives. I sensed that Tim reminded Hannah of the one thing she'd wanted to be but wasn't: a mother. Yet I had to give myself the chance to be Tim's father.

"You don't believe mediation is the answer?" John asked.

"I don't believe *I* am the answer. Nothing I do is good enough for Hannah."

The air conditioning rumbled to life, the ceiling fan continued to whir, and the conversation died with my words. Yet the unease it fueled in me didn't. I'd screwed up so much with Tim and Hannah. I wasn't sure of anything anymore.

The speakerphone buzzed. The receptionist said something about an important call.

"That's my kid's pediatrician calling. Be back in a minute."

He left. A rushing filled my ears and threatened to drown me with its sound. No way I could fix this mess. A mess I'd created.

My cell phone dinged and I checked it.

It's Adelaide, Hannah's ninay.

Adelaide Catacutan, my mother-in-law. She always identified herself as Hannah's *ninay*—Tagalog for "mother"—as if Hannah were still a child and as if I'd forgotten she was Hannah's mother. She liked mingling Tagalog with English too, or Taglish. When Hannah and I were still together, I'd always practice my Tagalog skills with her.

Kumusta, I texted. *How are you?*

Hannah was in a fire.

A shoveled out feeling settled in my gut. This must've been the fire at the community center. *Is she alive?*

When I called the hospital, they said all the victims were taken to Robert Wood Johnson's ER unit, and she's on the list. I can't get through to a nurse or a doctor to tell me her condition. I'm still out of town. Can't get there till tomorrow. Diyos ko!

No, I thought. *Don't let her be dead. Don't let her be dead. Don't let her be dead. Not her. Not like this.*

I'll go to RWJ to see if she's okay. Leaving now, I texted.

Pagpalain ka ng Diyos.

I smiled. *God bless you too.*

Guapa anak de bebe. She's my only beautiful daughter, she translated.

She was my only beautiful wife. I didn't type my sentiment. Too complicated. Was it too late? Had I missed my chance to reconcile with Hannah, the only woman I'd ever loved?

Hannah's mother texted her farewell, and my pulse climbed, along with my worry. I scooped my leather bomber jacket from the back of the chair and bolted through the waiting area.

CHAPTER 6

*S*itting in a hospital room all day gave me loads of time to think. I was like the Biblical apostles Paul and Silas when they were stuck in prison. Mama had told me the story once. Paul and Silas sang while in prison. Then there was an earthquake. The chains fell off and they escaped.

If only these tubes and medical devices and bandages would fall off. If only my skin would be perfectly healed.

If only I could sing… nah, that wasn't happening. If I sang, I'd crack the glass vase now sitting next to the television monitor. Singing wasn't my gift. Beauty was my gift. My only gift.

Guess I was stuck here.

No. Not stuck. I wasn't a vegetable. I had the power to overcome this disaster. I had the power to rescue my career too. I didn't have to worry and fret over modeling. I was gonna take action. I closed my eyes and imagined I was a brown-skinned Wonder Woman saving my own day.

Yaasss!

I picked up the phone to call my agent and salvage my

career. The only other option was to not call, say nothing, and be a no-show on Monday. That'd be worse. People had already spent a lot of time and money to get ready for the shoot. They hired the makeup people, the wardrobe people, the photography people, etc. Thousands of dollars had been invested in the fact that I'd show up looking fabulous.

When I touched the phone, my hand twitched. Anxiety built in a vacant part of my chest and trickled down my stomach, my legs, and my feet. "Call her. Just call the woman." I mumbled the words to myself, but I still couldn't muster the courage.

I had to call. Couldn't leave my future to chance. I slowly dialed the number and it rang on the other end. Everything in me pounded, pounded, pounded. What was I going to say?

"Click Models, how may I help you?"

It was Kristi, the receptionist and knower-of-all-things-office-politic-ish. "Hey girl, it's Hannah."

"Greta's been trying to get in touch with you. You've been checking your messages?"

"Um… no. She mad?"

"Pissed."

Rats.

"You have a bunch of go-sees lined up. One for a department store catalog, another for a stint in London, another for a trade show. Where you been?"

"Been good. Been… busy." I put on my best professional voice and stared at my bandages. Busy being hopeless.

"Too busy to call Greta back? Whatever you do, don't tell her you have personal problems. She doesn't want to hear it."

The blister on my hand was crusting. This wasn't a personal problem per se. This was more a health problem. Greta would understand if I told her the difference, right?

"I'll connect you," Kristi said.

"O… okay."

The phone played elevator music. My stomach churned and tumbled, and I hadn't even eaten the hospital's rubber meatloaf for lunch yet. I had to explain my situation to Greta so as to not count myself out of the possibility of future work. In my brain, I tried figuring how to explain, but my words mashed together.

The elevator music stopped. "Greta here."

She sounded all fast-talking and businesslike. "It's Hannah."

"How are you?" Her voice sounded cold and distant.

Yep, Greta was pissed with me. I should've had the nurse call her and explain as soon as I got to the hospital. Then she wouldn't have been as annoyed... or maybe that would've made her more annoyed. Argh! Too confusing. "Just a little under the weather." I wasn't supposed to mention my personal problems.

"Obviously, Kristi told you about the go-sees? I heard."

Man, this lady had eagle ears—or was it eagle eyes? Don't remember.

"You're calling to confirm the appointments?" Greta asked.

Confirm? *Dookies*.

Dookies. Dookies. Dookies. "Look, Greta..." I struggled to get the words past the lump in my throat, but they were stuck. I had to give Greta a reason for why I didn't return her calls right away. "I've been in an accident."

"Car accident? Where? When?" A piece of her business voice chipped and dissolved into empathy. Perhaps she really did care about me.

"No. Not a car accident." But someone might as well have rear-ended me too. "I was in a fire."

"Fire? The one on the news?"

"Yes." I peeped.

"You okay?"

I paused for a split second, still wavering on whether I should say the full truth. "I'm... recovering."

"What?! I'm so, so sorry. I saw the news last night and felt so horrible for the victims. My heart is breaking that you're one of them."

Her sympathy made me feel a tad bit better. Just a tad. Perhaps she wasn't the Cruella de Ville which she'd always portrayed herself to be. Perhaps she had a heart.

"I'll have Kristi send a care package. How's your recovery going?"

The question made my palms itch. Stupid palms. *Be careful how you answer, Hannah.* Yes, Greta was still a businesswoman, and I was the (now damaged) commodity.

"Oh, you know. The fire was minor for me. The doctor said after a short period of recovery, I'll be able to get back to work."

"Hmm... "

My heart did a backflip. "Hmm" wasn't good. Not good at all. I didn't like hmms, especially when they came from Greta. This had to be the end.

"How bad of a shape are you in?"

She already expected me to be in bad shape. I was pretty certain the news reporters had shared all the gory details. "It's not clear at the moment. The doctor wants to make sure I have time to heal."

"Guess you won't be able to make it to the photo shoot on Monday."

At least she said the hard part for me. The part I didn't want to hear. "That is correct."

"Keep me posted, okay? I want reports and everything. I want to see you get better so we can get you back to work." Another pause. "And don't worry about Monday's shoot. There's a new girl on board with us. Her name's Jacinta. I'll send her on the shoot. No worries."

That blister on the back of my hand was about to pop. I was being replaced with a girl named Jacinta.

"The recovery time should be short," I said.

"Focus on getting better. Take it one step at a time."

Why'd everyone keep saying that? "Of course."

"Look for the care package in the mail. Get well soon."

Dismissal laced her voice. I hung up and buried my face in my hands. Now what?

A soft knock sounded at the door, and I looked up. When I did, my heart sank to the ground. The one man I'd been pushing out of my life was now standing in the doorway. Jake.

My insides turned to stone, but my heart kept a-galloping, knocking around my chest, all uncertain and unsure. Not good. Not, not good. Jake was a jerk. No reason for me to feel that way.

His faded blue jeans were tucked into well-worn boots. A collared white shirt peeked from underneath a burgundy, crew neck sweater. A distressed leather jacket hugged Jake's chest.

And his eyes.

His eyes were chestnut with a touch of sunset, but the color had dulled, flattened, dimmed out. Faint lines bracketed his mouth, and I sensed they weren't from smiling but from stressing.

A mess of words stuck in my throat. Good thing I couldn't pry them loose or else I would've gushed about his high handsome factor, and that would've contradicted all my plans to legally separate. I took three deep breaths, a faint attempt to steady my reaction. "What're you doing here?"

"Your mom texted me that you were in a fire, and I wanted to see you." His voice sounded natural, poured out like honey.

My voice, on the other hand, croaked. "My mother?"

"The news may have released your name too." He leaned against the doorjamb awkwardly as if trying to figure out whether he should stay put or come closer.

I panicked. If the news released my name, then they could've also released the extent of my burns. I could see the headline now: "Supermodel Charred to a Crisp." All the gory details at nine. Was that why Greta was so dismissive toward the end of our conversation?

He stepped close and grasped the bedrail. "My gosh." He swept over my bandages and then at me.

So embarrassing. I wanted to shrink inside my bandages, never to return again.

"Are you hurting?"

"Of course," I said, trying to sound nonchalant at his reaction, but it pricked. "They give me morphine every once in a while. That helps."

"That stuff can be addictive. Make sure you don't—"

"I know what I'm doing, Jake, and so do the doctors who've prescribed my dosages."

"I know... I figured. I figured I lost you."

My brain almost fizzed out from his comment. Lost me? Lost me? So now he wanted to be all caring and considerate, huh? Jake didn't seem to care when he chose Tim over me. "You did lose me. My lawyer sent you a letter."

"Yes." He shoved his hands in his pockets and shifted from side-to-side. "I wanted to discuss that."

His expression held a faint longing which left me unnerved. I studied the window washers working on the office building across the street.

"I know," Jake continued. "It's not the time to discuss the letter given the situation, but it took me by surprise. I'm so sorry, Hannah. So, so sorry this happened."

I caught my breath. "Are you referring to the fire or are you referring to us?"

"Both."

The word landed like a fist to my resolve, rattling it to the core. I'd pretend I didn't hear that. He never apologized before, even when he'd first told me about his son all those years ago. Now he wanted to be sorry because I was in the hospital? I leaned over to put the cordless in the cradle, but I couldn't. "Can you put this up for me?"

He did and angled his body toward me, smiling. "You never do that."

"Do what?"

"Ask me to do things for you."

No way was I going to fall for his stupid attempt to bond. Why did people play nice when they saw you hurting? "It's a cordless, Jake." I tried making my voice sound as emotionless as possible, but his surprise visit settled beneath my skin. "When are you leaving? I need to be alone."

"I'm not leaving."

"So, you're just going to stay by my bedside, staring at me?"

"You're hurting. You need help while recovering." His volume lowered and his tone warmed me over, reminding me of the time when he first asked me out. Gah!

"Who's going to be there for you?" he continued.

"Don't know."

"Then I'll be there for you."

"No need," I waved him off, and the magazine flew off my lap and landed at his feet. "I'll figure something out."

Jake picked up the magazine, set it on my over-the-bed table, and then he didn't budge.

I really wanted Jake to budge—to budge his way out of my room—so I could continue with my fried-up little life. Having Jake around reminded me of the rest of my unsolved problems. "Don't you have to see about your son?"

He winced when I said "your son" as if it hurt I couldn't

say "our son" or "my son." Jake had brought that misery on himself and left me out as wreckage. I tried having a baby, okay? Tried, tried, tried. We went to fertility doctors and specialists out the wazoo, and nothing.

Guess his only answer was a one-night stand with some ho across town. My uterus wasn't good enough, and so he'd wanted a replacement—just like Greta wanted to replace me with this Jacinta gal.

"You look conflicted," he said.

I raised my eyes, and my entire being sighed. "Go on with your life. I'll manage." My defeated tone released a rush of sadness in me, and in its wake, a faint longing for what might've been.

Jake's attention switched from me to the door, and I drew a breath. He then refocused on me and I exhaled. He touched the bandage wrapped around my hand. I flexed my fingers inward and inched away, self-protective.

"I wish I could wave a wand and make all this go away."

"Don't patronize me, Jake. You never told me about the possibility of Tim living with us until his mother was court-ordered to rehab. You waited until the last possible moment. The moment where I'd look like a jerk for not agreeing to your idea. Guess what? Don't care if I look like a jerk. I have my life to live too."

"I know you do, but let's set that aside for now. Your recovery is important, and I care about you."

I tried my darnedest to flick away what I sensed as sincerity in his tone. It was my second day in this hospital. My body was still raw. I didn't need him picking at the scabs on my heart. "How kind."

"I'm serious," he said, sincerity deepening. "Who's taking care of you while you recover?"

"Me."

"Nonsense."

"Nothing nonsensical about it. If you really cared about me, we wouldn't be in the predicament we're in today." I reached for the remote, intent on proving I was perfectly capable of taking care of myself. I missed the stupid clicker by a few inches, and it tumbled to the floor. A sharp pain shot up my arm. Dammit.

Jake picked it up and handed it to me like an adulterous knight in shining armor. "Here you go."

"Thanks." I powered up the television, and it blared to life. I flicked through the channels and landed on an episode of a divorce court show. Perfect.

"You're completely bandaged from head to toe."

"Duh." I squinted at the television screen. The judge was getting to the part where he was about to slam the husband for running up secret debts in his soon-to-be ex-wife's name. I raised the volume.

"Hannah."

Commercial break. A smiling brunette appeared on the screen. She waxed eloquent about a lint roller. I feigned interest. Commentaries on lint rollers were still better than listening to Jake. His weirdo concern was making me all soft and squishy.

"Hannah."

"What?"

"What'd the doctor say?"

I paused. "Doctor said I'll be up and running in no time."

"Really?" Disbelief colored every inch of his face.

I turned my attention to the television. A lot of interesting commercials out there today. This new one was for forty-eight-hour deodorant. Forty-eight hours? Unbelievable.

"You're doing that thing with your eyes," he said.

"What thing?"

"That thing." He pointed. "You always do that thing when you're not giving the full story."

"You accusing me of lying?" I asked.

"Basically."

The man knew me too well. "Fine." I adjusted the volume on the television. "Four months. I have at least four months of recovery time, and I'll need some skin grafting surgery too." I looked away. Saying all that hurt.

"Four whole months?"

I didn't answer. Why repeat my helplessness?

"I'm helping you recover."

"Not looking for your pity."

"I'm not separating from you, Hannah. Especially now."

"You can't be serious."

He didn't change.

"You *are* serious. You're going to use this injury against me? You're going to try to make me dependent on you when I'm already in a vulnerable state. That's low. Lower than the lowest."

"I'm not signing."

"What?" My voice raised two octaves—not good when the rest of your body was crusting over from a fire. My loud voice was causing my body temperature to rise, hence the crust. *Blech.* "You're really going to try to keep me from separating from you? You don't have that power."

"I'm going to try, and you know why? Because I'm for you, Hannah. Yeah, I broke my promise to never see Tim again, but I'm not the kind of guy who'd leave you hanging. Especially at a time like this. That's not me."

"Then who are you?"

His face flickered, briefly, but it was there. "Who am I?"

"Yes. Who. Are. You. Are you the man who had a one-night stand after I'd taken fertility treatments for months—MONTHS—trying to have the baby I so desperately wanted?

Are you the man who'd said you didn't care that we couldn't have a child? Are you the man who'd said your marriage is more important to you than anything—even your illegitimate son? Who. Are. You."

He paused. "I don't know."

Why'd he have to sound so manly and vulnerable and…

"You believe in second chances, Hannah?"

All of a sudden, my eyeballs itched. "Look, I need to rest."

"Something's wrong and you're not telling me," he said.

If I could've gripped the bed sheets in frustration, I would've. Why was he trying to play the concerned husband now? There had to be some ulterior motive. "When did I ever tell you anything before?"

"You're right. I used to have to pry everything out of you. You've always shut me out."

I thought back to the time when I was so distraught about that dumb Italian photographer's racist comments. He had me second-guessing everything about myself. Even then, I didn't feel like sharing the experience with Jake, and if Jake hadn't found me dehydrated, I would've kept it a secret. What'd he expect me to do? Admit that I wanted to be accepted in an industry where almost-white Black girls were celebrated while those showing any ounce of "Negro-ness" weren't? Admit that deep down, I wanted to be accepted too?

"You're a fighter, Hannah. I know you'll get through this one."

"You're right. I will get through this one. On my own. Just like I always have in our marriage. Which is why I don't need whatever kind of help you think you can give me." I increased the volume on the television.

"I get it," he added.

I flipped the channel.

"I'm still not leaving you stranded, Hannah. I'm sticking

around till you recover. We can revisit the separation afterward."

"I don't need to revisit the separation. I've made up my mind."

He didn't flinch. "And I've made up mine."

"What?" I raised my voice. "You think we're going to have some happily ever after with your son in the picture?"

"I never said that… I haven't thought that far ahead."

"You never think ahead. You didn't think far ahead about how your one-night stand would affect our marriage. You didn't think far ahead about how I'd feel about you bringing Tim into your life. You just acted and let the casualties fall where they may, even if the casualty was your own wife. So no, I don't see a happily ever after, and I for sure don't see the three of us posing for a family Christmas picture at JC Penney Portrait Studios."

Jake's jawline relaxed—more like it surrendered. "Bye, Hannah." He left.

Not surprising. He'd left before whenever we'd fought, and I wouldn't see him for days. Still, I crushed him.

My tissue-paper heart crushed too.

CHAPTER 7

JAKE

A swell of anxiety washed over me. Her words rooted deep and scraped at wounds I'd been nursing for years.

Hannah didn't want me around. I tried everything to save us after I admitted to the one-night stand: counseling, date nights, keeping Tim out of my life. Now I couldn't convince her otherwise. Dammit.

Why was I such a chump? Was I hoping Hannah would easily take up my offer to help? Why'd I assume the gravity of her physical condition would override the gravity of our relationship condition? Stupidity cinched around my neck, tight as a noose. I exhaled, but the pressure increased.

No matter how much Hannah hated me, my offer to help her still stood. I simply had to figure out a way for her to agree to my help. Okay, it wasn't so simple now, but if I had to move back to New Brunswick to be nearer to and help Hannah, I would.

I was going to get all this resolved: my issues with Hannah, my issues with Tim, everything. Right now, I had to shift my focus to Tim.

On my way to the hospital, I'd texted him to meet me in the hospital lobby so we could find him a part-time job today. The "hospital lobby" being the operative phrase. I knew not to have him tag along on my visit to Hannah. I swiped the side seam of my jacket and headed downstairs. He wasn't there.

Empathetic stares followed me as I stalked past the people sitting in the hospital lobby and stepped through the revolving doors.

Outside, car horns, gasoline fumes, and raw tension filled Somerset Street and blended with my erratic thoughts of Hannah. In a matter of minutes, I walked through the cacophony and headed toward the stop light on the corner. He wasn't there either.

Sweat soaked through my shirt collar. Hopefully, the kid hadn't bailed on me. If he didn't land a good job and prove himself responsible, I'd look like the bad parent. I could even lose custody. Then where would he go? The social services system? Never.

A car horn beeped, and I started.

"Watch where you're going!" The cabbie flipped me the bird.

I moved out of the way and leaned against the light pole. Hannah's dismissal nestled in my conscience, and I wanted to scream. Couldn't do that. All the passersby would think I was out of it.

What did I care? I'd scream Tim's name and accomplish two things at once: attempt to find my son and let go of my stress about Hannah.

"Tiiiiimmmm!"

The name drummed against my teeth.

Nothing.

A few more steps and my unease about Hannah

increased. Would she ever forgive me? Would she ever understand that a father couldn't abandon his son?

Cigarette smoke weaved through the smoggy air. My nostrils tickled and itched. The sound of hacking stopped me, and I whirled around. Tim stood before me, a cigarette in hand.

The muscles in my left shoulder tightened to attention—more stress. When did Tim start smoking? He can't smoke. He's a minor and that's illegal. The last thing he needed was to break the law.

"Where were you? I was looking all over."

His wrinkled hip-hop T-shirt hung over his thin frame like a deflated balloon. "Needed a smoke break." He took a puff, the cigarette hanging on the edge of his lips.

"You can't go on job interviews wearing rap T-shirts, son. Who gave you those cigarettes?"

"No one."

"You bought 'em?"

Tim took another puff, and I grappled for the possibilities. "Someone gave them to you then. Unless you stole them."

No answer.

Understanding hit. "You stole them, didn't you?" I flung the question at him. "You can't steal, Tim." I reached for the pack of cigarettes in his back pocket, but he dodged me, his basketball sneakers shuffling against the sidewalk, his right hand barricading the cigarettes from my view. I almost stumbled but quickly righted myself and smoothed my hair, a poor attempt to play off Tim's countermove.

A few passersby turned into onlookers. A few onlookers turned into smirkers. Smirkers turned this into a circus show where I was the freak. The freak who couldn't earn his son's respect or his wife's forgiveness. I was a lost cause.

"Hand them over, Tim. I'm not arguing with you in the street."

"No."

The knot in my shoulder doubled. "Hand them over or else."

"Or else what?"

"Or else…" What else?

Tim rolled his eyes. "Can't think of it, can you? Playing the big bad wolf, and nothing will come from it."

"Stop being so stubborn. I have a say in how you'll get through this suspension too. I could tell the principal you stole cigarettes. I can tell the cops you're smoking as a minor. I can go right now if I want."

"You won't."

My resolve crashed in on me, landing in a pile of confusion. He was right and he knew it. "I sure would." I shoved my hands in my pockets.

"You can't tell me what to do."

Something invisible poked my side, the finger of powerlessness. He was right again. Couldn't tell him what to do. Couldn't yell him into submission. I yelled at Hannah once when she'd gotten into a funk over I don't know what. She was depressed over something, but she never told me. We'd spent all that money on therapy and she remained depressed. I shouldn't have yelled at her. It only deepened the chasm between us. I'd have to find another way with Tim too.

The strangers still stood there, watching. "This isn't a street performance," I said to the onlookers. "You can move on."

A hefty construction worker lugged two buckets of tools and drifted away, followed by a college-aged kid with dreadlocks.

I turned my attention on Tim. "What's wrong with you? I'm trying to help, but all you do is push me away."

"So, I'm the one to blame, huh? Everyone just assumed that… forget it."

"Everyone assumed what?" I asked.

Tim looked away. The wind rustled and my skin prickled at the coolness. "Tell me, son. I'm listening."

"Everyone assumed I was out for the kid. No one said anything about how he called my mother a crack whore." Tim took a drag of his cigarette. "Said that's why I couldn't do well in school. I must be a drug baby. When I told the teacher after the fight, the teacher said I was a drug baby too."

The air rushed out of me. Principal Grant didn't want to hear Tim's story, the whole story. My son was bullied. Didn't Grant say they had zero-tolerance for bullies at the school? Seems like the other kid was the real bully. "I didn't know. I'm so sorry."

"You ain't sorry because you asked me a few minutes ago if something was wrong with me. But back at the principal's office, you was all gung-ho about me and hopeful I'd make this big change. You ain't nothing but a faker. Like everyone else."

He was right. I was a faker. After I'd walked out of his life when he was a kid, I'd send him birthday cards where I'd write "I'm going to visit you soon." I never showed up till this past summer when I had to show up.

"Can't wait for Mama to get out of rehab so I can be away from you," he continued. "You don't care about me. Nobody cares."

I flinched. The truth he spoke cut me down to the bone and marrow. The evidence against me, clear; the inability to justify myself, real. So I did what any self-respecting man would do: I shifted the blame. "Just because people mistreat you doesn't mean you should let it eat you up inside. Smoking is self-destructive. You're underage. You can't smoke cigarettes. It's against the law. You can't wander away from me either. I'm your father."

"No father of mine would've left my mama."

Dread wrapped its cords around my ankles. If the ground could've split open and swallowed me, I would've wanted it to. Tim would hold onto my abandonment for the rest of his life, and I'd be at fault. "I'm doing what I can. Today."

"You ain't doing nothing but being fake. I tell it like I see it."

"You tell it like you see it, huh? I'll tell you how I see you. I see a kid angry at everyone. He thinks he knows it all, but he doesn't. And his know-it-all self is going to get him in big trouble unless he starts listening to the people who care for him."

"You don't care." His voice rose above the chatter on the street. "I do what I wanna do."

"Son." My throat grew hoarse. "Don't say that. I don't want to see you taken to places where you don't want to be. Keep up this defiant behavior and you'll end up in jail or worse, and it won't matter if you were the one bullied or not. Know why? Because people don't care about young Black men with bad attitudes."

"It's my choice where I wanna go. Can't stop me from choosing."

I wanted to punch a brick wall. "That attitude will get you nowhere good. A whole lot of nowhere."

Tim slid on his dark sunglasses and took another puff of his cigarette.

Dammit.

"I guess when your mother told you do good, you didn't care. I bet she could tell you about being taken to places she doesn't want to go."

"What's that mean?" Tim asked, his tone changing.

"You think she enjoys rehab? You think she's on vacation?

No. She's detoxing. Her mind doesn't want to mainline heroin, but her body craves it. Probably in her weak moments, her mind wants the drugs too. That's prison."

He stopped puffing.

"Your mom cares about you, Tim. If you don't want to put the cigarette out for me, then think of her."

"Since when did you care about my mother?"

I couldn't answer. Honestly, I never did. That one-night stand turned into a multi-year commitment when I'd learned she was pregnant with our son. Melinda and I had that connection for life.

When I'd found out a child would enter this world through my wrongdoing, I was overwhelmed and scared. I'd tried in the beginning to have some semblance of a relationship with his mother. However, the feelings weren't there, and Hannah's ultimatum was my escape. Still, I'd missed seeing my son.

"I figured you didn't care." Tim tossed the pack of cigarettes in the trash along with the one he was smoking.

I exhaled relief. "Thanks for tossing the cigs."

"Didn't put out my cigarette for you. Did so for my mama. What were you doing at the hospital?"

I paused. "Visiting Hannah. She was in the fire."

Tim's expression closed. "You about to visit her now?"

"No. Just finished." I shoved my hands in my pockets. "Let's go and look for a job for you."

Tim looked away. "Don't want a job."

"Excuse me?"

"Don't want a job," he repeated with more emphasis this time. "That hard to understand?"

His expression turned to stone. Sadness filled me like a stagnant, stinking pond. I lost him. Again. "Don't say you don't want a job. How about this? Let's go home and research something you'll be interested in. We can try again another day. How's that?"

"Don't matter what we research," he said, his voice quieter. "I tell you one thing. I ain't gonna be squeezed in between your hospital visits to your wife. That's for sure."

"It won't be like that, I promise."

"Promise? Like you promised me you'd come visit in those stupid birthday cards you used to send but never did?"

My heart deflated. The kid was right. No way could I win over Hannah and Tim. My grand plans of reconciling with both were flushed down the toilet. How can I fix this? I didn't want to choose between the two.

I exhaled. I wanted them both in my life. Perhaps moving back to New Brunswick would be a way to reconcile with both.

I wasn't going to give up on my son… but would I have to give up on Hannah to do so? Was that the price I'd have to pay?

No. Moving to New Brunswick was a reasonable action given Hannah's health predicament. I could still start the healing process with Tim too. I'd do something small, like make family dinner every night. I needed to bond with him first before he'd agree to anything I suggested like finding him a part-time job.

Still, another stark reality hovered in the background: maybe I couldn't have them both.

And that hurt.

CHAPTER 8

*R*econstructive surgery could be the solution to my problems.

Not *could* be the solution to my problems. It *must* be the solution to my problems. There wasn't any other way around it. None at all. Getting diced and sliced on the surgery table would be the only way to save my modeling career and get on the road to freedom from the prison called my marriage. I wanted to earn a decent income on my own, without Jake in my life.

Fool actually visited me in the hospital and insisted on trying to help me through this disaster. The nerve! The man had already rained disaster down on my life: one-night stand, having a baby from the one-night stand, then wanting the baby-turned-teenager to live with us. After I clearly told him no years earlier? What was he thinking?

I pressed the talk button on the cordless. I was smarter with the phone thing this time. When the nurse arrived, I had him prop up the cordless on a mini-bookstand and get the number to my health insurance from Google. Now the bookstand was smartly positioned on my food tray. No reaching. No chances of disaster.

My military ID, which got singed in the fire, had also doubled as my health insurance card. It displayed two names: Jake Hart, the sponsor; and me, Hannah Hart, the dependent.

I despised that word, *dependent*. It was a label that hinted —no, shouted—at the fact that no matter what I'd do in my life, I'd always remain connected to him for something.

I'd made sure I kept up with my modeling after marriage, because who knew what would happen with my marriage in the future? We could end up divorced and despising one another, much like my parents. I didn't want to be at some-one's behest if that ever happened.

Well… it was happening. I despised Jake. I even despised my burnt-up self. I was dependent too.

My situation gave me a case of the ickies.

I dialed the number to the insurance, and it rang and rang and rang. Had I called outside of business hours? What were the business hours? I didn't know. This could be a case of typical government sloth.

The phone still rang. Gah!

"Customer service, how may I help you?"

I explained my situation. "Does my insurance cover the costs of skin grafting and reconstructive surgery?"

"I'll check."

I heard rustling. "It should cover it," I added, desperate and worried about her impending verdict. "It's a medically necessary procedure."

More rustling and typing.

My stomach tightened. What if I wasn't covered? I couldn't pay out of pocket. I didn't have a pocket. Not a pocket large enough to contain the money it'd take to make me look perfect.

What would I do? I never even finished college. Even

when I had been a college student, I'd taken periodic leaves from school so I could travel to the European fashion shows on a moment's notice, despite the fact that I had a full course load. I'd wanted to be readily available for the industry. With the way I looked now, the industry definitely wasn't going to be readily available for me.

I used to have a Plan B once I reached my "old age" as a model. That plan involved finishing college and pursuing an academic career in mathematics, but that was before that stupid professor made me never want to pick up a school textbook ever again. The jerk… I pushed the thought aside. I'd had enough present trauma. No need digging up past trauma.

"You're covered eighty percent."

The tension in me loosened, and my body relaxed. "Thank you so much. Do you know how much it'd cost?"

"Hold on."

I sat as tall as I could, given my predicament, and noted my picture gracing the cover of the magazine. I'd tucked the issue underneath the plastic flower vase. In no time, I'd look like her again. I'd look like myself again.

But who was she, really?

The question came out of nowhere and pricked. Pricked so much it must've poked a hole in my brain. That was a dumb question. I knew exactly who I was. I was the wholesome woman on that magazine cover, smiley and sweet as apple pie. I was normal.

"I just asked my manager," the person on the phone said. "We don't have costs of procedures. You'd have to talk to your medical provider."

"I'm assuming it'd be a lot because I'm…" My pearly white teeth on the magazine smiled back at me, and I grimaced.

"Is there anything else that I can help you with?"

"Oh, yes, there's one more thing. I'm going through a legal

separation with my husband, and I want to make sure I'll still have coverage until I figure out something else."

"How long have you been married?"

"Sixteen years."

"You won't be covered if you're legally separated from your sponsor."

"What?"

"You'd have to be married for twenty years before you're guaranteed health care coverage and all other military benefits."

The picture of my perfect self taunted me. It shoved me in a corner and kept me there, stuck. "You're kidding me. I have to be with this joker for four more years before I'd get insurance for life?"

"Yes, but children are covered regardless."

Her mention of children struck a blow to my childless heart. "I have no children."

"Oh… well then. No coverage for you."

A stabbing pain formed at my temples. "You don't understand. I had to get a legal separation. It was my only choice. What else was I supposed to do? Just put up with… just put up with… " I blew out a stream of air, my words unable to catch up with my pulse.

The woman on the other end of the phone quieted. "Ma'am, I'm sorry that this is such an inconvenience. You have my deepest sympathies, but there's nothing I can do—"

"Of course you can't!"

"Ma'am?" The lady on the phone sounded bewildered.

"Yes, yes. I'm sorry." I forced myself to be present even though my thoughts were a pack of wild cats. "I'll have to consider this." Consider if I can go through with this separation.

I hung up and clutched my hospital gown. Okay, so that

71

whole reconstructive surgery-slash-health insurance thing didn't work out.

I reached over to get my glass of orange juice and yelped because the burns ravaged my skin. Should I sacrifice my independence from Jake for health insurance? Was that compromising? Ugh! This was complicated.

"*Anak*."

My pulse skittered. Mother. Here she came with her worry and her judgment. Somehow, she'd find me at fault for this situation.

She rushed to me, about to touch my hand when she hesitated, she must've thought better of it. Mama scanned the spread of blankets covering my bandaged body and smoothed the stray, dark hairs on her tight bun, exposing a fan of wrinkles around her eyes that confessed her age. Aside from her bright red lipstick, the fuchsia beaded chain dangling from her neck provided the only splash of color. Everything else was black. Black boatneck top. Black slacks. Black flats.

"Look at you. Look at you."

I looked the other way. Didn't look too good.

"My daughter. How'd you get caught in the fire?" Mama's expression held at serious.

"You make it sound like it was my fault."

"Didn't you look for a fire exit?" Her question-rebuke snapped in my ear. This was why I'd do my darnedest to recover alone. I didn't want to deal with her subtle blame. I steeled my lips shut.

"Never mind," she continued. "We will get you better. We will." Mama inclined her head, her eyes a murky pond of sadness and grief. "You must be in so much pain."

If only she knew. "I'll be okay, Mama."

"I'll pray special novenas for you. This is a bad, bad sign."

Oh lord, I thought. Here she goes with her religious stuff. "What kind of sign, Mama?"

"*Yawa* working his mischief. We have to pray him out. We have to stop him."

Yawa was Visayan for "devil." I knew some of that dialect too. Whenever I got in trouble as a kid, she'd call me *yawa-karon*, or "child of the devil." I wondered if she ever tried praying me out of her life. Felt like it sometimes.

"What'd the doctor say?"

I relayed to her everything that the doctor had said, but I left out the part about them not releasing me until I had someone who'd agree to help me during recovery. Didn't need any more eager volunteers.

"How are you going to take care of yourself once you're home?"

I left that bit out and she still asked the one question I didn't want to answer. "Mama, I'll find someone. Someone who specializes in home care."

"Is that covered by insurance?"

The insurance question. Ugh! "Don't know."

"Save yourself the time and energy. I'll go on a reduced schedule at work so I can be with you. I already mentioned it to my boss. I'm only working on Tuesdays and Thursdays, so I can be with you the other three days of the work week."

I felt like that little kid again, the one who Mama'd always tried to control. The one who'd been scolded for eating too much cake, for drinking too much soda, for having too much fat. She used to put me on all kinds of diets to get the fat to melt off or whatever. I'd tried those diets to win her favor, but those diets never worked. Frustrating. Now she was making decisions about how I'd recover once I got out of the hospital. Double frustrating.

But if she was around, I wouldn't have to spend money on a home care nurse. That was a plus. I wasn't going to let

Mama know how much she was helping. If I did, she'd become waaay too intrusive.

"You didn't even ask me if I wanted you to take off from work. How can you make those decisions without asking me?" I said, irritated.

Hurt flickered across her face, and all of a sudden I was entrapped in this passive-aggressive guilt trip roller coaster. This time, I wasn't falling for it. I remained silent.

"What's that?" She squinted at the letter which the nurse's aide had kindly printed out for me from my email account the other day. "Is that an email from a lawyer?"

My cheek twitched, and the edges of my mouth slid upward. How was she able to make me feel like I was a five-year-old again? "It's nothing."

"Those pariahs are trying to get you to sue someone, aren't they? I had swarms of them email me when I'd gotten a simple speeding ticket. They must've gotten your name from the news. The snakes." She arched her arms over me to get the copy of the email, and I inhaled the sweet scent of her face lotion, the same moisturizer she'd been using since forever.

"Mama. It's nothing."

As usual, she ignored me and read the email. "Why are you separating from Jake?"

"From our history, it should be obvious."

"You've been with him for years after he told you about his child. And?"

"And?" I puffed a sarcastic laugh that my lungs immediately pulled back in, a reflex to the pain. "What do you mean 'and?' He promised not to bring the child around me ever. Now, the kid's living with him. He broke his promise. End of story."

"You don't want to be like me, *anak*. After I left your

74

father, I had to start all over. That's why I'm working now. I'll be working till the day I die."

Oh brother. Why'd she have to be so melodramatic? I kept my mouth shut.

"Do you want to be working forever?"

"Actually, I do. I love modeling."

"You really think Greta will want you to model? In your condition?"

"Why not?" My voice splintered in response.

"You're... you're... "

A gush of moisture flooded my eyes, but I quickly blinked it away. "I'm what, Mother? Disastrous? Say it. Say it!"

The faint lines around my mother's face softened, and the intensity in her almond eyes unsettled me. "I had such hopes for you. To be married. To be happy."

She hadn't heard a thing I said. "I will be happy," I told her. "I'll be happy when I'm on my own. When I get through this injury and resume my life on my terms."

"You don't want to struggle like I did. Don't sign this paper. You'll ruin your life and—"

"My life is already messed up, Mama." I could hear my voice getting shaky. "Can't you see this is my way to salvage my life?"

Mama was silent, and I couldn't tell whether her silence was compassion or something else.

"When I came to America, I thought my problems would disappear. Life doesn't work that way. In many ways, my life got harder."

My eyes stung. I knew what she was referring to. She was in America, and so she had to do like the Americans: get rid of her accent, get rid of her traditions, get rid of herself.

She had to squeeze her first-generation Filipino ways into a third generation Filipino-American mold. I'd seen how Americans shamed her by doing things like making her repeat herself because, supposedly, they couldn't "understand her English." After a while, Mama had stopped speaking for herself, and so as a child, I stepped in and spoke for her. I was the transactional Ameri-Filipina, bridging the gap between American prejudice and Filipino shame.

"I know it was hard for you," I said softly.

"You have to work hard for your keep and keep what you have. Keep Jake. He's a good man, just made one bad choice. One."

Mama always had a soft spot for Jake. It started when they'd first met and Jake greeted her in Tagalog with a perfect accent. Mama was sold—and I was too.

She folded the email and slid it into her purse.

"What are you doing?"

"I'm making sure you don't go through with this separation. I'm keeping this letter."

"What? Are you serious? You can't tell me what I'm doing with my marriage."

"I sure can."

It was time for a stare down. I stared. She stared.

We stared.

Stared for an eternity.

First one to blink lost. Was that how that game went? I forgot. Things went a bit fuzzy after thirty-seven years, a fire, and a broken marriage.

How pathetic. I was engaging in childish staring contests with my mother. "Doesn't matter. My lawyer has a copy. Jake has a copy too."

After talking with the insurance company, should I tell Jake and the lawyer to put our separation on hold? At least until I finished with surgery? That would make me look like a big, fat loser. Jake would think I wanted him in my life again, which WAS NOT the case.

Mama interrupted my thoughts. "Darling, I'm only

thinking of your best interests. Remember when Lola—"

"I don't want to discuss Lola. That was years ago, and you're not going to make me feel incompetent."

"Incompetent?"

"Yes. Incompetent. You still… forget it." I choked. The memories resurfaced: Lola's gnarled hands slipping from mine when she breathed her last, Mother's coldness toward me afterward, the heavy sense that I could've called 911 sooner and prevented her passage into eternity. I could've still had someone rooting for me.

Lola had made me feel as if I was enough, imperfections and all.

Mama looked over at me and then tapped her foot incessantly. "Think of your future. Do you really want to end up like me?"

I didn't answer that question. Partially because I didn't know the answer. There were parts of Mama I'd never known. Parts of her I'd never know. Parts of me that'll remain unknown.

"You don't want to be like me," she said, barely waiting for me to even gather a thought, let alone formulate an answer to her statement. "You don't."

The truth was, I did. When I was in fifth grade, I'd wanted to learn Tagalog and Visayan, so I could speak it just like her. Mama had said that was unnecessary. In America, I had to speak perfect English. Being a rebellious child, I checked out a Tagalog and a Visayan language book from the library, intent on learning. I'd picked up a couple of words here and there, words like "child of the devil," but I'd wanted the whole enchilada.

Or was it the whole *pancit*? *Pancit*. I wanted the whole *pancit*.

Anyway, when I was at the kitchen table flipping through the pages one morning, Mama had taken the language book from me and slapped my face.

"It'll be hard enough for you in America, *anak*. You're brown. Beautiful, but brown. Brown is hard. Don't make it harder by learning my languages and picking up an accent," she'd said.

Beautiful, but brown. My burns have made me barely brown today. Was I still beautiful?

"Tagalog and Visayan will give you an accent like mine," she'd continued in that tiny kitchen. "Speak only perfect English. No accent like mine."

An accent like hers. If she'd only known, I'd wanted to be like her in every way.

When Lola died, Mama was all things Filipino. I wanted to know that part of myself too, but Mama smashed it out. To make things worse, two years after Lola died, Mama blamed me for negligence, insinuating Lola's death was my fault.

Afterward, I'd stopped wanting to be like Mama, and an emptiness filled me, an emptiness I'd filled with approval-seeking from my peers in school.

"This is my decision, Mama. I won't let you make it for me." I tried reaching for the letter, but *riiiiipp*!

The bandage fell off my arm, unraveled, actually. Cold air hit the exposed skin. I shivered and gasped.

A mottled sea of pink and white shone through, along with a trickle of blood and water where a blister had popped and oozed into the crook of my elbow. I cringed. So very gross.

"*Diyos ko!*"

"See? This was why I was going to look into getting a home care nurse. Can't have you paralyzed and in shock when something like this happens, Ma." (Okay, it wasn't the full reason I was going to looking into a home care nurse, but the other reasons were perfectly obvious.)

"Can you get the nurse?" I continued, irritated. "This could cause an infection."

After she left, I studied my arms. The blood drip-drip-dripped onto the white blanket and spread in uneven circles. I pressed the corner of the blanket against the wound, and it stung. I had to use the blanket or else I'd bleed all over the place. The stinging sensation seeped deeper into me.

I shattered.

Annoying, uncomfortable feelings flooded through, filled my chest, pushed out my air. My limbs were weighed down by the pressure. The pressure of having to fix myself so I could attain this perfect physical standard so I could work. The pressure Mama had placed on me to give up cake and soda as a child so that Mama would accept me. The pressure of trying to regain my independence after being so horribly betrayed by Jake. Pressure. Pressure. Pressure.

Reconstructive surgery would get rid of some of the pressure, but that meant having Jake hold off on signing the separation papers. Having Jake hold off on signing the separation papers would sacrifice my independence. This sucked, but I had to do it.

I'd make sure Jake knew I was only asking him to hold off on signing for health insurance reasons—not because I'd had a change of heart. I'd let him know this was a *temporary* hold. That way, he wouldn't assume he could invade my life like Mama was doing now.

This was the only way I could salvage my career, my life, my fight.

CHAPTER 9

*D*inners were family huddle times, right? Times to bond and connect. To relive the day with laughter, conversation, and fellowship. After feeling so alienated from Tim the other day, I'd made a point to have evening meals together at least four nights a week. If I was going to move closer to Hannah, then I had to reach out to Tim in some way too. I wasn't losing both of them.

"Want garlic bread with your spaghetti?" I asked, forcing Tim to look up from the book he'd brought to the table with him.

"Yeah."

Tim's voice sounded hoarse, probably because he hadn't spoken since our disagreement near the hospital. I'd taken off from work at the construction site today so we could hang out, but all Tim did was hide out in his room, away from me. Maybe I'd try humor. Yeah, humor could work.

He downed the sweet tea. Homemade spaghetti and a growling stomach changed his hiding-out plan. "You like my cooking?"

Tim forked more noodles and stuffed them in his mouth. Guess he was here for the food. Not the company.

"Still trying to play tough guy, huh?"

He stopped eating, fork stuck in his mouth.

I had his attention. Hmm. "I've been watching the way you slurp your noodles. Tough kids don't slurp."

"Ha ha." The fork jiggled as he laughed, and a smile formed at the edge of his lips.

"You know it's true." I crumpled up my paper napkin and aimed for the kitchen trash. Missed by two feet.

"Your aim sucked," Tim said, taking the fork from his mouth. "You used too much elbow."

"Oh yeah?"

"Yep. You go like this." He balled up a stray piece of junk mail on the kitchen table and positioned his arms at a ninety-degree angle. Made it in one shot.

"Whoa."

"No biggie." Tim shrugged. "Been practicing on the b-ball court."

"You like to shoot hoops? We should go out sometime."

"Maybe." Tim shrugged and went back to slurping up his noodles.

I squinted at the book next to his forearm. "Whatcha reading?"

"Not reading... translating." He grabbed a paper napkin from the napkin holder. "Algebra. I hate algebra."

"Lemme see. Maybe I could help." I flipped open to the bookmarked page and read the heading. "Differential equations."

"Don't know what that means. Don't care 'bout differential equations."

Algebra wasn't my strong suit. When I was in high school, I'd tried to get my father to help with my homework, but he was always too "busy" with work or whatever else was more important to him than his own son. "I care," I said.

He glanced up, and his eyes dimmed. "You're only saying that because you're stuck with me while my mom's in rehab."

I wish he could see how much I did care for him. I had a lot of Tim's assumptions to dispel. "Not true at all." I clasped my hands, rested my elbows on the table, and studied the pages. "This subject looks way above my pay grade, however."

"Told you it's hard."

"Not hard. If we can't figure it out, someone out there can. I'll pay for the best tutor in town if needed."

"If that's what you wanna do." Tim shrugged one shoulder as if lifting both required too much effort. "I don't care."

"You should care. School's important." I stared at the equations in the textbook, thankful for the possibility of connecting with my son through algebra. Of all the things that a father and son could bond over, mine was algebra. Hey, it was a start.

"You have anyone in mind for this 'best tutor in town'?" Tim asked.

Hannah. Hannah was the best tutor in town, but if she saw Tim, she'd be all kinds of angry. Still, Hannah was a human calculator.

When Hannah and I had been dating in college, she'd helped me pass calculus. I'd thought she'd make a career of solving problems, get her Ph.D., and be a math professor or something, but one day she'd abruptly dropped out of college. I was shocked. She'd said she wanted to focus on modeling before she got too old, but I always sensed there was something more to the story, something she wasn't telling me. I'd come to this conclusion because any time I brought up the possibility of her returning to school, she'd shoot down the idea. Tim had that same "don't care attitude" about math, and like Hannah, I didn't know the full reason. I'd figure it out.

"Earth to Pops." Tim snapped his fingers. "You have anyone in mind for the best tutor in town?"

"I may have someone in mind."

"Who?"

Best not mention Hannah, not when Tim was actually speaking to me. "I'll ask the person. If they agree, then you and I can talk."

"Why the mystery about this person?" Tim asked.

Dammit. This was another one of those trust tests I was in danger of failing. "No mystery. Simply don't want to make any promises unless they agree."

She wouldn't agree. No way would she agree, but I desperately wanted to see Tim improve, and Hannah knew math cold. I'd ask her once she got settled at her home.

"If you say so." Tim didn't sound too convinced.

"I got a notice in the mail. Principal Grant filed a vandalism report. You'll have a formal hearing with the school board and quite possibly a court hearing for vandalism too. This is on top of the kid who's pressing charges on you for the fight," I continued. "You can prove Principal Grant and the school board wrong by improving your grades."

"Ain't got nothing to prove to nobody." He crossed his arms and angled his head to the side, revealing a tattoo of a *Z* on his neck.

Hadn't seen that before. "I didn't know you had a tattoo."

"Yeah. Just got it."

"You have a *Z* etched into your hair too. What does it mean?" I asked.

"Nothing."

Yeah. Nothing. Was that how kids spoke these days? Because it was annoying.

"I keep it real." Tim tugged on his ear. "I'm just me."

"People aren't going to warm up to you simply because you're you. You have a bad school record. Employers, schools. They look at that stuff."

"Whatever. They look at me and see a Black kid. That's all they see."

He had a chip on his shoulder. Last thing he needed was a chip on his shoulder. "Don't pull out the race card unless you can rightfully use it."

"Rightfully use it? You mean unless I can prove I matter to folk? No way."

"No talking back."

Tim rolled his eyes.

"Focus on your work. Become a better student and let your improved record speak. Your color won't even be brought into the equation because your work will speak for itself."

"There you go with that old school 'we gotta be two times better' B.S. Don't care what records say about me. I know who I am."

I know who I am. His assurance unsettled me. Deep down, I didn't know who I was despite Hannah asking me the other day. *Who are you?* The question had been hanging around like a partially picked scab, unanswered.

"You know who you are, huh?" I asked.

"Sure do." He scratched his new tattoo.

"Do those *Z*s have something to do with knowing who you are?"

His face hardened. "No."

Ease up, Jake. Don't want to push Tim away again. This whole being a father after an eleven-year absence was tough. I rubbed my bare wedding ring finger.

Tim closed his textbook. A sticky note with a vaguely familiar address was stuck to the front cover. "What's that?"

"Address to Syracuse Behavioral Health, Mama's rehab center. I calculated it's about sixty-five miles from where we live."

"You calculated? Sounds like you're an A+ math student in the making."

"Ha ha. Addition and subtraction ain't the same as algebra. And this has to do with Mama so... of course I'd do whatever it takes to figure out our distance."

He sounded hopeful. Should I share that I'd found a new place closer to Hannah? "Your calculations are right." I cleared my throat, a vain effort to erase all emotion. "It's in Upstate New York. Out near farmland."

"That's far."

"It is. A couple of hours to drive." Even farther if we moved to New Brunswick to be closer to Hannah. I plucked the sticky note from the front cover, studied the address. Nice penmanship.

"I'd like to see Mama from time to time. Maybe every week. Can we drive there?"

Images of Hannah lying on that hospital bed, burned and bandaged, intersected with Tim's liquid brown eyes, eager and expectant. No time for long drives back and forth to the rehab center. Besides, Tim's mother probably wasn't ready to see him either. "I'm not so sure. When I last spoke to your mother she sounded very anxious and disoriented. Her doctors said she's still detoxing, so she's not quite ready to see you yet."

"She's not?" Dejection was all over his question.

"No." I exhaled, not wanting to delve into this topic. The kid didn't need to more to worry about. "You know... I've been barely getting by on my military check. I'm thinking of getting some contracting jobs in New Brunswick. We'd have to move closer to shorten the commute. You'd still be in the same school district. The lease will be ready for me to sign on Monday."

"You had this figured all out already? Could've just said so. Could've just said you don't want me to live with you and I'm a pain in the a—a pain in the butt and that you're tired of putting up with my sh—putting up with my problems." He dropped his fork on the table and it clattered and bounced, its tines pointing in my direction.

Sucker punched. "If I gave you any reason... If I *recently* gave you any reason to think I don't want you with me, I apologize."

"Then what'll I do while you move closer to your wife and earn this extra cash?"

I heard it in his voice. That sense of being abandoned. It sunk deep and laid roots, weeds that refused to leave. "Nothing will change. You'll live with me. Not sure what they'll decide after the formal hearing. They may have you attend an alternative school or do independent study. If they do, I'll still be here with you. Not leaving you, Tim. Not ever again."

He said nothing, and a jellylike feeling left me numb. I'd never been so honest with Tim. Over the years, there'd been many moments when I'd wondered how Tim was faring, when I'd wondered if he'd felt safe and cared for and loved. I didn't want him living the rest of his life wondering.

"Doesn't change a thing between you and me," I continued. "You're still my main focus. I'm only moving because Hannah's in bad shape. She'll need someone with her while she recovers. I want to be that someone." My voice got hoarser.

"Is that why you left Mama and me?"

I looked outside the window at the calla lily stalk that had sprouted up, no flowers. Not yet.

Tim didn't trust me. Not yet.

I didn't trust myself to be that good father, that good husband. Not yet.

The doubt in Tim's voice made me consider whether my "not yet" would turn into something permanent. Was I a forever failure? "I'm married, Tim. I should've never cheated on Hannah."

"You mean I should've never been born."

"I didn't say that."

"Don't have to. You can't have it both ways. Pretty sure she can't stand me."

He was right about that one. Hannah's words in the hospital about never being this picture-perfect family resurfaced. Yeah, Hannah had said she didn't see us taking Christmas photos at JC Penney anytime soon, but I wanted the three of us to have some type of cohesion. If Hannah tutored Tim, it could also be a way to gain that cohesion— although right now cohesion wasn't happening.

When I was a kid, my family had stopped taking annual Christmas pictures after Mom learned of Pop's multiple girl-friends. She was forever reminding him of his infidelities too, especially when he'd forget the small things like getting milk at the grocery store or filling her gas tank for the week or changing the light bulb for her bedside lamp. Would Hannah do the same? Would she forever use Tim against me as a reminder of how, for one moment, I failed her and our marriage?

Tim shifted in his chair, rustling me out of my musings. "I'll find somewhere else to stay while you help wifey."

Sweat warmed my scalp. I couldn't lose him. "You can't stay anywhere else. I'm your father and your legal guardian. The court order won't allow that either."

"Don't care 'bout no court order." He folded his muscular arms under his pits. "I got friends."

I glanced at that tattoo on his neck. "Gang member friends?"

"Good friends."

My right pinky twitched. He ran with the wrong crowd. The kind of crowd that could get him killed. "Ain't happening, kid. You're living with me."

"Why?" Tim drummed his fingers on the table.

"Because you're my son. The move to New Brunswick will be fine. You won't have to see Hannah, and she won't have to see you."

Unless Hannah decided to actually tutor Tim... Didn't think she'd be up for the idea though.

I backed myself into a corner.

"If we didn't live together, your only other option would be foster care." *Not your gang friends.* "You don't belong in foster care. You have a home and a family."

Tim's chin came down. For a moment, it seemed as if he was going to cry.

More than anything, I wanted Tim to see I wasn't that man who'd walked out on him all those years ago. Too bad I couldn't read minds. I could only read faces, and his face was —broken. Underneath the sharps planes and edges of his features was unease.

The unease of an accumulation of bad memories and experiences and disappointments that had become a fifty-car pileup. No telling how he'd rescue himself from the wreckage. Given his upbringing, his behavior could turn from school fights to more criminal charges. The way Grant was talking, it seemed to be headed that way now.

Tim had never had the chance to have a normal family upbringing. If things had been different, perhaps Tim wouldn't be acting out today.

Once I'd gotten a call from Social Services because his mother had been arrested for stealing food from a grocery store, and I was the next of kin. Tim was so small, a one-year-old at the time. He didn't remember. His mother had told Social Services about me for fear they'd put her kid in foster care. Hannah was working in Milan at the time, and so she didn't know I'd taken in Tim for a week. She didn't know about Tim, period. This had happened before I'd admitted the affair to Hannah. Those days with my son were some of the most memorable days of my life. We had bonded, Tim and me.

His mother was eventually released on bail, and she was quick to take Tim back. She'd said she didn't need me in her life, but I'd still see them for two years after the incident. I'd asked her then if she wanted help or more money than what I'd already been sending her for Tim. I didn't think she should resort to stealing. She refused and said she didn't need to be saved.

Which was why I was stepping in. *Tim* needed to be saved.

"I ain't living with you if I have to deal with you and your wifey. No way. Uh-uh. Don't need this kind of family." Tim snatched the sticky note from my hand and tucked it in his textbook. "I'll finish up my homework in my room." He left the plate partly empty, and I was left in the kitchen alone.

My legs urged me to stomp after him, but a series of questions overpowered the impulse. Was his mind set on other plans? Would his other plans put him around other, undesirable people? Did he value anything I said?

I got up and knocked on his bedroom door. "Tim? You okay?"

No answer.

"If you need anything, I'll be out here." Staring at the crack in the wall. I returned to the kitchen, tossed the left-over spaghetti in the trash, and loaded the dishwasher.

Time stretched into an endless stream of seconds, which

lengthened the distance between my son and me. I should've never brought up moving closer to Hannah. I could've waited until after I signed the lease, earned his trust a bit more.

Who was I kidding? Waiting wouldn't have garnered a different reaction from Tim. I tore off three paper towels and spritzed the countertop with cleaning vinegar. The acidic scent stung my nostrils.

Footsteps scuffing against the Berber rug gave me pause. I loosened my grip on the spray bottle. Tim stood in the doorway with a number two pencil positioned awkwardly between his thumb and index finger. He stared at his bright white sneakers as if to avoid eye contact.

"You okay?" I asked.

"Yeah."

Yeah. Here we go with that "yeah" again. I tossed the paper towels in the trash.

"Can't figure out a math problem," he said.

Relief ballooned inside me. Tim wasn't so mad at me after all.

"You serious about getting me the best tutor?"

Am I serious about Hannah? Because she was the best tutor. Was I still serious after the conversation we'd just had? "Yes. I am."

"Cool." Tim lingered, shifted his weight from side to side. "I want Mama better. I want her happy. She was never happy."

That night I'd met Melinda, she was happy, but her happiness was an illusion. How much could I have known about her after one night? When I'd later learned she'd been stealing groceries, I'd felt all kinds of awful. She was the mother of my child, after all. I didn't want her and my son to go hungry. Should I have given her more money, despite her refusing my offer?

These questions lingered all these years, but I'd been too afraid to answer them for fear of the burden those answers carried. I didn't want to be held responsible for her downfall.

"My mother is a good person," Tim continued. "Don't care what nobody thinks."

"I don't doubt it."

"I was thinking about it more. I might be willing to go along with your move if I can visit Mama on the regular."

This was my chance to reach out and make things better. "That's fair. I'll contact your mother and talk to her doctors, see if they can bend the rules so she can see you. How's that sound?"

"'preciate it." Tim headed back to his room, but before he did, I spoke.

"You really are okay with me signing the lease for the apartment in New Brunswick on Monday? For *our* apartment?"

He paused. "So long as you help me see Mama."

"I certainly will."

The corner of Tim's mouth curved upward. A seed took root in my chest—a seed of hope.

≈

So long as you help me see Mama.
That was my free pass. I could take care of Hannah as long as it didn't impede on Tim's relationship with his mother. A good deal. Hopefully, the doctors would agree or else I was screwed. A mother needed to see her son. As far as I knew, Tim was her only family.

Perhaps he'd agree to the idea of Hannah tutoring too—as long as it didn't impede on his relationship with his mother.

Didn't have to worry about that today. Today, I'd sign the lease. Then I'd stop by Robert Wood Johnson and check on

Hannah, tell her my plans. Yeah, she'd probably flip, but I wasn't going to ask for permission. I didn't care what she thought. She needed help while she recovered.

Know what? My bulldozing ways were part of the reason why Hannah was pissed, but in her current predicament, I didn't have time to think about her feelings. She needed my help.

I made my way down Easton Avenue and passed Buccleuch Park, the place where I'd proposed to her. We'd stood right outside Buccleuch Mansion. The proposal was a spur-of-the-moment thing. The memory pushed its way into my heart and mind.

"I'm moving to New York," Hannah had said as she fiddled with the gold chain around her neck, twisting it so much I thought it'd snap. "I want to be in the city when Greta calls for go-sees. Tired of trying to balance modeling and school."

"You're really not finishing up at school?"

"For what?" Defensiveness edged Hannah's voice.

"Models are smart too, you know," I said. "Beauty and brains. You're the total package."

Her eyes glistened. "Sometimes being the total package is a curse."

Curse? I stopped walking. "What does that mean?"

There was a slight tremor in her lower lip. "Nothing."

Nothing meant something, but this was the part of Hannah I never could reach. A part she'd kept locked in a tightly knotted package. I thought perhaps with time and love, she'd unravel it. "I understand."

"I knew you would." She hadn't removed the chain from her index finger. "I want to capitalize on my career while I'm still young. You could still take the train to Manhattan on the weekends to see me."

I'd snapped off a daisy from a nearby tree and tucked it behind her ear. "Marry me."

She startled. "Marry you?"

"Yes, marry me."

"You saying this because I mentioned New York?"

"Yes."

Her gaze lowered, disappointment etched into the edges.

"Things could change once you're in New York," I added. "You could forget all about me."

"It's only a train ride away," she said.

"That's too far. I love you."

"Love." Hannah's face softened. "You may be the only other person who's ever loved me."

"Is there some guy you're not telling me about?" I tried to sound lighthearted, but I really didn't want to know that answer.

Her face looked pained. "No. No other guy. I was thinking of my grandmother. Too bad you two never met."

"I bet I love you more than your grandmother did."

"You're crazy."

"Crazy about you."

She'd said yes to my proposal. Just like she'd said yes to a legal separation.

Was I stupid for moving back to New Brunswick?

The thought pinched, but I held on to the memory of us at Buccleuch Park. The memory of her smile when I'd said I loved her. That memory couldn't have completely died. She had to still hold some semblance of feeling toward me. Didn't she?

I made a left on Somerset Street. Just as I was about to step into the leasing office, my cell phone rang. Mother. "What's up?"

"Thank goodness I got a hold of you."

She sounded tense. "Everything all right?"

"No. That's why I'm calling you. It's your father."

Last time my mother had said "it's your father," he'd cleaned out the bank accounts before leaving on a "business trip." Didn't return until two months later. "What'd he do now?"

"Don't be cynical, Jake."

"I'm not being cynical. I'm being realistic. He doesn't exactly have a track record for good behavior." I turned. My reflection stared at me, and bile rose in my throat. Like father, like son.

"We're back from the hospital, your father and me. They're running some tests. Your father hasn't been himself lately."

Blood rushed to my ears. Please, no more complications, no more bad news to handle. Last thing I needed was more worry. I'd worry about Mom, not my father. She'd lose all common sense if something happened to him.

"He's been fainting a lot," she continued.

That could be anything. I listened, kept my mouth closed. Any hint of disagreement would make her worry more.

"I don't have a good feeling, Jake."

I stepped into the foyer of the leasing office and waved to the young woman at the counter. She was watching Jerry Springer on a mini-television. "I'm sure everything'll be fine."

"You think?"

Something in her words sounded oddly hollow. "I know."

"You should fly out here to Los Angeles and see us."

"Aw, you want me to visit? You could've asked," I said playfully. "No shame in asking."

"We'd like to meet our grandson too. I wish you would've told us about him when he was born."

My shoulders dipped slightly, and I shifted into a mild stress state. The shame in breaking my marriage vows still hovered. When Tim was born, I'd feared telling my parents about him. I was worried they'd tell Hannah since they'd been so close. It was twisted. Still was twisted.

"You're right. He needs to see all of his family, but he's concerned about his mother. I have to make sure he doesn't feel as if I'm taking him away from her. He feels alone."

"Sometimes knowing you have a lot of family helps with loneliness. Not good to walk around thinking you have no history. That'll make a person latch on to anything just to gain an identity."

That ugly tattoo on Tim's neck and that stupid *Z* etched into his hair were vying for my son's identity. "You're right again."

"So when can we meet him?"

"Not sure. Hannah's in the hospital."

"What?"

I explained the entire predicament and Mom gasped.

"Thank goodness she made it out of the fire safely. Where is she now?"

"I called and checked this morning. They transferred her to the burn unit. I'm going to visit her shortly and talk to her doctor. See how I can help."

"That's good. Very, very good. You know I'm not a fan of broken marriages. This is an unfortunate incident for her, but perhaps it'll bring you closer together. She'll need you."

A life-threatening fire would bring us closer together? Was this how she bonded with my father, through tragedy? "Uh huh."

"I'm not a fan of divorce either."

Her tone was mild enough, but I sensed every nuance. A subtle censure edged Mom's words. Stick it out, she implied. No matter how bad it is, stick it out. That was her method with my father. It would be my method with Hannah too, hopefully. "I know."

"I'll be praying for Hannah. Poor thing. You keep us

posted. When you can, fly out here and visit your father. It'll be good for you."

Can't make any promises. "Love you." I hung up.

Maybe Mom was right. It would be good for Tim to meet his grandparents. Yet this wasn't the time. Besides, why visit a man who reminded me of the worst parts of myself?

CHAPTER 10

I craved water.

I'd never known my throat could feel so dry. I tried calling out to the nurse, but my tongue had been caked to the bottom of my mouth.

A figure entered the room. Perhaps they'd help me. I tried sitting up, but razors ripped like a knife down my neck. I needed morphine. More morphine.

The figure did something to my IV and the pain slid away. Thank you.

I heard more shuffling and murmurs in my room. Burn units were depressing. I'd been in this place close to a week, and my feelings for the place hadn't changed.

They changed my dressings twice a day. Dressings? What was I, a turkey? Every time the staff came in to change me, it was like getting prepped for roasting. (Another bad analogy. Being stuck in a hospital gave me plenty of time to create bad analogies.)

This room always had a mountain of rubber gloves and paper masks and a trail of gauze that could wrap the universe. Between the smells of skin and the squeals and screams of patients and the sometimes screams of visitors, I had my fill.

Dr. Hutchinson said I needed to get someone to learn how to do all this for me at home. I agreed. After that incident with Mama the other day, however, I wasn't choosing her as my helper. No way, Jose. Still, I had to choose someone if I wanted to get discharged. Too bad I couldn't call Liza. Time to put my thinking cap on. It would take me a couple of days.

Harsh streaks of sunlight slashed through the Venetian blinds. I blinked at them. Part of me wanted to block the rays and hide in the darkness. Hide from myself.

"Hey there."

My insides somersaulted and I turned. Jake? What was he doing here? I wasn't in the mood to play Brady Bunch with the dude.

Then again, my insides felt all warm at the sight of him. It was like my burned body wanted him, though my mind knew better. Way, way better. Jake was getting all up in my feelings. "Why'd you come back?"

"Felt like I left you on a down note. I want to take you for a walk today." He held the door ajar with his foot and brought in the biggest contraption I'd ever seen.

"A wheelchair?"

"I spoke to your doctor outside. Dr. Hutchinson. She said you can get around with a wheelchair. We'll take a little stroll on the hospital floor. Whaddya think?"

I scrunched my face. "I don't need strolls."

"You need something. I wouldn't want to be cooped up in bed all day. If someone offered to take me out, I'd seize the opportunity. Make the most of the moment."

"Good for you, Zig Ziglar."

"What's that supposed to mean?"

The top of my skull itched, beneath the bandages, but I

knew better than to try to scratch at it. Already there was a pull at my singed hair. More bandages.

"Means I don't need a motivational speech."

"I get it."

Why'd he have to be so understanding? Good lord. All his niceties bugged the Beetlejuice out of me. "I don't see how being pushed on a rolling contraption and seeing other burn victims will calm and soothe."

"We can go down to the lobby too. Dr. Hutchinson said so."

Freedom. "We can?"

"Yep." Jake extended his hand and I stared at it for a split second. "I'll help you in the wheelchair. I won't bite, Hannah."

"I never said you bite."

"Sure are acting like it."

He laughed, and a part of me couldn't help but laugh too. My chuckle was deep and rich and it filled in an empty space within me. A placed I'd long forgotten.

Nope. Those types of feelings sucked me into places I didn't want to return. Happy places. Places where I'd forgotten all about his betrayal and his broken promises. Forgetting could lead to… reconciling. *Blech!* Ain't happening. Not with him.

"Okay, I'll go for one push on the wheelchair around the hospital," I said. "Preferably the first floor. Nothing more."

A shadow crossed his features, a shadow of disappointment. "Nothing more," he said.

Jake gently rolled back the blankets covering me and looked me up and down. All my self-consciousness returned. "I know. I look like a banged-up mummy. Get over it."

"Never said that." His voice was quiet.

Jake was right. He was never the type to negatively comment on my appearance, unlike Paco. But Jake probably thought negatively about my appearance. "Then what do you want to say about my appearance?" The words came out of my mouth, but I didn't want to know his answer. I'd seen my answer in the mirror. Hated it. "Tell me."

What was my problem? Didn't I just tell myself I didn't want to hear his answer? Methinks I'm a sucker for rejection.

"Ugly is impossible for you."

"Is that why you had that one-night stand? 'Cuz I wasn't ugly?" Even I was startled by the sound of my voice, harsh and cold and metallic. Was this what happened after trying for a child and having none? Was this what happened after carrying guilt over a miscarriage that you'd kept under wraps? A miscarriage from a college rape that was best left dead and buried with the embryo it produced? That math professor ruined my life in more ways than one.

"Let's not go there okay?" Jake said. "I'm taking you for a walk." He reached over and gently placed his left arm under my legs. "Let me know if you're in pain or anything."

I caught a whiff of his cologne. Mesmerizing. He carried me over to the wheelchair, and I kept inhaling his scent like a dog in heat.

"There you go, Mama." He placed me in the wheelchair.

I winced. I'd never be a mother. "Don't call me Mama." I tried swinging my legs into the leg rests, but that wasn't working out too well. Jake helped with that too.

After I was secured in the seat, he pushed me out the room, past the nurse's station, and down the elevators. I had to admit, it was nice being out of that blasted dark room.

"You okay?"

"Yeah."

Jake winked at me, and I sensed his warmth. Comforting. Once we were on the first floor, he parked my wheelchair near the waiting area overlooking Somerset Street. The world outside looked busy with a garbage truck rumbling down the street and a group of Catholic school kids waiting for the crossing guard to let them pass. The world continued on. Didn't need me for anything. If I wasn't model perfect, what else could I give the world? Nothing.

Jake studied me. There was a satisfied benevolence to him like he was a king surveying me, his subject. That was annoying. "Whatcha looking at?" I asked him.

"The medical staff said they can't release you until you have someone trained in caring for you full time."

"I know."

"I volunteered."

The words landed like a fist on the table. "You what?"

"I volunteered to care for you full time."

"You didn't."

"I did." He took a piece of paper from his back pocket. "Made it official and everything."

Everything in me stilled. I had to scramble to get out of this one. Quick. "Mama already said she was moving in with me."

"I know."

"Hold up." I raised my hand. "Y'all were talking to each other?"

"Texting over the past few days. That's all."

"Sounds like conspiring."

"She said that she's on a reduced work schedule, so I offered to fill in whenever she worked."

"So y'all just gonna come in, uproot me, and not ask me how I feel, huh? You always do this, Jake. When you found me in the bathtub that time, you went ahead and scheduled me for all the doctors and the counseling and never asked me how I wanted to go about things. You handled it as if I was something broke that needed to be fixed... quick."

He stopped. "You never told me this."

"You never asked!" My voice echoed and bounced off the walls, but I didn't care.

"We're not uprooting, Hannah. We're up-lifting." Jake frowned, slid forward in his chair, and his biceps tensed. "We care. I'm asking how you feel now."

No way I could get out of this one. Did I have money for a home care person? No. "I feel stuck like I have no choice."

"I understand where you're coming from. If you only want your mom with you, that'll be fine with me."

What was I supposed to do on the days Mama wasn't there? Gah. This man was really tightening my thinking cap. All of a sudden, the view outside the street looked terrifying. Unless I came up with another idea, once I joined the outside world, I'd have to rely on my mother and Jake. Two people I'd wanted to avoid the most.

"Did you have someone else in mind?" he asked.

Did I want to answer that question? Couldn't call Liza now and ask for help after a whole month. Me and my big mouth. Why'd I have to be so full of myself? I rested my chin in my hands. This was the pits.

"Doc said you're coming along nicely. Should be discharged in a few weeks. I can drive you home on your discharge day."

"How'd you get all this info from my doctor?" I tried to keep my tone level. "She didn't tell me, and I've been sitting in that room getting my bandages changed and staring at the ceiling all day."

"I am your husband, Hannah. That qualifies me to know about your condition."

Yeah, and I'll have to stay married to you for four more years to get to the magic twenty according to the insurance. Either that or come into a boatload of money. I touched my face, a lingering stroke with my fingertips. My jawline was rough and dry. Hadn't been on my regular skincare routine, but a fancy skincare line wasn't going to get rid of gross.

A warmth spread up my neck and face. Did someone turn

up the thermostat? I hated how something as superficial as my skin had the power to make me feel so—powerless. When I'd seen myself in the mirror that first day in the hospital, I vowed to never ever look at myself in the mirror again. Ever.

Jake checked his watch. "I'll take you back up. Doc said I only had thirty minutes."

I let my head loll to the side. All this new information was too heavy to bear. Doc said. Doc said. Doc said. What about what I said? What I wanted?

I wanted to be left alone. That wasn't going to happen.

I wanted my skin and my hair back to normal. That wasn't going to happen.

I wanted my career back too. Most likely not happening.

What was there left to want?

My hand dropped. Numbness seeped in, and it didn't have anything to do with pain or morphine or whatever. I knew the difference.

Nope. It had to do with lost hope. With having all of my wants explode.

≈

*D*ischarge Day. The day for me to exit one prison and enter another. Boo to the universe! You sucked at this little thing called my life.

I tossed the covers off my legs. (That was something I could do now.) And I took in the pile of bandages and gauze from last night. Nurse said she'd be here to show my care-giver how to change my dressings. My caregiver? Like I was in a nursing home wetting my diaper on the hour. Good gracious.

Anyhoo, my "caregivers" would be Mama and Jake. Mama was here already, rustling through my belongings and being nosy as all get out. Sigh.

I was gonna make sure it'd be all business too, especially when Jake picked me up today. I didn't need more moments of inhaling his cologne or staring at his eyes or imagining… Whatever. That was too extra.

"Morning, Miss Lady." The mahogany nurse from my first day entered the room. All smiles and joy. "Ready for freedom?"

"No."

She gave a Sunday dinner laugh, the hearty, fill-you-up kind where all the meat slid off the bone. "You're nervous, that's all. You'll be fine. World ain't changed much."

"But I have." That stupid frog returned to my throat.

The nurse stopped checking my IV. "You have."

I lowered my gaze, stared at the needle stuck in my forearm. The one connected to that bag of liquid that would soon be disengaged from my body. The one that supported me. For the first time, I feared myself. Feared my ability to… to be. "Think I can make it out there on my own?"

"Course you can. You'll be just fine." She reached over and disengaged the needle from my arm. I let out a tiny gasp like I was a deflated balloon.

"I agree." Mama crumpled my used hospital gowns and tossed them in the hamper.

"How do you feel?" The nurse wrapped the needle in a plastic bag and tossed it in the bio-hazard trash can near the window.

"Odd."

She reached over me and I noticed the gray hairs at her temple. She was much older than I'd assumed.

"What's your name?" I asked.

"Estella."

"That's pretty."

"A French name. It means star." She opened the blinds in my room. "My mother had said my eyes were shining brightly when I was born. So she wanted me to be named with the stars."

"That's lovely." Wonder why my mother named me Hannah? She never told me why. We never got sentimental.

"Anyone else picking you up today?"

Blech. "Jake."

"A friend?"

Oh. She was digging now. "My soon-to-be ex-husband." Soon-to-be meaning in four years, but that was beside the point.

There was a flutter of recognition in her eyes like she was finally putting together the pieces of my story. At least she could piece them together. I felt all scattered and discombobulated.

"Ah, yes. Jake. I remember meeting him the other day when he came in for caregiver training. He seemed to pick up on the procedures. Quick learner."

Oh lordy. I said nothing. Didn't want to get into all the reasons Jake picking me up was such a horrible idea. It wasn't her business anyway. "I need street clothes. Does the hospital have spare outfits?"

"I'll have to check. Usually, whoever is picking you up would've brought something."

That would've been Mama, but that obviously didn't happen. Having Mama around was helping and hurting. No way in the world was I calling Jake and telling him to go through my underwear drawer. A knock on the door stopped my musings. Jake, the not-so-love of my life, stood in the doorway. My heart squeezed into pieces.

"My son!" Mama called. She walked over to Jake and hugged him tight. Jake returned the gesture.

Ugh. Jake and Mama were like buddies now. Two against one.

"There you are, Jake." Estella clasped her hands and

looked at me and then at Jake and then at me again with this odd expression like she wanted to see us kiss and make up or something. I hoped she wasn't gonna try and play hospital matchmaker, 'cuz that wasn't happening.

"I was about to go and find some spare clothes for your wife, Jake."

She called me his wife. Ack! Stab me with a thousand knives, why don't you? I was technically his wife, but come on now. Didn't even dignify me with a name anymore? How annoying was that?

"Lucky for you, Hannah, I purchased a spare outfit." He produced a frilly pink shopping bag from behind his back and twirled it around and around and around.

How thoughtful—no, *not* thoughtful. It was a necessary gesture, nothing thoughtful at all. When I took the bag from his hands, our fingertips touched and the warmth tingled all the way to my heart. I jerked my hand back.

A tiny smile curved Jake's lips. Our eyes engaged. Stupid googly eyes. I looked away and rustled through the contents of the shopping bag.

"Do you want to try changing her bandages before you leave the hospital?" Estella asked Jake.

His smile grew wider. It grew double-trailer wide. "I'd love to."

"My mother already had that training too," I said quickly. "There's a strong possibility you won't have to concern yourself with changing bandages."

"And there's a strong possibility I'll have to attend to them," Jake said. "Better to be on the safe side."

"I agree." Estella winked.

Jake must've charmed the pants off her during that caregiver training 'cuz she obviously was on his side. Guess they were ganging up on me. "Don't I have a say in this matter?" I asked.

"It's for the best, Hannah," Estella said. "We want to make sure you're one hundred percent recovered. You'll spend more time at home than you'll ever spend here, so the continuation of care has to be as seamless as possible. We'll see how you fare at your follow-up visits." Estella smiled. "Let's have your husband change the alignate dressings on your legs."

Jake stepped closer and my heart beat rapidly.

"You okay, Hannah?" he asked.

"Yep. I'm perfectly fine."

Estella set out a bottle of antimicrobial soap. "We'll also have you clean the wounds, Jake, so you can practice."

"Clean wounds? As in Jake's gonna bathe me?"

Estella's eyes widened. "Well, um, no. This is for your extremities. The parts burned by the fire."

Good thing those other, womanly parts weren't burned by the fire. That would be… odd, seeing that Jake and I hadn't had sex since he told me he was considering taking in Tim. When he actually did, I knew he wasn't getting any from me. Neva!

Mama stood sat on the chair across from my bed. "Jake's your husband. He's seen everything. I've seen everything. The nurse has probably seen everything too."

Estella nodded her agreement. "I have."

Oh brother.

"This is only for your arms and legs," Estella said. "If you'd like I can have your mom do your core and neck."

That meant Mama was gonna wash my boobs. How was this a topic of discussion? So embarrassing. For one, I never liked Mama looking at my body. Not since the day she'd shamed me for being an overweight teen. Her critical eye always made me uneasy. For two, yeah, I was a model and all, but I was also a Type A perfectionist. Mix one and two together and I was left with a recipe for stress.

"I don't have to do this part if you're uncomfortable, Hannah," Jake said.

"No. No. No." Mama stood up and wagged her finger at Jake as if he'd been caught with his hand in the cookie jar. "You should do this part. You're the husband."

You're the husband? Did she forget what this "husband" did to me? Did she *care* what this "husband" did to me? Obviously not. See, this was the problem. Mama didn't care. All she held in her mind were these old-fashioned ideas of how a woman needed to suck it up no matter what the husband did. I'd had it with Mama's pushiness, but I was too worn out to fight. "Okay. Okay. Okay. Change the dressings, Jake. I'm tired of this back and forth."

I shimmied to the edge of the bed and carefully slid into the wheelchair. Mama wheeled me over to the shower and I paused. "I'm not stripping naked for you guys. This is only my legs and arms."

"Fair enough."

I rolled up the bottom of my hospital gown and made a side knot, holding the tail end of my faded gown. Jake reached over and turned on the water, his tricep muscle flexing just enough to make me notice. Why couldn't he be dog ugly? It'd be much easier to hate him, know what I mean?

"Water too hot for you?" Jake asked. The sexiness in his voice irritated me.

"It should be tepid," Estella said, standing off to the side.

"You can make it a little cooler." I held my breath, a reflex reaction to the water... or his tricep. Right now, I couldn't tell.

Jake squirted a couple of pumps of the antimicrobial soap into a clean washcloth.

"No washcloths, remember from training?" Estella said. "We use our hands. Washcloths are too rough."

I scrunched my nose. No washcloths? He needs a wash-cloth. I'm not ready for skin-to-skin contact.

The hesitancy in Jake's eyes told me he thought the same thing. And this audience of two wasn't helping me out at all. "Get it over with," I blurted. "Let's get this over with."

He unwrapped the bandages on my calves and thighs. My skin was red and crusty. I glanced at the nurse and almost asked her if it was wise for them to release me, but I didn't want to put any extra thoughts in her head. Staying in the hospital was like being imprisoned against my will. At least when I was home, I'd get a start on the road to independence.

Jake unloosened the shower head and ran the water over my legs. I shivered at his touch.

"Too cold for you?"

"Nope." I tried to sound normal too, but that wasn't working. His hands on my skin made me feel like a crazed teenage fan at a concert. When we first held hands a bazillion years ago, I'd undergone a similar sensation. I'd known then that he was The One, but I kept my cool. I was like a still pond. Zen and calm. Didn't want to let on that he was The One on the first date and all. That wasn't gonna go over too well.

Even now, I'd have to be all unmoved and businesslike.

Eeeeee! This was far from being businesslike. My mind was being all awkward-like, thinking these thoughts.

"Here's the ointment." Estella handed Jake a pair of latex gloves and a jar of Silvadene. "Don't forget to apply every ten to twelve hours. Once in the morning and once at night."

I nodded, but all I could think about was Jake's hands touching my thighs. Last time he was this close, it was like I'd died and gone to heaven—that was before the betrayal. I directed my attention to Estella. "Don't you think I should put on the ointment myself?"

"You'll need help wrapping the new gauze around your

legs, Hannah. That can be tricky given the burns on your arms." Estella took fresh gauze from a small box.

Medically correct reasoning was so annoying.

"Let him finish, Hannah. Don't be so stubborn." Mama gave me her mean-mama look.

"Fine," I said.

Jake had this borderline arrogant look on his face. Like he'd won this boxing round.

Whatever, cheddar!

He applied the cream to my legs, and his touch ignited a flood of memories. Like of the time when I'd had a complete breakdown after one gynecologist checkup. The visit where the gynecologist said I'd never conceive a child because my uterus wasn't shaped correctly. She said I'd risk serious health problems and possibly death if on the off-chance I conceived.

I'd been so annoyed with her "prescription" to simply stop trying to conceive like it was a decision I could easily make. The woman didn't understand. That college rape was traumatic, violent, and I wouldn't be surprised if it messed up my uterus. I never mentioned the rape to the gyno, however. Some things were best left unsaid.

The unsaid had become a soul scar, my taskmaster, and I couldn't help but blame the professor—and myself—for my inabilities to become a mother. Why'd I ever think it was okay to meet that dumbass professor at his office in the evenings to discuss homework anyway? Was I that trusting of folks? Obviously.

Who would've thought that a respectable man with a Ph.D. would be a rapist? Not me.

Perhaps if I'd told the gynecologist, she would've referred me to a shrink who specialized in trauma. But I'd figured it was best to let her think I was a woman anxious to conceive, not a woman holding in her body the memories of being dehumanized, violated, and later threatened. At the time, I was too distraught by her diagnosis and those memories to consider seeking a shrink on my own. Wasn't until Jake had caught me in the tub that day that I actually saw one.

I cried after that doctor's appointment. I cried for my jacked-up sense of self. Jake had taken me in his arms, and his touch had felt so comforting, much like it did now.

That was one of the biggest oxymorons of my relationship with Jake. The way he could be so kind but then be so hurtful. Perhaps it was true what they'd said— those you love the most know how best to hurt you. The day Jake said he had a son was the most awful day of my life.

When I'd said we could make our relationship work after he'd dropped the news of his one-night stand, I actually thought I could salvage the mess our marriage had become. When he'd decided to take in Tim, all my dreams of a happy marriage were crushed. Not only would I never have the chance to nurse a baby of my own, I'd never have a loving (faithful!!) husband by my side. The child Jake had with another woman would be the only child he'd have.

And I'd have none.

He finished up with the bandages, and I nodded my thanks at Jake and Mama. "Guess I'll finish getting dressed and packed," I said. "You guys have done enough." They were going to be around me all the time for the next few months. Why have them start hanging around me now?

After they left, I stood up and hobbled over to the shopping bag. When I did, I crossed the window and caught my reflection. I quickly lowered my eyes. It was shadowy, so I couldn't see much of myself. I didn't want to see much of myself.

I looked away. Estella was there, watching me. "Hard, isn't it?"

My eyes watered and stung, but I blinked away the sensation.

"It'll get better," she continued.

"When?" My lower lip trembled.

"In time. In time, the memories will fade. You'll forget."

The memories of my miscarriage during college hadn't faded. Not one bit. The memories of that terrible professor at Rutgers hadn't faded. Bad memories latched onto me like blood-sucking leeches and tried to drain me with each passing second. "How do you know I'll forget?"

She didn't answer, which meant she was trying to make me feel better about how awful I looked. They must've trained her to do that in nursing school. I ruffled through the shopping bag and pulled out an "I Love New York" T-shirt. Silly man. Jake knew how much I loved Manhattan.

"Guess I don't have to look for a spare set of clothes for you after all." Estella smiled. "That was nice of him to bring clothes for you."

"He can be nice when he wants to. Part of the reason I fell for him in the first place."

"Lemme see how he did your bandages." Estella bent and inspected my calves. "Very good of him. Very, very good."

That meant he was officially signed up as the Bandage Changer now.

"Think I'll eventually be able to do this by myself?"

"Eventually. But not today. I'll take care of your arms for now." She placed her plump hands on my forearm. "Be careful with yourself when you're on your own. I almost had a fit when I heard you ripped off your bandages a few weeks ago."

"Rip them off? I didn't rip them off. They accidentally unraveled. I was angry at my mother and was flailing my arms."

Estella gave me a look. The kind that said she didn't

believe me at all. "Try not to be so angry. You'll only end up hurting yourself."

Anger was good. Anger kept me from believing Jake would keep his word when, in fact, he didn't. Anger gave me the strength to go to the lawyer's office and file for a legal separation in the first place.

Yet now there was no way I could be separated from him—at least not immediately. What would I do? He'd already given me the shivers when he'd changed my bandages. Simply making a decision to keep things businesslike wasn't gonna work. Even though I couldn't stand him, the physical attraction was still there, and physical attraction could tempt me to toss all my separation plans out the window.

I needed boundaries with Jake. I needed terms too—clear, outlined terms. Maybe get them in writing. It could be my almost-separation agreement. Yes. That'd be perfect.

I headed to the door and saw my reflection in the window. A mirror image of myself shone in the sunlight.

Correction: That would be *almost* perfect.

~

*W*e left the hospital. Mama said she had to work the evening shift but that she'd return in the morning. Typical. I should've known that she'd set things up so that Jake and I would be alone.

Didn't matter. I was gonna set these ground rules with Jake and make them loud and clear. That was the problem in our relationship. Everything had always been so watery and unstable between us. Even when he'd proposed, it never seemed like he was ready to be married. I always sensed he proposed just 'cuz I said I was moving.

So why'd I say yes?

I hated thinking extra hard about stuff I didn't want to think about.

Today, I'd make the boundary lines of Jake's next few months with me clear, clear, clear. Our conversations would only focus on my recovery—nothing else. I didn't need to resurrect our skeletons.

He pulled his truck up in front of my house and turned off the ignition. "Home sweet home."

"My home," I said quickly.

He exhaled and twirled his car keys on his index finger. "Your home."

"This doesn't change a thing between us, Jake. I want you to know this doesn't change a thing."

"I'll get your bags." He hopped out of the truck and closed the door behind him.

Jake didn't acknowledge what I'd said. Whatever. He'd always been this way. When I tried to tell him about my concerns about having a baby, he always brushed me off, said the fertility treatments would kick in, and I needed faith. After he said that, there was no way I was gonna tell him about what happened in college.

We weren't done with this discussion about this being *my* home. That was for sure. I tapped my fingers on my knee and tried to figure out a way to bring this up again. Man, it was hot in here. I wiped the side of my face. That's what happened when you wore bandages 24/7 and there wasn't any air conditioning to be found.

I rolled down the window and glanced outside. The tail-gate slammed shut, and Jake made his way up the steps.

"Did you hear what I said?" I yelled. "This is my home. My burns don't change the nature of our relationship."

He set the nylon bag down and turned and looked at me, his expression full of hurt. I didn't care. "I get it, Hannah."

"Good." I crossed my arms and huffed.

Ten steps led to the front door of my house. Anxiety bore down on me, a heavy weight. I legit had to go through real life with these scars. Scars that wouldn't be completely erased.

To make it worse, I'd played all big and bad with Jake. How was I going to get up those steps without his assistance?

Good ol' fashioned grit. That's what would get me up those steps. Go, go, go, Hannah. Go, go, go, Hannah. I repeated the words in my brain, stared at my feet, and hoped for the best.

Jake tapped on my window, and I startled. "Ready to go inside?"

"I'll handle it."

He looked at me and then at the steps and then back at me. "You sure?"

"Yep." I unlocked the side door and hopped out of the truck. My legs went from feeling like needles at the hospital to feeling like wood planks.

Jake looked me up and down again. He didn't think I could walk up these steps, but you know what? I didn't care. He didn't have to believe. I'd climb those steps myself. He'd already been too close to comfort when he washed my legs with Estella and Mama watching.

I put one foot in front of the other. A sharp sting shot up my shins, but I took a breath and pushed aside the pain. Nonetheless, bending my knees was waaay tooo painfulllll. So I kept my legs straight.

"You look stiff." He said, a tiny smirk at the corner of his mouth. "You look like you need my help."

"I'm good." I took another step. Was someone banging an invisible hammer on my knees? Good gracious. I robot-walked to the foot of the steps and every single piece of me almost collapsed, but I kept pushing.

Jake stood off to the side, smiling at me. "I'll carry you up.

It'll be like when we crossed the threshold after our honeymoon." He wasn't joking either.

"Now that's cold-blooded. Taking advantage of my dire predicament."

"Don't be so melodramatic."

I grasped the railing and propelled my body weight up the first step. Felt like hauling bricks.

"Hannah, you don't have—"

"I said I'll do it, okay? Leave me alone." My voice turned sharp and tight.

I refused to depend on him for everything. If I did, he'd find some reason to hang around even longer.

I pushed myself up those steps nine more times. By the time I reached the top landing, I was breathless and my entire body stung.

Jake rewarded me with a slow applause. "Good for you."

"Your compliment sounds reluctant."

"It's not. You've always been a strong woman, even when you didn't believe you were strong."

Jake was charming. Still, he didn't know about how small I'd felt after that assault. Small and powerless and weak. That feeling had stayed with me all these years.

He jogged up the steps and stood next to me, and that blasted Irish Spring scent reared its not-so-ugly head. I tried not to inhale, but that lasted for a second before my lungs collapsed.

I loved his smell. I didn't love the person attached to the smell. But the smell... Yeah, Irish Spring on a man was my weakness.

"You're smiling."

"No, I'm not," I said, suddenly self-conscious.

"Don't worry. I won't tell anyone if you won't." A dimple formed on his left cheek.

Drats.

I loved his dimples. His dimples were very pokey, made him all handsome.

The breeze kicked up once again, wafting more of Jake's fragrance my way. I'd get through this next four months. I really, really, really would.

Really.

"You probably don't have house keys on you. Do you?" he asked.

"Nope. I lost those in the fire too." I jiggled the doorknob. "What? You don't have your keys?"

"Um, no. When you told me to move out, that's what I did. I moved out. I let go of the keys. I let go of everything."

My hands clenched reflexively while a muscle leaped in my jaw. His words sounded so—final.

Of course they sounded final. I kicked him out, didn't I?

I hated it when my conscience made sense. Still, hearing Jake say he let go kinda hurt (emphasis on kinda). Did that mean I was getting soft on the dude? Better not, 'cuz he definitely didn't deserve soft.

Jake rubbed the side of his chin, tapped his jaw. "Mind if I check around the side of the house?"

"What are you gonna do? Break in?"

"I can't be charged with breaking in. It's my… it's your house. And you're here."

He had a point. "What are you going to do?"

"When we first moved in, I hid a key around the side of the house, remember?"

I shuffled through my memory. "Oh yeah. I forgot."

Jake jogged down the steps and walked around the house. I heard leaves crunching and rustling. Another bead of sweat trickled down my brow. By now, the bandages felt like sticky goo on my skin. I'd be due for another bandage changing soon. Jake would have to do that since he was the only one here.

The. Only. One. Here. Eeek. I pushed the thought of him touching my extremities out of my head.

Seconds later, Jake reappeared, and he held up a shiny gold key. "Found it under the decorative stone."

He pressed it into my hand and lingered a little too long. The side of his mouth lifted into a smile, and my heart gained two pounds too much. I'd always liked his quirky little mouth, all luscious and full. I used to be able to kiss his mouth for seconds and minutes and hours.

Not hours, but pretty darn close.

"You're thinking about something," he said, his expression unreadable.

"I am?" I croaked. Why'd I croak? "Oh yeah. The keys. I'm thinking about the keys."

"Keep them." His hand gently squeezed mine. "That way you won't second-guess me, popping in unannounced."

Wow. And he was being trustworthy. Had he changed, or was he being extra charming? My heart said changed. My brain said extra charming.

Head? Heart? Head? Heart? So confusing. I went for extra charming with a touch of change.

(I know. I was horrible at making Jake decisions.)

I opened the front door and a shaft of light filtered through the side window along with a whole bunch of dust bunnies. I sneezed. More work to do. I usually dusted my house religiously, but the stint in the hospital left me with more housework. Housework that I couldn't do all taped up. Maybe Mama would help.

I took another step forward, but afterward, everything ached. Did I want to ask him for help getting inside my house? Like really. Did I want to ask?

Before I opened my mouth, Jake slipped his right arm underneath my legs and my skin stung. "Oweee!"

"Sorry, I'll be more careful."

Be more careful. How ironic. Was he careful when his ding-a-ling slipped out of his pants that night? The thought hurt more than my burns.

Jake carried me across the threshold. "You look like you're about to go in for a root canal without anesthetic," he said.

I twisted my mouth. This whole trying to set clear boundaries with Jake obviously wasn't working, 'cuz at any moment he could (1) piss me off or (2) make me all fluttery inside. Once we got settled, I was gonna tell him ALL.THE. RULES. 'Cuz we needed rules!

Did I forget to mention rules? Rules. Rules. Rules.

When we arrived in the living room, he set me down gently on my leather love seat and propped my feet up on a footstool. Whew, even his embrace made me heady. Reminded me of the time…

Forget it.

"There you go, ma'am."

I studied him up close. I'd forgotten how gorgeous his eyes were. How calm and assured his stance was. We'd only been separated for a few months but I'd missed that about him.

Jake's eyebrows made a slight movement. "Want me to carry you again?"

"What?" My tone was pitchy—more like squeal-y. "No way."

He bent and inspected the bandage wrapped around my left heel. "This one looks a bit loose." After tightening a bit, he said, "I'm hungry, and I know you haven't gone grocery shopping."

"Nope. And the food probably went bad too. I'll have to dump it out and wipe down the shelves and go grocery shopping and—"

"Don't you worry. I'll take care of those details. We'll

order pizza from Sal's." He left to make the phone call to the pizza spot, and I exhaled and rested my head against the headrest. Now that he'd carried me to the sofa and offered to help clean out my fridge, I was kinda glad he was around.

Yet the way I slipped into a natural attraction to him was annoying. I had to keep my heart on lockdown, no emotions whatsoever. He'd already completely shattered my life with that child. A child that would forever serve as a constant reminder of my own mistakes, my own failures.

"Pizza should be here in twenty minutes or so," Jake said.

"Good." Now would be the perfect time to discuss our ground rules and make sure it was super incredibly clear I didn't want to engage in any talk, interaction, or thing that didn't have to do with burn care.

No marriage relationship talk.

No "let's work this out" talk.

No Tim talk.

And definitely no Tim's mother talk. I didn't want to deal with baby mama drama. I had enough drama on my own.

"I signed a lease for a condominium two streets over. Tim and I will be moving in the next week. I figured it'd be best to be closer to you during this transition time."

Brain fart. More like brain indigestion. "What'd you just say?"

He repeated himself.

"Oh no, no, no, no, no. That isn't happening. If you think moving closer to me is gonna somehow get me to make nice-nice with you and reconcile—well, that isn't gonna happen. We agreed to you helping out whenever my mother couldn't. We didn't agree to you living so close you're practically breathing down my bandaged neck."

He looked like a little wounded puppy with his mouth drooping in disappointment. It was almost endearing.

Stop it, Hannah.

"You didn't hear a word I said when it came to you helping me, did you?" I continued. "Tuesdays and Thursdays. That's it. I didn't say you should move closer to me."

"I know what you said, Hannah. I've given it some thought. What you said was right."

Now I was confused. "What part of what I said was right?"

"I didn't move here to convince you to give us a second chance. You don't want a second chance, and so I won't push one on you. I'm only here for the four-month recovery time on the days we agreed. Me helping you doesn't mean I'm expecting us to reconcile. I've added another stipulation too so you know I'm serious. I'll be here only if you request I come over to help. That way you don't feel like I'm invading your space."

All of my words got stuck in my throat again. I coughed, tried to get them out.

"You okay?" he asked.

More coughing. More figuring out what in the world this man was up to. He was offering more boundaries than I'd planned. After a couple of seconds of my little episode, I sat straighter.

"Before, you sounded like you wanted us to reconcile. You were fighting me hard on the separation agreement. Now you're not expecting reconciliation. Why'd you change?"

"Being with Tim, talking with him."

Oh lord, here we go with the Tim thing again. Every time he said the boy's name I cringed. Then again, talking about the kid could counteract my attraction to Jake.

Hold up, did I just say ""my attraction to Jake" like I was owning this attraction? Oh, no.

He continued, "Tim made me realize I can't bull-dog my way into people's lives. People want what they want, and they don't want what they don't want. I can't change your heart toward me. So I wanted to give you the choice on how, when, or if you saw me."

When he first saw me in the hospital, he was all, "we need to stick together like Ike and Tina Turner." Now he was giving me a choice.

Granted, there was a high possibility I'd have to call him over, but at least now it was optional. That was good, especially since he still gave me the butterflies. I had to get my emotions toward him under control.

"Agreed. I'll call if I need it, and this'll only last for four months. Mama's help should be more than enough."

Waaay more than enough.

CHAPTER 11

JAKE

*A*fter the pizza arrived, I set out the paper plates and plastic cups for us.

I still wanted to bring up the tutoring idea with Hannah and offer that I'd only bring Tim along on days when she called for my help, but she was so annoyed I'd brought Tim up today. I was surprised she hadn't thrown a shoe at me when I'd mentioned Tim.

Once we'd gotten into a huge fight over how the cutlery should be arranged in the drawer—something silly. Well… not so silly seeing that a week earlier, I'd admitted to the one-night stand. I couldn't keep the secret from Hannah for much longer. Anyway, she got so pissed about the cutlery arrangement that she'd tossed a stiletto at me. I ducked and it banged against the white cabinet, bounced off the stove top, and landed on the tiled floor. So, yeah, I expected some shoe throwing to go down when I mentioned Tim today, but it didn't happen. Thank goodness.

To make things even better, I was still here. She hadn't kicked me out or anything. I had to make the most of this moment, but how? I may not get a chance later. No telling if she'd call for me when Tuesday rolled around.

My mother. I'd mention my mother. She and Hannah got along. Perhaps that would smooth the path to the tutoring idea. "I spoke to my mother the other day. She asked about you, and I told her about the fire. She sends her sympathy."

Hannah's lips twitched. "Oh."

Was she uncomfortable talking about family? Had something changed between them? "My father's not well." I bit into my pizza.

The smooth, shiny skin on her forehead crinkled. "What's wrong?"

"They don't know. They're running tests. Mom wants me to visit, but I'm kinda busy. I think she's overreacting."

"Still mad at your father, huh?" The crease on her forehead deepened, causing her eyebrows to slightly dip. My shoulders tensed at the mention. Hannah knew me *too* too well. She used to rail on me to get in touch with him, but on the real, I couldn't be bothered. His philandering butt could rot for all I cared.

Yeah, yeah, I had a one-night stand, but at least I was trying to change. Mom never mentioned that Pops made a commitment to do better. It seemed as if they were getting along to go along, and this whole threat of sickness seemed to cause my parents to bond like something abnormal.

Hannah went on. "No matter what he did in the past, Jake, he's still your dad."

She had a point. He was my father—nothing could erase the biological connection, but the emotional connection wasn't there. My relationship with my father was beside the point. Hannah and I didn't have a biological connection, but we sure had an emotional one. That mattered. That could be salvaged. "Just like no matter what I did in the past, I'm still your husband?"

A flash of hesitation scrawled across her face, and she caught my gaze. "You and I are different. I didn't contribute to your existence on the planet. Your father, however, did."

Her expression turned heavy and weighed my heart and mind. There goes that biological obligation thing again, but she was right. Tim was my son, and I wanted to connect to him. Yet this current turn of the conversation had nothing to do with Tim, and it had everything to do with Hannah.

"I know you hate me, Hannah."

"I don't hate you."

She didn't hate me? This whole time she'd acted as if she did. "Okay, then there's a strong dislike."

"Maybe a little."

We busted out laughing. I loved her laugh. I always did. The first thing I'd noticed about her all those years ago was her laugh. We were sitting in a trigonometry class in college about to take a quiz, and I was flipping through my flash cards one last time. Then I'd heard her laughter, melodic and light and free, almost like it bubbled up from her very soul. I had turned to see who was laughing like that, and I'd seen an angel. I'd never noticed Hannah before that moment. Afterward, I flunked the quiz while she aced it. That's when I asked her to help me out, and she did.

History aside, she'd be a great tutor for Tim.

"I want to discuss something with you. It has to do with Tim."

Her face shuttered.

"I know. I know. I know. Hear me out first." I bit down on my thumbnail. How was I planning to explain this? Didn't know. "You know Tim is living with me, and his school record is a mess. Behaviorally and academically. Remember when you helped me out with math in college?"

Recognition of where I was going with my argument

must've registered with Hannah because she shook her head as if she had Tourette's.

"I'm not tutoring your son in math. Ain't happening now. Ain't happening ever."

"You didn't hear me out. I would only have him tag along on the days when you specially called me in."

"Definitely not. If I call you to help me, you're helping me." She pointed to her sternum. "I'm not helping him. That's your son and your responsibility."

"Funny how Tim's improvement is my responsibility when before you didn't want me to have anything to do with him."

"Hey, don't guilt trip me into taking on your problems. You decided to take Tim in after his mother went to rehab. Not me. You get first dibs on all his problems. Not me. I ain't his mama."

O-kay. She answered that question loud and clear. Guess I better find a tutor elsewhere.

"And another thing," she added. "Maybe if you got your relationship with your father straight, you wouldn't be running to me for help with your child." She flicked her hair as if to accentuate her statement. "Visit your father, Jake."

"My relationship with Pops isn't related to Tim."

"It sure it's related. When was the last time you went to Los Angeles?"

My mind flipped through its mental calendar. Last time I saw Pops was when Tim was small—the same month as the last time I'd seen Tim as a child. Huh.

Hannah didn't need to know this info. No need for her to think she'd won this argument sans shoe throwing.

"It's been that long?" Hannah asked.

"Don't act all surprised, Hannah," I said, deflecting my cognitive dissonance. "We were living under the same roof for a good while, so you know how long it's been since I've visited. A long time."

A shadow crossed her features, and a part of me wanted to revise my tone, soften the edges.

"You're right. I could've encouraged you to visit your parents, but I didn't." Hannah rested her elbow on the armrest of the chair, her remaining black curls swaying to the left. "Too wrapped up in my own dilemmas to consider yours, I guess."

I thought of her struggles with self-image, our strained marriage, our failed attempts to conceive. "Don't say that. We did what we could. We did the best we knew how. No shame."

Her gaze shifted downward as if burdened.

Regret took hold. I'd messed things up, and here Hannah was carrying this silent weight.

"You're right," she said. "Sometimes, we have to accept them for what they are. As failures."

Although her tone was kind, the faint lines around her eyes tightened. Not a good sign. There wasn't forgiveness in her gaze, only anger and hurt over a trashed marriage.

When I promised Hannah I would never see Tim again, he'd been the deciding factor in her staying. When I took in Tim because Melinda was in rehab, Tim had been the deciding factor in her kicking me out. I pushed through my hair, shook my head. Hannah grabbed another slice of pizza.

Only an act of God could get Hannah and Tim in the same room. Was there a way to orchestrate acts of God? She definitely didn't want to tutor Tim. What else could I do?

Nothing.

The word slammed into me. Hannah would have to make that decision on her own. There was nothing I could do to bring Hannah and Tim and me together. I could only be here for Hannah, listen to Hannah—for as much as she'd let me.

Hannah ate the last bit of crust on her second pizza. She reached for a third. I remembered when she'd found out about Tim and was all kinds of angry and stressed. Was she stress-eating now or was she really hungry?

"This pizza is so good, Jake. I love Sal's."

"Do you?"

She stopped eating, looked at me. "Do I what?"

"You said earlier that you'd been too wrapped up in your own dilemmas to consider mine. Let's not consider my dilemma with Tim anymore. How has it been since I moved out? Apart from the fire, of course. You doing okay?"

She set down her plate and rested her chin in her hands. Her round nose wrinkled. Her left foot tapped on the hardwood floor and her front teeth tugged at her lower lip. Her stance screamed stress.

"You didn't like my question, did you?"

"No," she said. "I mean, yes. I mean. Ugh. Why is this so hard? My skin's all jacked up. I'm trying to rebuild my life. And then you're here wanting to know how I'm doing."

"I'll only be here again if you need me."

She paused as if second-guessing herself. "You're right."

Or perhaps not second-guessing herself. Her tone sounded like she may not need me anymore. Would we see each other again?

The question pricked, so I asked. "You and I, our marriage, it's a process, isn't it?"

"A very hard process." She picked up the pizza, looked at it, set it down. "Maybe I'm being too strict with the whole 'don't call me, I'll call you' thing. What do you think?"

My heart revved, but I took two deep breaths to steady my instincts. I could've really jumped on this opportunity and told her we needed to see one another every single day, but that wouldn't be right. "No. We'll stick with the original plan. That'd be best for you. You need space to be."

"Or all this extra space could cause me to be complicated and overthink-y."

I smiled. "I like you complicated and overthink-y. You're very self-reflective. I've always admired that in you. Your strength of mind."

"Strength of mind. Hmm." She sunk against the paisley throw pillows and set one on her lap. "Tell me how the rest of the pizza tastes since, you know, I'm here doing brain push-ups."

I laughed. "You're witty too."

"Thanks." She stared at the pizza. "You can take the rest of the pizza home. Give it to Tim or something."

She really wanted me to give pizza to Tim? Tim of all people. "You sure?"

"Yeah." Then she stopped herself as if thinking what I was thinking—her mention of Tim in a casual, non-angry manner was odd.

Odd. Odd. Odd.

She glanced away, apparently uncomfortable. "So, yeah. I'll call you if I need you."

I nodded once, stone-like and silent, but inside I was gasping for grace, the grace of one more minute, one more moment with Hannah.

But she walked me to the front entrance and closed the door.

No grace for me.

CHAPTER 12

HANNAH

The following morning, I struggled to sit up in bed. Those darn bandages were so tight, but I didn't care about the struggle. The comfort of sitting up in my own bed in the wee daylight hours far outweighed sitting in a hospital. No one here checked my blood pressure every five minutes. Alone in this house, I could figure out how to get control over my now wayward life. Alone in this house, I could make decisions on my own with regards to my career, my recovery process, and whether I wanted Jake to return.

If I didn't, Mama and Jake would be happy to make them for me, thus rendering me helpless.

That conversation with Jake lingered. Did I really have a crazy moment and say Jake could take extra pizza home to Tim? I mean, I hated the kid. All right, I didn't hate him, but he reminded me of the one thing I could never be—a mother. His very existence was proof that at one point in time, Jake had wandered from me. That sucked.

I should've kept all the pizza. All. The. Pizza.

At the moment, my offer sounded good, almost natural. That yummy pizza—my first non-hospital food in weeks—

must've made me so nice. Yeah, I blamed it on the pizza. What else was I supposed to do? Blame it on my heart? Nah.

It was just pizza. No feelings involved. (My goodness, I sounded like one of those female voice-over narrators on daytime television.)

A list. I needed a list, something to help me figure out what I should do with my career, my recovery, my marriage. Guess I'd start with Jake.

My journal sat on my bedside table. I grabbed it and a pen and drew a line down the middle of the page. I titled it: Pros and Cons of Calling on Jake to Return and Help Me Out. Even writing those words made me feel all weird.

Pro Number One: Mama wasn't going to be here every day. (Hmm. Okay, this reason could work.)

Pro Number Two: I'd get better faster. (Yes, I needed to recover faster. I needed to get my career on track quickly before the industry forgot about me. Things moved quickly in fashion.)

Con Number One: Jake would be helping me. (Meh. I wanted my independence.)

Con Number Two: Jake would know I needed his help. (A barf-worthy thought. He could start thinking he had an "in" with me or something.)

Con Number Three: Jake and I were on shaky ground. (Not completely in the dog house. Not completely in my house either.)

Hold up a sec. Did I admit Jake wasn't completely in the dog house? I must be on too many pain meds or something.

Or maybe it was all those nicey-nice things he'd done so far: moving closer to help me out, leaving the decision on whether we saw one another again up to me, bringing me that cute I Love New York t-shirt. So, so cute.

I bit on my pen cap. The nice factor posed a problem 'cuz it poked at the other set of feelings I had buried way down deep inside. The feelings that would take the skill of a brain surgeon to needle out—or the skill of a cute estranged husband.

All right, all right, all right. Perhaps I was making too much of my feelings toward Jake, but seriously, the guy knew me too well, like the whole math thing. He remembered how much I loved math. If I had a Con Number Four, his knowledge of my love for math would be it. Sounded more like a Pro than a Con. Like I said, it was complicated.

I loved math. My great-aunt Georgia was a math whiz. She earned a Ph.D. in Mathematics when Black women were a rarity in the field. So maybe math genius was in my genes, but after that mess with the professor, I became a fashion model. Not like that was a downgrade or anything—I loved modeling, but I certainly didn't love that calculus professor assaulting me or the repercussions.

At the time, I'd gotten pregnant with the jerk's kid, and he'd threatened to "mar my name" if I filed a complaint. I was so fearful and distraught and paralyzed that I left school. Jake was my boyfriend at the time, and he was trying to convince me to stay in school. I didn't tell Jake the reasons I had to leave. I wanted to be away from that professor and navigate life outside of college. The miscarriage made me feel more aimless so I threw myself into modeling. Tutoring Tim in math would be tough with all that baggage and shame.

I loved solving equations though. I could control equations. I couldn't control whether someone would hire me for a modeling assignment. That was the conundrum.

Seconds later, a car pulled up to the front of my house. I peeked through the blinds and saw a silver Volkswagen Jetta. My insides flipped. Mama. Not even six o'clock in the morning! I'd told her to arrive this afternoon. Gah! Thanks, Mama. Now I had no time to consider this whole marriage thing.

This whole career thing. This whole getting-around-on-my-own thing.

The doorbell buzzed. Oh, brother. "I can make this work. I can make this work. I can make this work." I left my bedroom and made slow steps to the front door, the slower the better.

Bzzz. Bzzz. Bzzz.

"Hannah, you in there?" Mama's muffled voice carried into the hallway.

"Yeah. Give me a sec."

Bzzz. Bzzz. Bzzz.

Good gracious. Hadn't I told her to give me a sec? I opened the door and there stood Mama in her usual black pants, black boatneck top, and floral scarf. "Hi." I put on my pleasant daughter voice and shoved my grown woman voice in the closet.

"Whew! So much traffic getting here. I ran into all the early morning commuters."

Well, she should've waited until later in the day to arrive. "Oh?"

"Yes." Mama bustled past me, dragging a rolling suitcase along. "That traffic is the worst. You haven't gotten dressed yet?"

"It's early, Mama."

"I always get dressed in the morning. First thing." She paused, tapped her foot. "Come to the kitchen, and I'll start breakfast."

"About breakfast. I hadn't gone grocery shopping, so—"

"No worries, *anak*. I went grocery shopping early this morning."

Of course. I pulled out a chair in the kitchen and watched her whiz around the space like she had ten cups of coffee. She poked her head in the fridge. "Phewy. This smells."

"Hadn't cleaned it." I waited for her to berate me about not yet cleaning the fridge.

She didn't. Surprise, surprise.

"I'll wipe it down with soap and water. Don't know what could've grown in there. Bacteria. Germs. Fungus."

My skin tingled. Yech. "I get it, Ma."

She took a note pad from her purse and started writing. "Clean fridge," she muttered and scribbled on the notepad. Then she took my place mats, my favorite place mats, and stuffed them in the drawer! "I like those place mats," I said evenly.

"They're cloth. Too hard to clean. I have plastic ones. Easier for me to clean."

Easier for her to clean. All righty. Since she put it that way, and she'd help me around the house, I let it alone.

"Good thing I bought non-perishables. I had a feeling things wouldn't be too good around here."

Mama said this as if I'd vandalized my own property or something. She set her pen down, looked at me with unseeing eyes. "In a way, I'm glad that I'm here to help you, my dear. I know we haven't had the best relationship, especially after your Lola died, but your recovery can be a new and better change for us. We're going to do things right this time, me and you."

She sounded very authoritative about the whole matter. Typical. "Uh-huh."

"I get to take care of you. Those sores are sensitive. They could be reinfected at any moment. I don't want you to endanger yourself. Remember what happened with your Lola? Remember?"

Discomfort edged its way past the borders of my soul, stirring up memories that were best forgotten. "I remember."

"Those sores can be deadly."

A picture of Lola's face, pale and gray, flashed before me.

134

When her skin cancer turned bad, her skin had become encrusted with lesions.

"They're not sores. They're burns."

"Sores. Deadly sores."

I exhaled. "Mama, they're not deadly. Lola's sores were deadly. Remember when she—"

"I don't remember anything." Mama picked up my flower vase on the end table and set it on the coffee table.

"Um, yeah you remember, Mama. You were the one who helped me clean her sores and made sure that—"

"No more talk about Lola." She took the stack of coasters on my coffee table and set them out as if we were expecting guests, which we weren't.

"Why are you rearranging my stuff?"

"It's out of place. Needs to be fixed." She dragged a chair clear across the room and set it in front of my thirty-two-inch television.

Mama was stressed. Was it because I mentioned Lola? "What's wrong?"

"Nothing." She draped a throw over the back of the chair.

"Oh yes, it's something. You said you wanted things to get better between us, and I agree. We should talk. You were so mad at me when Lola died, and I was young and—"

"No more of this talk. I focus on today. Not yesterday. Not years ago. Today." She pressed the power button on the remote, and it flashed to life.

"I don't watch television," I said.

"I do, and I can't miss my soaps. My eyes are getting bad so I brought the chair up close. You don't need to sit too close to the television because the window's close to the sunlight. In caregiver training, they said to watch your sun exposure. The sun can zap your skin off."

"Mama, we're inside."

"And the nurse had said there were a few brands of

sunscreen you could use, preferably the ones with zinc oxide and not oxybenzone. Your Lola never used sunscreen. She'd probably be alive today if she had."

I hated how Mama likened my skin condition to Lola's deadly disease. I wasn't dying. Yet the longer she spoke, the more I was dying inside, pieces of me crumbling off, bit by bit. "Mama, I'll have scars, but I'm going to try and live with them the best I can."

Did I say that? I did. Did I mean what I said or was it a defense against Mama's negativity?

"I know you will." She flipped through the television channels. "Wear sunscreen."

She wasn't going to stop.

"Wear this too." Mama grabbed her purse from the coffee table and gave me a flimsy piece of cloth.

"What's that?"

"A scarf for you. Matches mine."

I stared at it. Didn't look like a scarf. More like a rag.

"I'll help you put it on." She reached over and I flinched at her touch. Up close, her skin was smooth and wrinkle-free. Soft. My chest filled with heaviness. I'd never have perfect skin again. I remembered curling up in her arms as a child and inhaling her scent, cocoa butter and vanilla. I used to put my hand on her skin and compare my color to hers, innocent kid stuff.

"Mama," I'd said when I was six. "We're different colors."

"Beautiful colors. The way God made us." She'd smiled. "Never forget. Always beautiful."

Those "comforting" words sounded like a lie today. Since Mama blew up at me when I was eight, blaming me for carelessly "letting Lola die," I was always inadequate in Mama's eyes. I was always starting at zero on the approval scores and trying to work my way up to one hundred. Kind of like now with this scarf. I stepped away, tossed the scarf on the coffee table, and headed to my room.

"Where are you going?" she asked.

"To rest."

"But I wanted to—"

"Later, Mama." I left. My thick socks scuffed against the hardwood floor. I passed the hall mirror and stopped. In my reflection, I saw parts of my damaged skin the bandages didn't quite cover. Skin that was wrinkly and red-brown, deeper than my normal chestnut. Couldn't say that chestnut was my normal anymore. Scarred was my normal.

I stepped closer to the mirror and tugged on the edge of a bandage, revealing tender, pink skin. Skin that was almost as pink as the scarf Mama had given. Guess my neck could double as a mottled scarf, huh?

Okay, that was a bad joke.

I kept tugging at the bandage, careful this time not to cause an injury like I'd done in the hospital. Each tug revealed more pink.

Once, I had landed a lucrative contract with a major skincare company. The ads still ran on television and in print. Perhaps I could land a contract with a skincare line and a burn victim charity, which would draw attention to the real needs of women like me. Women who wanted to take care of themselves and feel beautiful despite their burns.

Nah. Wouldn't happen. When my skin was perfect, the skincare companies still airbrushed my face to make it look unattainably perfect. No way in the world would they go with my stupid little idea. I grimaced at my pinkish skin.

If they saw me now, they'd probably want a refund on the money I'd earned—plus interest.

"What're you doing?"

I startled. "Nothing."

"Looks like something." Mama stepped close, inspected my bandages. "Why are you taking them off?"

"I was just... just—"

"I can help with your bandages if you need them changed. You don't have to take them off alone."

Memories of that episode with Jake at the hospital resurfaced. I'd rather have him change my bandages now, ironically. Mama was being way pushier than Jake. "It's not time to change the bandages. Not for an hour or so."

"Then why'd you take them off now?" *'Cuz I wanted-to-see-but-didn't-want-to-see my real appearance.* I didn't answer.

"Anyways," she continued. "The nurse said you should change them morning and evening. It's morning." She pointed to my neck. "That exposed skin is an infection waiting to happen. I'll take care of the rest."

I stood in the hallway and waited. Looked at myself in the mirror. Looked away. My eyes stung. I looked horrible. No way would I be able to live with this warped version of myself. I looked like Lola in her last days, and Mama's mention of Lola's skin made me think twice about her changing my bandages. Mama had blamed me for being neglectful with Lola's care, but now I wondered. Was Mama's blame a cover for something else?

Mama returned with a roll of gauze, antimicrobial soap, and antiseptic cream.

I froze. "Mama. Let's wait. I can take care of this on my own. You wanted to clean out the fridge anyways. Can't you focus on the fridge?"

"No. No. No. We should change them now. You've been in them all night. Time to give your skin a chance to breathe and get cleaned. I don't want... " Mama lowered her gaze.

"You don't want what?"

"There was a time. One time when..." Her foot tapped, tapped, tapped on my dull, hardwood floor. Then she stopped. "I'm only trying to help. But you always push Jake and me away."

"Why are you bringing him up? All I said was it's best to clean out the fridge. What does my marriage have to do with cleaning out a fridge?"

Mama's eyes lowered. "If you don't want me here, I'll get out of your life. Like Jake got out of your life."

Blood rushed to my ears. Mama was taking this way too far. "Enough with the guilt trip." I stepped away from the mirror and ambled down the dimly lit hall toward my bedroom. Time to get dressed for the day, and besides, each footfall took me farther away from her.

"Not a guilt trip, honey," she called from behind. "It's pure and honest truth. Everyone who cares about you, you manage to push away. Your friend Liza. Has she visited you yet?"

"No." I stopped, switched the dimmer knob so the lights shone brightly.

"What happened with you two?"

Dog. Mama was nosy. I wasn't gonna tell her about our falling out. "With Liza?" My voice turned two notches too high. "I dunno. We got busy lately. Life happens."

"You should get in touch with Liza. She's a nice young woman. Tell her what happened. I'm sure she'd want to know." Mama walked in my direction and stood next to the coat rack on my left. "Always helpful and upbeat. She could help you navigate your career."

Not after I disparaged the plus-sized modeling industry. She hadn't spoken to me since I insulted her, and I didn't blame her. I was so full of myself. "We had a falling out recently."

"That's a shame." Her reprimanding tone lunged at me. "It's a good thing my love for you won't change. You can't push me away."

How in the world did she manage to turn this back on me? All I said was clean out the fridge.

Mama breezed pass me and gestured to the couch in the living room "Hannah, sit down. I know you're in a bad place, but it's not over for you. Do you think you'll be able to model?"

Greta's dismissive tone when I'd told her of the fire stayed with me like an annoying itch. "I'm meeting with Greta next Tuesday."

Mama took her seat at the chair in front of the television. "So soon?"

Ack. Her question irritated me to no end. Like she didn't believe I should be on my own. I remained standing. "Yes. So soon. I'm mobile, and it's not a long trip."

"Okay." Mama didn't sound entirely convinced. "I'll be at work. Is Jake driving you?"

Good point. "I'll call and ask him today." There goes my pro-con list. Jake was now pro by default.

"What's the purpose of meeting Greta in person?"

Again with the questions. She wanted an explanation for everything. "I want to sit down with her and strategize my return to modeling." I stepped inside the living room, pressed my hand against the fireplace mantle. "I have to show Greta I've not given up on my career or else she'll think I don't care. She'll think I'm replaceable. Not happening. Hopefully, she'll keep me on as an inactive client until I fully recover."

"And if she doesn't?"

Didn't want to face the possibility. If Greta didn't take me on, I'd have no other options for modeling. I'd be a nobody. A nothing. "She has to."

"And if she doesn't? What's your Plan B?"

Tutor Tim? I shook my head. The thought sounded so flippant.

"What will you do?" Mama repeated. "What will you do if

people in the industry aren't accepting of the way you look today? What if Greta doesn't want to work with you anymore?"

Still couldn't answer her. I leaned against the wall, wrapped my arms around my waist as if to comfort myself. The idea of contacting Liza to see about the nontraditional modeling thing popped into my head, but again, we weren't talking. If the mainstream didn't want to deal with me, then I'd find the people who would. Yet I'd look ridiculous if I called Liza after dissing her work. "I don't know," I said softly.

"I know you don't know." She gave me another smile that didn't reach her eyes. "Let me take care of things."

Mama guided me back to the couch. I tried blinking back the tears, but I couldn't. One got away. Didn't have control over anything anymore. Not my career. Not how I would recover. Not anything. I'd thought maybe coming home from the hospital would change things—make me feel like my life was getting back to normal, but it hadn't.

And I hated it.

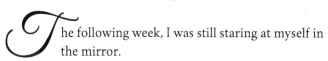

The following week, I was still staring at myself in the mirror.

Okay, okay, okay. I wasn't staring at myself in the mirror for an entire week. Every single day since I'd talk with Mama about Greta, I'd been glancing at myself in the mirror more often than usual. I became super self-conscious about my appearance, but I also did other things like call and ask Jake to drive me to see Greta. He agreed. I sensed glee in his voice when I called.

When he arrived today for my appointment with Greta, I was gonna point out this ride into Manhattan was a one-time thing, not something he should expect. In a few weeks, Dr. Hutchinson would hopefully clear me to drive again. I couldn't wait for that day—independence was a beautiful thing.

The bandages still needed to be changed twice a day, but I'd decided that today I wouldn't wear bandages around my neck. It had healed decently, though the skin was still pink and mottled. I just couldn't show up with bandages and look completely crazy at the modeling agency. I needed to wear a cover-up for this discoloration. Mama's scarf. Mama's ugly pink scarf.

It would have to work.

I rustled through my drawer and shifted my mumbo-jumbo black makeup box out of the way. Where'd I put that scarf?

If only I could try concealer instead, but makeup wouldn't work at this stage of the healing process. My makeup box had everything a woman could want: lipsticks, foundations, powders. Well, anything a woman without burns would want. Nah, I'd have to cover up. Perhaps I'd see if there was makeup specially formulated for me later. Something to add to my to-do list.

The scarf was tucked in the drawer between my under-wear and my bras. I wrapped the thing around my neck, once, twice, three times, and stood in front of the mirror.

Yech. I looked like a strawberry mojito, and it was hot as Hades outside. Greta knew I'd been burned. Maybe I should just let her see the full extent of my burns. Maybe trying to hide what had happened was stupid. Cover up or bare all? Decisions. Decisions.

Dr. Hutchinson's advice about wearing bandages floated in my brain. The parts about taking my time and not rushing back to work and making sure I fully healed.

What did the doctor know? My emotional and psychological well-being hinged on knowing where I stood in my modeling career. That was as important as my physical well-being. So for today, no bandages.

I sat on the edge of my bed and thought about Dr. Hutchinson's words. They taunted me. Could I really do this today? I had to do this today. I had to know Greta's thoughts or else I'd erupt—mentally erupt. I sighed.

"When am I going to win?" I held the question out there in the ether, the unseen space between the sky and the universe, the unseen space where wishes lie.

No answer.

I had wanted to win at being a math professor, earn my Ph.D. like my great-aunt, and solve complex equations for the rest of my life. Didn't happen. I wanted to win at being a wife and mother, having a happy, stable family. Didn't happen. I wanted to win at being a high fashion model, earning fame as one of the tops in the industry. Would this happen?

I had hoped it would. I always believed if I got enough sleep, and used sunscreen, and ate the right foods, and exercised, and wore hypo-allergenic makeup, etc., etc., that I'd maintain my beauty on my own terms. A sleazy professor and Jake's one-night stand couldn't take those things away.

"Is being a successful model too big of a wish?" I asked the empty space around me and awaited an answer. Nothing.

"Can I still improve my appearance?" I asked.

Nada.

I was getting a little kooky. Whatever. Kooky came with the territory of surviving a fire and being on the verge of losing your career.

I mentally deleted the last two questions and held onto the first. *When am I going to win?* That's what I wanted the most. I wanted to win. Win with modeling by securing a huge contract with a major brand or by being featured in the fashion spread for a national magazine. Win with my skin by not having any scars. Nada. Zip. Zilch.

If I could win at one (or both) of those things, I'd be complete. I'd finally feel like I'd gained the respect I deserved, respect I hadn't received from that professor or Jake.

And maybe I could win with the whole math thing too. If (a big if) I tutored Tim and discovered that math didn't dredge up all those horrible memories, then tutoring would be a baby step toward going back to school and working on my degree. Hmm.

Nah, the idea wouldn't work. I'd have to also get over all my feelings about Tim. Ain't happening.

A knock at the door startled me. Must be Jake. My neck was partly covered in an ugly scarf while the rest of me was a mess. Wonderful. Now he would see me all messed up.

Hold on a sec. He'd already seen me messed up. This time, he'd only see me half messed up. I left my bedroom and answered the door. His white button-down collared shirt and faded blue jeans hung nicely at his hips. Delectable.

No, *not* delectable. Practical. Having Jake around was practical. After all, I needed a ride to the modeling agency. Dr. Hutchinson had said I'd need a driver for my first few weeks because all the movements involved with driving—turning my head, turning the wheel, etc.—could stretch the new skin.

"Hey." A piece of hair had slipped out of my ponytail and I pushed it out of the way, used it to cover my neck.

"All set for our drive?" Jake asked.

"Kinda-sorta." I checked my watch. "I know we have to leave soon and all, but I can't figure out how to make myself look normal."

"You look better than normal. You look gorgeous."

My stomach back-flipped. I hated gastrointestinal back flips because it proved that my mind and my heart weren't

144

on one accord with Jake. I didn't like contradicting myself. "I'll need about twenty more minutes." I tugged on the piece of hair that had fallen out of my ponytail, a nervous tic.

"Sure thing." He paused. "You don't have to be so nervous."

"Who said I'm nervous?" My voice croaked.

Jake reached over and loosened the tendril of hair from between my fingers. "You look gorgeous."

My insides flipped. "We'll see if Greta agrees."

"If Greta doesn't want to work with you through this hard time, that's her loss. Not yours."

Oh, brother. What was I supposed to do with that statement? I mean, Greta was Greta. Everyone wanted to work with Greta.

As if reading my mind, Jake added, "Know your worth."

Okay, now that was super-duper confusing. The man who had a one-night stand was telling me to know my worth. Ironic. But that was waaay too much to ponder at the moment. Time was ticking and I had to get ready. "Do you mind waiting for me in the car while I finish getting ready? Shouldn't take more than twenty minutes."

He didn't move. He just stood there, looking and smiling. Smiling and looking.

"What?" I asked.

"You're so nervous." A delicious dimple formed on his cheek.

My goodness, he was cute. "Am not."

"Am too."

Wasn't it supposed to be "are too?" Gah. I hated when Jake tried to get all cutesy with me. "Am not," I repeated.

"We sound like school kids. From what I know of Greta, she'll be understanding of your situation. You've known her so long. You're like a daughter to her. Can't cut your daughter off, can you?"

"People cut their daughters off all the time," I said, but in truth, my relationship with Greta was funny. In many ways, I was closer to her than with my mother. Mama never seemed to mind, however. "Look, I've known Greta for a very long time. Long enough to know I'm only as good as my last magazine spread."

"No. You're good. A good model and a good person. Period."

There he went getting all squishy and romantic again. "What do you know? I'm the woman who tried to give you marching orders."

"This is true." He ran his fingers over his buzz cut and recognition swelled. The shadows in his eyes retold a story I'd already known. Before he continued speaking, I was pushing away his words. Still, they arrived. "There's still room in my heart for forgiveness."

My heart rate raced from a gentle trot to a strong gallop. Forgiveness. Ha. Jake wasn't the one who should be offering forgiveness. I was the one who'd been slighted, after all. I was the one who'd been asked to help raise the child of my husband's one-night stand. But sure. Jake could forgive me. That was rich!

"Get outta here." I jabbed his arm. "I'll be ready in a moment." I needed to collect myself.

He left, but my heart was still galloping. The fact that Jake was willing to talk forgiveness got me feeling all weird. Who cared if Jake had room in his heart for forgiveness? I didn't.

Then why was I so annoyed with the comment? Had my stance toward Jake changed in some stupid, illogical way? Did I want to reconcile? Did some part of me appreciate that he offered?

Nope.

Still, my foot jittered like I'd caught a case of the itchies. Whateva. I had to get ready. I walked to my bedroom and stared at myself in the full-length mirror. The little piece of hair that had fallen out of my ponytail didn't hide much because the other side of my hair was burned. I'd need a Sherpa scarf and a haircut to even the length. A bun would have to do for now.

You don't look that bad.

Mama's words from the other day played with my brain and I started second-guessing myself. Or maybe it was all these mirrors. Maybe they were making me second-guess myself.

That was it. No more mirrors. I lifted the full-length mirror and set it in the hallway. Then I went to the bathroom and lifted that one off its hinges.

Then I removed the hall mirror.

And the mirror in the guest bathroom.

All the mirrors.

Tears welled. Each time I removed a mirror, a part of me withered and died. Ain't no amount of watering could resurrect this ol' plant. I was done.

For most of my life, I'd measured my worth through a piece of glass, an image of myself, not my true self. Whether it was a camera or a mirror, if I looked good, then it was all good.

But now that I didn't look good… what? I removed another mirror.

Why are you erasing yourself?

Where'd that come from? Now I'd done gone cuckoo. "I'm not erasing myself," I said.

Yeah, you are.

"Am not. I'm erasing… I'm erasing this version of myself. That's it. I don't like the 2.0 Burned Version."

That's the only one you got.

My heart pounded. What was up with my conscience? "Stop talking. Stop it now." I swiped up my teal pea coat and house keys from the hall closet. I had to leave. Talking to myself wasn't getting me anywhere. Or rather, it was getting me to a place I'd been avoiding all this time: The Imperfect Place.

The place where imperfect fires eat perfect skin, where imperfect math professors assaulted perfect math students, where imperfect emotions erode perfect marriages.

No way was I gonna let my career turn sour. I had to convince Greta that I still stood a chance in the modeling world. I left my house and almost tripped over my feet. Stupid feet always got in my way. Couldn't go anywhere without them tripping me up.

Kind of like how you're tripping yourself up now?

"Shush!"

$\sim$

An hour later, Jake and I were booking it down West 54th Street on our way to see Greta. I had to make a good impression, and that meant I couldn't be late. I weaved through the busy New York crowd. This time there weren't any trippy feet.

"Hannah, you're walking fast."

"I have ten minutes to get there. Greta hates tardiness."

"And I like my legs."

"I like being on time."

"You took longer than twenty minutes to get ready," Jake said.

"I was busy."

I'd left out the part about how I'd spent an extra fifteen minutes at home taking down every single mirror in the house 'cuz it didn't matter.

My skin was tingling without the bandages, like really, really tingling. But I pushed aside the feeling and kept walking. I'd already made the decision to go sans bandages and I was running late. I couldn't turn back now even if I wanted.

The tall metal skyscraper that sheltered Click Models came into view, and my heart beat faster. This was almost like finding the missing component of a thousand-piece jigsaw puzzle, except I hoped to piece together everything about myself.

We went inside the building and I nodded at the door-man, told him where I was going. As we made our way up the elevators, Jake grasped my hand and I instinctively held onto his.

"You'll be okay," he said.

My thoughts tracked back to all the mirrors now leaning against the wall in my living room. "I'll have a good and productive meeting with Greta." I plastered on a smile for extra effect, my cheeks tightening. I never faked happiness very well.

The elevators opened to the third floor. A sheet of paper announcing open calls with an arrow pointing to the right was taped on the floor directory. We walked down the hall, and hopeful young girls were packed into the lobby of Click Models. Tall. Skinny. Young. Perfect. "It looks busy today. I should've picked another time to see Greta."

"Don't worry. Once those models see that the famous Hannah Hart has stepped into the room, they'll have to take a backseat to greatness."

I gave him a *get-real* look. Dude never seemed interested in my career when I was actually working and successful. Now that I was jacked up, he wanted to be my champion. I kept walking.

Moments later, I slipped through the doors to the agency. One model hopeful saw me and her eyes widened. It wasn't because I was the famous Hannah Hart. More like because I was the scary-looking Hannah Hart.

My resolve squeezed into a tiny little ball. I didn't belong here. Not anymore.

Jake followed behind me, then stopped. "Oh, wait a second, I have to feed the meter."

I whipped around. "What?! You can't leave me alone. I need—"

"You need?"

There was a note of anticipation in his voice. I did not need Jake. I did *not* need Jake. I didn't. I didn't. I didn't. I pressed my lips and gave him the bug eyes.

He waited for me to finish my non-statement.

"I don't need anything," I said. "Feed the meter. I'll handle this meeting. You can wait in the lobby for me when you return."

"You're gonna do fine." Jake pecked me on the cheek and I clenched my jaw, veering my attention to the carpeted floor. Why'd he kiss me? Now I was all distracted and stuff.

Before I could say something about Jake's surprise smooch, he deserted me with a bazillion impossibly gorgeous girls.

And me, the burned woman.

The receptionist's phone trilled and mixed with the chatter around me. My nerves were on edge as I squeezed through the crowd. All the pretty in the room set me on edge. In my head, I immediately pulled out the invisible tape of the world and measured myself against it—I came up lacking. Sorely lacking.

I finally made my way to the desk. Kristi was on the phone. Thank goodness she was working today and not a stranger. "Hey, girl."

Kristi squinted at me, a guarded shadow cast over her eyelids. "Hannah?"

Courage deflated, I tucked my chin. She must've caught a

glimpse of the scars on my neck and jawline. I pressed out my words. "Yes." I was the same person inside. I was.

Her face changed. It was as subtle as ice melting into water, but I noticed. The lines around her eyes erased into seamless ivory parchment. Her shoulders rounded and relaxed, even her smile sang. "Hannah!" She hopped out of her office seat. "Hannah! Hannah! Hannah!"

Kristi's excitement jolted me. I'd felt this way before, in the in-between instants in high school where I'd been second-guessed for being overweight, rejected by peers. Those instances when the thing I'd wanted so much—acceptance—changed and turned real and solid. Kristi accepted me because of who I used to be, not because of who I was today.

She extended her arms over this invisible expanse separating her normalcy from my not-normalcy. Kristi wanted to hug me, but then she held back: "Is it okay if I—can we—"

"Hug? Yes. We can hug." I embraced her quickly since I had to smash all that awkwardness. I hated that Kristi didn't recognize me the first time.

After I released my embrace, Kristi took two steps back. "I can't believe this happened to you. I'm so sorry."

That sounded like the final death sentence to my career.

"I'm recovering smoothly." My laugh was high and pitchy and... high. "I have four months max and then I'm back to work."

"As a model?"

My heart took a tumble and roll like being banged up in a car accident, crashed into by my own insecurity. "That's what I'm going to see Greta about now."

"I'm sorry. I didn't mean to—"

"No worries, friend," I responded with way too much sugary affection. "I have to get used to people tiptoeing around me, I guess."

Her hands flew to her mouth. "Oh! I feel soooo awfuuulll. I shouldn't have said what I said. I'm so stupid."

"No worries. It's a natural response."

But really, I hated the words as they tumbled from my lips. I didn't want to be immune to people staring at me funny. I wanted it to remain uncomfortable so I'd have something to shoot for: a more perfect version of myself.

That's when I noticed—the room was hushed and everyone was staring at us. Or rather, everyone was staring at *me*.

"What're y'all looking at?" Kristi tossed up her arms. A wisp of hair fell across her crystal blue eyes, and she flicked it aside with a jerk of her head. "Do you even know who this is? Do you?"

No one answered, and something within me deflated.

"This is *the* Hannah Hart. And if you hopeful models were smart, you'd study her career because she's a role model in this industry."

The girl who'd looked at me funny from earlier stepped forward. "Oh my. Hannah Hart. I've been following your career for the longest time. I can't believe I didn't recognize you."

I can believe it. "No worries," I said. This little catchphrase, *no worries*, was becoming my fall-back response.

"All you girls can ask Hannah questions later. Come with me." Kristi grabbed me by the hand and led me to an empty office—empty except for a desk and a chair. "You can wait here away from the crowd. Greta's busy seeing models, but I'm sure she'll stop once I tell her you're here."

The phone kept ringing and ringing and ringing. "Don't you have to answer those calls?"

"Nah." She waved me off. "Those calls can wait. Although you may have a point. Greta's been on a rampage lately."

"A rampage?"

"Yep."

I must've made some kind of funny face because Kristi added, "I'm sure Greta will change her stinky little attitude when she sees you though. You're her favorite."

The phone kept ringing. "You sound so optimistic."

"I am. This little snafu of yours will make headlines as an inspirational story of triumph against the odds. Oh, girl, they'll eat that stuff up."

"I'm not feeling too inspirational right now," I said.

Pity was written all over Kristi's face.

When would everyone stop pitying me? "Don't feel sorry for me." Surprised by how vulnerable I sounded, I turned away.

When Kristi wrapped her arm around my shoulders, a tear threatened to surface from my right eye.

"Let me know when you're ready for Greta," she said.

"I'm ready. I can do this."

"Then I'll tell her you're here." She gave my shoulder a gentle squeeze. "You're a rock star."

She left and I took several deep breaths. With each inhale and exhale, I calmed myself and then replayed everything I planned to say to Greta.

Twenty minutes later, there was a tap on the door, and it creaked open. Kristi poked her head inside. "Greta's ready for you." She whispered as if speaking too loudly would make Greta change her mind.

I slipped past her and headed to Greta's office. Greta sat behind a massive metal desk, hands clasped. She wore her usual outfit: tailored suit with added shoulder pads, diamond studded earrings, and a diamond watch. Here in Manhattan, it was a look perfectly suitable for a banquet, a fancy restaurant, or a courtroom. As one of the most successful modeling agents in the industry, Greta had been to all three.

"Hannah, dahling. You've come to visit." In one seamless

movement, she stood, air-kissed me, and sat again, her face crinkling as she assessed my appearance. I looked down for a millisecond, ashamed. "What brings you in today?"

"I'd like to go out on go-sees in a few weeks. What do you think?"

Greta screwed her face sideways as if she were trying to chew on this dilemma a moment longer before deciding what to tell me. "You're very... very—"

"Scarred. I know. After my initial four months, I should get some reconstructive surgery. That'll help."

"But we don't know how much it'll help." A deep, vertical line pulled between her forehead, and her face held a mixture of emotions I couldn't quite unearth. "In the meantime, there's a young woman whom I'd like you to mentor."

"Mentor?"

"Yes. She looks similar to you. A real cutie. Very ambitious too." She held up a snapshot of the woman.

Yeah, we had some similarities: dark hair, dark eyes, chestnut skin, except I was older and dented while she was younger and smooth. "What's her name?"

"Jacinta Roberts. I mentioned her to you when we spoke on the phone a few weeks ago, remember?"

"Sort of."

"She's a very enthusiastic young woman. She hopes to model full time, but I wanted to see how she fares before I decide to sign her. I've had my share of flaky, unprofessional models. I don't want to take my chances on Jacinta until I see how she does in a mentee capacity."

Wonderful. Now I'm out of work, and I'm training my replacement.

"When I brought up the possibility to her, she was beyond thrilled. Jacinta adores you. Completely adores you."

"What would this entail?" I asked.

"She could be your assistant, basically doing whatever

154

you need administratively. Posting on social media. Filing. Answering emails."

I twisted my mouth. "Where does the mentoring part come into play?"

"I figured it'd be on-the-job mentoring." Greta shrugged. "Whenever she had questions, you'd answer, point her to resources, give her tips. That sort of thing."

"Would I be paid?"

"Of course you'd be paid. I can only do twenty dollars an hour, about ten to fifteen hours a week, depending on how much help you need."

I'd go from earning three hundred dollars an hour modeling to twenty dollars an hour being a "mentor." I might as well tutor Tim too.

Hmm. What would Jake think if I did this whole mentoring thing but refused to tutor Tim? Would he think I was a hypocrite? Ugh. I hated these stupid dilemmas. Best not to agree to mentoring Jacinta. "I won't be able to mentor Jacinta. I'm still recovering."

Her eyes slanted for a millisecond. "You're absolutely right. Forget that I brought it up." She checked her watch. "Guess I have to see the rest of the models now. Nice chatting with you."

My skin prickled. "What about my modeling? After I'm recovered of course."

"I don't see many ad agencies looking for your... type at the moment. Things could change." She rested her elbows on the desk and gave me the kind of direct look only my mother and Jake had given. "You really should consider mentoring Jacinta. It's a great way to invest in someone's career. And it'll be a great way to stay in the modeling loop while you recover."

"Is your offer a deciding factor in my staying on as a client post-recovery?"

She twisted her mouth. "Can't say for certain. We have to see what your doctor says, of course. But it's nice for models like yourself to contribute."

This whole mentoring thing could be a way to keep me from blowing up at the real news: that my career was toast. Yet how would I know for certain?

"I would really like for you to be on staff," Greta continued. "Your experience would be invaluable to Jacinta and other models too depending on how you like the gig. If you don't like the gig, well… "

Yep. Greta was basically saying this was the only way I would have my foot in the door with modeling. Beggars can't be choosers. "Fine. I'll work with Jacinta."

Great.

CHAPTER 13

JAKE

I worried for Hannah.

Sitting downstairs in the lobby of that big New York skyscraper, waiting for her to return from her meeting with Greta, made me worry.

I worried because I saw the hope and trepidation in her face as she'd stepped into the waiting area of that office building. Hope that, yes, she'd be able to go after her modeling dreams in full force, and trepidation that her dreams would be squashed to bits.

Before she left for Greta's office, I wanted to hold her as I did in our honeymoon years, tell Hannah no matter what Greta's decision, Hannah was enough. But to Hannah, my words were tarnished pennies. They could be tossed to the ground and she wouldn't miss them.

An hour after I told Hannah I needed to feed the meter, she was riding the down escalator. She craned her neck, pretending to look around, but her distant eyes said she wasn't looking at a thing. From afar, she looked like the old Hannah with her charcoal black hair and golden-brown complexion. As she came closer, her skin morphed into spots of red and small patches of white, burned. Even now, I tried not to stare too hard for fear of making her self-conscious.

In reality, I was the self-conscious one, always making sure I didn't do something to push her away, always making sure I treated her with care during this fragile period. I'd already done a lot so she could feel comfortable around me, comfortable and safe. I didn't want to lose her trust.

The despondency in her face said she was especially vulnerable. Her wild, wandering eyes were at the point of tears, her cheeks swollen red. She'd been crying.

"Hey, you," I said, my voice gentle and kind. "What's wrong?"

"Everything." She sat next to me on the wooden bench and her weight deflated into mine. Moments later, hot tears pitter-pattered on my shirt.

My worries were true. "What do you mean?"

"Greta said I wasn't ready. Said I needed to wait." Her fingers gnarled into tight fists. "Said I should spend some time mentoring the amazingly ambitious girl she replaced me with at that last photo shoot I missed—"

I didn't respond right away. Instead, I grasped her hand and looked around, remembering the first time I'd seen her walk through this busy lobby as a younger model. Her electric energy had buzzed through this space, assured and confident and strong, unlike today.

Yet the space was the same—the security guard still sat behind the center podium, the porcelain-like floors shone to a polish, bright rays filtered through the sunroof. The only addition to this space was a painting, a replica of the Mona Lisa, hanging in a blue glass frame and adjacent to the building directory.

Mona Lisa's gamine smile greeted all who entered. Her smile greeted us now—rather, it greeted me. Hannah was a puddle of grief.

My task was to comfort, and I would. "Mentoring can be fulfilling work."

"Yeah, for people who've accomplished all they wanted to accomplish in their career. I have yet to live out my career to its fullest."

Mona Lisa didn't flinch. I, however, did.

"Hannah, you still have time. Don't set your expectations for yourself so high that—"

"Why should I have to settle?" She sat up and her voice echoed through the lobby, causing a temporary quiet among the crowd. "I'm not settling, okay? I don't care what you or Greta or Dr. Hutchinson says. I deserve to have a fulfilling career. I didn't deserve this fire." She pointed to the reddish-white scar stretching across her neck, bare for me to see. "What did I do to deserve this?"

The question was sudden and unplanned, and she lowered her eyes.

"You did nothing to deserve anything wrong that has happened to you." I exhaled and the truth of my words, the truth of our life together, settled into me. "Nothing."

Her brow crinkled and a shadow of sadness flitted across her face. She was quiet for a long time, the chatter of the crowd filling the tension between us.

"Nothing," I repeated.

"You don't know. You don't know." Her breathing quickened. Her chest rose and rose with each heavy breath.

"What? What is it, Hannah? I want to know." I reached for her hand, grasped it gently. "Tell me what I need to know."

She paused. "Nothing." Finally, she rested her head on my shoulder.

"You don't have to settle." I kept my voice low and gentle, even as I pressed on with the words I knew she wouldn't want to hear. "Yet you have to realize—everything's changed. You're not the same Hannah."

Mona's Lisa expression was stagnant and shadowy now, almost mocking. As if she loved being captured in time, never aging, never changing. That's something I'd never understand about Hannah, her need to stay in this small container. Yeah, she'd had some success as a model, but she was so much more.

"Seems like everything I've ever wanted gets snatched away," Hannah said. "There's nothing in my life that's certain. Modeling is the only thing I have left."

Her shoulders tightened, and so did I. Wasn't I here? Why couldn't she get out of her own head and recognize that, although things looked bleak, I was here for her, supporting her?

After I'd told her about Tim, Hannah had placed herself inside this self-imposed bubble, and I couldn't reach inside and say the truth: that though I messed up once, I loved her. My love never stopped. I'd told her as much before, but she wouldn't hear me then. It was unlikely she'd hear me now. I didn't protest, waiting for her to continue.

"When my face graced the cover of a magazine for the first time when I was in high school, I felt important. I was treated better. I wasn't the fat girl. People befriended me. People saw me."

There was a sense of awe when she'd said "me," as if she still didn't believe in her magic.

"I felt completely awful in Greta's office just now. People saw me, yes, but they were repulsed. Like I was some kind of freak."

My chest filled with rage. Freak? I should've stayed up there with her, forget the parking meter. I took a deep breath, willed myself to be patient. I didn't want to interrupt and stop what could be a moment of real connection for us.

For what seemed like hours, I waited for Hannah to speak, but she remained silent.

Finally, I couldn't stand it anymore. "You're not a freak, Hannah. You're beauty and light. If others can't see, no need to prove yourself. That's their issue, not yours. Don't absorb their disdain."

Her tears dripped, dripped, dripped. I nudged my shoulder from under her chin, grasped her face in my hands. "Don't absorb their disdain."

A map of red veins colored the whites of her eyes. Her lip was tugged between her teeth, and her eyes moved from side to side, avoiding contact. "You're more than that hate, Hannah. You are."

"Greta not-so-subtly said that if I didn't mentor Jacinta, then I would—"

"You'd what?" I cupped her chin in my hand and drew her close. Her cocoa butter fragrance filled my senses.

"I'd be taken off the roster." Her gaze lowered. Shame colored her expression.

White-hot rage stirred in my belly. "She said that to you?"

"Not directly. Indirectly."

"What'd you say?"

She paused. "I agreed."

I never understood logical fallacies before, but in this moment, I did. "You what?"

"I agreed. Jacinta will be at my house tomorrow morning."

"Why'd you agree?"

"I need to save my career, Jake. This'll give me an edge."

Hannah was magic. Hannah was magic. Hannah was magic. Why was she settling? When I'd accompanied her to a fashion show in Soho, she'd been so nervous and worried about doing well at the event. At first, I'd thought she was joking. She'd been in many fashion shows before. Yet Hannah was serious—a tightly wound ball of insecurity and fear.

The moment she stepped on the stage, all of that melted away. The crowd loved her and she loved them. There was this synergy in the air that night at the fashion show, a force emanating from her spirit. Magic. Why couldn't she see this? "You don't need to model, Hannah. I wish you'd see that. Can't believe you agreed to Greta's offer."

"What else do you want me to do, Jake? What? Stick it out with you and hope you don't betray me again? I need to take care of myself. I need my independence."

"Sooo your independence is agreeing to Greta's veiled threats." I put my hands up in surrender. "Explain to me how that's being independent."

"Whatever." She stood up and rushed for the exit.

"Hold on a sec, Hannah." I ran after her, but she flipped me the bird and passed through the revolving doors. I pushed through the doors. She'd turned the corner onto the busy street. "Hannah!"

Didn't even stop.

Dammit. I shouldn't have been so hard on her. I'd hoped by doing so, she'd see the point of my reasoning. Guess not. I booked it to the corner of 56th Street and Lexington Avenue and pressed through the mass of people on the sidewalk, those sweaty, stressed bodies. When I was within three inches of her, I touched her arm. She jerked away. "Leave me alone."

"How are you going to get home?"

"I'll figure it out." Her gaze lowered to the littered sidewalk. The wind picked up and an empty soda bottle bounced by. A small crowd of people walked around us.

"No, you won't. You can't travel around Manhattan alone when you're upset. Let's work this out, you and me. Besides, I brought you here today. I'll bring you back."

She folded her arms, stubborn.

"Don't you know you're worth more than Greta's flimsy

162

little opinions?"

Hannah shifted from side-to-side and wrung her hands. "Leave me be. I know my worth. Don't need you philoso-phizing on me."

"There's more ahead for you than what she's giving you."

"What? What more?" Her lower lip trembled. "I tried other things. You remember me at Rutgers. I wanted to get my Ph.D. I wanted to teach at the college level."

Yeah, but you quit because you never believed you were smart enough. Too insecure. Just like you didn't believe you'd do well at that fashion show. "But you didn't. Why?"

She tapped her hand against her left thigh, a nervous tick. She was a volcano about to erupt. "Told you why," Hannah said. "Modeling. Now I'm-a take the subway to Penn Station and catch the train to New Brunswick. Don't need a ride from you."

"You're being melodramatic."

"Am not." Hannah crossed her arms and huffed.

"You sound like a two-year-old, but I'm not even gonna fault you. I know how much you love modeling. Ain't gonna grill you anymore. You do what's best for you. I said I'd be here for you only if you needed me, and I'm sticking with my promise. I won't play counselor anymore." I extended my hand to her. "Peace. Can we make peace?"

Hannah looked at my hand as if it were leprous. "Fine. You can drive me home."

"Wonderful. And I'll make you dinner as my peace offer-ing," I added.

"You cook now?"

"After you kicked me out, I had to eat. So yeah, I cook now." I added a wink for extra effect, and she chuckled.

"Fine, Jake. You can drive me home and make one dinner. That's it. And the dinner better be good. Real good."

I smiled. Small victories. I'd have to take what I could get.

CHAPTER 14

J dreaded this new morning. It wasn't because it was another day filled with changing bandages, managing aspirin doses, or dealing with my mother. I dreaded today because this Jacinta girl was showing up for the first time. My "mentee." She supposedly idolized me. How much would she idolize me after seeing my helpless state? Not much, I suspected.

The more I thought on it, the more I'd wished that Tim was arriving this morning instead of my fangirl. Yep, that was how bad I didn't want to see this girl, but with all of Greta's talk about helping the new generation coming up, what choice did I have? Especially when Greta also hinted I'd be taken off the roster.

Hold on a sec. If Jacinta was the new generation, then what was I? The old generation? The fading out generation? The "has been" generation? The idea left a weird taste in my mouth.

I had to "mentor" Jacinta. I couldn't come across as a non-team player. Then I wouldn't get on Greta's good side. If I wasn't on Greta's good side, then it didn't matter whether I got reconstructive surgery or not. I wouldn't be sent on any go-sees, period.

Ugh! This was going to be so hard. Maybe I needed some positive self-talk from one of those motivational speakers on the internet. "Be a good sport, Hannah. Be a good sport, Hannah. Be a good sport, Hannah." I clapped really loudly each time I made the statement to get it into my subconscious or whatever. Didn't help. Jacinta's approaching arrival made me as grouchy as a single old lady with a house full of cats.

Perhaps I should touch base with Jake's mom and see how Jake's father was faring. That'd get my mind off this modeling stuff.

The doorbell buzzed and I jolted. "Don't let her be as gorgeous as her photo. Don't let her be as gorgeous as her photo. Don't let her be as gorgeous as her photo."

Did that count as positive self-talk? I mean, it would positively affect me if she was dog-ugly in person.

I was such a meanie. I was.

I looked through the peephole and my jealousy meter shot up ten thousand degrees. Girlfriend was gorgeous. All ethereal and birdlike and stunning with her long dark hair, sepia-brown skin, and round, liquid eyes. Yeah, I discerned all that through a peephole, so I could only guess her gorgeousness would be amplified once she stepped through the door.

My not-so-gorgeousness would be amplified too. Drats. I'd spent hours trying to look presentable this morning: set the nice part of my hair in curly twists, wore a lightweight scarf to cover the rest and long sleeves to hide the scars, slapped on some lipstick and everything. I flung opened the door and plastered on a plastic smile.

"Hello. Jacinta, right?"

"Yes, is Hannah here?"

My plastic smile froze in place. Did I look that awful? Yes, I did. I remembered the stares from everyone at Click Models. "I'm Hannah."

"Oh… oh, sorry. I didn't realize. I mean. I thought—"

"My skin's healing. I gestured to my bandages to show that her faux pas didn't faze me at all, even though it really did. "It's a slow process. Come on in."

She breezed past me and I caught a whiff of herbal shampoo and fruit perfume, two of my favorite scents. I hadn't been able to wear any perfume because of my skin, and the last time I tried herbal shampoo it stung, so her scent was depressing, to say the least. Jacinta looked how I wanted to look, and she smelled how I wanted to smell. "Are you using Aveda shampoo and Romance perfume?"

"Uh-huh." She swung her oversize Kate Spade bag over her shoulder and twirled around. What was she? A kinder-gartner? "I read in a magazine once that you use them too. Well, actually, you're my inspiration for trying them out."

Oh, joy. Girlfriend was a copycat. *Find your own shampoo and personal fragrance, missy!*

She surveyed my place. "This place is rad. Love the art deco feel."

Love this art deco feel, I said in my inner whiny voice. *Whatcha gonna do? Copy my home décor too?* I kept all these thoughts to myself, however. Didn't want to look as if I wasn't a team player.

Then again, mentoring Jacinta would benefit me in other ways besides saving my own career. I'd been a nervous new model before myself, insecure and worried about whether I'd be successful in the biz. Perhaps I'd quell her anxiety too.

Yes, giving back. That was a much more noble purpose.

"Let me show you around." When we stopped at my home office, I flung open the door. "It's a little messy in here. Haven't been working in a while, but this is where you'll set up shop. Greta had suggested you'd be my assistant. Filing. Posting on social media and stuff. That'll be so helpful since my mobility is limited." I pointed to the empty card table and chair. "Good for you?"

"More than good. Thank you. I never had my own workspace before." She set her purse on the desk.

Did Miss Missy just say "my own workspace" as if she owned my office? No way.

Jacinta looked at me. "So, what's it like?"

I hoped her question didn't have anything to do with my burns because I was not in the mood for a heart-to-heart with Miss Chipper. "What's what like?"

"Full-time modeling. The photo shoot I had—"

"You mean the one I was supposed to go on?" I sensed the snark in my voice as soon as I posed the question, but I couldn't help it. How are you going to work on the photo shoot I was supposed to work on and then ask me a dumb question like that?

"I felt so honored just to go on the assignment in your place. It was a dream come true."

Her dream was my downfall. I immediately busied myself at my desk, shuffling around papers for no particular reason, moving the pen cup to the left, and then moving it back to the right. "That's great." I put on my valley girl voice, not liking how I sounded but knowing I had to wear this mask. If word got back to Greta that I was less than helpful and friendly, she could drop me. Greta was all business with a touch of friendly.

"Tell me." Her maroon lips curved into a much-too-eager smile. "Are there any pointers you have that could help me on future modeling assignments?"

Pointers? Why would I give you pointers? "You've signed with Click Models?"

"Freelancing with them and a few other agencies for

now." She wrapped her perfectly pin straight ebony hair into a loose bun. "She said they're not taking on new clients."

"Oh." Not really sure what I was saying "oh" to—the fact that Greta wasn't taking on new clients, or the fact that Jacinta was freelancing. If the client slots were full, then was I taking up a slot? "You looking to sign exclusively with an agency?"

"Signing with Greta would be a dream of mine. I told her she was my top choice, even though she's not taking on new people. So freelancing helps me to continue booking assignments." She paused. "I'm still working through the whole signing-with-an-agent thing. I was hoping you'd help."

I paused. "Help how?"

"Could you put in a good word for me with Greta?"

Put in a good word? We just met. Girl, I was trying to get in good with Greta myself. "I don't have that much pull. Besides, you're right. Freelancing is better when you're new."

"Is that what you did when you started out?"

Now I wanted to kick myself. Note to self: don't give out advice you haven't tried yourself. "No. Greta actually discovered me at a pharmacy."

"Oooh, one of those starlet discovery stories." She giggled. "I love it. I'd love to be signed at Click Models one day. You still exclusive with her?"

I paused. Was I still exclusive with her? The way Greta was talking when we'd met, I kind of, sort of wasn't. And could I be completely frank with Jacinta? Was she trustworthy? "I've been working with Greta for a long, long time."

"I know. I've been following your fabulous career for a long, long time."

Yeah, I wasn't going to trust her with too much info. Fangirling and ambition made for an odd mix. Or was I the insecure one? Didn't want to answer that question—and so I kept my mouth shut.

"You are such an inspiration to me," she added.

Jacinta waited for me to say something like, "Oh, that's wonderful." Or "Thank you." Or something else equally cordial. Thing was, the question of whether I was insecure gave me a brain fart. Better to change the subject. "You have any more modeling work?"

"I have a photo shoot coming up for a makeup company," Jacinta said. "They have a new line of lipsticks coming out. They have an Italian photographer named Giancarlo on the assignment."

Giancarlo. I seriously wanted to barf all over my desk, something which I'd actually done after that photo shoot when he made the most demeaning, racist comment I'd ever heard in my life.

"Sounds like a… nice gig," I said, not really wanting to relive the depressing details of my last gig with them. Word could get around that I badmouthed him, and then *I'd* get blackballed. Yep, that's how it was in the fashion industry. "Be careful with Giancarlo."

"Oh, I heard he's the best. The shoot will be in Central Park next month when the weather gets colder. Brr." She gave a fake little shiver, which was followed up with a fake little giggle. "You did an ad campaign with them before, right?"

Why was she asking me this question when she already knew the answer? "Right."

"I loved your pictures. You looked so gorgeous. And your lips were divine, girlfriend. I just about cleared out the department store's makeup counter of their Rave shade after I saw you donning the lipstick. My goodness. It is sooo fantabulous, and you look absolutely amazing in that ad."

The memories of that horrid day bubbled to the surface. Giancarlo was talking about my lips like there was no tomorrow. Then when they'd had me wear that awful bright red lipstick and foundation that didn't match my skin tone, I was beginning to think I was becoming more of a blackface caricature than a fashion model.

Why'd I even put up with that nonsense? Why'd I stay for that photo shoot?

Because gullible me wanted so hard to be a "professional." Giancarlo fell off the civility meter when he'd commented on my appearance. Stupid head.

I'd put up with a lot to be liked and accepted. Now I was beginning to see how naïve I was for doing so. I sacrificed my sense of self-worth to be well-liked by a jerk. Like this whole mentoring thing. Was this how I wanted to spend my time? I was beginning to think not, but how else would I get to stay on Greta's roster? And if I wasn't on Greta's roster, then what would I do with myself? Get that math degree I'd put off because of that rapist professor? Tutor Tim, the kid who reminded me of the worst betrayal ever?

"Hello?" Jacinta snapped her fingers. "Earth to Hannah."

"Yes, yes, yes. I'm here." I tucked my lips in between my teeth subconsciously. Then I thought better of it and pouted. Even the memory of that lip comment made me self-conscious. "You know, Jacinta. There's a downside to the modeling industry. Are you ready to be criticized and evaluated and judged all the time?"

Jacinta gave me a blank stare. "Yeah. What's your point?"

This young lady wasn't getting it at all. She probably didn't understand. Ambition blinded. "My point is that you should consider what you want to accomplish in your own career. Or someone else will be more than happy to decide for you."

Another blank stare, but this time it was accompanied by a split-second side-eye. Girlfriend didn't want to understand. Why try?

"So, let's get to work, shall we? I was thinking you could help out with my social media and—"

"What makeup do you wear now?"

I blinked at her random question. We were working. No more makeup talk. "Excuse me?"

"What makeup do you wear?"

I scratched my head and looked at her up close. "Why do you want to know?"

Jacinta shifted her weight from side-to-side. "I'm your mentee, so I figured you'd share your secrets to success since you're not recommending me to Greta, your boss and agent."

Oh, no. Girlfriend was trying to nice-threaten me into giving her beauty tips? I don't think so. I wasn't gonna tell her nothing. "I don't wear much makeup now. Just tinted moisturizer when I can."

"That's obvious you don't wear much makeup. I was talking about before. When you were successful."

When I was successful? What the… ? And girlfriend sounded snarky too. "Whaddya mean by 'that's obvious' and 'when you were successful?'"

"I mean. You know. Your face is fine and all, but you're not modeling now and models wear makeup on photo shoots and—"

"The more you talk, the more you sink deep into the mud," I cut in. *Your face is fine? Your face is fine?* Her pity-comment didn't score any points in my book. "How about we stick to the work at hand? Filing and posting on social media."

Jacinta nodded quickly, her head bobbing up and down as if she were caught stealing. "Sure. Sure. Sure. Sorry. I didn't mean to offend you."

I ignored her apology, refocused on my computer screen, and clicked on the mouse. "Here's my public Facebook page."

I paused and looked at her. "You do have a Facebook page, right??"

"Yep. I don't have many likes, though. I'm not as famous as you."

I wasn't sure whether she was complimenting me or being snarky. Girls like Jacinta were usually well-versed in both. "I'm not that famous."

"Pish posh." She waved her French-manicured hand at me. "Don't play humble. You are a star, baby. A. Star. Girls would kill to have the kind of fame you've had as a model."

"Girls like you?" Did I say that aloud? Oh, yes, I did.

Her mouth twitched. Ha. I knew it. This girl was all ambition and no heart. She'd do anything to get ahead.

"What's that supposed to mean? 'Girls like you?'" Jacinta asked.

"You like modeling, don't you?" I put on my happy voice, and my pitch elevated by a couple thousand feet. "You seem pretty passionate about fashion."

We stared at one another, and in that tiny space of a moment, I felt odd. Odd because somewhere in this little interaction, the game got flipped, and I was the one walking on eggshells because I wasn't sure whether her compliment was real or faux.

Did the modeling industry make me this edgy of a human being? The question made me feel the weirdest. I didn't want to be one of those toxic people who were burned by the industry and spread bad vibes wherever they went. No, I wanted to be a do-gooder. "I'll help you get more engagement on your public page and give you tips on what to post."

"Really?"

Her excitement gave me the warm and fuzzies. "Sure. You can see the types of things I post on my public page. I don't post on my personal profile. I used to post fun pictures of my life and stuff, but—" Now there's nothing fun about my life.

"But what?" Jacinta asked.

The bandages around my neck felt hot and sweaty all of a sudden. "I like to maintain my privacy nowadays. Things get quite uncomfortable the more I'm in the public eye."

"I'm so sorry. Are you going to post about your, you know… " Her eyes empathy-flicked to my bandages. One thing I had to get accustomed to from this burn fiasco? The stare-not-stare people gave me all the time.

The stare-not-stare happened when Jake and I were walking down the street in Manhattan. Folks tried not looking at me too much 'cuz I was so odd-looking with my bandages on my neck and arms, but then they'd give an obligatory glance to prove they were cool with my mummi-fied presence. Yeah, it was complicated.

Kind of like when White people said they weren't preju-diced because they had Black friends but then rolled up their windows and locked their doors when (or should I say "if") they ever ended up driving through the ghetto.

Complicated.

"So are you gonna post about your accident?" She gave another empathy-flick.

"Nope."

"Your fans want to know more about you. Maybe you could post about your skin care regimen, after, you know?"

My skin care regimen after the accident? Was she out of her mind? "Not ready."

"People love you, Hannah. I bet they'd be really interested to compare your before- and after-photos. I mean after you have reconstructive surgery."

Know what? I wasn't mentoring someone if all they were going to do was sit here making me feel like I was broken or inadequate or something. Nope, not doing all that. "Post about my burns? Post about the fire? Post about the fact I'll never be able to feel fully myself ever ever again?"

173

Her eyes changed from empathy to stunned, and fresh shame dumped on me once again. Shame was a bucket of mud I'd never fully wash off.

Jacinta's mouth downturned in this "you poor thing" way, and my shoulders rounded. My stomach bloated from ingesting her pity. That, along with the empathy-flicks did me in.

"You know what? No. This isn't going to work out—this mentorship." I scrambled for composure and tried gluing it back to my voice. Didn't work. "I don't need this. I need more time to process everything that's happened."

I'd never admitted I needed time before. I'd been so quick and fast to jump back into modeling, to meet Greta, that I hadn't given myself the space.

Space was scary. Space was empty. Space didn't hold any goals or plans or fast tracks to success. Space was space.

"Don't cancel the mentorship. It means so much to me. I always looked up to you, Hannah," Jacinta said, taking me out of my thoughts again. "You're an inspiration for me and a lot of people."

My vision turned blurry. Lately, I'd been feeling more desperation than inspiration. "Really?"

"Definitely." Jacinta's pity-smile didn't leave her mouth, yet she sounded sincere.

Maybe I'd misjudged her. But did I still want to do this mentor thing?

"You're inspirational and positive," she added.

Yeah, she was definitely referring to an alternate version myself.

She squinted at the computer screen. "You have a bazillion likes on your Facebook page. Told ya people were waiting to hear from ya."

Problem was: I wasn't eager to be heard. Would those folks in social media land still "like" me if they knew what I really looked like? Did it even matter what they thought? I wasn't sure if I liked myself at this point. Didn't my view of myself matter more?

Space and time would help me sort this all out. Not mentoring. Not reconstructive surgery. Simple space. What would I discover in the emptiness, in the no-plan-for-the-future-ness? Part of me was too fearful to find out.

~

ake and Tim arrived for dinner.

Yep, Jake and Tim. I was completely stunned Jake had brought Tim. As soon as I saw the kid, I pulled Jake aside and grilled him on the reason for Tim's presence. Jake had said he didn't want to let Tim out of his sight, considering Tim's behavior problems at school and all. So naturally I was thinking: Why bring the kid with the behavior problems around me? What if he flipped out or something?

Jake didn't have an answer. He only seated himself next to Tim at the dinette.

Whatever. It would only be for a few hours. In the middle of the meal, I braved one last swallow of that pot roast, thankful my plate was empty. Jake couldn't cook. My jaw might come off its hinges if I had to chew another bite of his cardboard meal.

It was the intentions behind the meal that counted—I guessed.

Nah. Screw intentions. Jake needed to go to cooking school or watch the Food Network or something. This was something awful.

"Sorry we ran out of pot roast. I should've bought more," Jake apologized.

Why was he being all nice and cooking for me when he

obviously didn't cook anyway? Was Jake feeling bad about my meeting with Greta? Perhaps later I'd tell him I was having second thoughts about mentoring Jacinta. If I didn't mentor, then I'd have more time to focus on math. Do something like tutor Tim.

Did I just say that? The kid was a terror. I drummed my fingers on the table.

Tim. I had already resolved to keep my cool and not let all my resentments spill over and take the form of tense conversation and angry innuendo. So far, my resolution was working. That was a miracle in itself.

Hmm. Maybe I was maturing or something. Or maybe the fact Tim hadn't said anything all evening had something to do with it. Kids were better seen not heard anyway. I tended to be old-fashioned when it worked in my favor.

"Next time, I'll bring more pot roast," Jake repeated.

"It was more than enough for me," I assured him.

Tim nodded in agreement, then returned to mopping the seasoned meat juice from his plate with his biscuit. The kid could've been made of dough, all of his features round and cushy. Tim favored Jake in a lot of ways: the round eyes, the full lips, the straight posture. Yep. Jake must've been a spitting image of Tim when he was a kid. Or rather, Tim was a spitting image of Jake as a kid.

The sentiment needled and poked. Partly because it came so naturally, and everything about this scenario was highly unnatural. The only reason I'd agreed to this dinner was because I'd wanted Jake to know I appreciated him taking me to Greta's. Yet after that first day with Jacinta, the time spent seeing Greta seemed more and more like a wasted effort, like a "visit" as Greta had said. Greta was done with me before I had a chance. Yeah, I was still grateful for Jake driving me there and all, but I could've done away with the rest of it.

I could've done away with Tim being here at dinner too.

Every time I looked at Tim's face, I was pulled into this nice-mean dichotomy that flipped me inside out.

The mean side of me wanted to sit at that other end of the table, far, far away from Tim. The nice side of me wanted to appear civil and stay put.

"I still have grilled asparagus left. Want to finish it off?" Jake reached for a serving spoon, but I held up my hand to stop him.

"Thanks for the offer, but no thanks," I said.

"How about you?" Jake asked Tim.

"Nah, man." Tim smiled, accentuating the dimples in his cheeks. "Your cooking is horrible."

I laughed out loud.

"My cooking isn't horrible." Jake set the serving spoon back in the dish and some of the pot roast juice stained the white doily which he'd brought over. Interesting table décor. Jake never came across to me as a doily man. Must've snagged those at a garage sale or something. "What do you think of my cooking, Hannah?"

"Tim's right. Your cooking sucks." Tim and I smiled at one another, and for a few blissful moments, our painful history disappeared. It was comforting, like being wrapped in a floaty bubble of peace.

"Told ya," Tim added.

I giggled through my nose, a girly laugh that had never faded. "Jake, remember when we went out to dinner on our anniversary, and that waitress recognized me from the magazines? She nearly flipped when I said I did all the cooking in the house. She didn't think all those big-time models did normal stuff like cook and that my cooking must be as good as my looks. Never heard that comparison before." I chuckled. "Wasn't sure whether to take that as a compliment or what."

Jake's eyes lit. "I'd take it as a compliment. You definitely have cooking skills. And you're a beauty."

I sighed inside. How was Jake capable of making me feel good? Dilemmas, dilemmas.

"Wonder what my mom looks like in person after months of detox," Tim said. "Must not be good with the withdrawals and all."

I bristled at the mention of his mother. Where'd that come from? We were having a perfectly good time and Tim ruined it.

A shadow fell over Tim's face, his thin form molded to the chair in a slouch. He moved his fork through the scattered peas, a kaleidoscope of circles. Every spiral drained more levity from the room.

Forget about draining levity from the room. With that one statement, this kid had drained levity from my brain. I adjusted the collar of my shirt, ready for this dinner to be over. I should've listened when my instincts reared their oh-so-wise head earlier when they'd arrived.

"Tim, I'm sure your mother is getting better and better each day." Jake smoothed his rumpled cloth napkin. His lips upheld a worn smile. "Trust in a good outcome for your mama."

The scraping of his fork was Tim's only reply.

I rested my chin in my hands and tried to muster up an ounce of empathy. We were just talking about a fun time, something Jake and I hadn't done in ages, and Tim ruined it. What was I supposed to do? Comfort Tim because his mother was a mess? Wasn't happening.

Jake looked at me as if I was supposed to say something sympathetic. Wasn't happening! I was gonna let this silence hang around until forever. I made eye contact with Tim and gave him a smile. That was all he was gonna get out of me.

Tim looked over my shoulder as if overcome with guilt at his inappropriate comment. "What's all that?"

I turned around. The mirrors I'd taken down were still propped up against the wall. I should've put those things up. "Mirrors." My right foot jiggled on instinct.

He got up and made deliberate steps to where all the evidence of my insecurities remained. My pulse climbed into my throat and threatened to choke.

"What're you doing, Tim?" Jake asked.

The kid didn't answer. He simply held up a mirror, stared at his reflection. "I was wondering where the mirror was at when I washed my hands in the bathroom. You remodeling?"

"No." I kept my voice careful and even and emotionless, pushing against the pressure closing in on me. I definitely didn't want to discuss the reasons I'd taken down the mirrors.

"Set the mirror down, son." Anxiety seeped into Jake's words. Jake must've sensed all my discomfort with my appearance and how I'd been so torn. He was defending me.

It was as if Tim sensed he was onto something because he set that mirror down and picked up another. Clutching the frame of the mirror with both hands, he pointed it at me, his forehead a torture of grooves above those mocking eyes.

My reflection. My scarred jawline. My incinerated hair on the left side of my head. My bandaged self. My upper lip twitched as if tugged by a thread, and I studied the grooves on the wooden dining table. Tim knew what he was doing, holding up that reflection of me, and I couldn't stand him for it.

"Did those scars—did the fire, did it hurt?" Tim asked.

Why was he being so nosy? What a ridiculous question to ask. No, no, no way would I tutor this kid. Who did he think he was? "What do you think?"

Tim looked away. "I know. Dumb question. Pretty sure it was very painful. That why you took the mirrors down?"

This new question nailed me. "Er. I, uh. They told me there was going to be physical scars, but they didn't tell me about the—the other scars. The unseen ones."

I said too much. I said too much. I said too much. Why'd I say too much?

"What unseen scars?" Tim asked.

"It's been hard looking at myself after the fire." *As hard as it's been coming to grips with the fact that you're now in Jake's life.*

"Sucks you feel that way," Tim said.

"Yeah. It sucks." I shrugged, my voice shaky.

"Do you still feel beautiful?" Tim asked.

I hesitated, chewed my lower lip, then I rotated the silver thumb ring on my left hand. Rotated it around and around and around. Yeah, he asked a simple question, but did he have to ask it now? I so wasn't in the mood for a therapy session at present. I looked away from the mirror and gave Jake a look that said you-betta-control-your-kid.

"Put the mirror down, Tim."

He didn't.

"Put it down!" Jake snapped. His low gruff stiffened my spine.

Tim's grip loosened on the frame. His eyes—and the mirror—lowered.

Jake leaned forward. "You know how much trouble I went through making this meal and trying to get all of us together here, Tim? Least you can do is show some respect."

Jake remained motionless, his eyes on Tim. The air gained the weight of molten lead, the stifling intensity of a smothering blanket.

Not that I wanted anyone to smother in a blanket or anything. That was how it felt.

More silence. Welp, this was way too awkward.

I shot to my feet and began gathering the plates. "I have a store-bought pie here for dessert. Have a seat, Tim, and we can all enjoy it together."

Together. Did I say that too? Humph. I must be maturing. Perhaps that moment of laughter we'd shared gave me a glimpse of what was possible—perhaps I was starting to like the possible.

Either that or I didn't want Jake to get in a brawl with his son in my dining room. I wasn't going to be stuck in the middle of a father-son standoff. I made hesitant steps over to Tim, and slowly, slowly, slowly touched his shoulder. "Everyone relax now. We have a pie in the kitchen. A. Pecan. Pie. And I don't want it to get cold. Have a seat."

"Don't wanna sit. Can I hang out outside?" Tim murmured.

My disappointment must've shown because Jake looked as if he was gonna erupt, and so I jumped in. "Of course, but don't go far, Tim. Hang out on the porch. I'll save you a slice of pie. Maybe you can take it home."

Tim slowly inclined his head. His eyes, though shaped like Jake's, reminded me of a polluted pond. The black-brown mixture clouded the depth and truth that lay beneath the surface. Tim must be experiencing a lot with the changes in his own life.

Maybe I was wrong. Maybe I could tutor Tim. He needed someone else besides his father to encourage him to get better. Should I be that someone else?

"I'll be outside on the front porch," he said to Jake.

Tim crossed the room. With silent footfalls, he floated down the darkness of the hall. A shaded figure, then a sketch, he gradually disappeared. The front door clicked behind him.

"Still up for some pie?" I asked.

"Um—yes, that would be excellent." He spotted my hands filled with dishes. "Let me help you with that." Rising, Jake

181

reached for my impressively balanced tower, but I stopped him quick.

"You have a seat. You've already made a full meal for the three of us." I quickly rinsed the dishes and placed them in the dishwasher.

Upon returning with two plates of pie in hand, I mined for conversation. "So, how are you adjusting to living in New Brunswick again?"

Not responding, he gazed at the small bouquet of tulips on the table, long enough to count each and every petal. This dinner was dead in the water.

"I have to apologize," he said suddenly. "Tim has been going through a lot."

There was a certain level of comfort in knowing that Jake had apologized. I lifted my shoulders and offered, "Maybe once he settles into his new life with you, he'll—"

"I don't know if Tim will ever settle into life with me. I believe he should get his life on track, but what I wanted… " Jake shook his head.

"What did you want?"

He shrugged. "Doesn't matter what I want."

This was weird. I didn't know what to say, and I definitely didn't feel qualified to give Jake parenting tips on his son. I sighed.

"Anyhow." Jake's tone indicated that we delved too far into the topic for comfort. He lowered his chin and peered at me. "I better get going."

Until tonight, my only fear had been that Tim was going to be weird—and he was weird with his mirror shenanigans. With Jake bidding me goodbye, I worried about something else: I was allowing myself to care about Jake. He'd taken my side tonight when he told Tim to put the mirror down, and he could've kept quiet. Before I would've stubbornly pushed against this sentiment. Now, I was letting myself slip in the sensation.

≈

wo hours after Jake had left, I was still thinking of him. I shuffled into my bedroom and closed the door behind me. I didn't like this change I was undergoing. These feelings of allowing myself to care about Jake were confusing. They could only lead to disappointment.

His son complicated what would've been a perfectly good (almost perfectly good except for that yucky pot roast) dinner. If I was really going to be honest with myself, I enjoyed having a home-cooked meal for once. Traveling all the time for work had made me accustomed to microwave dinners and quickly eaten meals. Sitting down to eat was a delight.

I sat on the edge of the wooden chair and twirled what was left of my shunted curls. The fire-ruined side didn't show any signs of new growth or recovery—although my feelings for Jake were definitely growing, definitely recovering.

This was the most disorienting feeling ever.

What possessed that kid to hold up that mirror to me? Didn't make any sense. Why did I act all scared when he did? *I* didn't make any sense. Seemed like Tim zeroed in on my insecurities and capitalized on them. I hated how a teenager had so much power over me, but Tim wasn't simply any teenager. He was proof that for one moment in time, Jake had strayed.

The phone rang and the caller ID showed Jake Hart.

My stomach flipped. I answered the phone. "Hey, Jake."

"Tim wants to talk to you."

He wanted to talk? My pie-as-peace-offering must've

affected Tim—in a good way, I hoped. Was I ready for what Tim had to say? I clenched the phone. "Um, okay."

Muffled sounds filtered through my end of the phone and I tried imagining what they were saying. Perhaps Jake was all: You better be nice to her. And then Tim was all: Whatever, man.

Was that how guys spoke? I didn't know. Speculating was pointless.

"Hello, Ms. Hart." Tim cleared his throat, and I was silent, waiting. "I never got to thank you for having me over today," he said. "I wanted to apologize if I did anything—"

A voice whisper-shouted in the background.

"I mean," Tim continued. "I *am* apologizing about the whole mirror thing and for being nosy with my questions. That was wrong of me."

A lump lodged at the base of my throat. The pie thing worked, and now I didn't know what to do with Tim's gesture. Seemed like he should have resented me as much as I had resented him, and now?

Tim's apology made me feel all weirded out. His apology was an unruly thing I couldn't tame or contain. I could only let it be—free. "Apology accepted." My voice was hoarse and I patted the armrest of my couch as if Tim were here in person, and I was patting him. "These things happen. I was glad to have you over." *Not really, since you were pretty rude.*

"You were?"

I toe-tapped the floor. "Yep." I meant it this time. If we needed to experience an awkward dinner to make amends with one another, then all the awkwardness was worth something good—

even the awkwardness of looking myself in the mirror. Tim's actions made me face the truth about how I looked, and yeah, I wasn't ready to cope with the truth.

I still wasn't ready, but at least I knew my limitations.

With my shaky free hand, I brushed the curls from my face. "Thanks for calling. And for coming over. I hadn't had guests in a long time."

"Cool," Tim said.

Should I ask? Would I be a complete sucker for asking if Tim wanted me as a tutor?

Then again, I loved math, and Tim had apologized. If I asked, I'd be asking for me. I paused, sniffed once, and puffed out a breath. "Your father told me you're in need of some algebra help?"

"Yes."

I bunched up the hem of my t-shirt and tipped my head to the side, still wavering. This was so awkward. This was so awkward. This was so awkward.

No, not awkward. I was considering delving into math again anyway, and Tim needed help. He seemed at odds with his father at times—not sure how well they gelled when (or if) Jake helped him with homework. Besides, the look in Tim's eyes right before he'd left my house said everything. He was in need.

Not to mention how I'd resolved to release my defenses around Jake. I wanted to show Jake I cared too.

"I'm pretty good at math. If you need a tutor, I can help." I allowed the words to rush out of me so I wouldn't take them back.

"You will?"

"Uh-huh." I'm doing this for me. I'm doing this for me. I'm doing this for me. "As long as you don't hold mirrors to my face."

He laughed. "I mean, sorry. I didn't mean to laugh."

"Not a problem."

"Wanna be clear though. You're my tutor. Not my mother."

My cautions flew up. "Mother? Who said I'm your moth-

185

er?" My voice stopped short, and choppy, silent breaths flowed in and out, out and in.

Tim paused. "My mother warned me when I was moving in with Jake that you'd try to be my mother."

His tone sounded comfortless. The sound scratched at my heart. "What? That's nonsense. I am not trying to be your mama. You only have one of those and—"

"What?"

I'll never be anyone's mother. An emptiness filled me, melancholy and familiar. "Never mind."

"Looking forward to tutoring with you though," Tim said, his tone sheepish.

"Me too." My voice squeaked.

"I'll get Jake."

There was more rustling in the background, more whispers. I craned my neck to discern the words, but I couldn't. Too scratchy.

"Soooo, you're tutoring Tim. Ha. And all I'd hoped for was an apology."

"His apology was generous and kind. He meant it."

"Oh, you have a knack for detecting insincerity, huh? Didn't know that about you."

"You trying to be a jerk again?"

"No. I'm serious. Do you think I'm insincere?" Jake asked.

A silent beat passed before the ridges in my forehead faded. "You try your best."

"But my best isn't sincere enough. Even after that lovely, scrumptious pot roast. What's a man gotta do to win you over?"

I sensed the playfulness in his voice and smiled. "Your pot roast wasn't all that now. Tasted like cardboard."

"I can't believe you and Tim didn't like the pot roast I slaved over. I DVR'd the recipe on the Food Network so I could get it right."

I grabbed my glass of water from the kitchen counter and sank into my cushy couch. The grainy leather squeaked in response. My glance fell on our wallet-sized wedding picture sticking out from the mass of magazines scattered on my coffee table. I must've stuck it there in a fit of rage and later forgot about the fairy-tale image. Were we worth salvaging?

"Earth to Hannah? You still on the other end?"

His voice jogged my awareness. "You must've skipped a couple of steps in the recipe 'cuz whenever I tried Food Network recipes, they came out perfect."

"So you're blaming the cook?" he asked.

"Welp, yes."

"Then the cook needs a do-over."

The cavalier way he'd said it left me struggling for a response.

"And you should cook with me next time," Jake added. "So I won't skip any steps."

The man was coming on strong, and I had to admit it was pretty darn charming. "Can't make any promises. I'll have to check my schedule." I put on a proper, English voice. "Very busy these days, you know? Changing my bandages and all."

"You didn't like my bandage-changing skills at the hospital?"

The bass in his voice hit all my low notes. "They were all right," I said, nonchalant. "If you insist on a dinner do-over, then perhaps I can squeeze you in. I've been considering no longer mentoring Jacinta."

"Good for you. I like seeing you take a stand."

His confidence thrilled me, but I kept my tone even. "I haven't quit yet, so my days are still filled."

"And your nights?"

Oh, lord. "I'll be asleep at night. Sound asleep."

"Joking. Joking. Joking. I'll take whatever time I can get.

Perhaps Tim can have his tutoring session during this dinner do-over."

"We'll start two Tuesdays from now. Goodbye." I hung up and stared at the wallpaper on my bedroom wall, warmed by his words, which had evaporated the coldness between us. How was Jake able to do that so seamlessly?

Despite our chasms—from our falling out over Melinda, to our falling out over Tim moving in with him, and even to the strained way we'd related to one another after this fire, he still made me smile. The notion sent a heated shiver up my arms.

Left to my quandary, I leaned against the wall. Was I so naïve to think our marriage could be restored? Even the pot roast had spoken its disagreement. Then again, Jake had made the yucky pot roast. Perhaps Jake should get an E for effort?

How'd I get on this mental detour?

Deep within, a tiny part of me wanted to give Jake another chance. The connection we'd shared seemed to have survived all those chasms. I'd fought him so hard with the separation papers, with Tim, and with setting terms on my recovery. Yet he still accepted me no matter how hard I fought him. He still accepted me despite my burns. Jake never once said, "We'll talk after you get the fire stuff sorted out." No. He wanted to sort the fire fiasco out *with* me.

And that's what we were doing.

CHAPTER 15

JAKE

*H*annah was going to tutor Tim. Perhaps dreams did come true.

Maybe I sounded a little too Kumbaya for my own good, but her willingness to help with Tim's homework was huge. Once she started tutoring Tim, I'd be free to focus on some father-son bonding, and we'd no longer butt heads over school.

Better yet, once Hannah started tutoring, we'd all bond. Now *that* was dreaming. I smiled at the thought. In the meantime, I'd brought Tim to the office with me today in the hopes of inspiring him to think about his future possibilities, possibilities that didn't involve gangs or jail time.

"Tiny space you have here." Tim shoved his hands in his pockets and surveyed my office, which teemed with unpacked boxes.

"Yep." I heaved a banker's box from the seat and dropped it on the floor. "Although it's better than trying to meet with clients at our new condo. That wouldn't appear too professional. This new rental space will have to do. When I signed

189

the lease for the condo closer to Hannah, I knew I'd end up renting an office too."

"Is the rent expensive?"

"Always, but I have some contracting work lined up here in New Brunswick, so no worries." I cleared the cardboard boxes from my desk and tensed. Until Hannah started with Tim, I was the interim tutor. "Ready to work on some algebra today?"

Tim rumpled his brow, then twisted his mouth.

"I want to see you excel at school. If we have to stay here all day until you figure out these math problems, we will."

"I'm not so sure about all day," Tim said.

"Hey, man, whatever it takes, you and I have to keep pushing." I scanned my phone for the assignments given by Tim's teachers so he wouldn't fall behind. After reading the document, I flipped open his textbook to the correct page. When I did, my skin went cold.

Lines were scribbled all over the place—angry, slashed lines. Looked like an overzealous toddler had drawn on the pages—at least I hoped an overzealous toddler had taken over the text. The stick figure drawings illustrated images of getting stabbed and shot and maimed. It was as if Tim wanted people to think the worst of him when they connected the owner of the textbook to the illustrator of these disturbing images. He was asking to get permanently expelled for defacing school property. "What's this?"

"Dunno."

"Dunno? What kind of answer is 'dunno?'" I faced him, and our gazes did more than meet. They were at a standoff. Yep, I was ready to fight over this blatant act of self-sabotage.

I could've been more empathetic and worrisome. I could've asked, "What happened? What was going on with you?" I didn't. Tim didn't need understanding. He needed a swift kick. When I was on the verge of ruining my life as a kid, my father didn't play nice and understanding with me. He knew the world would be ten times harder on me, a Black man, and so I wasn't going to be easy on Tim.

"What kind of answer is 'dunno?'" I repeated. "Did you or did you not destroy this book?"

"I did." Eyes on the text, Tim shook his head, a grimace etched onto his face. "I was mad. So mad I wanted to punch a wall. That there," he pointed to the textbook, "was nothing."

I held back a response and ingested his gloom and his misery, feelings which colored every syllable he spoke. My gaze sloped down to the puncture marks on the edge of the pages.

"You can't destroy stuff because you're angry, son."

(I already knew that I should've had this talk about caring for your belongings when Tim was in kindergarten, but I'd missed that bus. Perhaps a swift kick wasn't in order at this point. I hadn't put the time in as a father to earn that right. Better talk this one out first.)

"What happened?" I asked.

"Don't wanna talk 'bout it."

"Come on, man. How you gonna improve if we can't get to the root of the issue?"

"Wasn't nothing serious." Tim tugged on his earlobe, unperturbed.

"Sure was something serious if you drew these horrific images." I rested my elbows on the desk and stared him down, unwilling to let up.

Sadness flickered across his expression. "I kept trying to call Mama. They kept telling me she couldn't talk, so I was pissed. Don't know what they're doing to her."

"So the algebra book suffers." I closed the text, walked in his direction, and placed the book in his hands. When I did, a steeliness edged up my sides. I readied myself to tell him the truth, to tell him the way the world worked. "Don't you realize the school officials have the right to sic the school psychologists on you? Those psychologists could use those pictures as evidence to expel you. Your assault hearing is next week, and if they find this evidence, you're done."

"What? I can't express my anger anymore? I can't be mad over what's happened to my mama?"

"Naw, man. You can't. You're a young Black man in America. Anything you feel—good or bad—can and will be used against you. I was like you once. Pissed at the world because my father was a class A jerk. Didn't do me any good. It only gave the teachers a greater reason to target me. This algebra book is your only hope. You can't destroy it no matter how mad you are, no matter how unfair life gets. Why don't you channel your anger by taking up a sport or something?"

"Ha. Ha. You saying that's why there are so many of us in sports? We're channeling our anger?"

I shrugged. "I just want you to do something positive with your life, son. Not something destructive."

"Easy for you to say. My mama ain't your mama. She ain't even your wife."

I took that hit. It was well-deserved. "I told you I'd call her. What made you call?"

"Gets tough for me." He gave a one-shouldered shrug.

At that moment, I saw the world as Tim did, through a harsh camera lens. Where a young Black boy down on his luck lived unhappily ever after. Where prejudice stood at attention the moment he entered a room. Where he'd always be judged for every mishap and misstep, even the ones that occurred through no fault of his own. Where sometimes it didn't feel worth it to even try, because the deck was already so stacked against him.

Tim deserved better, a fair shot, a happily ever after. Yeah, I'll reserve swift kicks for later. My son's emotions were complex, and I had to understand him first before I cast a quick, harsh judgment.

"I'll email your teacher and see if I can get some copies of the ruined pages. I'll call the rehab place too. See if I can get through." I used my desk phone to dial the number to the rehab center. After speaking to the receptionist, I waited and lifted my chin in acknowledgment. "They're checking now."

"Cool." Tim smiled feebly and opened the textbook to the marred page, ran his fingers over the edges.

While I waited, I debated whether to email the teacher and ask if they had a replacement textbook or call my mother to get her advice on this matter. The phone clicked, and I twisted the telephone cord around my fingers. "Melinda."

Tim's eyes shone, reminded me of a kid at Christmas— except I wasn't around when he was a kid at Christmas, so…

"No, this isn't Melinda. This is Dr. Jackson's assistant. May I help you?"

"Oh. Yes." I studied the business card I was given. "I'm— I'm family to Melinda, and her son wants to speak to her."

"I'll have to check her file and see if she's cleared to talk to family members."

Tim's gaze stayed on me, expectant.

"Can you check now?" I asked the assistant on the other end. "Her son's here with me."

I waited a few moments and quickly explained the situation to Tim. He nodded. Seconds later, the lady returned on the line. "Melinda's cleared to speak to family. I'll see if she's available."

My pulse quickened. The idea of speaking to Melinda had me nervous. As long as I focused on Tim, I'd be okay. She answered. "Melinda, it's me, Jake. Tim's here. He wants to speak to you. That okay?"

"Sure." Her voice was gravelly and hoarse.

193

My son's face held hope. "What'd she say?"

"She wants to talk," I said, holding out the phone.

"Yes!"

Sadness shrouded my shoulders. Melinda had a bond with Tim I'd never match. There'd always be this gap between Tim and me, a gap spanning from the day I decided to play absentee father to the day I picked him up from Social Services. Those years in between would remain unknown to me, no matter how much I wanted to relive them. I handed him the phone, but instead of putting it to his ear, he pressed it to his chest.

"You mind if I talk to my mother alone?"

A bond I'd never match. "Sure thing." I slid my cell phone in my back pocket. "I'll give my mother a call too."

Questioning colored Tim's features. "Why?"

"Can't a grown man call his mama?" I asked, imploring Tim to agree. A slight dimple indented Tim's cheeks.

Once out of the office, I strode down the hall toward the conference room, bridling the urge to return and press my ear against the office door. I could hardly feel my shoes making contact with the threadbare carpet, I was so anxious. What were they going to discuss? Would Tim speak highly of me?

What if Tim's conversation with his mother made him even more angry about her situation? He was already getting in trouble at school, defacing textbooks. What was next?

An empty conference table awaited me. I hopped onto it and pressed my hand against the window. Across the street, a window washer worked, cleaning another office building. I wanted to be like that guy, focused on my tasks instead of focused on what was now transpiring between Tim and Melinda.

My mother would give me some wise advice. Besides, if I wanted to be a better father to Tim, then I needed to be a better son to my own father. I should see how Pops was faring health-wise anyway. That was a first step. I called, and Mom answered on the second ring.

"Son! How are you?" Her voice vibrated with a forced optimism. "I was thinking of you. Was thinking about you a lot lately."

I shifted my weight from side-to-side. "What's going on?"

"Too much. Your father."

A snatch of sunlight pierced the clouds and poked through my window. I veiled my eyes from the light. "Everything okay?"

"Cancer. Your father has lung cancer."

The C-word.

I felt nothing. I did nothing.

Then a subtle shock tinged my skin. My hopes of reconciling with Pops would never come to fruition.

"Cancer, Jake. Did you hear me?"

Loud and clear. "What stage?"

"Stage three lung cancer, but what does it matter? Your father has cancer. Lung cancer. I told him all these years to stop smoking. This changes everything."

Not the infidelities. Not the fights. Not the cruel words spoken. That didn't change anything. Lung cancer did. Lung cancer only shortened the time available for me to make amends with Pops. That was all. "What do you mean, it changes everything?"

"Isn't it obvious? I can't keep working while your father is dying. He'll need regular chemo treatments. I'll have to go on an extended leave."

Mom sounded like she was the one with stage three lung cancer. "One step at a time, Mom. You sound panicked."

"I am panicked! I gave my whole life to that man. Gave up everything. Now he's going to die on me?"

She was right. Mom gave up her autonomy, her dignity,

her self-worth. Hearing her say this was hard because Hannah could say the same about me. In many ways, I'd caused the same damage. I'd been a prick too.

The realization was difficult to admit. Untangling these threads would be hard. "It's not the end of the world. Medical science has advanced." I sounded like a commercial for a men's hair replacement shampoo. "Where will he get his chemo treatments?"

"I'm flying him to Sedona, Arizona. They have the best cancer center in the country."

Her heart was an endless well of compassion. "You're a good woman. I couldn't do it."

"No, you couldn't. You hate your father."

Her words sliced into me. Was she trying to guilt trip me for all the years I refused to speak to Pops? "I don't hate him."

"You do. But my grandson should meet him. Have you decided when you're flying him out here?"

She really thought I was some ungrateful prick of a son. "I'm not a monster, and I told you my reasons for not bringing Tim."

"I don't think you're a monster. I do think cancer is a bigger reason for you and Tim to see him."

My heart contracted, skipped three beats. Death waited for no one, but how did someone mend years of damage?

I could've said the same for Hannah and me. Two hard situations where I didn't know the answer. "Cancer isn't a bigger reason. Cancer is cancer. That's all I'll say." I gazed outside at the passersby, wishing I could drown myself in the crowd and become a nameless, faceless one.

Between Tim on the phone with his mother and my mother on the phone on the verge of a breakdown, I'd reached my limit of problems. Hopefully, Tim's conversation with his mother was going better than my conversation,

because if it wasn't, well, I didn't have the emotional reserves
to cope with Tim and Pops and Mom.

Couldn't forget about Hannah—yeah, I was at my limit.

"What if your father dies?"

The question stung. Could I live the rest of my days
leaving my relationship with Pops the way it was now? If I
flew down, would I make it in time to try? I couldn't handle
all of these relationships all at the same time. I had to priori-
tize. Tim and Hannah were my priority. "If you're taking him
to Sedona, then he has a chance."

"Nothing's guaranteed."

Her comment led my mind to an image. Tim's textbook
page, poked and mangled beyond repair. Perhaps Mom was
right—nothing was guaranteed. Rallying for Tim could get
me nowhere. He could self-sabotage his school assignments,
flunk out, and live his life drowning in a never-ending hole
of regret. What difference would helping Tim in school
make? What difference would a visit to his grandparents
make? Nothing was guaranteed.

This was getting more depressing by the minute. Still, I
wanted to feel good knowing I'd given my relationship with
Tim my best shot. I didn't want to drown in my own regret
over being a sucky father, but I couldn't focus on Pops and
Tim simultaneously. Something had to give.

"His first chemo treatment is on Monday morning. I've
already got our plane tickets. In the meantime, he'll be on
painkillers. I'll be home with him from now on." Mom
sighed, a reluctant surrender to this unwelcome stage in her
life. "Let me know if you decide to visit. I need the support
too. It'll be hard going at this alone."

When she put it that way, gosh. Still, Tim and Hannah
came first. "I will. Love you, Mom."

I got off the phone and returned to my makeshift office,

thoughts flurrying in a haze. I didn't want to see that man, my father. Was I awful for feeling this way?

It was there, in the numbing silence, when I dared to wonder: was unforgiveness a brittle seed that would grow into something worse? I ran my thumb over my empty ring finger. Not having closure with my father could somehow, some way, carry over into my relationship with Hannah. These relationship webs were more connected than I'd imagined.

Tim sat at the chair in front of my desk, his face rigid. "Mom told me the truth."

Confusion tugged at my conscience. "What truth?"

"You never told her we were moving to New Brunswick. You hid it from her on purpose. You're trying to make sure I won't see her again."

"Wh… what? Where'd you get that idea?" I spoke only loud enough for Tim to hear. People occupied the offices nearby, and so I didn't want to cause a scene. "If I wanted to hide your whereabouts from your mother, I wouldn't have bothered to call the rehab center today."

Tim shifted from left to right, his demeanor clouded with uncertainty. "You're telling me what I want to hear, not the truth."

I combusted. "Know what?! You're right. I don't really want you to see your mom again. Not if she's addicted to drugs. Not if she's going to let you wander the streets and skip school and whatever else. And yeah, we also moved so you could be in a better place, away from the bad influences in that neighborhood. I'm not going to lie and say I'm sorry for moving you. Because I'm not. Because I did it to try to help you succeed."

"So you're a sellout, and you wanted me to sell out too? Wanted to turn me into a White boy or something."

"Wh-what? Turn you into a White boy? Are you outta

your mind? When're you going to see I'm not against you? I'm for you. I'm more for you than you'll realize in your lifetime."

The irony of my words landed on me, a dead weight. Did Pops think the same of me? Had he been for me more than I'd ever realized? The question pinched.

"Whateva, man. I ain't trying to be no square. I knew you didn't want me to see Mama too."

This conversation showed no signs of progressing, stuck on its circular path. Nothing's guaranteed. Mom's words pressed into my heart.

Weariness set in. This kid was going to think the worst no matter what I'd said, and that would be his main stumbling block if he kept it up. Principal Grant's veiled threats to Tim resurfaced, implications that Tim was doomed to failure.

The world was ready to guarantee Tim's failure. That wouldn't be anything unique for the six o'clock news.

"I'll make sure you see your mother. I'll go up to the rehab center myself and visit Melinda in person. I'll see if we can work out some sort of visitation schedule."

"Don't bother. She already said she doesn't want to see anyone, including me."

I paused. How could Melinda say I was keeping her from her son and then refuse to see him? Didn't make any sense. I approached my reply carefully—hearing that from his mother must've stung. "She's not rejecting you, Tim. I'm sure she's experiencing a lot of pressure. Give her time. She wants her son to see her at her best. And I'll still visit her in person regardless."

He looked unconvinced.

"I'm going to email your teacher and see if we can get those fresh pages sent to us." I peered at the scribbled page. "Can't read the equations at all."

"Yeah."

"Like I said, your formal school hearing is coming up." I closed the textbook, not wanting to look at the evidence of my son's pain, evidence that could crucify him. "We're gonna have to show your efforts to improve, not worsen."

Tim nodded. "I understand."

Solving the problems in our relationship was going to take more than a trip to my office or extra tutoring sessions.

It was going to take all of me, just like Mom was giving all of herself to help Pops through cancer. Yet Pops was a dying man. Was Tim's potential for improvement dying too? Those disturbing scribbles in the textbook suggested so.

But since I was around, I wasn't letting that happen. Not to my son.

CHAPTER 16

"You have a lot of followers on your Instagram page too." Jacinta clicked on the computer mouse and her eyes widened. "You are so, so lucky."

If only she knew that all that attention brought with it an ever-increasing pressure to remain appealing to a fickle crowd. If I was to have any semblance of a modeling career, then I'd need to keep up with their demand.

With the way I looked now, I definitely wasn't keeping up. "You really think I'm lucky?"

"Oh yeah." She flipped her long, black ponytail in my direction and gave me one of those frenemy smiles, half-fake and half-sincere. "I'd kill to get this kind of feedback on my social media."

I wasn't sure whether to be happy or flattered or weirded out. I certainly wouldn't kill for a Facebook like. That was too extra for me. I knew those "fans" wanted to see me because I hadn't posted a picture of myself since before the fire.

I sighed. Totally didn't want to even think about all that. All I needed to do right now was mentor Jacinta. Worry about public photos of myself later. I had my doubts, but after thinking about it more, I figured it was better for me to stick this mentoring this out. That way I'd keep my options open. I mean, what if things fell through with math and tutoring Tim? They'd fallen through before. Yep. Better to not place all my bets in one area. "So, you have any questions for me? I'm here to help you out, so shoot."

After I'd said shoot, I immediately thought of her "kill to get a like on Facebook" comment. Yeah, maybe I shouldn't have said "shoot."

Jacinta twirled the edge of her ponytail around and around and around, and I could see the hesitation on her face.

"What do you want to ask? There's no question too hard."

"When I was talking about freelancing last time I was here, I kept thinking about wanting to sign with a modeling agent. I really, really, really want to sign with one. I understand you don't want to give me a recommendation, but how do I get one?"

Except that question. That question was too hard. How was she going to ask me how to get a modeling agent? I was on thin ice with Greta myself with my injuries and all.

I sighed. Mentoring was complicated.

"Except for the two assignments Greta sent me on to fill in for you and one other model who had pneumonia, I haven't been regularly booking assignments even though I've gone on a ton of go-sees," Jacinta said.

Listening to her predicament made things sound more hopeless. If things were hopeless for her, then they were even more hopeless for me.

Get the thought out of your head. Helping Jacinta is helping you get in Greta's good graces. Focus on mentoring her. "If you fare well in the mentorship, you might get signed with Greta."

"You think?" Her eyes widened.

Jacinta's hope deflated mine. "You should always keep your options open though. We can do some research for agents. See who's open to taking on new clients. Sound good?"

Jacinta paused, studied me up close. "Are you retiring?"

"Retire? Um, no."

"Sorry, sorry, sorry. Didn't mean to be nosy or anything." *But you did.*

Time to change the subject. Back to mentoring mode, even though that retiring question made me want to cut the workday short—cut the workday off now. "Ready for me to show you how to use your Facebook fan page?"

"Sure."

I had a bazillion notifications on my page. "That last meme you created got me a whole bunch of likes. Let's see what the hullabaloo is all about."

"Yeah." Jacinta let out a high-pitched laugh, and I clicked over to check the post. When I did, heat lit my face and spread down my neck.

A picture of Jacinta was all over my Facebook page, a very flattering picture. She wore a tight red dress, low cut to reveal her push-up-bra boobs. The photo definitely had a filter on it. Her skin looked a tad smoother and dewier than it did in person. I clicked on the caption. It read, *Check out this gorgeous up-and-coming model. She's a person to watch. The total package. Beauty and brains.*

"What is this?" I asked.

"I, uh—"

She'd need a lot of chips in the bucket with me if she ever wanted me to promote her on my page. Since she snuck behind my back, I was *never* going to promote her on any of my social media.

"Did you post this yourself? You posted this like I'd given

you an endorsement. When? I never gave you admin privileges."

"Um, I posted it when you were still logged into Facebook. I thought it'd be fun."

Fun? Seriously? Undermining me and being a backstabber was fun? No way. When I first started in this modeling game, I was all for buddying up with my fellow models. Then I'd offended one and she never spoke to me again. I tried to gain that model's forgiveness, but she didn't listen. That experience taught me one thing: business was business. I couldn't get buddy-buddy with my fellow models because feelings were easily hurt in this hard industry.

"You thought blatantly self-promoting yourself on my Facebook page without my permission was fun?" I squinted, trying to figure out if this girl was sincere or faking me out. The way her eyes were doing that rapid-fire back and forth movement meant she was faking me out. "Don't ever. Ever. Do this again."

"Okay, okay, okay." She put her hands up like I was the wrong one. "Not a big deal. I'll delete the picture. That's all."

Whateva, girl. "I'll delete the picture." I did and quickly logged off, still pissed. My leg was still twitchy. I was done with this girl. Done. Done. Done. "That's all for today. We can recoup tomorrow."

"What about showing me how to use my Facebook fan page?"

Was girlfriend serious? Like, really? "Not today," I said, deadpan.

"I didn't mean anything by it. I just thought it was something fun to do." Jacinta wrung her French manicured fingers and giggled like a nervous little idiot.

She'd just put my reputation on the line, and if she did something screwy in the future, people would look at me as the person who first championed her.

Wait a sec, she already did something screwy by posting her picture on my page without my permission. What else was she capable of doing? Perhaps I needed to rethink this relationship. "We'll pick up bright and early tomorrow morning," I continued.

"Okay." A frown was etched on her face. "Again, I really want to apologize."

"You're only apologizing because you got caught. Did you not think I'd check my own Facebook account?" My words seethed between my teeth, hissed really.

"I didn't mean any harm by it. Promise."

"Jacinta, I'm supposed to help you out. It'll be hard for me if you do this type of thing." *Or really, I don't want to help you if you're going to do this kind of stuff.* "Got it?"

Jacinta did a one-two-three blink. "Are you really saying you're going to stop mentoring me because of this teeny-weeny faux pas?"

Teeny-weeny faux pas? Um, you broke my trust. My trust!

"I never said that I'm going to stop. You're putting words in my mouth. I said it'll be hard for me, and I want this to be the best working relationship that it can be." Sheesh.

Girlfriend kept blinking, one-two-three, one-two-three, one-two-three. "If you're not going to mentor me anymore, go on and say it. Go on and say it!"

Jacinta's voice turned a little too frantic. I kept silent.

"Maybe I'll tell Greta to switch me to someone else."

My skin got a case of the pricklies, and it wasn't because I'd added a coat of anti-microbial crème to my skin an hour ago. Nope, it was 'cuz of this wannabe-model's subtle little threat. Now I was the scared one. If she told Greta about this problem, she'd frame it in a way to make me look like the bad guy.

Question was, would I succumb to her threat and look like the sucker? No way.

"Do what you want, Jacinta. I know what I said, and if Greta has any questions about it, then she can contact me herself."

"Fine." Her voice turned to steel.

"Fine." My tone matched her intensity.

"Fine." Jacinta dialed up the volume a few decibels.

She left my house, slammed the door too. The nerve! Who did she think she was, catching an attitude? I gave her all the advice. I offered to show her how to create a social media presence. Was she outta her mind?

Or was I outta mine? I rested my chin in my hands. Nope. I was gonna stand my ground. She didn't have a right to post that picture to my page when I never approved.

I logged into my email account. I was gonna tell Greta about my "fabulous" time with Jacinta. Yep, that was how I did it, never complained about anyone. That way, if perchance Jacinta did complain to Greta, she'd look like the awful one.

Not me. Never me.

CHAPTER 17

*A*t the end of my conversation with Tim the other day in my office, he appeared to have understood the serious nature of messing up his textbook. If Tim could see the flip side of why messing up the textbook was so bad, then perhaps the judge could see the flip side of what would cause a kid like Tim to get in so much trouble.

One could hope.

I finally got the summons from the other kid who was pressing charges for the school fight. When I'd read the summons, I'd almost wanted to toss it in the trash. The words sounded so accusatory, so wrong as if punches hadn't been thrown at Tim too. Yeah, I'd seen my son's black eye in the principal's office, but no one had mentioned Tim's injuries in the formal documents.

Here I was in the courtroom, waiting to see if the judge would refer Tim to a trial in juvenile court. I hoped not. I hoped this entire school fight fiasco stopped right here, and that the judge would throw out the case.

My buddy John wasn't a criminal lawyer, but he'd referred me to George Allen, the man seated next to us, a man who seemed very young and green to this whole lawyering thing. We'd only spoken on the phone last week, and so I hadn't met George.

Now, I wished I'd met him in advance. If I had, I would've found another lawyer in an instant. I needed someone with experience. Couldn't do anything to change the present though. The only thing I could do was give Tim my best fatherly self and support him in any way necessary.

I placed my hand on Tim's shoulder. "You're not alone in this, Tim. I'm here for you."

"I know." He cracked his knuckle.

He knew? The other day at my office, he was fighting me and doubting me and second-guessing me. Maybe things were starting to improve, slowly.

George tightened the knot on his tie and then took out a yellow legal pad and started scribbling nervously across it. Was this his normal way of prepping for trial, or was he nervous because this was his first case—ever? I hadn't even asked the man because I'd been so busy thinking of Hannah.

"How long have you been practicing law?" I asked him, trying to sound nonchalant and not as if I questioned his abilities.

"At this firm, three months." George cleared his throat and started clicking his pen incessantly.

"And prior to those three months?" I prodded.

"Um, prior to those three months I was in law school."

My mouth twitched. Law school? What kind of referral had John given me? I tapped the pen on the desk in a rapid-fire pace. This couldn't turn out good, not with this guy on board.

No, no, no. I'd paid good money for this lawyer. A whole lot of money, and I had to believe we'd get what we paid for. This would result in something good.

"Tim, this is your first charge, and so I doubt the juvenile court officer will take you to trial," George said. "You'll have to be completely careful with how you answer. A lot of times the judge's decisions for these kinds of cases are superficial judgment calls based on appearance and attitude. That sort of thing."

I took one look at my son and knew he was bound to be a target with his slumped don't-care posture, that *Z* shaved into his head, the *Z* tattooed on his neck, and his dark complexion.

On my first day at Wilberforce Preparatory as a freshman, I remembered how awestruck I'd been about being only one of three Black kids in a school of over a thousand students. We were even outnumbered by the Asians, but hey, they had it better than Black people anyway: owned all the stores in the 'hood, sent their second-generation kids to Ivy League schools, all of that.

Yeah, on that first day, I knew I had to step up my game. Any misstep on my part and I'd be kicked out in a minute, and all of my parents' hard-earned money, all of their deferred dreams, dreams they conferred to me, would've gone to waste.

I knew what was up, and so I spoke the King's English, stayed clean-cut, always kept uniform regulations. Men like me weren't given second chances.

Now, I looked at my son with the wrinkles in his t-shirt and his devil-may-care demeanor, and I wanted to pull him to the side and give him a strong talking-to about his chances, and how he couldn't let up or give anyone a reason to write him off.

But it was too late for all that. Besides, I'd chosen the "be the best father I could be today" corner, not the "I'm gonna save you from systemic racism and injustice" corner. Ain't much saving from the other corner anyway.

I rubbed my temples and tried to read the chicken scratch

George seemed to be writing on his legal pad. He sat across from me, so the chicken scratch was upside down. I couldn't read a thing. For all I knew, he could be doodling and trying to play off that he was in control of this whole situation. I sure wasn't.

Upside down chicken scratch. That's what this whole assault-charges situation was turning out to be. Upside down.

"Give Tim my all. Give Tim my all. Give Tim my all," I muttered.

"All rise," the bailiff said.

Everyone in the courtroom stood, and Tim remained seated. Oh lord, here we go. Tim was already being defiant, and the rookie lawyer didn't help my confidence much either.

I nudged my son and gave him what had become my practiced father eye, the one that said *get up or else*.

He took off his headphones and stood too. The judge, a sixty-something man with Santa Claus white hair and a beard to match, sat behind the bench. I doubted he'd be giving out any presents this season.

"All right, let's see what we have here." He slid on his bifocals and looked at the docket. "Three cases. We'll start with Khalid Rogers."

Whew. Tim wasn't first.

Khalid had a chip on his shoulder. I could tell by his stance. He shifted his weight to one side, thumb in the belt loop of his jeans, hat turned to the back. Yep. If what George said was true about judgment calls being made on appearance and attitude, then this kid didn't stand a chance. So much about life was subjective. The judge could have had a bad morning and send Tim to trial. Please, I thought, don't let that happen.

After a couple of moments of back and forth, the judge

slammed his gavel. "Referring your case to the juvenile court trial." He announced.

Yep, I was right. Khalid didn't stand a chance with those baggy jeans and that hip-hop t-shirt. At least Tim wore a suit. A wrinkled suit, but it was a suit.

"Tim Ramirez."

My stomach clenched at the mention of my son's name. The last time I felt this emotion was the day I'd found Hannah semi-conscious in the tub. I was nervous, worrying if she'd make it, worrying if I'd make it without her.

That familiar worry suffocated me now. How would I manage if Tim received a harsh judgment? I'd never forgive myself for contributing to his fate.

George stood but dropped his briefcase, papers spilling everywhere. He quickly bent to gather them. I exhaled and counted the seconds to see how long it'd take for George to get himself together. The seconds turned into minutes.

The air started getting heavy and thick. Each second our lawyer took was a second too long. It was more seconds for the judge to make value judgments that wouldn't be in Tim's favor.

Yep, Tim should've ironed all the wrinkles out of his shirt.

Finally, our oh-so-smooth lawyer made his way to our side. "Your Honor, I apologize for the delay." He adjusted his glasses on the bridge of his nose.

"We have an assault charge," the judge said. "Taken place on school property?"

"That's correct, Your Honor. I want to file a motion for dismissal since this is Tim's first criminal charge," George said.

The judge didn't say anything, simply kept flipping through a thick file before him. "The plaintiff's representative sent us this school record. Seems like he's been in trouble before?"

The judge's voice held an undercurrent of doubt, not doubt at the evidence but doubt of Tim. I was familiar with that change in tone. All the words sounded flat and monosyllabic except the one at the very end—that last syllable would end on a down- note or an up-note, but either way, it indicated doubt.

"Yes, Your Honor. He does have some blips on his school record, but his father has informed me that Tim has made some strides after meeting with the principal a few weeks ago. Grades are improving. No new offenses at school. Looking to start a job."

The judge didn't respond. He only flipped through pages and pages of records. Stuff even I didn't want to read.

"Looks here like you like to fight a lot, Tim? Vandalize school property?" the judge asked.

There was that tinge of doubt in his voice again. This time, the judge directed the question at Tim, and I hoped he'd say the right thing.

"Those are on my record, sir," Tim said.

Phew. Good, good, good. He added a "sir" to his statement.

"You plan on this happening again?"

A pause from Tim and my pulse quickened. I'd recalled our conversation where he'd said the other kid had bullied him about his mother. *Don't try and justify your actions now, Tim. Don't do it.* If he did, then the judge could think my son was being defensive or trying to hide something.

"So long as I'm not provoked," Tim said.

My jaw tightened and I tugged on the cuff of Tim's suit. Tim ignored me, which was annoying because I'd prepped him for this hearing, told him not to show any attitude.

The judge did a double take. "Excuse me? What'd you say?"

"The person who filed charges provoked me, said some rude things about my mother, Your Honor."

The lawyer's neck reddened. "Your Honor, this—"

"Provoked you?" The judge raised a brow. "Explain."

Now I was getting sweaty and uncomfortable. As soon as Tim opened his mouth to explain, a rushing filled my ears, and my hearing instinctively shut down and blocked whatever was coming from Tim's mouth.

"So you punched first?" The judge asked after Tim "explained."

Oh no. Oh no. Oh no.

"Your Honor," George stepped forward and gave a nervous laugh. Why'd he sound like a rookie? Man, I could've found a better lawyer than John. "This is Tim's first criminal offense. I recommend he not go to trial for it," George repeated.

That's all he could say? That was it?

"You involved with gangs?" the judge asked Tim.

Tim's eyes widened. "No, Your Honor."

"Says here you were seen colluding with gang members on school property. Gang members who were way past the age of attending school. What were you doing?"

"A lot of people hang out at the school. That ain't nothing new."

That ain't nothing new? Where'd all the slang come from? I wished the ground could open up and swallow me. I nudged Tim again, but he didn't take notice—or he was purposefully ignoring me.

"A lot of kids who end up in juvenile detention go on to have criminal records as adults," the judge said. "It's a statistical fact. The company you keep doesn't seem to be on the road to being model citizens."

He was right. Juvi typically meant a criminal record later

on in life, but I was still holding out hope this judge would be lenient on Tim.

The judge redirected his attention to me. "You keeping him out of trouble?"

There it was: the whole parental-responsibility thing. The thing I'd missed for ninety-nine percent of Tim's life. "I'm trying, Your Honor."

The judge looked Tim straight in the eye, his gaze steely. "This'll go on your record, young man. I won't take it to court. But if you're ever in here again for anything else, I can't guarantee you'll be so lucky. You'll have to get a job. Volunteering. Community service. Something. Five hundred hours of community service at a verifiable non-profit to be completed in six months."

Now that was a problem. A big problem. We'd tried volunteer work and not one non-profit or business in this area wanted to take him in. Tim's poor reputation had gone before him.

"If you don't complete the hours, we'll take this to court," the judge added.

"Your Honor, I—" Tim said.

"That's my final judgment." He slammed the gavel. "Six months. And the court will need a written record of Tim Ramirez's volunteer hours. Six months is more than enough time."

CHAPTER 18

HANNAH

*A*fter I had sent an email to Greta, she'd responded with a short, sweet response: *Glad to hear things are going well.*

Whew! I was worried Greta would inquire further and then I'd get all nervous and blab my worries, making me look like the insecure one. Greta's response must've meant Jacinta didn't contact Greta. Haha! Jacinta was such a chicken.

Now we'd see if Miss Prissy Pants would show up for work today. I checked the clock on my wall. Five minutes till her official start time, and she wasn't here yet.

I opened the blinds to my kitchen and sunlight streamed inside, highlighting the dust speckles in the air. Mama had been right about me having to keep up with dusting and stuff. I needed a super-clean living space so that I'd heal up nicely. I was doing pretty well with keeping things spic-and-span now that Mama had bought me this super-duper, suck-up-everything-in-sight vacuum cleaner, plus she'd been helping dust in the areas that I couldn't. In a lot of ways, this fire had brought us closer together despite the differences between us.

215

If Jacinta arrived today, I'd be the civil one. I'd make sure I set clear terms and rules for how she handled my social media accounts and of course, being the better person, I'd rise above her blatant abuse of my social media account, and I'd forgive—'cuz I wasn't petty. I was learning how to supervise petty people with maturity and grace.

See? Not petty.

The doorbell buzzed, and I jolted. That must be Miss Thing. *Be civil, Hannah.* Seconds later, I greeted her with a polite "good morning." I sounded so fancy I could've been holding an audience with the Queen of England.

"Hey," she responded. Today, she wasn't wearing that oversized handbag. Instead, she had a small wristlet. Cute.

"Glad you're here," I said and opened the door so she could enter. "It's a new day, and I'm ready to work."

She didn't budge from her position on my front porch. "Yeah."

Jacinta's voice took on a drawl I hadn't recognized before. That's when I knew something else was up. Had she posted a picture of herself on my Instagram too? Hmm. I would've checked my phone, but I'd left it on my desk.

"We need to talk." Jacinta tugged on her wristlet strap. Her nails weren't French manicured today. They were short and bare. She must've removed them since seeing me yesterday. "I've been doing some thinking since we last spoke, and I wanted to apologize."

Ah, how nice. "Apology accepted." I smiled and my shoulders relaxed. "Guess we can get on with the day."

"Yeah, about that too. I wanted to tell you in person because I felt it more appropriate. The short time I've been with you has been fabulous, and I was truly honored to model in your place at that photo shoot over a month ago when you were in the hospital, but this mentorship isn't quite the right fit for me anymore."

I raised my brow. "Oh really?"

"Yes, it's time for me to focus on something else."

Something else? Greta didn't mention a something else when I'd sent my email. "You're not pursuing modeling?"

"Actually." Her fingers twisted around her wristlet again. "I'm pursuing modeling full time. That's why I'm stepping down from this mentoring thing."

This "mentoring thing?" She'd made it sound like it was some terrible disease.

"I hope you'll find someone who's a better fit for you," Jacinta said.

Blood rushed to my head. The girl was rejecting me, and I'd had my fill of being rejected. Rejected by Jake. Rejected by my mother. "Does Greta know?"

"Yes, she does. I told her this morning."

Told her this morning? I got an email from her this morning. Someone was obviously lying.

"I better get going. Have a nice day, and I hope you heal up nicely. You're already looking fab." She turned to leave quickly, a little too quickly.

"Hold on a sec," I said, curious. "So, you'll still be freelancing full time, I assume."

She twisted her mouth and her eyes bugged out like she'd been caught. "Greta offered to sign me on this morning."

"This morning? What the what?"

"Yes." She jumped up and down and did this stupid two-step shuffle with her feet. "I'm so excited I could pinch myself."

I could pinch you too. I bit the inside of my cheek. Pinching her would've been incredibly uncivil.

"Greta has three go-sees lined up for me for next week and then I want to take some studio shots to add to my portfolio. Eeee. This is sooo exciting."

Again with the two-step shuffle thing. Good grief!

Someone needed to tell her to stop reveling in her career success in front of my house. How rude. Rude and hurtful. My heart crimped. I'd worked so, so hard to build up my career, and one freak accident compromised my career, but Jacinta had a chance. I hated how she had a chance, and I didn't. Maybe that was bad to say, but it was true. Would I get a second chance?

"Have a good day." I waved, shut the door, and slunk against the wall.

A pressure built inside my ribs and my breathing constricted. Mean-girl-with-ruthless-ambition was moving on to bigger and better things, and here I was burned—in more ways than one. This sucked meatballs. Why didn't Greta mention Jacinta's new status in her email? *Breathe. Breathe. Breathe.*

Eeee. This is sooo exciting.

Jacinta's words wrapped around my neck like a choke hold. I needed space to breathe. I pushed myself off the ground and headed over to my laptop, ready to focus on my work. I didn't need Jacinta's help with my social media accounts. I could handle them myself.

I logged into my Instagram, something I hadn't done in a while, and a private message notification popped into my inbox. Humph. I didn't get PMs on Instagram. Folks typically PM'd me on Facebook.

I clicked on my inbox and a long stream of messages exchanged between Greta and Miss Prissy Pants clogged up my Instagram inbox. What in the world? Did Jacinta accidentally-on-purpose add me into this exchange?

I clicked on one message from Greta:

Tried sending you an email, but my messages kept getting bounced back to me. So I'm trying you here. I have the representation agreement ready for you to sign. I'm so sorry about the mistreatment from Hannah. My apologies. I wished it would've worked. You never know about these things.

Bile formed in the back of my throat. Jacinta *did* accidentally-on-purpose add me into this exchange! She *would* do something cruel to irritate me. What did Jacinta tell Greta? I had to find out.

I fished my cell phone from the side drawer of my desk and dialed Greta's direct line. She answered on the second ring.

"Hey, Greta."

A two-second pause. "Hannah, how are you?"

Our working relationship was so close, she'd recognized my voice. No way Greta could've believed whatever Jacinta had told her about mentoring. We'd had our trust, hadn't we?

"Jacinta told me this morning that she quit."

"Oh. So sorry to hear."

So sorry to hear? I reread her message to Jacinta on my Instagram. "She said she signed with you this morning or whatever. I'm checking my messages here and it reads like you knew she was going to quit. You knew she was unhappy. Didn't you?"

"You know I don't get into those things, Hannah."

"You certainly knew something or you wouldn't have offered for me to work with her in the first place!"

Calm down. Calm down. Calm down.

"Hannah, since the first time you called me from the hospital, I've been beyond worried for you. We've been together for a long time, but I think it's best for us to part ways."

"Part ways?"

"Yes. You need to focus on you and your recovery. I need to focus on making sure this business is running smoothly. That means I need all of my clients at their best."

My skin tingled. *And you think I'm at my worst?* "That's

how you're going to end this, Greta? After all these years, you're dropping me from the agency?"

"Not dropping you. We're simply moving on. You've had a long and beautiful career, Hannah. Keep that with you. Always."

My eyes stung. *Long and beautiful career?* I'd given up my whole life for this stupid industry, and she was kicking me to the curb for some hot young thing?

I sounded like a bitter ex-wife. Whatever.

"If you ever need any referrals, Hannah, feel free to let me know. I'm more than happy to give you a glowing recommendation for whatever path you decide to take."

Greta meant whatever path I was forced to take because Greta dumped me.

Yeah, yeah, yeah: bitter ex-wife.

I mumbled something incoherent and hung up. Rejection was the pits. My hand trembled, my lower lip trembled, everything trembled. "It's just a stupid career," I said to my empty house. "It's not the end of the world." Except it was. Modeling was the one thing I had left that was truly mine, truly—

My eyes stung and my vision turned blurry. I was crying again. The doorbell buzzed.

Bet Jacinta was returning to tell me something snarky. I shuffled to the door and looked through the peephole. Jake? What not-so-perfect timing. Guess this wasn't the day for getting work done. I opened the door. "Hello."

Jake stood before me and did a double take. "What happened to you?"

"Everything happened to me." I let him in and we sat on my living room couch. I relayed the events of the morning, choking on my tears.

"I told you, Hannah. You're worth more than what Greta was offering you." He cupped my face and looked gently in my eyes. "You'll get through this too. Just like you're recovering from your burns. You're so strong. And you can still model, you know. Why don't you ask Liza how she made it in the industry?"

"Um, I burned that bridge." I told Jake all that had happened with Liza.

"You know, Hannah. I'm learning how worthwhile it is to reach out and say you're sorry for any hurts you've caused. Why don't you try that with Liza?"

I had too much to think about. Mending friendships was the last thing on my mind. "Greta was right. I can't model. I'm done. I'll always have the scars."

"But they don't have to have you."

The words landed like a gavel, strong and sharp and true.

Jake reached over and took my hand in his, gently rolling up my sleeve to reveal my bandaged forearm. I shuddered against his touch.

"It broke my heart when you'd taken down all the mirrors in your house," he continued. "When I saw you in the hospital the first time after the fire, I was shocked. But I never flinched at your appearance. I love your scars."

He loved my scars? What?

Jake kissed the back of my hand, the skin that was welted and warped. Something in me melted. He was standing here, kissing my scars when I couldn't even look at myself in the mirror. This man did see me. This man did love me.

"Come with me." He got up from the couch and flicked on the light in the side hall, the hall leading to the room where I'd hid the mirrors. "You need to look at yourself in the mirror and see how beautiful you are."

I stopped walking. "No."

"If you ever want to stand any chance of moving past this Greta ordeal—this fire ordeal—you'll have to be able to face yourself, scars and all."

221

I shook my head a thousand times. "Wrong. Wrong. Wrong. You of all people shouldn't be giving me advice."

He went into the room where I'd hid the mirrors, and my pulse pounded. This joker was really getting a mirror. I wanted to run away, but it felt as if my feet were stuck to the ground. Deep within, Jake was right. I couldn't live the rest of my life hiding from myself.

There it was, the mirror in his hand. And here I was, nervous.

"Come on, love." Jake wrapped his arms around me. "You should do this for you."

If my heart could bust through my rib cage, it would've. "The first time I looked at myself after the fire, I broke."

"This time when you look at yourself, you'll begin to rebuild."

"Begin?"

He winked. "Everything's a process, love. Your scars. Us. It's a process. I was thinking about us, and I wanted to know if you'd be interested in marriage counseling."

My alarms went off. "Why?"

"I want us to get better, to be better. I want to be a better husband to you."

"Humph. I'll have to think about that one." I took the mirror from him and slowly turned it over. When I saw myself, I gasped, lighter this time. The welted scars on my neck seemed to have made their home on my healing skin, forming new grooves and dents that could've only been tried by fire.

Every part of me wanted to toss the mirror aside, but I knew I needed to stand my ground with myself. With this. With Greta. With Jake. With my future. I wasn't going to live the rest of my life hiding from my own self. No matter how long it took, I was going to learn to live with my skin.

When I first saw myself in the mirror at the hospital, I'd

been so disgusted by my appearance. My feelings didn't change the day I was getting ready to meet Greta or the day Tim held the mirror to my face. But when I looked at my image this time, I didn't shudder.

I traced my index finger over a map of welts that had imprinted my neck weeks earlier. The welts were now replaced by a grid of scars, white-pink lines that reminded me of mesh netting, tiny and tightly knit.

"No amount of body makeup could conceal this mess. This isn't model-perfect," I said, my voice cracking. "Then again, even when I was so-called model-perfect, I didn't feel that way."

"People are tired of perfection. People want real," Jake said. "Do you have to be model-perfect?"

The question floated in the air, waiting for someone to catch it.

I didn't. I deflected. "I get tired too," I said, holding the mirror closer. The scars were settling in and making their home on my body. "But this is too real. I'll scare people off if I ever model looking like this."

"You're referring to the onlookers. Who cares about them? Do *you* have to be model-perfect? Is that a requirement for your happiness? Can you even tell yourself that you deserve to be happy?"

My hand trembled, and the mirror trembled along with it. I hated getting all emotional in front of Jake. Last time I did was when I'd told him about Giancarlo.

"Try saying it," he repeated.

He was turning this into some pop-psychology, self-love, positive-thinking moment. "You're corny. Is this your way of being a better husband and all?"

He chuckled. "Perhaps, but you're only saying that as a defense. Try it."

Again with the shaky hand thing. "I'm fine. See?" I waved

the mirror back and forth like it was one of those funeral fans people used in those hot, stuffy wakes as if to prove that Jake's words meant nothing to me, that they didn't affect me.

(Oh, and to keep him from noticing that my hand was shaking from feeling supercalifragilistically put out by his question.)

He didn't budge, and my hand still trembled. I was being a fraud with myself. I'd worn a mask all these years as a model, tried so hard to bend to people's expectations. It'd gotten so bad after Giancarlo's comments about my lips, I'd tried getting the extra fat sucked out of my lips, but the cosmetic surgeon said the procedure was too risky. Instead, I'd learned to keep my lips pursed. In doing so, I'd also silenced my voice.

I sat on the settee that was positioned at the end of the hallway. When I faced myself in the mirror, I recoiled from a version of myself that no longer fit. My skin was like an old sweater I'd outgrown. Yeah, I could tug at the sleeves, pull at the collar, but still, the fabric wouldn't accommodate. In the end, all that was left was an old garment that had to be released. An old self that had to be released.

I could get deep with myself when I wanted.

I held the mirror close. A woman I hardly recognized stared at me. Although the redness from the fire had faded from my skin, dejection had down-turned the corners of my mouth. Sadness had replaced the light in my eyes. And I knew this wasn't caused by a fire. It was from living on the hamster wheel of striving, striving, striving.

I jutted my chin slightly for a closer look. My features were like my mother's, a woman who had bowed to life's disappointments. A woman who'd lost her faith. Would I end up the same way?

The question clung to me as I glanced at the old photos

hanging on my wall, snapshots of Mama and me at the fair, at high school graduation, getting ready for prom.

Those were photos of the young fashion model me. I'd looked radiant and glowing with the expectancy of an unwritten future, a future that I'd hoped would be powerful enough to erase my past.

I stood and ran my finger over the gold picture frame and studied the photos of myself up close. My makeup was pristine. My hair was perfectly coiffed.

That woman breathed beauty. Still, even then I hadn't believed in my beauty. I hadn't believed in myself.

Although Jake had spoken all those reassuring, rah-rah-rah words, he failed to realize he'd been talking to the young woman in the picture. A woman who, despite indescribable pain, had fought to clothe herself with strength and dignity, to laugh without fear of the future.

That woman was in me. Hurting, hiding, but in there. The fire, the affair, the rape, the endless striving toward acceptance in a superficial industry had nearly snuffed her out.

But not anymore. I was reclaiming her.

"I'll be back," I said and left to search for a dress in my bedroom closet, a dress I hadn't worn since before the fire. It was a sheath dress, no sleeves. Wearing it could be a beginning step.

"Where are you going?"

Jake was probably thinking I needed to escape so I could ugly-cry, but I was through with ugly-crying. "To my room." Once there, I exhaled and glanced at the tattered slippers on my feet, the ones I'd always worn around the house, the ones providing me comfort, the ones never challenging me to change.

I padded to my closet and pulled out the designer knock-off. It was unique and eye-catching with its form-fitted shimmering blue fabric. Maybe if I got out of these grubby house clothes and wore this dress, then I could inspire some-thing, a new outlook, a new objective. Things I didn't possess.

In the full-length mirror, I held the dress to my body and forced my mouth into a smile, not resting until it matched the one in the photos of the wall. Only someone close could differentiate between the two. Someone like Jake. Ugh. So frustrating. I couldn't convince myself to be happy with this fakey-fake smile, and Jake would see through my false happi-ness. He knew me too well—little use in me denying that.

Nope. I was gonna stay here till my smile was real and full and belly-deep.

I kept smiling until, in a subtle second, I settled into my scars and knew—I'd never match those photos on the wall, but that was okay. Why live pretending?

CHAPTER 19

JAKE

S he wanted to be alone. All righty then. I could respect that. I hoped she wasn't in her bedroom having a complete breakdown. Maybe I'd pushed too hard with the mirror thing, and now she wanted to get away.

What if she was having a breakdown? What if the break-down was because of me? Then what? Not going to let that happen. Better check on her.

My dark boots clunked against the wooden floor as I made my way over to her bedroom, worried I'd said the wrong thing. "Hannah?" I knocked on her door.

No answer. Flashbacks of that time when I'd found her in the bathtub gutted me. I flung open the door and saw her standing in front of a full-length mirror with a pale blue dress held against her body.

Radiant.

"You okay?" I asked.

"I am now."

"Mm. You look fine in that dress. Always been my favorite."

A smile curved her mouth. "You never told me this was your favorite."

"Never told you a lot of things."

"What things?" she asked.

"Like how you have the best laugh—not even a laugh. More like a snort-giggle."

Hannah scrunched her nose. "I don't snort!"

"Oh yeah, you do."

"Whateva." She flung her hand at me in that way she'd done when we were dating, playful and light. It was nice seeing her this way again.

"What happened?"

Hannah blinked. "What do you mean?"

"You're all happy and stuff."

"Something wrong with being happy?" Hannah chuckled. Her laughter filled me and reached all the way inside. "No. I'm happy you're happy."

"Perhaps I'll wear this dress. Perhaps I'll go to marriage counseling with you too." She walked over to her closet. "I'll definitely go to marriage counseling with you."

My ears twitched. Was I hearing her correctly? "Really?"

"Yep. Why not give us the old college try?" She rearranged the empty hangers on her clothes rack.

I loved seeing her this way. Made me think of the first time I'd kissed her many years ago. I'd taken a chance back then because I wasn't sure if she'd felt the same way, but she did.

I'd take another chance now. Yeah, we had a rocky history, but the chemistry was still there. As she was about to hang up the dress, I touched her elbow, pulled her close into my embrace.

Our lips touched. I'd forgotten the taste of her mouth, salty and sweet. I'd forgotten the way she'd felt in my arms, strong yet soft.

That's when she did something which I'd never have expected. She tilted her head to the side as if beckoning me to kiss her neck, the place where her scars were most visible. I hesitated. "You sure?"

"Positive."

Her voice was steady, but her words dropped low. Low and deep and way too familiar, like she'd been waiting to say those words from the start.

I kissed her collarbone, the top of her shoulder, right underneath her ear, and she shuddered against my touch. "Should I stop?" I breathed Hannah in and kept my mouth close to her ears so she could hear my every word.

"No."

And so I didn't. I traced my index finger along a jagged scar line, a complex map of intersections which were like a guide to her heart: the bumpy paths, the smooth paths, the paths unseen.

She wrapped her arms around my neck and liquid love filled my body. The warmth on Hannah's lips boiled over, and she rubbed the pad of her jittery thumb against my palm.

I touched her chin. The air stalled in my lungs, awakening attraction out of hiding. The feeling spread to my jawline, covering my cheeks, touching the tips of my ears. It tumbled inside and somewhere in the backseat of my mind I acknowledged it was more than physical. It was love. Love smoothed the kinks in my shoulders. Love beckoned me to stay through her recovery. Love called me to kiss her today.

I sealed her eyes with a kiss that drained my strength, but I didn't care. My fingers slid through her hair. A flash of a moment, and my mouth was on her chin, her jawline, her ear.

We slipped away and our breathing slowed. Heat from her skin burned through my clothing, and the whisper of my name rose, spoken against my collarbone. I was Jake. And she was…

Alive.

≈

*A*fter we made love, I spent the next few hours cuddled next to her, my wife. I returned to my condo to shower and dress, promising to bring Tim for his tutoring session, not mentioning my plans to visit Melinda tomorrow at rehab.

The following morning, the taste of Hannah lingered when I parked in front of the rehabilitation center. I didn't want to be here. I wanted to see Hannah again and have lazy conversations about nonessential nothings, laughing and joking the entire time. Would Hannah think I was betraying her for visiting Melinda? Would she understand that I had promised Tim? Would she understand I was doing this for Tim's sake?

No. Hannah wouldn't fully understand. Holding her, kissing her, touching her was everything I'd ever wanted and more. I wouldn't risk losing last night, and so I wouldn't mention the visit to Hannah.

I looked at the picturesque brick building that housed Melinda, Tim's mother, and shook off those feelings because now, I had to see if she was up for seeing her son. I'd made a promise to Tim, and I intended to keep it. If I didn't, I'd risk losing his trust.

By seeing Melinda, I was risking Hannah's trust. If she found out… no, she wouldn't find out.

After stepping inside the rehab center, I smoothed my hair and straightened my polo shirt. Didn't know why I was nervous. Yeah, I knew why. This meeting could turn out to be a disaster. Dust motes danced in the sunlight streaming through the cracked doorway. A metal detector, a security guard, and a gang of visitors crowded the place, leaving little room for my pulse to steady and settle.

I hadn't actually seen Melinda since the day I picked Tim up from Social Services, but Tim had said whenever Melinda had mentioned me, a few choice word phrases weren't far behind. Hopefully, she wouldn't make a scene.

"All cell phones, keys, computers, and jewelry on the conveyor belt."

The guard's booming voice made my stomach spiral. I set my leather wallet on the conveyor belt and tossed my cell phone in a plastic bin.

After going through the security check, I turned a corner, and my thoughts went haywire. The skin twitched under my lips. Coming here wasn't an easy decision, more like an agonizing one. When I'd visited Hannah at the hospital after the fire, I knew it'd be a troubling visit, troubling on many levels, but my love for Hannah remained, no matter how much she had pushed me away. I didn't love Melinda.

Lordy. What if Melinda pulled a funny and said she didn't want to see her son like she'd done on the phone the other day? I would've come all the way out here for nothing.

No. Not nothing. This wasn't in vain. It was for Tim. I'd keep the conversation focused on him. Seconds later, I arrived at the visitor's area. A scant smattering of people filled the room. Correction: a scant smattering of people and the color beige. Lots and lots of beige. Beige walls. Beige tables. Beige chairs. Beige carpet. Blech. For all the greenery and beauty outside, the inside of this place looked beyond bleak.

I waved to a man wearing a wrinkle-free blue shirt, creased black pants, and a shiny badge. Must be the security officer. "I'm here to see Melinda Ramirez."

"Are you family?"

I hesitated. Trick question. What should I say? We share a child together? She's my baby mama? Nah. "Yes. I'm family."

The officer must've sensed the hesitation in my voice because he angled toward me, mouth opening to reply, but he stopped. His eyes filled with awareness.

"Oh yeah, I remember—"

"Remember?" I asked. "I've never visited here before."

"Yep. Yep. Melinda's been waiting for you all morning." He nodded to the closed door. "She's sitting right inside that room."

I went inside. An older, feminine version of Tim sat hunched at a rickety table with a colored pencil and sketch pad in hand. Flat, jet black hair hung over one side of her eye. A heart tattoo imprinted her left forearm. The green pencil she held was the only splash of color in the room—a lifeline.

She wasn't the woman I'd met at the bar that night, fearless and carefree. Now, she was broken.

"Melinda," I said slowly.

Something flashed across her face. A flicker of an expression which, in another situation, I may not have noticed.

It was care. Pure, unadulterated care. She still had feelings for me, feelings I didn't share.

My right temple pulsed. I hoped I misjudged the look. No way could she feel—care—it was just one night. "Hey, Melinda."

"Hey."

I scooted out a chair, its legs skidding against the threadbare carpet, and sat across from her. The fabric of my chair was stiff and sticky like it was stained with soda or juice. I'd hoped it was soda or juice. Anything else would be gross. Yep, for all that beauty outside, the place was seriously unkempt.

"How's it going?" I asked.

Melinda's head got caught in the gray area between a nod and shake. "Why'd you want to see me?"

All righty then. We can get down to business. "I'm here for Tim. He wants to visit you. I spoke to your doctors, and they said you were fine enough. That'd it be up to you. You wanna see him?"

"You wanna stop lying on me to my son?"

Oh great. Here we go. "I never badmouthed you to Tim. Never was like that, Melinda. And I ain't beefing with you today. I'm here for Tim. You wanna see him or not?"

She opened her pencil case and dug through everything—pens, markers, colored pencils, the works. She took out a black colored pencil and examined it up close.

Was she purposefully ignoring me? "Did you hear a word I said?"

She flipped open her sketchbook.

What was up? I swear if it wasn't for Tim, I'd leave right about now. Instead, I waited and absorbed the depressed surroundings—the iron-barred windows, the flickering fluorescent lights, the dented metal doors. The place was two steps lower than the pits. How was anyone gonna recover in this dump? Those photos on the internet were misleading. "How long you been here now?"

"Don't know." Melinda adjusted as she sketched the profile of a feminine face. "Stopped counting."

"I picked up Tim about two months ago. So it's less than two months."

"Then why did you ask me?" Her voice was steely and edgy.

"I'm trying to be civil here, okay? Can we talk? Can you let me know if you want to see your son? He wants to see you. Talks about you all the time."

Behind her dark bangs, her forehead creased in puzzlement. She erased some sketch marks and blew the shavings across the table—in my direction. I must be a magnet for pissing women off. Hannah. Melinda. Well, at least Hannah wasn't as angry as before.

"I want to see him too." She stared at the dents on the table instead of my face. "Not like this though. I don't want…" Her voice cracked and she tugged on her chapped lower lip.

Empathy welled. Sitting here with her, seeing her in this state, hurt me too. Maybe if I had kept in touch, she wouldn't be here now. I couldn't change the past, but I could make today different. I could show empathy.

"I understand. Focus on getting better, Melinda. I'll tell Tim you're not ready. Before you know it, you'll be out of here and living the good life."

"You think it's that easy? You think a stint in rehab's gonna change anything? I'm better off dead."

Something in me collapsed, and I felt powerless, powerless and unable to give her the perfect response. My choices had affected her too. "Don't say that, Melinda. You're a mother. You have a son."

"He's all I have." Each syllable was stuttered out in slow succession. "All. I. Have."

I inhaled, afraid I'd shatter the paper-thin glass which held the conversation together. "You have a lot."

"No, I don't. I don't have you."

The glass shattered.

"Me?" I asked, my voice another shadow in the dimly lit room. "It's been years since that one night. One night. You don't need me."

"You needed me once. You said so yourself. You said you needed me when you were married."

Melinda was right. I'd said it once when I dropped off a check for Tim's daycare fees. It was after a nasty fight with Hannah. I thought I needed Melinda, but I needed to get things right with Hannah. Melinda was an innocent casualty. I fidgeted.

"Don't you need me, Jake?"

Her words sank in, layer after layer. Words that touched a wound inside. A wound I wanted to cover. A part of me was pained when I stopped all contact with Melinda because I didn't want her completely out of my life. Not because I loved her, but because we brought life in the world together. A bond had formed between us after Tim was born, but if I didn't keep a distance, Melinda would want more from me. Hannah would be hurt too.

"I was wrong when I'd said I needed you, Melinda. I shouldn't have said that to you. I better go."

"Don't leave." Melinda held up her hand. "Stay. Please."

I stopped. Memories of the time when I'd left her before flooded me, but I had to keep this about Tim. That was our common bond. "You said you didn't want to see Tim yet. That's all I need to know."

"Did you ever love me?" Melinda asked.

My throat screwed tight, and I took another step back. Hannah and I were just now reconciling, and so I wasn't going to get into all this. Melinda and I were only a one-night thing. Nothing more.

"Did. You. Ever. Love. Me?"

Hurt filled every edge of her face, and my heart screwed tight. I never loved Melinda, but I couldn't tell her that. That'd break her heart, and she was already broken. Melinda needed to focus on detoxing from drugs, not on her feelings for me. "That doesn't matter."

"It does. Dammit!" Her words echoed through the visitor's area, and she stabbed her pencil into the sketchbook. "Tell me."

Everyone turned to stare, and a rushing filled my ears. If I left, I'd look like a real jerk. Or maybe her demand made her look like the jerk in this moment. Couldn't tell.

"Did you?" she repeated, softer.

Melinda's tone settled into my skin, lowered my chin. I rubbed the pad of my fingers against the inside of my hands, causing the tension to tighten.

"You gave me a child, Melinda. I'll always respect you. You'll always be a big part of my life story."

"Your life story? Stop sounding fake." Melinda's expression tinged with hurt, a thread of hurt, woven through a fabric of numbing pain.

My resolve to hold in my thoughts about Melinda unraveled. "It was my fault. Everything was my fault."

The faint lines around Melinda's eyes deepened.

I got up and crossed the room, staring outside an iron-barred window. The morning light was dimming. Striving to keep it aglow, I stood off to the side to allow in more light.

"I can't begin to imagine what all my screw-ups have done to you. I'd like us to be on speaking terms."

"Speaking terms? What about your wifey?" she asked without looking at me.

"She's my wife, Melinda." *And I love her.* "We can manage, you and me. For Tim's sake."

"That's what you call it? Managing?"

Melinda's question conveyed more disbelief than sarcasm. Despite the challenge, I replied quietly, hoping to soften the impact. "It is what it is. It's not perfect. Just life."

She opened her mouth as if to protest, then closed it again and looked down, defeated. Was there something I could say to reassure her?

No. No amount of reassuring could be said, and this whole rabbit trail that Melinda started felt like a betrayal to Hannah. I wasn't crossing over into exploring-my-old-feel-ings-toward-Melinda territory.

"Melinda, you don't need me. You're strong on your own."

Melinda swiveled toward the same window, throwing me a glare before staring at the dented table. Perhaps coming here wasn't the wisest choice. It only opened wounds that should be sealed shut.

"That's a nice drawing you have there," I said.

"Don't need pity compliments." She lifted her head.

"Not giving one. It's the truth. You have a talent. Something good could come from it. You could… " Here I was, trying to fix stuff. "Never mind."

Seconds later, the security guard strolled by. I expected Melinda to tell the guy to kick me out, but she didn't. She simply kept staring at her drawing.

"I wanted to go to art design school once," she said.

A trace of guilt pressed into my chest. "Never too late."

"I'm an old druggie." Her face darkened and snuffed out any flicker of hope. "Ain't nothing left for me."

My eyes stung. When I met Melinda, she was so vibrant and hopeful. Then my choice to not make contact with her and Tim messed up her life. I was so selfish. I should've never jumped into bed with her that night. I could've figured out my marriage problems without adding Melinda into the mix. "Isn't true, Melinda. You can go back to school once you're free from addiction."

She bit her bottom lip, shook her head. "You better leave. Tell Tim I love him, but I can't see him now. I'm still tryin' to get better."

The guilt rooted deep, and I needed to slap myself. I should've let this relationship alone. Now I was leaving her to battle her demons alone—demons I'd caused. It was the only thing I could do at this point. I had to keep the lines between us for my marriage's sake.

"I will." I checked my back pocket for my car keys.

Seeing her like this broke me up inside. I wanted to do

something to fix her pain, but this kind of thing wasn't quickly fixed.

"Go on home." She cleared her raspy throat and closed her sketch pad.

Home. The word sounded distant and hollow.

CHAPTER 20

*A*fter Mama and Jake had suggested I contact Liza, I finally sucked up my pride and did. Liza quickly forgave me 'cuz she was gracious like that. She'd agreed to meet me today at The Coffee Cup, a local café and diner. Mama was coming along too. Liza and Mama were very close.

Two days had passed, and the memory of making love to Jake reached inside, touching me more deeply than any love song or sonnet. I wanted to kiss him again. And again. And again.

I was falling for the man, and I didn't want to get up. The ache to kiss him grew, along with the desire to forge a new path for my modeling career, a career where I'd be accepted for my scars.

Instead of spending quiet evenings mindlessly flipping through channels on the television, I'd discovered this newfound purpose and started logging in hours at the computer, searching for modeling agencies that worked with models who didn't fit the mold, differently abled models like me. I'd found a few that I wanted to ask Liza about when she arrived at the café today.

A gold jangling bell announced my arrival. The scent of sausage and bacon mingled with the chatter of diner patrons in the crowded little space. Gray-white cooking smoke hovered at the ceiling and caused my eyes to smart.

Customers occupied every booth, table, and seat. I squinted and looked for Mama, but I didn't see her anywhere. Odd, because Mama was early for everything. I hung out near a gumball machine and waited for them.

Seconds later, Liza arrived. "Hey, Hannah!" She waved at me all excited and stuff. Her dark eyes shimmered with friendship, with forgiveness. Man, she was the best.

"Hey yourself!" I ran up to her and we hugged. Then my earring caught on her curly black hair. "Ack, girl! My hoop is in your hair."

"Stop wearing those big earrings." She giggled and gently unknotted my earring.

"Stop wearing that Diana Ross hair." I tossed a smile at her, joking.

"Whatever, sister. I can't stop wearing my hair because it's my hair. I don't wear weaves, okay?" Liza paused, stared at me. She was thinking, evaluating my appearance.
"Honey. I—"

"Don't worry. I won't judge you for your reaction to how I look." My shoulders relaxed. "I'm used to it by now."

"Sorry." Liza's eyes lowered, and the sunlight from outside shone brighter through the windows, highlighting her sepia-brown skin.

"Nothing to be sorry about. If anything, I should be the one apologizing for being a jerk to you."

The corner of her full lips up ticked into a smile. "Oh, girl." She hugged me, and all at once I felt at home. It had always been like that with Liza, chill and relax. "It's crowded here today."

"Always crowded here." She laughed and adjusted the designer sunglasses which sat atop her head. "That's what I love about this place."

I stood on my tippy toes and spotted Mama sitting at an empty booth down a narrow aisle. "There she is," I hollered amid the noisy crowd. "I knew she'd be early."

We headed down the aisle. I scooted in the booth and sat across from Mama. My bottom squeaked on the white, vinyl seat. Self-conscious at the noise, I straightened my place mat. Hmm. I was more self-conscious about my butt-squeak than I was about my scars. Perhaps this was a step toward recovering.

Liza and Mama hugged and chatted while I flipped through the menu. I had to admit it was nice not to be the focal point of Mama's attention. Still, I had to get Liza's take on this differently abled model thing. As soon as I figured out what to order, I opened my mouth to speak, but Liza interrupted me.

"Okay, Hannah, spill it. You're glowing." She patted her thick hair. "Are you preggers?"

Mama's eyed widened. "You're pregnant!"

I wish. "No, Mama. No way."

"Newly engaged?" Liza asked.

Mama's eyes doubled widened.

"No. I'm technically still married to—"

Liza slammed her hand on the table, and I jolted. "You and Jake did the deed, didn't you?"

My face prickled and blood rushed to my cheeks. Oh, lordy. Did she really have to ask this question? In front of my mother? No shame, y'all. She had no shame.

Mama looked as if she was going to have a heart attack,

PRESLAYSA WILLIAMS

and if she dropped dead in this diner because we were talking about my sex life, then all blame would rest on Liza.

"Well, did you?" Mama asked.

Oh. My. Gosh. "We are married, you know."

Liza hopped up and down in her seat as if her butt was attached to a pogo stick. "This is faaabulous! Simply faaabulous. When I was getting ready this morning, I was thinking about the two of you, and how I wanted y'all to get back together."

"Why? You knew everything he'd done."

"Yeah, but I'd been telling you all along to give him a second chance. The first time I saw you two, I knew you were meant to be," Liza said. "The one-night stand was wrong, very wrong, but I always knew he loved you. That never changed."

"I'm so, so glad you two have kissed and more than made up!" Mama added.

My mother had tears in her eyes like she'd won the Power Ball Mega Millions or something.

"Er, thanks," I said.

"You're positively glowing too! And healing up so nicely from the fire. And—" Liza reached over the table and hugged my neck.

I startled. "You okay, Liza?"

"Yeah, yeah, yeah. I'm fine. Sorry about the open display of affection. I'm just so happy." Liza raised her brow. "So y'all are living together again?"

"No. It… " I flipped through the menu again. "Just happened. Once. It happened once."

"Once?" Mama said. "You need to have sex at least three times a week."

Someone kill me now. Seriously, someone please kill me now. Anyone?

242

"Don't be so hard on her, Mama." Liza nudged her. "Once is a start. A very good start."

What in the world?

Liza laughed and rested her elbows on the table. "But you should seriously consider when y'all are going to do it again."

I balked at the question. Why hadn't anyone come over to our table and killed me yet? "Are you serious?"

"Hey, if your marriage is going to work, you need to plan ahead for these things. Set some goals."

"Yes." Mama folded her hands on the table. "I'm always early for things. Like today at the diner. I had the seat reserved and arrived early. I plan ahead. You know?"

What kind of conversation was this? "No, I don't know." I glanced around for a waiter, someone to interrupt us. *Puh-leeze?*

"That's your problem." Liza pointed at me. "You were holding out on sex. The beginning of a breakdown for any marriage. Plan ahead, honey. Trust me."

Says the woman who's been married three times. Liza was right though. The busier I'd gotten with modeling, the less Jake and I had sex. Then I'd found out about Melinda, and I surely wasn't going to get intimate afterward. Wasn't happening.

The waitress finally arrived and we placed our orders. After she left, I shoved my hands underneath my thighs, ready to talk modeling. "Greta let me go from the client roster."

"What?" Liza and Mama said in unison.

"Yep. Said it was time for me to retire. Something I disagree with entirely."

"Perhaps it is time for you to retire, *anak*. Think about another job. Just a suggestion."

The muscles in my neck tightened. I was not in the mood for entertaining Mama's "suggestions." I pressed on. "I'm considering working for another agency, Liza. An agency that's open to working with models that may not be—main-stream—you know?"

"Ah." Liza winked. "You wanna come over with me to the flip side and be a normal-people model."

Come over to the flip side? She made it seem like I was taking a step down, but for me, it was taking a step up. It was a chance to help other people too and feel proud of my career in a way I hadn't before. "You think there'd be a market for someone like me? Someone with… " I looked down at my skin. "Someone with scars?"

Liza's gaze steadied on me, evaluating me, and I glanced away, nervous. If I could give a penny for Liza's thoughts, I'd empty all the change in my wallet.

"Do you really think you'll be up for this type of modeling work? It's not going to give you the acclaim you once had. In fact, you may get criticized more."

"Criticized?"

"Yeah, everyone expects models to be perfect. Skinny and tall and not a flaw to be seen. Even though the consumers aren't skinny and tall and flawless, high-fashion models are an escape from real life in a way. You'd be going against that mold. Are you ready for what goes along with breaking the mold? The haters? The questioners? And the ones who'll champion you but would never go and put themselves out there in a similar fashion?"

Liza made this sound like I was going out to battle or something. "I don't know."

"Don't do this, Hannah." Mama unrolled her utensils from the paper napkin and set them in a neat little row. "Better to find another job."

"Not so easy, Mama." Liza shrugged. "If modeling is Hannah's passion, she can't just up and dump it for a nine-to-five. She'll be miserable for the rest of her life. Is modeling your passion?"

"It's something I've always liked, but I've liked it for the wrong reasons. I liked it for the praise. Now, you're saying if I go this alternative route, I may not get praised."

"Nope." Liza rested her chin in her hands. "I can't tell you how many times I've gotten nasty emails and social media comments about how I should be ashamed of myself for modeling as a 'fat' girl. If I wasn't a strong person, I probably would've had a mental breakdown."

I'd already had a couple of breakdowns as a skinny model. What would happen when folks criticized me for being a scarred model? Going this route would be harder than I thought, especially if those in this new market niche didn't want to work with me.

No, I couldn't worry about that. If I wanted to, I could model with scars. All my life, I'd been trying to live someone else's image of myself. It was time to be who I was, the real me. "Modeling is what I want to do, regardless of the naysayers." I sat up straighter, squared my shoulders, and nodded once.

"No. No. No." Mama shook her finger at me. "Don't do this. Too dangerous. You've already been through so much, *anak*. Not this too. Stay home and be a wife. Have a baby."

I shuddered. A baby? Not possible, even though I'd wanted one. Mama knew that Jake and I had tried. Mama didn't know about the rape though. The miscarriage of my child with that professor had sealed my fate.

"Can't do that, Mama," I said softly.

"You're so stubborn with your husband. You know this, *anak?*" She shook her head at me as if I should be ashamed and slipped out of our booth. "So stubborn. I'm going to the restroom, but you better not ruin your life."

She left, and there I sat with Liza. Would Mama think I was so "stubborn" with my husband if she knew I'd agreed to go to marriage counseling with him? I didn't want to mention it to Mama because I was tired of trying to defend myself to her. "See the kind of nonsense I have to go through? You see?"

Liza reached over and patted my hand. "I'm sorry, hon. I know you're dealing with a lot. A lot of decisions to be made. Perhaps your mom is right. Perhaps you should—"

"No," I said quickly. "I've made up my mind. I'm living with how I look, and I'm not giving up on modeling just because I can't be the same kind of model I used to be. If I have to deal with hecklers and haters, then I'll deal—starting with my own mother." I poured myself a cup of black coffee from the carafe. "That's my final decision."

"You sure?" Her statement screamed uncertainty.

The waitress returned with our food and carefully set it before us. Steam rose from each of the plates. They sure knew how to pile on the food around here. My plate was the hugest.

Liza jammed her fork into the pancakes and dug right in. I needed to try another tactic to convince her I was serious because obviously, she didn't believe me. "How about if I do a photo shoot?" I asked. "Just the way I am?"

Girlfriend barely held back a grin. "You're really serious, aren't you?"

"I'm serious. I mean, yeah, Mama has her reservations on the matter, but this is for me, not for her."

She stopped eating and studied me, then she did some squinty-eyed thing that got me feeling all weird.

"What?" I asked.

"There was a time when you would've flat-out refused to be seen on camera without everything in place."

"I know what you're getting at." My chewing slowed, and I set my fork down. "It's a change, but I'm set on modeling. I can't toss years of work in the trash. I'll work hard."

"What if this attempt fails? Then what'll you do?" Liza asked.

Man, why'd she have to be so realistic and level-headed? "It ain't gonna fail. It just ain't."

The waitress returned. "Is there anything else you'd like to order?"

"No," I said, thoroughly pissed Liza was making me think about the possibility of failure. I'd already failed with motherhood and high-fashion modeling and math. Wasn't failing this time.

"Is this one check or two?"

"One. I mean two. I mean three," I said, doubly pissed.

Liza gave the poor waitress a kind smile. "It'll be three checks."

Wasn't that what I just said? Whatever. I sliced my bacon into tiny little pieces for no reason other than to keep my hands busy and my mouth shut. The waitress nodded at Liza and left.

"I have an idea, Hannah." Her forehead tensed, revealing the smudged foundation at her hairline. "Why don't you visit me on one of my photo shoots and see what it's like for me as a plus-sized model? Then maybe you'll see whether you'll be as comfortable in front of the camera as you were prior to the fire."

"When would this be?"

"Next Monday at two o'clock."

"That works since I'll be tutoring Tim on Tuesdays."

Her eyes flashed. "You're tutoring Tim?"

I shrugged and tried playing it off like I tried playing off the whole sex thing. "Yep. Our first session is next Tuesday."

"Girl, you really are getting soft on Jake."

She was right. I was tutoring Tim and going to marriage

counseling with Jake, but that wasn't the point. "I'll be at the photo shoot. End of discussion."

It wasn't the end, but it felt like the beginning of something good, real, real good, both with Jake and this career move. I just didn't want to talk about the Jake-sex stuff, and I was done talking about changing up my modeling career. I knew what I wanted.

Liza gave me one of those "yeah, right, I don't believe you" grins.

Whateva. I didn't give a patootie.

~

*Y*eah, buddy. Tim was set to arrive at any moment, and then I would tutor him in All Things Algebra. Me, the disgruntled wife-woman scorned. This could be the smartest thing I'd ever done—or the dumbest, depending on how I looked at it.

The smartest because I'd be moving forward from our mangled marriage. The dumbest because I'd be moving away from my goal of independence. Liza was right—my soft meter toward Jake was growing to new levels of fabric-softener softness.

Silence buzzed in my bedroom and swelled to parachute-like levels. I upswept my hair in a loose bun and inspected my skin in the mirror. It was still mottled and shiny, but not as tight and sore as it had been. The scars had stretched, dimpled, and pulled where scabs and wounds had been. The red-pink color had leeched away and was replaced by a walnut color—not my original hue, but then again, nothing was as it had been—not anymore.

At my next follow up visit with Dr. Hutchinson, she'd determine whether I was ready for reconstructive surgery. Now that I had this refocused angle on my career, reconstructive surgery didn't seem as urgent, but I'd still go through the process because Dr. Hutchinson had said it'd help me with mentally recovering from the fire's trauma. She was right. I was getting better with accepting my appearance, but surgery would help. Besides, the surgery could give me a leg up in this new, differently abled modeling venture of mine. I'd be scarred, but good-scarred.

Hold up, Hannah. What was good-scarred? What a twisted line of thinking. How can a person look the best among the—wasn't even going to ponder the word. That was twisted.

But enough of that. Tim was due to arrive, and I had to be his tutor. *His tutor.*

Last time I tutored was at Rutgers. I had made the dean's list every semester since freshman year, and so I'd been tapped on the shoulder by the head of the math department (not by Professor Gropes-a-Lot) to help in study hall. I became a tutor for my work-study job as a junior. Despite being a 4.0 student, tutoring made me nervous. It was one thing to learn mathematics for myself but quite another to teach someone else.

Why? 'Cuz the longer I tutored, the more of a personal stake I had in seeing each student improve. Whenever they didn't, I blamed myself and figured I should've drilled them more or tried different learning techniques.

I'd blamed myself whenever I was overlooked for a modeling assignment too. Always used to think I could've lost two more pounds or done my hair differently or some-thing. Greta's rejection still stung because I'd seen Greta as a mother-figure too. When she'd replaced me with Jacinta, a younger, more "perfect" version of myself, the rejection lingered and threatened to drown me in the Sink Hole of Self-Blame, but I wasn't sinking down nothing. Not if I had any say.

I left my bedroom and the summer humidity drifted through the open windows, laying a thin blanket on my skin. Another day without wearing bandages 24/7. No trying to figure out how to hide my mummy wrappings. Only the quiet freedom of settling into my mottled skin.

From my side window, Tim's bike rounded the corner. My heart stuttered. I wanted to tutor him well, just like those days at Rutgers. I greeted him before he had a chance to make it to the top of my concrete porch. "Ready to rock out these math problems?"

Rock out these math problems? What is wrong with you, Hannah? You sound like a valley girl. I added an apologetic smile even though he had no idea what my cheeseball smile was trying to convey.

"I guess," Tim said finally, an unchanging monotone in his voice. "You know I'm only here for an hour. I have to find some volunteer work out in town because of that court order. Knowing my record, that may take all day."

"Volunteer work?" I gestured for him to come inside.

"Yep. The judge said so." He slung his backpack over his shoulder. "No big deal."

"Sure about that? Sounds like a big deal to me."

"Nope. Not a big deal," he said. "Better than a jail sentence. Granted, I won't be getting paid for my time. But whatever. Volunteer work is supposed to fix me or something."

The court saw him as a problem that needed to be fixed, a Black problem that needed to be fixed.

My gaze snapped to his dark, liquid eyes. I tried discerning the emotions lying there, but his expression was too murky to figure out. Wasn't my problem to figure out anyway. I was the math tutor, nothing more. "What do you want to work on first?" I asked.

"Guess we can start on my homework. I have a test next

week on chapter five. Differential equations." He perused a home and garden magazine on my wicker coffee table. Kid could probably not care less about the magazine and was probably just avoiding my gaze or something. At least that's what I'd figured.

"Ah, yes. Jake mentioned that to me. Differential equations it is."

He took out his worksheet, which I quickly scanned. My brain went into Voltron Mode—all my synapses fired off, and that buried knowledge bubbled to the surface. "Make sure you factor the equations first."

"Lost me already." A scratch to the back of his neck punctuated his frustration. "I told Pops I wasn't going to get this stuff. It's pointless. He's been bugging me to get my grades up. I think he wants me to be some kind of whiz kid or something."

"Parents always want the best for their children." I tried, tried, tried to lose all the would've, could've, should'ves from my voice this time around. I should've been here helping my biological child (wasn't happening). It would've been a possibility if it weren't for that professor but worrying about that wasn't worth my time. Tim was Jake's son and that was that. "Let's get you started. Did you bring your textbook?"

Tim rustled through his backpack, and the way the light hit his face made him look so young and innocent. As Tim handed me his book, I saw his vulnerability shaded with discomfort, anxiety, heaviness. Made me wonder what burdens he carried inside, what heartbreak, what story. "You ready?"

"Yes. We're on page 172."

I squinted at the page. "Okay, the easiest way to remember how to factor an equation is the FOIL method: first, outer, inner, last."

"No clue what you're talking about."

"FOIL? Your teacher didn't tell you about FOIL?"

Tim shook his head, looking at me like I was confusing him.

"Okay, look. FOIL is basically just a way to remember the steps you take to factor an equation. I'll demonstrate for you." I grabbed a piece of scratch paper from my desk and solved the first problem. "See?"

Puzzlement zipped across his features. He mumbled something and looked away. "I'm too dumb for this stuff."

My heart crimped. He sounded so defeated. "If you take it in bit by bit, a piece at a time, then it's not so hard. Try the second problem. Try factoring the six first."

He tried, and the little grooves on his forehead tensed as he did. Then his forehead relaxed and I could see that something clicked. "I did it!"

"I knew you could. Those folks at school were wrong. You just needed to learn the method, that's all."

He paused, set his pencil down. "Why'd you decide to help me?"

I shifted my weight from side to side, uncomfortable. "I know you can do better. You're a smart kid."

Tim twisted his mouth as if he didn't believe me. "Is that the real reason?"

"I was mad at you when you held that mirror up to me, but when you apologized, I was like wow, this kid is pretty decent."

A shadow crossed his face.

"What?" I asked. "You don't think you're a decent guy?"

Tim's jaw rattled, and he veered his attention to the tiled floor. "No. Sometimes I think I'm pretty awful."

"Because of some bad school records? They won't follow you into adulthood. You can always make a better way for yourself. That's what you're doing today."

"Some perfectly solved math problems ain't gonna help me change my past. Ain't gonna help me at all."

My jaw slackened. No way was he going to learn anything with that outlook. I flipped the worksheet over. That's when I'd noticed a camera bag tucked in his open backpack.

"You take pictures?"

He dropped back in his seat, drew out a sigh. "A little. Just started."

"How about you take some pictures? Get your mind off the complexities of algebra. I know we've only done one problem, but maybe it'll help. We could even brainstorm volunteering ideas." I grabbed the door handle to my patio. "Wanna take photos outside?"

"You serious?"

"Yep. I heard from photographers it's sometimes best to take pictures outdoors in natural light and hey, you'll get to spend part of your tutoring time not thinking about differential equations. Then, when your mind is fresh and clear, we can tackle the work."

"Don't think I'll take good pictures in natural light. Not good at much of anything."

His dejection tugged at me, halted my breath for a second. Was he always this down on himself? He was too young and —too young. Life hadn't had time to pull him into the soul-sucking bleakness I'd been carrying. "It was a thought. That's all. You don't have to go along with it if you don't want to." I slid my hand into the pocket of my peach wraparound dress. A shred of hope stained the tips of my fingers, hope which, for some unknown reason, I wanted to give to this kid.

Tim leaned across the coffee table and set the magazine in place. Still no answer. This kid was Fort Knox.

"Okay, well then. You decide whether you want to take pictures or talk equations or whatever. I won't push anything."

As I turned to get my cell phone from my purse, I pulled my hand from my pocket. I'd been holding a stray thread, the first sign of a seam unraveling. Mama would've said this was a bad, bad sign. A sign that pointed to more bad luck and *yawas* and stuff. I'd already had my share of bad luck, didn't need any more.

"I can take some photos," Tim said. "Mama got me this camera last year for my birthday, and I haven't used it since she left for rehab."

My bad luck detector turned to static. The mention of his mother got me all in my negative feelings—didn't want to think of her and all the stressful thoughts she'd brought into my life. "Let's go outside," I said to mask my feelings and get my mind off Melinda.

We stepped under the canopy on my back porch and I shaded my eyes to see the best spot for nature photos. My gaze landed on my maple trees. There, a row of chrysanthemums grew in a neat row, a colorful spread of purples and lavenders and pinks.

"Is there anything here you'd like to photograph?"

Tim scrunched his mouth. "I'll take some photos of your flowers." He took the cover from his camera lens, headed over to the tulips which lined my fence, and started snapping away.

I couldn't help but smile at his intensity and his focus as he knelt closer to the flowers and shifted to try different positions. Why'd he say he couldn't learn anything? He'd learned something about snapping photos with that DSLR camera.

Minutes later, he stopped and scanned through the pictures on his viewfinder.

"Can I see what you've taken?" I asked.

"Sure." He handed me the camera. The photos were closeups of the petals, all different in their shape and angle and curve, something the natural eye wouldn't have noticed from a distance. "You have a photographer's eye. These are unique." I thumbed through the shots. "Do you have any other lenses in your camera bag? You can experiment with them and see how the flowers look with different lenses."

"I have one, but I don't know how to put it on correctly. Can you help with switching out the lenses?"

"Sure."

Tim handed me the camera bag and I peeked inside. A picture of a woman was on the bottom. I squinted and took out the picture to examine it up close. Despite the humidity, my skin went cold. The woman in me recognized the other-woman in her. Tim's mother.

Ebony waves cascaded past her shoulders. Dark, long lashes framed eyes the color of the obsidian skirt I'd worn the day Jake had told me her name. A butter-yellow dress graced her trim, petite frame. Butter-brown skin. Oval-shaped face. Full, round lips. But it was the dejected slope of her shoulders—as subtle as a shadow cast in a dimly lit room —that left me pissed. Why was she dejected? She had the son. She'd had Jake for one night too.

No need to go there. I was moving on, being a better person, and all that positive mess. I grabbed up the remnants of my resentment and pressed it into an invisible, tight ball.

"That's Mama." Tim angled his head to the side. He stared at the photo, heartbreak written all over his features. "Her name's Melinda."

"Oh. She's photogenic." I forced as much neutrality in my voice as I could manage. I pulled a deep breath. Sounding nicey-nice was hard. "Camera loves her face."

"That picture was taken before she had me. I had snapped a photo of the photo with this camera. Them drugs messed Mama up real bad. Don't look the same."

Yep, she was a pretty woman.

"She was having money problems before she went to

rehab too," Tim continued. "Said she was having trouble managing the bills and the rent. I promised to keep up with her bills while she's in rehab. She had given me the checkbook, and I been paying the bills and stuff. So far, I've done good."

Could I be any more of a cad? Melinda was struggling, and here I was, bitter over something that occurred over a decade ago.

Self-awareness tugged on my conscience. I'd never considered Melinda's side before, only mine. "How's she doing?"

"Wish I could tell you. Haven't seen her. I only spoke to her once. Whenever I called afterward, they say she can't talk." He leaned against the trunk of the willow, tucked his hands underneath his armpits. "They say she busy in treatment. But I know she don't want to talk to me anymore. I ain't no fool."

He must feel so rejected and lost. I could see why he didn't feel like trying at academics. "Don't feel bad about what she said. Detoxing must be tough for your mother. She needs time. I know she loves you because you're her son."

"I'd do anything for my mama. Anything to make her better." His voice was a whisper.

I returned the camera, and he stared at the image of his mother, lonely.

I'd known The Lonely that Tim now nursed, a sense of feeling rejected or abandoned by those you loved. When I was a young gal and Lola died, loneliness planted its first seed. The seed, small yet sharp, hurt, but I'd learned to befriend its accompanying pain 'cuz folk like Mama had nothing for me but silent blame for Lola's passing.

I'd carried that blame around like a full-term baby who refused to be ejected from my body. I'd sought respite in modeling and adulation, but it never went away. It was only now that I was slowly releasing The Lonely from my soul. It was only now that I was choosing modeling for a higher purpose.

So yeah, The Lonely and I were BFFs, but it led to The Nowhere, an endless cycle of striving for acceptance with a bunch of fickle people. I knew all this in my head, but it had weighed down my body and caused me to second-guess myself. Standing in the backyard and staring up at the cloudless, open sky made me even more aware of how scaredy-cat I had been before this time. Before, I didn't want to go through the labor pains to eject the dead baby. Holding pains were much safer. Now, I was willing to make that sacrifice.

"You shouldn't give up on seeing your mama," I said. "No matter how much you think she's pushing you away. You only get one mama in this life. I pushed my mother away. The only reason I see her now is because she insisted on helping me heal."

"Word?" Tim raised his brow.

"Word. Don't push your mother away. Those relationships are important." Even as I said the words, my heart started changing toward my mother. No matter what had happened in the past, she was still my mother.

"Maybe you're right. Maybe I'll give her time. I like looking at these pictures of Mama. I like seeing her happy. I hated seeing her addicted and struggling with the bills." He quickly cleared his throat as if to silence a sob.

Tim's reaction combined with my feelings about my mother coagulated into a thick, sorrowful soup. I squashed my tears too. "Want me to call your mother?"

His expression shifted, doubt etched into his features.

What's wrong with you, Hannah?! You're the tutor. The tutor!

Tim's eyes welled with tears, and he swiped at them. "What good'll it do? I've tried calling lots after that one time we'd spoken, and I got nothing. There's no point."

I swept a glance over my lawn, trying to muster my response. Dredging up those old memories was hard. "When my father died, I would've given anything to speak to him one more time. To hear his laugh. To see his old eyes crinkle when he smiled. To hold his rough, weathered hand. Now, the only place I can remember him is in my imagination, my memories." I pulled a deep breath and my father's face appeared in my mind. There he was, as vivid as if he'd been sitting in my living room today. I almost heard his belly-deep laugh and my eyes stung. "Make the most of every moment. That's my only point."

"I see what you're getting at. Don't want to think of it like that, but yeah, you never know." Tim released a sharp sigh. "I'll try calling. See if she wants to talk."

He followed me into the kitchen where I grabbed the cordless. "Want me to Google the number?"

"Nah, I know it by heart."

Of course he would. That was his mother. I pressed a hand to my belly. If the baby I was pregnant with by that college professor had lived, she'd be a little older than Tim, about nineteen years old. Wondered if she would've been a math whiz too, or if she would have had another talent.

If my baby had been born, would I have ended up marrying Jake? Would he have loved me still? Would Tim have still been born?

Although everything in me wanted to be a mother, I couldn't do anything about my miscarriage and infertility today. I could only focus on what I had—a marriage on the mend and Tim, a kid that desperately needed to feel as if he mattered.

Tim pressed the numbers on the keypad and held the phone to his ear. After talking to the receptionist, he cupped his hand over the receiver. "They're looking for her," he said, hopeful.

A stirring of regret moved from my stomach to my chest. I could've had this kind of relationship with Tim earlier. I could've let go of my resentment over Jake's infidelity and helped Tim when his mother was in the throes of her addiction. Best not to ponder what ifs. Better to focus on what was. I was helping Tim today. "That's wonderful. I'll be in my office if you need me so you can have privacy." I headed to my office and shuffled through the papers in my overflowing inbox.

Seeds of doubt bubbled to the surface. Tim was talking to his mother in my house. Was that nutso or what?

If I were any other person, this would've been viewed as a perfectly normal, generous gesture. After all, what sane adult wouldn't want a young person to talk with his mother who was in a dire situation?

I glanced at the clock on my wall. Twenty minutes left in this tutoring session. We'd have better luck next Tuesday. Perhaps this was a perfectly sane gesture. Sorely needed if Tim was to gain the mental focus needed for algebra.

My door creaked open and Tim poked his head inside, his smile radiant.

"What happened?" I asked.

"She was there. We spoke."

"That's wonderful. What'd she say?"

"Dad visited her."

My stomach clenched. Jake visited her? After Jake and I had—ugh. I'd poured my heart out to him so much it formed puddles on the ground. Was this man screwing with me? I mean, I was glad Jake helped Tim out and all, but Jake and I had just started piecing together our broken marriage. Why'd he see Melinda? "He did?"

"Uh-huh. Told him she wasn't ready to see me yet. Still wants to get better. Mama had said it was Jake's visit that had led to me and her talking on the phone again. Before she wasn't even gonna do that." He stepped inside and sat on my yellow bean bag. "But I feel better. I wanted to hear her voice."

Obviously so did Jake. "I understand. Every child wants to hear their parent's voice sometimes." And every mother wants to… Who was I kidding? I wasn't a mother. But Jake was a father. No matter how much Jake and I reconciled, the facts wouldn't change my status: my never-ever-gonna-be-a-mother status. The notion still stung.

I dug my nails into my palms and wrestled my thoughts into submission, even though every ounce of me wanted to get Jake's butt on the phone and tell him what was what. Who did he think he was, sleeping with me and then running off to see his baby mama? Didn't our night together make him second guess contacting Melinda? Obviously not. When we made love, I thought it was the first step in truly fixing our marriage. Guess it wasn't.

"She told me to call her whenever I wanted to talk." He checked his watch. "Guess my time's up for today, and we didn't do my homework."

"Ah." I raised my brow. "Now you want to discuss homework?"

He shrugged and a grin formed on his face. "Next week we'll talk differential equations. I'll wing it for tomorrow's test."

"You sure?"

"Uh-huh." He checked his watch. "Dad said y'all were going to some marriage counseling or something?"

I sorted through my mental files and stopped at the last conversation we'd had, the one coupled with kissing and kissing and (ugh!) kissing. "We are." Unfortunately. Now counseling seemed pointless. Why go? He obviously had wanted to see Melinda. He obviously was never going to change—was never going to let that woman go. And I wasn't sure I could let *that* go. How could I trust him if he was still seeing Melinda? And how could he stop seeing her when they had a child together? A child. The child I'd wanted so bad to give Jake.

"Cool. See you next week." He left.

Despite the sunshine blazing through the windows of my home office, I started feeling slightly cloudy with a chance of crazy. Who did Jake think he was, pulling me along? I should've never gotten soft on him. Stupid, stupid me.

CHAPTER 21

JAKE

I still hadn't told Tim a thing about the details of the conversations I'd had with Melinda when I visited her at the rehab center. Quite honestly, I feared his reaction. Would knowing his mama wasn't ready to see him cause Tim to retreat? He'd taken a big step by getting tutoring from Hannah. Would he reject any effort toward improvement once he knew?

I needed some parental advice. After powering up my phone, I dialed the number to my parents' cell phone, hoping to chat with Mom about the Tim situation.

"Hello?" The voice was gruff. Dad's.

I shivered. For a split second, I wavered between hanging up and talking further. Resentment had settled into my bones and made its permanent home. Last thing I wanted to do was get in a standoff with him while he underwent cancer treatment. Then again, I might as well talk since he answered. I'd keep the conversation cool, casual, carefree—as much as I could. "Hey, Dad."

"That you, Jake?" His voice turned hoarse. "Whatcha doin', son?"

"Checking in on you. Mom said you were very ill."

"That woman. I tell you. Overreacts about everything."

The sharpness in his tone made me second-guess Mom's assessment. Then again, why would she tell an untruth? "So, you're not sick?"

"The doctor says I am, but don't feel that way. Not at all." He hacked out a phlegmy cough. "Life happens. Sometimes you gotta roll with it and not worry. Your mama worries. Whatcha call for?"

I smiled. For a man who had been the consummate business professional during his working years, he sure sounded like he was from the country. Guess cancer diagnoses made a person not care much about keeping up appearances. "I called for some parenting advice."

He guffawed, like really guffawed. Never thought I'd use the word, ever, but that's what he did.

"You asking me for parenting advice after you done said I was the worst father in the world?"

Actually, I was calling to ask Mom, but that was beside the point, especially given his situation. "Yes."

"How you and Hannah doing? Your mama told me you were helping her recover."

I thought of our time together the other day. "We're doing real good. Real, real good."

"I hope y'all can keep your marriage together."

"Me too."

Awkward silence, a silence I didn't want to fill because talking to my father about marriage was odd for obvious reasons.

"Marriage is tough. I shoulda done a better job with your mama. Maybe cancer's my curse for being a jerk to her. I don't know. Something I been thinking 'bout lately."

If cancer was Dad's curse for his infidelities, what would

my curse be? Didn't want to know the answer to that
question.

"Can't change the past though. Gotta fight this cancer
fight. That's what I'm gonna do. I thank the good Lord
your mama's by my side. She doesn't have to be, and I told
her so too. She is determined. Said she'd forgiven me." His
voice cracked. "Good woman, your mama. Real good
woman."

"I know." *Glad you're realizing this too.*

Hannah was a good woman. Determined and strong like
Mom. And I had cheated on Hannah like Pops had cheated
on Mom. I'd do better too. Do better by Tim and Hannah.

"When your mother was pregnant with you," Pops
continued. "She'd gotten in a bad car accident. I was away on
a business trip. When I'd gotten the call and confirmed it
wasn't fatal, I didn't leave right away. I waited two days to
leave my trip and return home. I've been so selfish."

This would've been the perfect time to make a smart-ass
comment about the reasons he didn't see Mom right away,
but I didn't.

"Your Mama though, she's different. Soon as she learned
of my cancer, she took unpaid leave from work and has been
at my side ever since. Made me feel like an awful human
being, I tell you. I don't deserve your mother, just like you
don't deserve Hannah."

His words cut, but I couldn't fight them because they
were true. "I know."

"Take care of your wife."

"I am."

"No, you don't understand," he said, a hint of accusation
in his voice. "Take care of your wife."

What did he mean by that one? I was taking care of
Hannah. Helping her recover from the fire and everything. I
hadn't left her side. "I. Am."

"You said you were calling us for parenting advice. That boy still with you?"

That boy? He wasn't gonna address Tim that way, and what was up with all this loyalty to Hannah? Pops was never loyal to his own wife. "You mean my son. He's not 'that boy.'"

"Yes. Your son. Not Hannah's son."

"My son's living with me now, and I suspect he'll be living with me for a while."

"His mother's still on crack, ain't she?"

"Why you have to be so harsh? She's not on crack. She was on heroin."

"Same difference. Still a druggie."

The adulterer was judging the drug addict. Was he serious? This man had that superiority thing down pat. "She's trying to get better. She's in rehab. I visited her the other day, and it's tough, but she seemed like she's willing to do what it takes to improve."

That wasn't entirely true. She sounded hopeless when we'd spoken, but I wasn't going to let my father in on the details of the conversation.

"Are you defending her, Jake?"

"No. I'm telling you how I see it from my perspective, and she's doing her best with what she has been given."

"You have a marriage."

He was pissing me off now. Really pissing me off. "I know I have a marriage. I'm working on it too. We're going to counseling and everything. I also have a son. And he has a mother he needs to have a relationship with. If I can help with that—"

"Counseling won't help if you have this woman's son—"

"My son."

"Whatever. Counseling won't help if you have this woman's son waiting in the background. They're threats. You have to make a choice. Who will it be, them or Hannah?"

"Where is all this coming from, Dad? My son and his mother aren't threats. They're part of my life. I thought I had to make a choice too, but that's a lie. Even Hannah has been helping Tim with homework and—"

"Don't be so naïve. Women don't forget a thing. They hold the past and will take it to their grave."

"You just said Mom forgave you."

"Your mother's the exception. She's a different kind of woman. Most women ain't that way."

Oh, brother. There he went with his sexist psychology. I cracked all ten knuckles and restrained myself from hanging up in his face. He did have cancer, after all. Wasn't going to be rude to the man.

"Just because that woman hit a string of bad luck doesn't make it your problem. She should've made better choices."

My ears burned. "Better choices? Like the kind of choices you'd made when you decided to spend nights away from us so you could be with your women?"

"Watch your mouth, Jake."

"No. You watch your mouth, Dad. I wasn't going to let Social Services take my child. I'd figured you'd understand the value of family by now, but it's clear you don't. Even Mom wanted to see Tim. He's your grandson. The only one you're ever going to have."

"You and Hannah don't plan on having children?" he asked.

I contemplated the room, regarding each piece of furniture and taking a long time before answering. Hannah and I couldn't have children for medical reasons but maybe— possibly—Tim, Hannah, and I could live together? Maybe possibly? That was one way we could be a family. Hannah could grow closer to Tim. I could bring up the idea with Hannah. Pops didn't know about our infertility issues, and I wasn't in the mood for explaining everything. "Hannah and I haven't had a child yet. I don't expect us to have a child in the future. Anyways, Mom suggested Tim visit you two, but I see the interest was one-sided."

"She suggested he visit?"

"Yes." I switched the phone to my other ear. There was an extended silence on the other end as if he was mulling over Mom's suggestion.

"I never finished my story about your mother's car accident. When I finally saw her in the hospital hooked up to all those machines and pregnant, I knew I had to make a choice. I could've lost my family to some freak accident, let alone my bad choices. I broke it off with the woman I'd been seeing at the time. But as we know with time, it causes you to forget. When you were three, I'd resumed my horrible ways."

My father really was a piece of work. No need to seek parenting advice from him or my mother. Still never figured out why'd she put up with him.

"Do whatever it takes to keep your wife, Jake. She's number one."

So said the serial adulterer. I exhaled. The thing about Pops was he had his share of marriage regrets and from what I saw, he knew them full well. He was saying the right thing, but had he really changed? "What have you done to prove you did 'whatever it took' to make things right with Mom?"

"You want proof, huh?" Pops asked.

"Yep."

"Your mother wanted a divorce three years ago. When the realization I could lose her hit me, I changed up real fast. I'd taken her for granted, thinking she'd always be around. I broke off my affair, and I got serious about putting your mother first. I went to counseling too. It was working for a while, but then this diagnosis interrupted our weekly appointments."

Pops going to marriage counseling? He was not the pour-your-heart-out-to-a stranger type.

"I'm not the jerk you're making me out to be," Pops said. "I want to meet my grandson too."

"You do?"

"If your mother insists on its importance, then it's important to me too. I'll be more than happy to cover the plane tickets."

The man was serious, and he was making Mom's opinion his first priority. As far as I knew, he'd never done that before. When Mom requested something from him, he'd always made some excuse. "Mom has that much of an influence over you, huh?"

"I told you, son, she's a different kind of woman. When you have someone good, you don't make it easy to let them walk out on you, and you make them number one. Number one. I realize that now. I hope one day you will too."

Frustration resurfaced. He still had to hint at my need to make this "choice" between the two. After Hannah and I connected the other day, I'd decided I was done with guilt. Yeah, I was still struggling with the feeling, especially when I visited Melinda, but I wasn't going to allow guilt to rule me like it had in the past. "I'll think about making that trip."

I hung up, annoyed I hadn't gotten to talk to Mom, to ask her for the advice I'd been hoping for. Annoyed at Pops for insisting I had to make this choice between Tim and Hannah as if he knew how to fix my marriage. Annoyed he could still be such a hypocrite. They were both out of their minds.

Mom should've had her bags packed a long time ago, and Dad—well, he never changed. Didn't matter what he said. Guess as far as parenting and marriage advice, I'd have to trust myself.

For the first time, that was okay with me because it was working. Tim and Hannah were connecting, and Hannah and I were taking steps toward healing. Life was looking up.

CHAPTER 22

I tried to cancel the marriage counseling appointment, but the lady on the phone had said they'd charge us a hundred bucks for the short notice.

So instead, here I was in the waiting room, waiting to talk about problems best suited for a made-for-TV movie. Jake hadn't arrived yet, and I wondered whether I should strangle or shoot him upon arrival.

Joking, joking, joking.

Not joking. Not, not joking. Jake was gonna have a hard time explaining his little rendezvous to rehab. If we had to start off marriage counseling with a fight, then I was ready to fight 'cuz no way in the world was I playing scorned-woman victim.

"Hannah."

I startled at the sound of his voice. He looked all cool, calm, and way too cute in his white button-down shirt, khakis, and shades propped atop his Caesar haircut, but guess what? Who cared?

"Been waiting long?" He slid in the chair next to me, and I

caught a whiff of his scent, Brut this time. Who wore Brut to marriage counseling? Dumbo Jake, that was who.

"Earth to Hannah." He snapped his stupid fingers in my face. "I asked you a question."

"I heard a question." I tried my hardest to get the snark out of my voice, but I couldn't. His jerk meter was high, and so was my anger.

His thick brows dipped. "You okay? Something happen?"

You tell me. I pursed my lips and saved all my words for the boxing ring—I mean, the counseling session.

Seconds later, a redhead welcomed us into her cozy office. I took one look at the place with its potpourri sticks, vanilla candles, and vase of tulips, and thought I was inside the lounge of a bed and breakfast instead of a therapy office. Was this an effort to keep down the levels of bickering?

"I'm Rebecca Starnes, a licensed marriage and family therapist. Have a seat on the couch." She clasped her hands and sat across from us in a rocking chair, resting her gold-bangled forearms on her thighs. "I like to keep a casual, friendly atmosphere."

I like to keep a cantankerous, fiery one.

"Me too." Jake sat next to me and scooted a little too close. I swear his aftershave was going to make my nostrils bleed.

"Let's start off our session by first discussing your goals for counseling."

To kill Jake.

"I want us to stay married," he responded in this calm, socially acceptable tone. "Not in name only, but in friend-ship… and love."

Did he really say that? After he hauled his butt to the rehab center to see Melinda?

"And you, Hannah?" Rebecca's focus shifted to me. "Are those your goals as well?"

"Seeing that I was the person who originally filed for the separation, no. Those aren't my goals."

"No?" Jake and Rebecca asked at once.

"No."

"What are you talking about?" Jake asked, incredulous. "We discussed counseling the other day at your house. What happened?"

"Your visit to Melinda happened. Tim told me you saw her at the rehab center and—"

"Who is Melinda?" Rebecca interjected.

"The other woman Jake has a child with."

Rebecca scribbled notes in a pad, and my foot got all jittery. I was going to let this fool have it. "You were talking all this stuff about wanting to reignite our friendship and love. If you want to do so, then why don't you first try by not visiting Melinda."

"The only reason I went there was Tim was worried about not being able to see his mother. I was trying to arrange a visit."

"I know," I spouted back. "He told me."

"So why the anger?" Rebecca asked.

"Why the anger?" Now I redirected my attention to Rebecca. "You hear this man? He'd told me time and time again that he wasn't going to have anything to do with Tim or his mother. Fine. Cool. I can deal. Then Tim's mom—"

"Who's Tim?"

I hated having to explain everything. "The child!"

"Oh." Rebecca's shoulders rounded. "Sorry, go ahead."

I continued with the story of the fire and the drug abuse and even the tutoring. (I left out the sex part.) As I did, Rebecca scribbled a whole bunch of notes on a legal pad and then she looked up. "That's a lot to unpack."

"I know," I said, deadpan. She wasn't telling me anything new.

"Showing up today tells me there's some semblance of trust, Hannah. We can build from there," Rebecca said.

My insides felt hollow, scooped out and empty. "There's nothing about Jake I trust. I only agreed to counseling because I thought he'd changed. He didn't."

"That's unfair, Hannah. I have changed," Jake pressed. "You have too. You're kinder. More patient. I was blown away when you agreed to help Tim with algebra." Jake shook his head and angled his posture away from me. "But you know what? There comes a point when Hannah has to decide whether she wants me or not. If she's that annoyed with me, we could've canceled this whole thing and saved ourselves a whole bunch of money."

"Actually, there was a hundred-dollar cancellation fee." I scratched my palm.

"I would've paid it," he snapped.

Whatever cheddar! He would've begged and pleaded with me to try and change my mind. Ain't nobody got no time for that mess. "You can't play Casanova with me one day and then see Melinda in rehab and think there won't be any repercussions and buried resentments, Jake. Doesn't work. I'm not gonna bend to meet the screwed-up choices you made in your life and get my feelings hurt in the process. Ain't happening."

"I'm not tossing you around, Hannah, but this is my life. Tim's in it. Melinda's in it. I want you to be in it too."

Oh, so we were all gonna be this one big happy, dysfunctional family. What crack pipe was he smoking? "Who would be first?" I asked.

"First?"

"Yeah, who would have first priority? Me, Tim, or Melinda?"

He was silent. Couldn't answer. My soul pinched. This man couldn't even tell me where I stood on his priority list. I knew he wasn't about nothing, and I was tired of being a second-class citizen in errbody's life. I was his wife and he cheated on me—second-class citizen. Dumbo photographer didn't like my lips—second-class citizen. Greta thought my skin was too jacked up to model again—second-class citizen. Ugh.

"Actually, Hannah, I've been thinking." Jake's voice steadied. "If counseling goes well with us, Tim and I could move in with you."

My brain screeched. "Whaaat? Are you out of your mind? No way. Is that why you wanted us to come to counseling? So I'd soften up enough to let you and Tim live with me?"

He was silent. My insides pinched again because I was right.

"Okay, Jake and Hannah." Rebecca intervened before we grabbed our guns and started a duel. "Let's not come to any hasty decisions here or stop this conversation before we make some good ground. You've both said a lot. Moves are huge leaps, Jake. We'll need to unpack this all, and that won't happen in one session."

"We haven't unpacked it in all the years we've been married." Jake exhaled. "Don't know if that'll ever happen."

Hearing him say those words hurt, but they were true. The very reason I tried to file the separation in the first place. The kiss and the intimacy we'd shared the other night was fleeting.

"You've told me a bit of your history, Hannah. I've seen you two... communicate," Rebecca said. "When Jake set up this appointment earlier, he told me a little about his side. Now can you tell me what you want most from Jake? From your marriage?"

I'd never asked myself those questions, but I knew the answers. "I want someone who'll tell me the truth about everything, even that visit to see Melinda in rehab."

"If I would've—"

Rebecca raised her hand. "Hold on, Jake. Is that all, Hannah?"

I nodded. "That's all I can think of now."

"If I would've told you that I was going to visit Melinda, you would've blown up in my face," Jake said.

"I did blow up in your face."

"This is true," he said.

There was another question buried underneath my protective sarcasm and anger that I wanted answered but was too afraid to ask. Might as well ask it anyway. "You love her, Jake? Do you love Melinda?"

He looked away.

"You did love her!" My voice shrilled. "You did!"

"I never loved Melinda. Honestly, I never did." His volume lowered as if he was trying to make up for his feelings or something.

"Sorry, buddy. But you can't flip-flop between us. I'm not risking my heart for this nonsense again. Ain't doing it. She doesn't have to be part of my life."

"I can't write her off, Hannah. We have a son together. If I want him in my life—and I do—then Melinda is going to be in my life too. She's in bad shape, and she's important to Tim. I want to see her get better. But I don't love her. Never have. Never will." His head bowed a second and sorrow flashed across his expression. "This is the lot I chose. I'm not rejecting it or avoiding it anymore. You'll have to decide if you want this lot too. I'll understand if you don't—if you don't want me."

So now Jake was saying I had to take him and the whole entire package that came along with him: Melinda and Tim. Before I knew of his visit to the rehab center, I had figured our marriage was on the up and up, but I didn't want to deal with him talking to Melinda on the regular, even if it only concerned Tim. He made things hard.

My conversation with Tim during our first tutoring session flitted through my head. There was a reason Jake never mentioned his intentions to visit Melinda in rehab earlier, and I was gonna figure it out. "I want to be in a relationship with someone who'll tell me the straight truth. I've always had to eke it out of you or prove you were lying."

"So, what happened with us the other day? The kiss. Meant nothing?"

Oh brother. Why'd he bring all that up? In front of a counselor! No, not ready to discuss the physical parts. "Married people kiss. Or at least they should kiss." I tossed a smile in the counselor's direction. "Among other things. It's expected."

"Even with a husband you've kicked out of the house and with whom you've had no interactions with *at all* since June, until this fire?" Jake asked.

I angled my posture away from Jake and toward the counselor. "Communication tips, please?"

She tapped her pen on the desk. "I have no tips because this is really good. You've brought up a good point, Hannah, about Jake being forthright with you. Carry on. This is sublime."

What in the world? Jake paid her over a hundred bucks an hour to say our bickering and mistrust was sublime?

"You're talking about an issue you probably wouldn't have discussed had you not been in a safe space to explore," Rebecca added.

Explore? She spoke as if we were a couple of kids learning how to use fidget spinners for the first time.

"I would've confronted Jake 'bout all this regardless. The thing is, I think Jake would've dodged the point if it were one-on-one." I folded my arms, pissed.

"No way, Hannah. I would've answered you no matter who was present." Jake clasped his hands together and tapped his thumb on his knee.

"Then answer. Why didn't you tell me you were going to see Melinda? Why'd I have to hear it from Tim?"

"Because I knew you'd hate me all over again. You hate me now, don't you?"

I balled my fist. I didn't hate him. "I strongly dislike your actions. Strongly."

"Time's up," the counselor said. "We can resume next week."

What?! Time's up? We were just getting started. "Um. We'll resume whenever I feel like getting my answer since Jake says he'll answer no matter who's around. I'm finishing this. And not paying you for it. You can hear how it went next week. How 'bout that?"

Rebecca looked at me, dumbfounded. I put my purse on my shoulder and headed to the waiting area. Jake followed close behind.

"We had a good first session," Jake said.

"Are you serious? Nothing was resolved. Obviously, this counselor lady doesn't care 'cuz she ended the conversation when our time was up."

"I wasn't expecting a miracle. I'm glad you told me you're pissed about the rehab visit."

I crossed my arms, gave him one of those bully-at-the-playground stares. "How are you going to fix it?"

He touched my jawline, his fingers warm and kind. My skin might as well have shriveled into a wrinkly little ball because PDAs were not my thing, especially when I posed a serious question. "Stop trying to gloss this over and answer my question." I stepped away.

"That's why I visited her—I was trying to fix it. Tim wanted to see his mother and—"

"I know the story. He told me everything. I was referring to us. You said Melinda was going to be in your life, and I had to decide whether I wanted to accept Melinda. You hid the visit from me, Jake. Do you plan to do hide future visits from me?"

"No, I don't. I don't want you to hold them against me, however. The visits to rehab will only be for Tim's sake."

I crossed my arms. Jake had made promises before and had broken them.

"Hannah, I know the road ahead for us isn't easy. I never expected it to be, but you're the one I love. There's little else I can do to prove this to you. You'll have to press the 'I Believe' button."

I have to press the "I Believe" button? What was he, a greeting card writer or something?

"Whaddya say? Are you going to press that button or not?" He gave me another one of those Shemar Moore smiles.

He had a point. (Maybe.) Jake was trying. (Perhaps.) This could simply be the old Hannah returning from the dead, trying to get me to have a major freak-out. The old Hannah would've written him off completely, would've never wanted to see him again. Old Hannah was gone. I'd dumped her and her insecurities in the trash bin that day when I'd looked at myself in the mirror head on.

I rubbed the scar on my collar bone. This time, I wouldn't run away. "I'll press the 'I Believe' button."

Jake smiled.

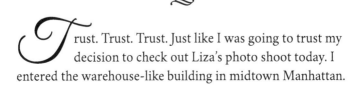

*T*rust. Trust. Trust. Just like I was going to trust my decision to check out Liza's photo shoot today. I entered the warehouse-like building in midtown Manhattan.

The inside—spacious and filled with natural light—belied its outer appearance.

Liza stood in front of a beige backdrop, looking Sasha Fierce as she posed for the camera. Jealousy pinched my insides. It'd been so painful to even look at old magazine photos of myself, knowing that was no longer me. Yet here was Liza, all fabulous and content with her size sixteen curves.

And she was getting paid for it too?! Why was I was so self-conscious about my appearance? I should've eaten a tub of Blue Bonnet ice cream and found myself a commercial modeling agent.

She was working that camera like nobody's business. Go girl. Yet it was easy for Liza to do so since she'd always been secure in her skin. Liza wasn't dealing with this huge change in appearance like me. On top of all that, I was feeling insecure in my body before the fire, so I had it double-bad.

"We'll take a five-minute break, Liza, and you can do a wardrobe change," the photographer said. "Great work."

"Hey, girl." I waved.

"Hannah!" She squealed and ran toward me and wrapped me in a squishy hug. "You're here."

"Of course I'm here. What'd you think, I'd chicken out or something?"

"Hmm… I did." Her smooth brown cheeks stretched into a smile. "But you're here. Go Hannah. Go Hannah." She moon-walked around the studio. Embarrassing.

"It ain't that serious, girl."

"It sure 'nuf is. You're here. You're moving forward. I'm proud of you."

Now my eyes were getting all watery. I blinked a bazillion times and looked around the studio. The photographer, a good-looking Latino man in his thirties, was busy adjusting the lighting, and I was busy hoping he didn't recognize me as *the* Hannah Hart.

I was complicated like that.

"I'll be back, beautiful. I'm gonna change for the next session." She air-kissed me and disappeared into the dressing room.

I turned my back to the hot-looking photographer, self-conscious all over again. What was I doing here? Playing "Take Your Burned Former Supermodel Friend to Work Day"? Liza was plus-sized, but she wasn't scarred. Big difference.

The faint sound of the photographer's footsteps grew louder and closer, and my heart beat faster and worser. Yeah, worser.

Then he was standing next to me. I pretended to stare at an invisible spot on the wall and leaned against the radiator. Hopefully, the heater wouldn't turn on or else it'd light up my butt like something serious.

"You look familiar."

The leaning-against-the-radiator-while-staring-at-the-wall trick didn't work. "I do?" I modulated my voice like those phone operators on the TV shopping networks.

"Yes." He squinted. "You're Hannah Hart, aren't you?"

I got a case of the prickles. I hadn't gone out too, too much since the fire for this very reason. I hadn't figured out how I'd respond when someone recognized me. Now that the moment had arrived, I was weirded out. It was one thing to look at myself in the mirror and quite another to have someone looking at me, studying me. Would he compare how I looked before to how I looked now with my scars? Would he see something missing in how I looked today? That worried me, not being seen as enough today. "Yes, I am."

"Nice to meet you. I'm Miguel."

Miguel gave me that photographer's eye, the one where

their eyeballs turned into makeshift camera lenses that studied every crack and feature of my face with laser-like precision.

"I heard about the fire," he continued. "Glad to see you're doing okay."

How thoughtful. He didn't see me as a freak. I held my arms close to my body in a self-protective stance.

"You look great."

"Now you're lying." I laughed nervously.

"Not lying at all. You've changed, of course, but I still see the same Hannah Hart, beautiful as ever. Have you been modeling?"

The muscles in my neck tensed. Greta's final, rejection-filled words still stung, and although I was all gung-ho at the diner the other day, today I was hesitant to speak my heart's desire. "No. I haven't, but I'm considering the very faint possibility."

Very faint possibility? Get a backbone. Even my confidence had drained.

"We'll have to get you back in the game." The words came so easily from Miguel's mouth, I looked behind to check that he wasn't talking to someone else.

He wasn't.

"I'm serious," Miguel continued as if reading my mind. "Your comeback is going to be the biggest yet. The phoenix rising from the ashes. Yes, yes. Yes! You need to do a fashion spread with that very theme. I could do a test shoot and pitch the idea to the fashion editor at *Vogue*. She's a friend of mine, so you won't need agent representation." He held up both hands in a rectangle and evaluated me through his mock camera angle. "My goodness, girl. You'll be absolutely divine."

Words stuck in my throat, a whole bunch of words.

Thank you!

Are you serious?

Vogue!

OMG!!

I stood there, dumbstruck.

Liza came out of the dressing room in a bandeau dress, which showed every curve. She was working it. "Hannah's gonna be in *Vogue?*"

"Not promising, ladies." Miguel held up his hands. "Simply tossing the idea out there. I want to do a test shoot."

"Eeee! Hannah's gonna be in *Vogue*. Hannah's gonna be in *Vogue*. If Miguel said so, it's a done deal."

"Oh lord, I done started something." Miguel powered up his camera.

"You sure did! You started my girl's comeback." Liza pumped her fist.

"Girl, why you have to be so melodramatic?" I shook my head. "Miguel said he'd do a test shoot. Having me in a full-page spread in *Vogue* would be the risk of the century."

"It'd be the smartest risk of the century. If they knew what was good for their company, they'd start putting imperfect models in the magazine. Women are tired of all that photoshopped garbage. They want to see real," Liza said.

Liza's conviction was contagious. Perhaps my foray into modeling wasn't about me. Perhaps it was about something bigger. It could challenge the status quo, change people's perceptions of beauty.

"Girl, you don't know how much success I've had with plus-sized modeling," Liza continued. "At first, I was definitely worried, but folks loved seeing me in a catalog or a magazine. I got so many letters from people saying that I had given them hope."

Hmm. Liza had only mentioned the haters when we were at the diner. Guess haters were gonna hate, and I'd have to learn to only listen to the inspiring voices.

"How'd you get into modeling?" Miguel asked Liza.

"I was going through a rough time, completely unhappy with working a dead-end job in cubicle nation. I saw this notice online for an open call for models, and I showed up. I was the only plus-sized woman there, but I didn't care. I worked that room, and I booked my first print ad for a local clothing store. That led to more bookings and things took off."

"Can you lend me some of your swagger?" I sighed. "I need a dose."

"You've already got swagger; all you need to do is own it." She nudged the man. "So, will you supply the best wardrobe for my girl? I know you can hook her up, Miguel."

"I sure can. I have lots of designer friends," Miguel said. "But remember, Hannah, the clothes don't make you. You make the clothes. You are everything you need to shine."

I am everything I need to shine. Hmm. I liked how that sounded. Now to simply slip into those words and own them.

Easier said than done. The clothes would definitely help. I wasn't gonna lie.

"Hannah, you look like you swallowed a lemon." Liza gave me the side-eye. "Don't be all worried. Miguel's gonna work his magic."

"Can you stop by bright and early tomorrow? I have another shoot scheduled for late afternoon, but I can definitely start early and work till a bit past lunch." Miguel gasped. "Oh my. I can see it now. I'll call my favorite stylists and makeup artists to see if they can stop in tomorrow morning. Your scars are fine art, honey. You're gonna be so gorgeous. Say yes."

Yes?

I was taking a risk with reconciling with Jake. And now Miguel was asking me to take a risk with being on camera, scars and all. Yeah, I'd been considering this all along, but now he was asking me to make a decision. Could I really make myself vulnerable on all fronts?

I wanted happiness at home and happiness in modeling. To do so, I had to take these risks. "Yes."

~

*T*he next morning, standing outside Miguel's warehouse studio again, doubt turned into a Mack Truck and slammed into me.

A test shoot? For *Vogue*? Miguel wasn't paying me for this test shoot. *Vogue* could reject me. Anything could happen.

I tapped Miguel's business card on the inside of my palm, reconsidering.

Stop being such a wuss, Hannah. You're not hurting anyone, and no one's hurting you. It's a bunch of pictures.

I pressed the buzzer.

"That you, beautiful?" Miguel called from the intercom.

"Sure is." I answered to "beautiful" without a second thought, not something I'd done in the longest time. That whole stint with Giancarlo from years ago had me questioning my beauty. He spoke of me like I was chattel or property or a commodity. I'd ingested Giancarlo's words unconsciously, believed them to be true when they weren't. Today, I wasn't gonna beat myself up over it. I was then, and I am today, beautiful, belly and lips and all.

After I'd gotten over my initial awkwardness after meeting him yesterday, I'd concluded that Miguel had a way of making me feel at ease with myself, a sign of a talented photographer. Many were egotistical jerks.

Miguel buzzed me in, and I made my way into the now familiar space. "Where are you?" I called.

"Over here, love."

I rounded the corner and saw Miguel. He brushed his long bangs away from his face. Miguel looked as if he should've had a starring role in Miami Vice with his creased linen pants and blousey, button-down white shirt. I could definitely see how women would toss their panties at his feet.

"Ready for your closeup?" He gave me a side-hug. "Suzanne! Lucinda! She's here."

Seconds later, two women came from the dressing area, one brunette, one redhead.

"Here she is. Suzanne's going to do your hair and makeup. Lucinda's your wardrobe person."

"And do I have the outfits for you, honey. Soon as Miguel called me last night, I said yes. You're gonna have those editors at *Vogue* eating out of your hands."

Or laughing at my ridiculousness. *Nope. I was gonna be positive here.* No time to be negative whatsoever.

After the women got me all primped, I took one look in the mirror and my mouth dropped. (It didn't literally fall off my face and drop to the ground, but I gaped.) I looked like Nefertiti extra-crispy. I was—

Divine. The scars were there—every crevice, every dent— but they didn't make me wince. I was like a piece of broken glass fitted back together. Unique.

"I can't believe you did this for me. I need to look like this every day. How'd you do it?"

"Tinted moisturizer with a dab of powder. No founda- tion. No concealer. Nothing to cover you up. I only accentu- ated your skin tone and let everything else show," Suzanne said, smiling.

"That's amazing." I grinned extra-cheesy at my reflection in the mirror.

"Ah, don't sweat our skills," Suzanne said. "We had great raw material to work with… you. Come on, let's show

Miguel."

We left the dressing room, and Miguel was busy arranging the backdrop. It was fiery red with a huge, multi-colored phoenix painted onto the backdrop. The air rushed out of me—the image was vibrant and alive. It spoke to my soul and said, "Rise up, woman. Be who you are."

Be who you are. The words reverberated through my chest and filled me. I'd try. I'd definitely try.

When Miguel turned and saw me, he did a double take. "Amazing! You are killer."

"Killer-good? Or killer-bad?"

"You know what I mean. Come on." He reached over and took my hand. "You need to be in natural light."

I stayed put. "You sure about natural light? People will see every little scar on my body with natural light."

"That's the point. Don't worry. You're magic."

Magic, huh? I waited for my fairy godmother to show up, wave her wand, and let everyone know I wasn't this special person that Miguel had said. But there weren't any fairy godmothers who showed up. Instead, I stood there absolutely real. Terrifying.

"You're scared. I can see it in your face."

I stuck my tongue out him. "Boo!"

Miguel laughed. "You're silly. Come on, lady. Let's get these pictures taken. We can experiment and play around. Get artsy. This is the best part of my job."

I checked the clock on the wall. We had plenty of time for this shoot.

"All right, gorgeous. Let's go."

I stood in front of the camera feeling all exposed and plastered on a tight smile. "Cheese."

"Cheese? Cheese? Hannah, you're a model. Don't give me cheese." Miguel set down his camera. "How about this? Think of a happy memory that you've had recently. Something good, not stressful. Then look outside the window so I can catch your profile."

I thought of Jake. Not of our counseling session, but of when we made love, the pleasant time. My shoulders relaxed as I melted into the memory.

Jake's exhale had danced across my cheek and tickled the tip of my ear. My belly had flipped, and I melted into him.

Jake's lips blanketed mine, and I obligingly went undercover and returned his supple and soothing kisses. Fireworks.

With an exhale, I pressed my hands into his muscled back. I could've stayed in that position, wrapped in him. Forever. I loved my husband.

"Attagirl." Miguel clicked more pictures, and I was jolted back to the present.

When these photos got developed, I'd show them to Jake, see what he thought. He'd probably say something short and succinct like "nice," and then I'd try to get him to be more descriptive so he'd end up saying something like "nice photo." Man, that'd make me laugh. Jake was like that at times. I giggled.

"There you go. That's it. Smile and be free." Miguel's camera clicked away.

Funny how the good memories with Jake made me feel as if I could fly to the moon. The sensation settled into my bones. The other time I'd felt this way was on my wedding day. My nerves were spiraling out of control on the days leading to the wedding. I'd been so nervous and worried that I'd mess something up, but when I saw Jake standing at the other end of the aisle, the worries dissipated. I was embarking on a new, perfect life, a life far away from those memories of that college professor and my miscarriage.

We may grow old together, but I won't have babies of my own. We'd had some huge rifts, and our marriage was far from perfect, but perhaps marriage wasn't about perfection. Perhaps it was about progression, about getting better with each passing day.

Despite our mess, Jake had his good side. Early in my career, I was worried about landing this big modeling assignment. No one thought I'd get it because I was an unknown, but Jake said I should believe in myself, even when no one else did. It was hard to believe in myself back then, perhaps because I'd placed all my hopes in that big-time advertising agency that'd be deciding whether I should be hired.

Yet this time around there wasn't a huge ad agency making a decision on my fate. There wasn't money riding on my appearance. It was just me, Miguel, a camera, and a strong sense of this newfound freedom and belief in myself. I giggled again.

Then the doorbell rang.

"Hold on a sec." Miguel left to answer the door. I rested my bottom on the ledge. The residue of hope gathered in my chest and spread through my limbs. Liza and Miguel were right. I was gonna rock this modeling thing.

"Thought I'd stop in a bit early so I can get a head start on the photo shoot. Get my makeup ready and stuff."

That voice. That mousy little voice. Jacinta!

"Er… " Miguel's voice sounded very stumble-y and unpolished. "I'm in the middle of a photo shoot right now. Only one person can use the dressing room 'cuz it's too small. Can you return in an hour or so?"

"An hour or so? No way. You told me I'd be the only person you'd be working with today."

"Yeah, I made a last-minute change. But I promise it will in no way impede on your scheduled time. Promise."

"Sorry, Miguel. That won't work. I'm here. I'm not leaving."

My ears pricked. Was this girl for real? Miguel just said he wasn't changing anything about her photo shoot. How obnoxious.

Seconds later, I heard her heels clickety-clacking inside the studio, and my skin got all clammy. I immediately shoved the feeling aside. No need to get all nervous. Jacinta was the one interrupting my time. When she saw me, she stopped.

"What are you doing here?" Jacinta asked.

"I'm here for my photo shoot." I erased all hesitation from my voice.

"So am I." Jacinta gave me the side-eye.

What? This chick was giving me the side-eye like I was invading her space. Oh no. Oh no.

"I thought you were done with modeling, looking like you do." Jacinta smacked her lips like she was the boss lady in this studio.

My cheeks turned hot, and my face was more than clammy. "What's that supposed to mean? Looking like I do? Looking like what?"

"Dog-ugly." Jacinta didn't even blink. "Don't even have any makeup on. You—"

"Hold on a sec. Hold on. You talking about me?" My sistah-girl voice was in full effect. "You talking about *me*? You ain't nothing but a fake little girl wannabe model."

"Look ladies." Miguel jumped between us. "Jacinta, I will not have any altercations in my studio. I said you can return later. Your shoot isn't for a few more hours. Nothing changed. Now I'm going to finish this *Vogue* shoot with Hannah, and you're going to return at your scheduled time, Jacinta."

"*Vogue* shoot?" Jacinta raised her brow as if shocked that I'd be on a shoot for a major fashion magazine. "Did you say *Vogue* shoot? You?"

"Yeah, me, Miss Thang. Me." This chick. Was she serious?

"Don't nobody wanna see your crispy self in the *Vogue* magazine." Jacinta put on a cruel smile.

My heart clamped up. Her words slammed into me, taking all of my resolve and squishing it into a tiny ball.

Don't let it get to you, dear. You're fully capable. Fully capable.

Lola's words, words from long, long ago, bubbled to the surface. She'd said them to me when I was a kid, and I wanted so hard to believe them in this moment, but it hurt. I exhaled. No matter how I felt inside, I wasn't gonna let this chick get away with dissing me.

"Crispy? Who you calling crispy?" I balled my hand into a fist, and Miguel's eyes widened.

"Ladies, stop. We are not about to have a wrestling match up in my studio." He waved his finger at us like we were two ungrateful children. "Now Jacinta, I'm asking you for the last time. Please leave."

Jacinta's hurtful words lingered and drowned out all of Miguel's rah-rah-rah support. No point in me continuing this photo shoot. My confidence was shot. "I'm about to go. I'm through."

"We still have a few hours left," Miguel said. "You were just getting started. You sure?"

"Beyond sure." I headed to the dressing room. "Thanks so much though. It was fun while it lasted."

While it lasted. Truer words had never been said. When Jacinta stepped in that room looking so—so perfect, that had been enough for me, and then she had said all those nasty things. Stupid of me to even show up today. Very stupid.

After I changed, Miguel talked some nonsense about developing my photos and emailing them to me in a week. Whatever. I made my way home.

I shouldn't have gone there in the first place. No one wanted to look at someone like me. No one wanted ugly. There wasn't any room for ugly.

That's when I stopped walking and cried.

~

*T*he next day when I was getting ready for my next tutoring session with Tim, I was still crying.

I wasn't bawling my eyes out or anything, but I was definitely reeling from Jacinta's cruel remarks. Gah! I hated that Miss Thing's words had an impact on me.

The problem was that her words still hurt. *Don't nobody wanna see your extra crispy self in the* Vogue *magazine.*

What a hater.

After changing my bandages and getting dressed, I checked my email. Miguel had sent a note asking if I still wanted him to send in my pictures to the *Vogue* shoot. I said yes. Ain't gonna let Jacinta's bullying hold me back from greatness.

I scrolled through my emails and saw two more from the makeup artist and hair stylist from the shoot. They wanted my permission to talk me up to some industry folks too. Yes. Yes. Yes.

Hmm. Maybe something good will come from all of that. Hopefully, Jacinta won't try to sabotage my chances with *Vogue* by telling Greta and then having Greta botch up the opportunity.

Gah. I hated thinking like that. I really did, but it was a reality in my cutthroat industry.

The doorbell buzzed. That must be Tim, ready for tutoring. I answered the door and gasped.

The late-afternoon sunlight bounced off his face and highlighted his black eye and bloodied mouth. A trickle of red dribbled down his chin.

The sight of him punctured my chest. "What happened!"

"Nothing. Just a tussle." He checked his watch. "Sorry I'm late. I got, um, sidetracked."

"You're fine. Come on in." I motioned him inside and then I looked onto the street, cautious. "You safe?"

"Now I am." He walked down the hallway with his backpack slung over his shoulders.

"We'll get you cleaned up." I headed to the half-bathroom and grabbed my mini first aid kit. "Tell me about this tussle."

"Wasn't nothing. Some kids were ragging on my mama. Saying some stuff. I got pissed and punched one out."

I thought about his school record. "Was this on school property?"

"Nah. Nah. I'm smarter than that. We were at the convenience store. Well, we were outside the convenience store."

"Good." I caught myself. "I mean. Not good. That you were fighting. What did they say about your mama that you got all riled up?"

No response. His expression was calm, but it hardened around the edges.

My breathing thinned just enough to cause a tingling in my sternum. This kid was going through some bad stuff. Stuff he didn't want to discuss. My empathy welled. "You don't have to talk about it if you don't want to."

"Ain't nothing. Just some money stuff. Mama was always struggling with money, and that kid was calling me a poor bastard child." He shrugged. "That made me get all up in my feelings and punch him out."

I flexed my fingers around the zipper of the first aid kit, gulping down the nerves crawling up my throat. Yeah, this kid's problems stemmed from a deeper root. "I know you were angry but try not to punch people next time. Your father is going to have a fit when he sees you."

"Pops? No. I can't let him know."

"What do you plan on telling him when he sees your

face?" I handed him the antiseptic and some cotton balls. "That you fell?"

"Nope."

The care in his eyes almost caused me to melt into the carpet. "Here are some bandages. It's kind of warm in here." I fanned myself, hating how my brain turned to scrambled eggs at Tim's helplessness.

"I'm fine."

"I'm not. I'll turn on the air." I walked across the wooden floors and fiddled with the thermostat. The air conditioning rumbled to life.

"So you ready to get started on algebra?" I asked.

"Sure. Oh, and I got a B on my math quiz." He crumpled the dirtied gauze in his hand.

"That's awesome!" I clasped my hands together. "See? And that was just from a little bit of practice. Wait till we progress. You'll get better in no time."

"Miss Hannah?"

"Yes."

"Promise me you won't talk to Pops about this. Even the part about them calling me a poor kid. I just don't want to get into it with him."

The cool air from the vents wafted against my skin. Trust. He wanted to know he could trust me. If that's what would help him cope, then I could give him that. "I promise."

"Thank you, ma'am." He gave me a kid-innocent smile, and my heart spilled all over the place. In that moment, something happened that I didn't think would ever be possible.

We connected.

CHAPTER 23

JAKE

"*I* got these pictures from a photo shoot I did the other day," Hannah said. "Miguel—the photographer—loved them. Then the makeup artist and the stylist wanted to use them in their portfolios. They said they'd spread the word about my new look. So I gave them the okay too. Tell me what you think. Be honest."

Honest. Honest. Honest. That's all I'd tried to be with Hannah since the fire. If she wanted honest, I could definitely give her honest, especially since I hadn't told her about my visit to Melinda. My lesson learned? Even if it was going to make things uncomfortable, we were going to have to learn how to deal with honest together. After her decision to keep moving forward in our marriage, I was looking forward to bonding with her, not just as lovers, but as friends. This was the perfect moment to do so.

I squinted and studied the photos up close. Dapples of sunlight streaked through her hair, shone on her skin. Skin that was smooth in some areas, pitted in others, but authentically beautiful nonetheless. Her russet-brown skin glowed in the light. The red-orange dress accentuated every curve on her lithe body and reminded me of a phoenix, long and lean and lovely. "You're amazing. Amazing. When were these taken?"

"Last week." Hannah had this faraway look in her eyes as if worried about something. "Liza hooked me up with this photo shoot with Miguel, a famous photographer."

"That's wonderful, right?"

Hannah twisted her mouth. "Kinda."

"What's wrong?" My volume lowered, a measly attempt to ease her anxiety.

"Nothing."

Her foot was jiggling. Something was definitely up. "This have to do with counseling?"

"Ha. Ha. I wish. Well... no. I don't really wish." She paused.

Her hesitation was getting me nervous. "What is it then?"

"Um, Miguel was going to show them to the fashion editors at *Vogue*. I think they look ridiculous though. Not *Vogue*-worthy. Do you think I look like a freak?"

"A freak? Why'd you think that?"

A shadow of shame flitted across her features. I could see it clearly, and it broke my heart. Those insecurities were hard to release.

Hannah relayed her confrontation with Jacinta, and my empathy meter rose a thousand notches. She definitely didn't need to feel inadequate and freakish, because she wasn't.

"Lemme ask you something." I nestled close to her on the couch, and the scent of her hair almost caused my heart to stop. *Calm down, Jake.*

"What?" she asked.

"When were you happiest?"

"Ever?"

"Ever." I echoed.

Hannah tapped her finger against her chin as if cycling

through all her memories. Part of me hoped a memory of us would come to mind first. "When I was with my grandmother. She made me very happy."

I couldn't compete with a grandmother. "Go on."

"Like this one day, I'd come back home from school feeling like I was the dumbest student in the world. I'd been failing miserably in all my subjects, especially math." A smile curled her lips even as she recalled the incident. She'd never shared this with me. There was still so much more to know about my wife. I listened.

"Lola probed. At first, I played it off, but she called my bluff. I showed her the F I'd received on my math quiz. I'd told her I couldn't do this. I was too dumb. Et cetera. Et cetera. Even as a young girl, I was very insecure about myself and my abilities. Then Lola had said the kindest thing to me. She said I was fully capable. She said I was smart. No one had ever said I was smart."

Her mouth curled into a tiny smile, kind of like it had that day I'd asked her out for the first time.

"Afterward, she purchased flash cards, math workbooks, everything, and we practiced together. Each day after school, she'd help me with homework. Each day, I was getting better. Kind of like how Tim has been getting better during our tutoring sessions. Much better."

"Practice makes perfect," I said. "Cliché but true."

"Her support helped a great deal too. I got an A on my next quiz. It was surreal. That A meant everything. I wouldn't have been able to get it without her help, her encouragement, her love. I told her as much." She exhaled. "Know what she said?"

"What?"

"That it was in me all along. I had what it took to ace my math tests. She simply prodded me in the right direction. I never believed her though. Seems like most every moment after her death, I'd been seeking that same feeling from someone… or something."

"You don't have to anymore." The words came slowly. A part of me had wanted to be something to her, but the best way for Hannah to grow was for her to grow on her own, with or without me in her life.

The thought was revolutionary. Yeah, I wanted us to get close and be lovers and friends and all that, but I wanted Hannah to be her full self even more.

Much, much more.

"I shouldn't have let Jacinta bully me out of my time with Miguel," Hannah said. "I should've stood my ground and stayed. If Jacinta or anyone else tries to get in the way of my dreams, I'm gonna give them what's what."

"You're an amazing woman, Hannah Hart." I smiled.

"And you're a pain in the butt of a man, Jake Hart." She nudged me playfully.

"I can be. That's why I've been hounding you for us to reconcile. You know this, right?"

Hannah looked away, and a flit of sadness swept over her. "I know."

"A while back, I promised I'd take you dress shopping. You still up for a trip to your favorite store sometime next week?"

"You sure?"

"Positive. I remember you flipping through those dresses in your closet the other day," I said.

"You never went shopping with me, even when we lived under the same roof. Why the change?"

I pursed my lips. "Just trying to make things better with us."

Her eyes lit. "Yeah, I'd love to. I know you must be changing if you want to go shopping."

"You're right. I am changing." I laughed, but my conversation with Mama sprung to my memory. The one where she'd talked about all she'd sacrificed through the years to keep their marriage, and her fear of losing Pops to cancer. I'd always sensed Mama had wanted to do more with her life, but she stayed by his side. She had made her choice to forgive Pops and stay in the marriage. I wondered how things would've turned out if she felt free to leave without any hang-ups or regrets. I didn't want Hannah to feel that way too.

"I'm not so sure what'll come of us, Hannah. We're going through counseling and all. We're getting close. That's good too, but living has told me one thing—nothing's guaranteed. Even if you and I don't make it for whatever reason, know that your grandmother was right. You always had it in you to do amazing things." I studied those pictures she'd taken one more time. "You're beautiful. No matter a fire, a crazy-ass husband, or a Jacinta. You're beautiful."

"You think so?"

"Yes. Your personal growth is the most important thing to me." The only time I'd felt more sure was the day I'd asked her to marry me. I took another look at the picture. "*Vogue* would be stupid not to take you on. They'd lose so much. You'd open them to a whole new level of branding and readership." I smiled at her. "They'd be the ones losing out. Not you."

Hannah nodded. "I know. Guess I'll contact Liza and ask her if she can recommend any agencies that represent differently abled models. I'll need an agent in case *Vogue* is interested." Hannah still stared at the photos.

"Do you. Follow your dreams."

Even as I said all this, part of me wanted to take back my words and tuck them into the invisible closet in my mind. What if she really took all I'd said about her growth being more important than our marriage to heart? What if all my attempts to reconcile our marriage came to nothing?

But it was worth it. I still loved Hannah. I wouldn't stand in the way of her freedom to be her fullest self.

~

*L*ater that day, Tim and I had a follow up meeting with Principal Grant, a progress report of sorts where I'd let Principal Grant (or Grant, as I called him) know about Tim's progress.

I had to focus for this meeting, but all I could think about was what I'd said to Hannah about being free to be herself, even if our attempts to work on our marriage weren't successful.

That was scary. All this time, I'd wanted to reconcile Hannah and Tim, but I'd never conceived of the possibility that Hannah's own dreams would take her away from me.

When I'd proposed to her all those years ago on campus, I was worried she'd choose modeling over me too. Perhaps that was my old fear popping up again. Perhaps there was nothing for me to worry about.

Couldn't think of that now. Focus, Jake. Time to show Grant that my son had been improving.

A dull gray light pushed through the smudged windows of Grant's office, outlining Grant's shiny, bald head and his bulbous nose. Ain't nothing changed about him since our last encounter. He was still as greasy looking as he could be.

"Principal Grant." I sat in the chair across from him. The same chair where I'd almost knocked him out months ago. "Tim's been sending in his homework on time to the teachers, and his grades have been excellent. The judge at the court hearing granted him reprieve too."

I figured I might as well lead with something positive since the last time I was here, Grant wanted to bury my son.

"Yep. Grades are up." Grant scratched his head, and the few scant white hairs shifted around. "Especially math."

Because of Hannah. Who would've known that all that time spent going over flash cards with her grandmother would've led to it helping Tim too, years later? Life was funny like that.

"That being said. . . " Grant raised his eyes from his desk blotter and tapped his pen on the edge of the scratched up desk. "There has been an increase in gang-related activity here at the school. More vandalism. More destruction of property. Of course, I'm not blaming your son. It's just something I want you to know."

My defenses shot up. Grant wouldn't have mentioned something if he didn't mean to imply Tim. "Why are you mentioning blame? Tim has been on the straight and narrow since our meeting."

Grant frowned, and he laid the pen on a pink slip of paper. He then edged himself to sit up straighter in his executive chair. His button-down shirt was bursting at the seams, verifying his clothes were too tight. "Like I said. Not blaming anyone for this mess going on, but the school board is looking into it, and they are questioning every student. Including Tim. That's why I wanted to have you here today."

This buster was implicating my son. "Hold on a sec. When we were going back and forth via email, you never mentioned the need to question my son over gang-related activity."

"The memorandum went out yesterday." He placed the pink sheet of paper before me as proof. "There aren't any hidden agendas on my end if that's what you're hinting at."

I read the memo, and it mentioned the possibility of outsiders—not students—as the culprits. My heart sank. I'd tried my best to keep Tim nearby at all times. There couldn't have been a way for him to leave the house, vandalize school property, and return. No way.

In his creaky leather seat, Grant adjusted his necktie and propped his elbows on the desk, arrogant, as if he'd already tried and convicted my kid as the perpetrator. This man was wrong.

I looked over at Tim. "Tim? You know anything about this?"

"I didn't do anything." My son ran his thumb over a tattoo of his initials on the fleshy part of his hand. "I haven't messed around on school property since that suspension."

"Do you know who vandalized this place?" I asked.

No response.

"Not responding isn't gonna cut it. You either know or you don't. What is it, Tim?"

Tim lowered his eyes to his grip on the armchair, and his brown cheeks shadowed. The silence between us shouted for what seemed like an eternity. I wanted an answer, but I couldn't force one out of him. This was the line that I, as a father, couldn't cross. It was a line where Tim would have to decide, on his own volition, to answer his father's question. I waited.

He didn't answer.

Grant leaned back in the chair, his pot belly spilling over his belt. "The interior gym has graffiti. There are gang symbols all over the outside walls. This is serious. Our school is not a gang zone." He aimed his words at Tim and fired straight at him. "You understand?"

"I ain't in no gang," Tim said.

The *Z* shaved into his hair and the *Z* tattoo on his neck told another story. I'd questioned him about it before, and he'd said nothing. Where'd he get that stupid *Z* from? Screw the graffiti on the walls. If Tim was messing around with gangs, his life could be at stake. "Tim, do you know anyone involved in gangs?"

"I said no." Tim's eyes hardened. "You believing this mess that whitey's talking?"

Oh, lord. Every time I tried to get some truth out of him, he'd either get defensive and not answer or pull up the race card. "This isn't a race thing, Tim. It's a safety thing."

"No, it ain't." Tim stood, and the chair he sat on squeaked behind him. "I don't see any other White kids around here in this office being questioned about graffiti. Only me. Well, I ain't did nothing, and I don't know who did."

"You sure you don't know?" Grant narrowed his eyes at Tim, eyes which were slit like razors, cutting and sharp. I hated how Grant carried this sense of superiority over my son like he should go unchallenged.

"The Eighth Street Kings have been behind a lot of petty crimes in this area: petty robberies, counterfeiting cash," Grant continued, and his brow creased. "They are also suspects in the fire at the community center."

My ears pricked. This gang was implicated in the fire that burned my Hannah? They harmed my wife? That was inexcusable. Inexcusable and criminal. "Whoa. Whoa. Whoa. What are the names of the kids in this gang?"

Grant looked at Tim. "Ask your son. He's friends with them."

A fire arose from inside, a rational anger that moved from my stomach to my chest. "Mr. Grant. You just said you weren't focused on my son with regards to the school vandalism, but now you are focusing on him."

"Not focusing." Grant gave a smile that didn't reach his eyes. "Stating the facts. He knows them. He hung out with them on school grounds."

My heart went into overdrive. Last thing Tim needed was to be associated with a bunch of gang members.

"Tim, you've seen Hannah's condition. You know her. If you have any information on that fire, you have to report it."

"I told you already," Tim said. "I don't know nothing. I stopped hanging with them."

My mouth gaped. "You stopped hanging with them. That means you were hanging with them before. No one's accusing you, son. But you have to do the right thing. Gang members won't have your back if you get in trouble. Why are you protecting them?"

"Why are you blaming me?" Tim shot back.

I was about to reply with a string of curses and questions and anger, but reason took hold and I muscled the impulse down.

"Look," Grant said. "I don't know anything about that fire. The school is my responsibility. Like your father said, don't try to protect your friends. They won't help you."

"I'm tired of this mess!" Tim glanced at Grant's devil-may-care face. "You're already accusing them. You're even accusing me."

I sensed the pain in my son's voice. Pain mixed with anger mixed with confusion mixed with a simmering rage.

"No one's accusing you. No one," I said quietly, but I gave Grant the side-eye.

"No one's accusing you, yet," Grant added. "Law enforcement will be investigating the graffiti incident. They'll be questioning students too. They want to speak to you, Tim. You should visit the police station, preferably by the end of the month, and tell them your side of the story."

My alarms went up. Visit the police station? Tell them Tim's side of the story?

"That's too much. I have to… I have to."

Grant's eyes flickered. "You have to do what, Mr. Hart?"

My insides seized. What should I do? What should I do?

What should I do? I obviously wasn't winning at showing this man Tim's improvement. I was failing. Failing miserably.

I'd have to figure out something. I couldn't simply let Tim meet with law enforcement unprepared. One thing I'd definitely have to do—contact a lawyer for Tim. Somebody better suited than George Allen, that joker straight out of law school. Perhaps I could squeeze in a phone call to another lawyer's office before I took Hannah dress shopping tomorrow. No way was I gonna allow his chances of graduating high school and making a better life for himself get ruined. Not on my watch.

CHAPTER 24

HANNAH

*I*t wasn't until two o'clock that I realized my mind had been roaming all day. I was thinking about Jake saying it was okay if things didn't work out with our marriage. I was cool with what he'd said and all, but another part of me wasn't cool with what he'd said 'cuz I was starting to like Jake, love him, again.

I just admitted it to myself. I loved the dude. Sigh. And where was Jake anyway? He said he was gonna be here at one o'clock to take me dress shopping, and he wasn't even here.

I scooted out from my desk, grabbed my purse, and headed to the front door, peeking outside the window. Jake's white GMC truck was parallel parked in front of my house, so I stepped outside and stomped down my red brick steps. He was busy swiping his thumb across his phone while Tim sat in the back seat. Both looked pissed. Seconds later, he tossed the phone in the empty seat next to him.

I headed over and tapped Jake's window, and he rolled down his window.

"Hey, y'all." I kept my tone light, but for some reason, I felt as if I was stepping into a quiet minefield. "Ready to go to the mall?"

Jake averted his gaze. "Uh-huh. Hop in."

I did, slamming the door behind me. The silence in the car suffocated me. Something was definitely up. "What's wrong?"

Tim huffed and drummed his fingers against the door handle. "Ain't nothing."

"It is something, Tim. Let's not deny the facts." Hand beneath his head, Jake exhaled and leaned against the driver side door.

This wasn't good. In my mind, I saw Jake back in the early years of our marriage when he was working his tail off to secure some general contracting work for his business. No one wanted to deal with Jake for various reasons, but deep inside, he knew. They didn't want to work with him because he was a Black man who owned a business. If he had been a worker bee, everything would've been okay. They saw him as a threat.

I hope Jake didn't bump up against some racist mess in his business again. That would suck.

When Jake relayed to me that Tim was accused of vandalizing school property, my jaw dropped. "That ain't no fair. I mean, you've been improving and getting better. Studying hard."

"I know he is. I got in contact with a new lawyer to be present during questioning. But he's not available so we're stuck with the same joker that John had recommended. On top of all this, this principal said… " Jake's voice trailed off and he bit his bottom lip as if he'd said too much.

"What?" I asked. "What else'd he say?"

"Nothing," Tim said quickly. "Just the graffiti stuff."

"The principal was—"

"Just. Some. Graffiti. Stuff." Tim slanted his eyes at the back of Jake's head. "I ain't talking 'bout no mess I ain't got nothing to do with."

Jake wrapped his fingers around the steering wheel and let out one of those boy-you-got-on-my-last-nerve exhales.

My throat tightened, and I tugged on the red ribbon tied around my loose ponytail. This was weird as all get out. Being around these two made me feel like I was in a jacked-up episode of the Twilight Zone or something. "Look. If y'all two need to focus on working this out, you don't have to take me shopping today. It's okay."

"Nah. I promised I was taking you and so I'm taking you." Jake turned on the ignition and proceeded to drive down my street.

The ride to the mall took longer than an eternity, and the stifling quiet in the car had me feeling all cray-cray. I was like the kid caught between her parents when they were in the middle of a fight.

Part of me wanted to tell Tim not to worry about the graffiti stuff, but that wasn't gonna work none 'cuz he was obviously worried. Know what? I wasn't worrying about it, at least not for now. Today was my day to try on a dress that would show some skin, and I needed to get my head mentally ready for that one. Couldn't have my brain stuck in two places. Not good at all.

Jake exited off Route One and turned into the lot at Quakerbridge Mall. Tim continued to sit quietly and text on the phone. After Jake parked, we headed inside.

"The dress shop is over there." I pointed right, and Jake followed me while Tim veered left. That made me stop. "You're not coming along with us, Tim?"

"Nah. I'll grab a pizza or something." Tim shoved his hands in his pockets, and a shaft of light from the sunroof shone on his high-top fade. "Y'all probably need y'alls time alone anyways."

"Tim, you don't have to make yourself the third wheel. We want you to be with us." Jake gave his son a smile. "No matter that mess at school, I don't want you isolating yourself."

"I'm a-ight."

"Don't wander too far," Jake added. "I'll call you when we're finished."

Tim left without a second glance.

They had the oddest father-son relationship. First, Jake and Tim were super-tense in the car and then Jake wanted Tim to hang with us while I went dress shopping.

"You set to go the store?" Jake asked me.

"With the way you two are acting, this whole trip feels like an exercise in futility."

"It isn't. It's an exercise in me trying to make things work with you and Tim." Jake crossed his arms. "I know we won't have a smooth path to reconciliation, but I'm trying my best to get there."

I scrunched my mouth. Yeah, he was trying. I had to credit Jake for that.

∽

*W*e arrived at the dress shop, and I rustled through the clothes on the rack. The weight of Jake's gaze was on me the entire time, and it made me feel all self-conscious. "Whatcha looking at?"

"You," he said without hesitation.

Now my stomach did a triple back flip. "I know you're looking at me. Question is, why are you looking at me all weird like that?"

"'Cuz I think you're hawt." He winked.

I laughed and laughed and laughed. "I'm supposed to be picking out dresses here."

"Go on ahead." Jake hung back. "I'm not stopping you."

I shuffled through the dresses on the rack, hoping to find something that would look natural against my dimpled skin.

"Can I help you find something, ma'am?"

I turned in the direction of the friendly voice. A petite brunette stood next to me and she smiled.

"Sure can. I'm looking for a sundress. Size six."

"We have a pretty nice selection." The sales lady searched through the same racks that I had searched through. Nothing. Then she went to the dress displays on the back wall and pulled out a couple of dresses. "Here you go. These should fit you perfectly."

I held up a sleeveless butter-colored dress to my chin and looked at myself in the mirror. "They look a little… revealing. Shows too much skin, don't you think?" I asked the sales lady.

"A little skin never hurt anyone." Her tone was casual and calm.

I thought of the photo shoot with Miguel, how comfortable I'd felt before Jacinta had shown up. "You're right. Nothing wrong with showing a little skin. I'll try them all on."

"Go for it." She smiled.

Once in the dressing room, mirrors surrounded me on all sides. I took a deep breath. I'd done this before, I could do it again. No more shame.

There was a light knock at the door. "It's Jake. You okay?"

"Uh-huh." I pulled the dress over my head and studied myself in the mirror.

"I'll be out here waiting for you. Can't wait to see what you look like," he added.

He was being all charming and stuff too. Perhaps he was

making up for the tension between him and Tim. After I put on the first dress, I studied myself in the mirror. Not bad. Skin was healing up nicely too, and if I didn't love my skin, who would?

No way would I shy away from my appearance again. No way would I let some stupid comparison to a girl like Jacinta send me in a tizzy. Not happening. Why should I let some young upstart have so much control over me?

"What are you doing in there?" Jake called. "Trying to figure out the meaning of life?"

"I told you I'm getting dressed." I tugged on the hem of the dress and adjusted the crooked shoulder strap. Much better.

"Then let me see your outfit."

Screw it. I'll show off the dress. I stepped out onto the storeroom floor, and the air conditioning rumbled to life and blew through the overhead vents, tickling my skin.

Jake's eyes spoke hunger, ravenous and deep like he wanted to… to… My pulse jolted, and I smiled.

"My, my, my. You're a beauty." He took two steps toward me, and a shiver surged up my arm. I rested my hands on my hips and tried for a casual stance but that wasn't working out too well. This guy had the ability to make me feel like I was Cinderella—before and after midnight.

"You look amaze-balls," the sales associate said.

All righty. The sales lady was ruining the moment. "Amaze-balls could work too." I straightened my posture and twirled. The flow-y part of my dress swished and swayed. Part of me felt like singing "I Feel Pretty" from West Side Story. I hummed the tune, but I wasn't the singing type.

Jake growled and I stopped twirling.

"Did you just growl at me?"

"Me?" He held up his palms and shook his head. "No way. Where'd you get that idea?"

"Um… by that lion-like noise that emitted from your mouth." I smiled.

The sales associate nodded. "Yep. He definitely growled, girl. That's 'cause you look hawt." Her mouth formed an exaggerated "o" when she said "hawt." I giggled.

"Thanks, y'all."

As I was about to go to the dressing room, Tim returned from wherever he wandered to. When he saw me, his face stilled, and his eyebrow did this twitchy thing.

"You okay?" I asked.

"Nice dress," he replied. Something in his voice sounded oddly hollow. I tried picking it out, naming and identifying the sound, but I couldn't.

"My mom has a lot of marks on her arms too."

Not burn marks, I was sure.

"Those look like druggie arms," Tim added.

Jake's face hardened. "What's wrong with you, Tim?" His voice was tight, controlled.

"I was just saying." He shrugged.

"'Just saying?' You don't have to say everything that's on your mind, okay?" Jake redirected his attention to me. "You still want the dress?"

Was he serious? Tim just compared me to a drug addict, and Jake wanted to know if I was interested in getting this dress? A drug addict, y'all. Like all those compliments and gawking from Jake and the sales lady were enough to erase the boy's words from my memory. I smushed my lips together because this was a lip-smushy moment.

I changed into my street clothes, and Jake paid for the dress anyway. Not sure if I wanted to wear the thing after Tim's comment. I mean, anyone could mistake me for a drug addict. Ugh! I surely wasn't going to explain the scars. The drug addict comparison was embarrassing enough.

No, no, no. This was a new Hannah Hart. The new Hannah Hart empathized with Tim's situation, both with his mother and now with the school. She (the new Hannah Hart, that is) would want to ensure that Tim was on the road to wholeness. The new Hannah Hart would want Tim and Jake to move into her house.

Huh?

The new Hannah Hart would want Tim and Jake to move into her house.

What in the Hades? Did my brain actually produce that corny thought?

Yes, it did.

Sheesh. The notion sounded wonderfully fluffy, but the tension in the car had been thicker than three stacked mattresses. No way could we live under the same roof. I knew that when Jake and I were in counseling and I confronted him about visiting Melinda in rehab without giving me a heads-up.

When Jake finally returned to my house, I was glad to get out of the vehicle and away from them. I needed to be alone so I could process the druggie comparison—and maybe process the idea of us all living together. The kid was hurting, and we had connected during the tutoring sessions but living together was something else entirely. Besides, living with Jake again, that was moving in an entirely new direction.

It would mean my original intentions to separate would be null and void. Was I ready to go all in with Jake? I didn't know.

Jake followed me out of the car and up the walk, his Brut aftershave trailing my every step, clinging to the humidity and settling on my skin—my druggie-esque skin. The sound of cicadas echoed and skipped along with my trippy heartbeat.

"Guess I'll see you later," he said. "I enjoyed shopping with you today."

I turned and grabbed the metal railing on my front porch, trying to reclaim my cool. "I enjoyed shopping too… until Tim wigged out on me."

His face flickered. "Don't mind him. He's going through a lot."

"Yes, I know. You explained. And he explained to me during tutoring. His mom has a lot of issues." My voice was tight and terse.

Jake shifted his weight from side to side, shoved his hands in his pockets as if hesitant. We stared at each other like a pair of dumb cows.

"Yes, thank you for helping him with school work despite his odd comments at times." Jake glanced down. "Tim and I have a lot to prepare for in the days ahead. I hope I can do right by him during all this school stuff."

His vulnerability shone through. "You will."

Jake didn't look convinced. Thoughts of my original intentions to separate resurfaced, thoughts that didn't hold as much power anymore. He needed my support as he traversed this tricky area as a father, and I needed… I needed him. The thought was scary and freeing at the same time. I needed a new direction, one that included Jake —and Tim.

Should I say as much? Jake had offered earlier, so it wasn't like I was doing something completely unexpected.

"You know. I've been thinking about that offer you had made when we were in our first marriage counseling session. The one about moving in. It would be a good idea."

Jake stared at me, eyes wide. "Really?"

"Yes. I've gotten to know him better, and he's not such a bad kid. I can forgive his remark at the store." I cracked my knuckles as if that would delay what I was about to say. "He must have a lot of bad memories pent up inside his head. Memories that come out at the oddest times."

Jake said nothing for the longest. When he spoke, his voice sounded the way it had when he'd first asked me on a date all those years ago. "I'd love that, but I'd need to ask Tim."

"You changed your mind about the idea?"

"No. No." He wrapped his hands around the staircase and leaned toward me, speaking in confidential tones. "I'd love to move in with you. I just want to ensure that Tim is comfortable with the idea. So, we'll see."

How did this conversation get turned around so I sounded like the needy one? He's the one who'd offered first. "If you changed your mind, that's fine too."

"I didn't change my mind." He stuck his thumb in his belt loop, moving slowly as if he'd aged since I brought up the idea. "I'll need to leave the bulk of the decision to Tim. If he says no, then I'll stay put."

If he says no, then I'll stay put? What the what?! Jake was putting Tim and Melinda's needs above my own again, and I was his wife! "Forget it, Jake. I don't need any courtesy moves. If you don't want to move in, don't."

"I'm not saying that."

"Then what are you saying?" I yelled again. I couldn't help it this time. This dude was irking me.

"I'll ask him." His tone lowered two notches, all calm and reasoned. Jake stepped close enough for me to see the flecks of light in his eyes. "Promise."

I didn't answer because I didn't want to get my hopes up.

As Jake headed to his truck, I imagined a hundred reasons why Tim would say no to the notion. Those hundreds turned into thousands and those thousands turned into ten thousands. I hated that Tim had all the power in this thing right now. The decision was up to him. Gah!

I tried my darnedest to flick the concern aside. It was late, the heat was rising, and my feet were moaning from walking around all day.

But then an image of Tim's face at the clothing store returned, along with his words about my "marks." The recollection stung like a slap, and the slap hurt.

Would living with Tim include him probing into the awkward areas of my life? I hoped not.

CHAPTER 25

"Whatcha watching?" I sat next to Tim on the leather sectional and gave him a grin befitting a horse, way too wide and awkward.

The Lakers versus Pistons game lit up the television screen.

"Nothing."

Nothing. Wasn't gonna let the one-word-answer teenager ruffle me. I needed to hear his thoughts on moving in with Hannah and convince him if he refused the idea. I needed to convince him, because I wanted us to move in with Hannah too. I glanced out the window and at the sky, surprised to see it an endless blue. Somehow a dull gray seemed more appropriate. *Don't be so negative, Jake. You haven't even asked him.*

When Hannah'd mentioned the possibility, I was beyond happy. All this time, I'd wanted the three of us to live under the same roof, and the possibility was now strong. I didn't want to miss my chances.

"Nice outside. Wanna go shoot some hoops?"

He turned up the volume on the television. "Ain't in the mood for shooting hoops."

"I hope seeing the principal and then Hannah didn't get you shook." I flopped my feet up on the beat-up coffee table.

"Ain't that. Just watching the game, man."

Kobe dunked the ball, a three-pointer. Things were picking up for the team. They'd been on a losing streak. Felt like I was still on my losing streak. Everything about Tim was sealed shut—his posture, his conversation, his mannerisms. "I spoke to the lawyer, the one with us at the hearing. He'll be with us at the police questioning."

"For what? Dude had no pull at all. If you hadn't been there, them White folks would've strung me up a pole. You was the one who knew how to talk to 'em."

Tim had a point.

"I've had my share of court cases in my thirty-something years on this earth."

He turned away from the TV and toward me. "You have?"

"Yeah. Petty stuff. Speeding. Broken taillight. Judges always charged me crazy-ass fines though, but that was better than jail time. One judge told me I could pay the two-thousand-dollar fine or spend a couple nights in jail."

"Really?" Tim asked.

"Really. Black man can't catch a break in this country."

"I feel you."

"That's why you gotta do your best when they question you. Don't give them any reason to think you're involved in that gang mess."

Tim straightened on the couch, and with his chin set, flipped the channel.

"I thought you liked the Lakers," I said.

"I do."

"Then why change channels?"

"Wanted to watch something else," he said.

The opening credits to *Days of Our Lives* rolled on the screen. "You into soap operas?"

"No."

"Then why—"

"Why you gotta ask me all these questions?" Tim's tone wiggled between aggrieved and outraged.

Tim was slipping from my grasp and so I gathered myself quickly. My red Dixie cup crinkled in my grip. I put the cola away and cleared my throat. "All right, I'll cut the small talk. Hannah wanted to see if you'd be interested in moving in. I had mentioned it to her a few weeks ago because I think it'd be a great idea. Your mother isn't coming out of rehab any time soon, and you and Hannah were getting along in tutoring so I—"

"No."

His response surprised me. I'd figure since they'd had a few successful tutoring sessions, they were getting close. "No?"

"No. Bad idea." Tim coughed, sounded like one of those fake coughs people make when they were trying to pretend like they were sick, but they weren't. "Ain't ready. And don't be so quick to write Mama off as a lost cause. She could get better faster than any of y'all think."

My fists clenched reflexively while a muscle leaped in my jaw. Snippets of my conversation with Melinda at rehab sprung to mind. The expression on her face when I told her there would never be more between us weighed on me still, and my shoulders slumped. "I wasn't writing her off."

"I have faith in Mama even if you don't."

Melinda's words pressed into my conscience. No matter the falling out between us, I wanted her well. I wanted her to find her way.

"I never said I didn't have fa—"

"Anyways. My answer's no."

"I thought you and Hannah were getting along."

Tim went still for a moment before raising his head.

"Ain't gonna work." Sorrow stretched his words, his eyes. Why all the pain?

I nodded as if receiving an unspoken message through Morse code, a message I didn't want to decipher for fear it would be a message I didn't want to hear. I really wouldn't be able to take hearing more negative news from or about my son. The school stuff was bad enough.

"This have to do with what happened at the mall the other day? When you asked her about the marks on her arms?"

After tossing the remote on the coffee table, the remote that dinged the heel of my loafer, Tim produced a deep frown, not the caricature kind, the really hurt kind. Dejection tugged at the edges of his eyes and settled into his stony cheeks. "Hannah's cool as a tutor, but I don't think we should all be living under the same roof."

"I thought because she's cool as a tutor it'd be okay. Boy, what's going on?"

A down-to-business look tightened Tim's face, an ounce of regret leaked through. Tim must've been thinking about how he didn't want to jeopardize his relationship with his mother. Moving in with Hannah could possibly do so—but nothing was certain. He glanced at the television screen. "Don't want to make any sudden moves after talking to that principal."

"Aw, come on man. Don't let Grant's accusations about the community center get you all down and color your decision on whether we should live with Hannah. Y'all were doing well." When I reached over to nudge him, the expression on his face stopped me. "Those accusations got you, huh?"

"They do... because they're true."

My chest hollowed, emptiness echoing my fear and disbelief. The sound tapped against my ears. "Excuse me?"

The vein in his slender, brown neck pulsed, the movement traveling up his temple and making his expression tight. "They're true. I set fire to the community center. I snuck up there, locked the exercise room so the fire wouldn't spread, and started the fire. The locked door ain't stopped it from spreading though. It was a gang initiation thing." He stood and began to rock, his body language underlining his guilt.

I tried ignoring the chill that licked the back of my neck, but I couldn't. I fisted my hands. "You tried to kill Hannah? Kill her?"

"No. No. I didn't know she was in there. It was only after you'd told me she was in the fire that I figured it out." More pacing. This time Tim weaved between the coffee table and the lamp stand as if somehow he could pace away all that he'd done.

"Whatever." I stood in front of him, stopping him in his tracks. "You knew people were in there. They have hundreds of members. What were you thinking?"

"I was only setting fire to the exercise room, nothing else. I didn't see no one in there." Tim's voice took on this frail quality, but there wasn't anything frail about what he'd done.

"People were seriously injured from that fire. Forget the White man trying to hold you down. You're doing a good job of that yourself. The White man's simply going to come in and give you the worst sentence. You ain't getting off on this one."

The realization of what I'd said hit and a tremor hit my fingers. What was the worst sentence? Life in prison? The death sentence? Either way, I'd lose my son... lose him before I had a chance to fully know him. "Why'd you have to do this? Why?" I pleaded.

"Mama was in rehab. I was stuck with you. I don't know.

They're my friends. The only ones who cared." He turned and glanced at the opened blinds.

"Cared? You'll see how much they care after you turn yourself in, Tim. You'll see." I popped the side of his head. "Have you lost your mind?"

"I was so scared when Principal Grant said those things. That's when I understood I'd done wrong."

"*That's* when you understood? You only understood when there was a chance you'd get caught? Come on, man. This isn't a game. This is real life. It ain't a joke. So, when you saw Hannah all messed up you didn't feel guilt, huh? When she tutored you in algebra, you didn't feel guilt? When she helped you get in contact with your mother, you didn't feel guilt? You held a sick satisfaction in knowing—"

"It ain't like that! I didn't know she was in there."

My resolve crumbled. All that I'd done to try and help Tim came to nothing. "You'll have to confess. You'll have to tell the truth."

"Then what?"

"I told you what'll happen. You'll get the worst sentence. No getting around that one." My stopwatch ticked by the seconds, and I gave my shoulders a weary rub. Leaning against the wall, I tried for a pseudo-casual stance—took too much effort. "You'll tell Hannah too."

"No."

"Oh, so you're going to chicken your way out of that one too?"

"I can't tell Hannah." There was a hitch in his voice now. "I'm too ashamed."

"Dammit, Tim. You weren't ashamed when you set fire to the place." I threw a sketchy glance across the living room and continued in a hushed tone. Felt as if the walls were listening, recording, judging—judging my failure as a father.

"You'll have to tell the investigator. No way you're getting out of that one."

He nodded once. "I will."

"As far as Hannah... I'll tell her."

Tim didn't answer.

The bile in my stomach spiraled, and my body went dead limp. My thoughts shifted to the time when I'd taken Tim to church with me for the first time. He was a baby. He had on a dapper suit with a blue bow tie and a blue hankie tucked into the front pocket. He was a fine little man with a bright future ahead. I was so proud.

If there is a God in heaven, please don't let the system take away my son. I buried my face in my hands, knowing I'd lost Tim. I was going to lose Hannah too.

Why? I tightened my arms around my stomach and willed the image of my baby boy away. "I can't deal with this. I can't." I stumbled out of the room and rushed to the phone to call for... for what? There was no one I could call. No one who could help.

I couldn't restore Tim's past or his future. And no one else would.

CHAPTER 26

HANNAH

"*Y*ou talk to Tim about the move?" I chopped the bell pepper into tiny little bits at my kitchen counter, eager to settle the details of their move. After he'd left the other day, I started getting comfortable with the prospect of the three of us living together. A peace had settled in my heart when I thought of all the ways I'd be able to be a good influence in Tim's life. I'd really wanted a better life for myself in all areas.

"Yes, I spoke to Tim about the move." Jake produced a tight smile and shrugged.

"I figured Tim can take the guest room. I rarely have guests so if we ever do, then he can crash on the couch or something. What do you think?"

"Good."

I took the diced peppers and tossed them in a skillet with my egg whites. Cheese and veggie omelets were my favorite, easy to make and healthy. "When do you think the two of you will be able to move in?"

Jake sat on the barstool next to the breakfast table, his expression bent.

"What's up? Talk to me." I jiggled the skillet a tad to even out the layer of veggies.

"Um, Hannah. We need to discuss—"

"That's what we're doing. You don't think Tim should take the guest room? The only other room is my office and well, that's stuffed. I don't want to switch my furniture around."

"Tim doesn't want to move."

I stopped all my skillet jiggling. Stumped. Despite that hiccup at the mall the other day, I thought we were getting along. "Why not?"

Jake uncurled the edges of a magazine near his hands and studied the front cover which, I assumed, was an avoidance tactic. My thoughts cycled back to my last conversation with Jake about this. He was hesitant even then.

"Long story." Jake lowered his voice and ran his hand over the dark shadow of his two o'clock stubble. "Remember I told you of his behavioral problems?"

"Yeeesss." My voice was doll-like and shrunken, scared.

"Tim said he set fire to the community center."

The words shot right through me, swift, vicious bullets that riddled me in pieces. I raked my mind for a response, but it was lost somewhere between shock and disbelief. "Tim tried to kill me?"

"He said he didn't know you were inside." Jake looked away.

Didn't know I was inside? Was that true? Or was this kid vicious enough to knowingly try to kill me and then have me help him factor algebra equations when he'd failed? I'd let a dangerous kid in my house. Forget the omelet, my mind was a scrambled egg. Who was I kidding? Tim was his mother's child, and his mother didn't like me too much. No telling what kind of lies she'd spread about me to her son. "I don't believe that. You think I was born yesterday? You think I'm an idiot?"

"No."

"So you believe Tim's garbage?" My voice shrilled and would've cracked my wine glasses had they not been hidden behind my cupboards.

"Not quite."

Hurt. A gnawing sense of hurt seeped past my skin and touched my bones, marrow-deep. How weak of a response from Jake. *Not quite.* The man couldn't even give me a straight yes or no answer. He was always protecting his bastard son. Who'd he think I was, some stupid woman he could cheat on, lie to, and then dump more garbage into my life?

Jake was intent on ruining my life. Bad enough he'd had a kid with another woman. Now that child wanted me dead. I should've never, ever, *ever* accepted his offer about moving in.

"What does 'not quite' mean, Jake?" I squinted as though I was missing prescription glasses, too blinded by Jake's dumbass charm to see this one coming.

No answer.

White hot rage filled me. "What does 'not quite' mean?!" I screamed. "Tell me now! Stop lying to me. Stop ruining my life. Stop!"

Jake took two steps back as if trying to duck for cover, but I wasn't letting him off the hook. "You knew what Tim had done all along, didn't you? I can't believe I've been such a fool. I should've never entertained you or any of your stupid ideas. I should've stopped you when you came to pick me up from the hospital."

"Don't say that, Hannah." His eyes flashed pain, but I didn't care. I wanted him to live with this pain I'd been holding. I wanted him to carry this pain for the rest of his life.

"I'll say it, and I'll say it again. I should've stopped you when you came to pick me up from the hospital. Stupid me for even thinking we could've worked things out. Perhaps that miscarriage and infertility was a sign from the beginning."

"Miscarriage?" he asked, his voice quiet.

The word had slipped from my mouth. Why'd I mention the miscarriage? "Nothing."

"What miscarriage?" His tone hardened.

"It was before us. I mean, in college. When we were dating." I stopped. "Never mind."

"No." Jake stepped closer to me. "Not never mind. What happened, Hannah? You cheated on me in college, and you have the nerve to stay mad at me for—"

"I was raped!" The words pulsed through my blood, made me sick. "I didn't cheat like you. I was raped. Raped. Raped. Raped!"

He stood there, quiet. I stood there, woozy. I just vomited years of buried memories, and it spilled on the ground, stank up the space between us.

"Who?" Jake's voice simmered rage. "Who did this to you?"

"A math professor. That's why I left school." I looked away, still ashamed, still hurt. My body still held the pain after all these years, and it loomed larger now in Jake's presence.

"I'm so sorry, I—"

"Cut it, Jake. Just cut it." My breathing turned heavy and belabored. "That's the past, and what you think of what happened to me in college doesn't matter anymore. What matters is today. That kid of yours is the real reason I'm not modeling. It doesn't have anything to do with Greta or Jacinta. Or even me. That hoodlum kid lit the match, and you knew it all this time. Get out of my life. How sick of a man can you be?" I shoved past him and walked quickly to the entrance, ready to get Jake the Jerk out of here. I flung open the door. "Get out!"

"Don't do this, Hannah. Don't kick me out of your life." His voice turned quiet. "We've come so far, you and me. I swear by everything in me I didn't know what Tim had done. Believe me. Please believe me. And the rape... the rape. Hannah, I'm—"

"That's your son. Not mine. There's not a vindictive bone in my body, but there's a whole lot of vindictiveness in yours." There was a ton of steel in my voice now, and Jake backed up two steps. "I don't want to see you or your son again. You hear me?"

He walked past me and stood in the tiny space between the doorjamb and the coat rack. "I'm sorry. I didn't know! I'm here telling you this because I just found out. I don't know what to do. I don't want to lose you. I don't want to lose my son."

My eyes stung and my vision grew blurry. "Whatever. I don't care about what you lose. I've lost everything. Everything! I almost lost my life because of your son. Stupid me for thinking we could've worked out our marriage. All those reasons you'd given me for visiting Melinda were lies. Lies!"

"No, they weren't, Hannah. The reason why—"

"I don't care about your reasons, Jake. Get out of here."

He left, posture slumped, face downcast, eyes dulled with dejection, but I didn't care. My soul unraveled. The walls stretched and swayed, and all the blood drained from my head and pooled at the soles of my feet. The betrayal seeped deeper and deeper until it choked and stifled my breath. Hot tears trickled down my cheeks.

That night we'd made love bubbled to the surface. That night I'd decided it was safe to be with Jake again and mend our marriage. That night I'd decided to trust.

Safe. Mend. Trust. All stupid, stupid words. Words that led me to feeling unsafe, broken, and consumed with distrust. If I'd never made that decision to give my heart and body to Jake that night, I wouldn't feel ripped apart and shredded to pieces at this moment.

"Never again will I give my heart to anyone," I said to the empty space. "Never again."

I slid against the wall and rested my face in my hands, crushed.

CHAPTER 27

JAKE

I had to stand with Tim.

He didn't have anyone else, and Hannah wasn't going to stand in Tim's corner. She said herself she didn't want to have Tim or me in her life ever again, and I needed to do all I could to stand by my son during this time. I couldn't lose him. Not like I'd lost Hannah.

Hannah, sweet Hannah. When she'd told me of the rape, everything came together in an all-too-awful way. I understood why she was so intent on having a child. I understood why Tim had been a source of pain. I understood her snap decision to leave college.

Despite it all, she'd somehow found room in her heart for Tim as they went through tutoring. She must've felt so betrayed. The finality of our last conversation settled in me like a dead weight.

The pain in Hannah's eyes didn't leave me as I set foot in the police station. I surveyed the space filled with officers and administrative staff, hardworking people. People who cared about the community. People who cared about their children's safety as much as I cared about Tim. People who, like Hannah, had been harmed by Tim's actions. My stomach knotted. I'd let her down. My inability to be a good father to Tim ended up hurting Hannah in the end. Tim would have to confess the truth to the investigator, but right now, the truth was Hannah was hurting. I'd failed her, and I couldn't see a way to winning her allegiance or love back this time.

I couldn't dwell on that loss. If I did, I'd get angry at Tim, which would make me unable to advocate for him before the police officers. I refocused on the four officers, our lawyer, and a middle-aged woman, who sat in a neat row across from Tim and me at the rectangular conference table.

Officer Wasser, the senior police officer, rested his spectacles atop his silver hair and gave Tim and me an eagle-eyed stare. "First off, I want to let you know this conversation will be recorded, and I will state your Miranda rights." He pressed a red button on a digital recorder.

As the officer read Tim his rights, each word nicked at my heart. This wasn't how my son's life was supposed to go. Well, society said this was how my son's life was supposed to go, but not me, his father. I'd had hope. Now hope was getting snuffed out.

"Can you tell us about the vandalism at the school, Tim?" the officer asked.

"Okay." Tim's voice sounded scratchy. He placed his index finger next to the first of ten bullet points he'd typed out the night before. We'd practiced his confession late into the night. How he'd always felt lost growing up, especially when his mother turned to drugs. How he'd befriended some kids in the neighborhood afterward. As time passed, they invited him to be in a gang, and he got jumped into the gang. Shortly thereafter, they wanted him to set fire to the community center.

But Tim didn't want to hurt anyone, and so he started a small fire in the exercise room. He'd spilled too much kerosene and the fire spread quickly. Tim got scared and ran off.

He read from the card verbatim, each word driving me deeper into a pit. I saw his future getting bleaker and bleaker. These officers will have no sympathy for Tim.

"And that's my confession." Tim set the card down. "Does anyone have any questions?"

One officer in the crowd scribbled furiously on his yellow legal pad. Another turned the volume up on the voice recorder.

Guess we were in for a long meeting.

"You're confessing guilt in the arson of the community center?" Officer Wasser placed his steno notebook scribbled with notes in front of Tim. "And you're saying it's gang-related. That correct?"

"Yes, sir."

My heart pounded hard and slow, and I was pulled in two different directions—one, proud of Tim for telling the truth, and two, sorrow, deep sorrow.

"Those kids are riffraff and thugs. All of them." The middle-aged woman popped out of her seat, hands on hips, scowl on her face. "They're disruptive, disobedient, disturbing, and dangerous." She held up four fingers to emphasize her points. "They're nothing but trouble."

"Who are you?" I asked. My tone was mixed with accusation and anxiety.

"I'm Laura Roberts, the manager of the community center. My building has been shut down for months because of your son's crime. Many were injured."

I opened and closed my mouth twice before deciding what to say. Saying the truth was best. I'd run from the truth before when I was a kid trying to dodge my petty crimes. The running hurt. "Tim's done wrong, but he's been working hard to do better in school and improve his behavior."

"Nothing he can do to improve his behavior. He's an arsonist." Laura crossed her arms.

Her words pecked at my resolve as if I were standing beneath a stream of pellets—my skin was jelly, my muscles useless. Stand your ground. "I'm not justifying my son's actions. I'm simply saying that he's trying to right his wrongs. He didn't intentionally harm anyone. That's what he said in his statement… in case you missed that one."

"Okay, Ms. Roberts," the officer said. "I'm in control of the questioning here. I know you're angry about the center, but we'll handle this."

I took a deep breath and strengthened my knees under the weight of Laura's accusations. Those were recorded on tape, and they'd probably paint an even more guilty picture of Tim.

Officer Wasser wiped his face with a dirt-smudged hankie. "Fact remains your son burned the community center down. Injured many too."

"I know. My wife was one of the injured. Second-degree burns."

The officer's face flickered. "You burned your mother?"

"She's not my mother."

I didn't know whether I heard bitterness or neutrality in Tim's tone. He'd sounded even-keeled.

Dead quiet settled over the room. Everyone must've been absorbing the untold story in what Tim had said. "Yes, yes, yes." I wanted to say. "It is what it is."

"One of them died according to the report," another officer said.

Died? When did someone die? I flipped through my notes for information on a death. Never heard of a death.

"That hasn't been confirmed," Officer Wasser said. "But three victims are still in critical condition."

This was bad. If any of those victims die, Tim could be

charged with murder. The possibility settled in and worried me even more.

I closed my eyes and Hannah's face appeared: the soft edges of her cheeks were hardened. She'd worked so hard toward recovery, only to feel betrayed by me in the end. Not sure which burns were worse, the physical or the emotional ones.

"Let's refocus." Officer Wasser tapped the table.

George Allen flipped open his memo pad. "Officer Wasser, I've discussed the options with Tim and Mr. Hart. We'd like to reach a plea bargain with you."

The officer steepled his fingers, and Laura shifted in her seat. I hoped they weren't dead-set on crucifying my son, but their silence indicated that was the case.

"What charges do you intend to pursue?" I asked.

Officer Wasser deferred to the prosecutor. "Jim."

Jim scratched his temple. "By his own admission, Tim went to the community center with the deliberate intent of setting fire to the building. Regardless of whether he intended to harm people, many incurred serious bodily injury. That's first-degree arson."

My heart flipped upward and punched the base of my throat. Dammit. Tim's life was ruined. I chewed my lower lip and then curled the edge of the page that listed my notes.

"If we went to trial," the prosecutor continued, "Tim would have to prove he didn't intend to do harm to people. Given the number of victims, that would be hard. Tim could get anywhere from two to thirty-five years in prison. If any of the victims in critical condition die, it could also be a voluntary manslaughter charge."

Oh no.

George nodded in agreement, his face solemn, and a cold sweat formed at my brow. I failed my son. I should've been in his life earlier. I should've been there for him through every-thing. I could only blame myself for this moment.

Officer Wasser leaned back and whispered to the prose-cutor, who was busy scribbling notes.

Then the prosecutor redirected his attention to us and said, "We can do a plea bargain. If Tim pleads guilty to second-degree arson and involuntary manslaughter, or if Tim pleads no contest to the same, he'll get a lower jail sentence. That's up to the judge at the sentencing hearing."

"It definitely won't be more than ten years," Officer Wasser said.

Ten years? That was long. Way too long.

George tapped his pen against the oak desk. "That's a good deal."

A good deal?! Whose side was this guy on? Mine or the cops? Getting stuck with George was going to be the end for my son. This lawyer wasn't going to fight as hard for my son, whether consciously or not. I could do a better job here.

My son would spend ten years of his life around felons. Yeah, he'd be in juvenile hall, but once he became a legal adult, they'd transfer him to prison. Who knew what treat-ment he'd get… and what kind of man he'd be when he was released? I knew what kind of man he'd become—a man crippled by the prison system.

"What if Tim gave names of gang members? Can we get the judge to make a lighter sentence or have Tim charged as a minor, not as an adult?"

"Pops!"

"I got this, son." I held out my hand, a gesture to silence him. "That's what you want, don't you? Knowing who the gang members are will enable you to stop them from influ-encing kids like Tim, could prevent the spread of similar incidents."

The prosecutor looked at Tim. "You'd be willing to give names?"

Tim looked down for a moment, and a conflicting set of emotions played across his features. "Yes."

"All right then," the prosecutor said, adjusting the glasses on the bridge of his nose. "If you give names, then you can get a five- to seven-year sentence and have you charged as a minor."

George seemed surprised by this change in events. "That's an even better deal."

Was he serious? That was not a better deal. Yes, it skimmed off a few years, but those would've been Tim's college years. The years where he'd become a free young man. Now he was going to be an incarcerated young man.

"Can you tell us names?" the prosecutor asked again.

Tim was silent as if considering the consequences. "All right. I can tell you names."

I checked to make sure the recording was still on. I was going to hold the prosecutor to his promise. Tim said five names, and the prosecutor and the police scribbled them down.

"Thank you," the prosecutor said. "This is much needed."

After looking at tentative dates for the sentencing hearing, I grabbed my notebook and headed to the exit, nodding goodbye to the officers, the prosecutor, and Laura. Once outside, Tim and I hooked a left toward the parking garage. "You've snitched on your gang friends. You'll have to watch your back."

"I know."

"You did good though, son. I'm proud of you. Very proud." The tightness in my voice could've strangled a cat. He would still do time. He'd still have a record. I still lost my son.

"Only would shave a few years off my sentence." Tim's

tone flat-lined and so did his expression, but I pretended not to notice. I only wanted to focus on the time I had left with him before he was sentenced to juvenile hall.

Seconds later, Laura waved us down, her face lit with fire. "Hey. Hey. Hey."

"Hoo-boy," I said. We stopped in the middle of the street. "What does she want?"

Seconds later, she stood before us. The coldness in her expression made me tense. The tension spread to the bridge of my nose and my cheekbones. I gulped. I'd known that kind of judgment. I'd known that kind of hate. I'd lived it every day when I attended prep school as a kid.

"Keep your kid off the streets," she said. "He's a danger and a disgrace."

"He won't be in the real world for much longer," I said, trying my hardest to maintain my cool. "No need for you to rub it in."

"And I'm glad for it. Not everyone deserves a second chance."

"Let's go, Tim. Don't need to hear this." I mustered my most non-threatening voice and kept walking. "Remember, son. You made some bad choices, but I'm here with you. I'll always be in your corner. You're not alone in this world."

But I was alone.

The thought hit hard and ricocheted through my body.

Hannah didn't want anything to do with me. Tim would be behind bars. Then what? I had my mother, but she lived far away.

This was my payment for my screwed-up choices. I had no one.

CHAPTER 28

*D*ays passed, but my hysterics didn't. I'd mastered the art of curling into a fetal position on the couch. I'd also mastered the art of being a weeping, sobbing mess. Today, Mama shuffled into the space, sat next to me, and wrapped me in a warm embrace.

"I'm so sorry, *anak*."

First time Mama didn't blame me for something Jake had done. It was nice, bittersweet, but nice.

"We have to get you moving forward though. You can't be stagnant forever. I need to see you progressing, not regressing. What do you want to do with your life now?"

Mama's sentiment flipped through my stomach, rattling all my resolve to live the crying-couch-potato life. I burst into sobs that shook my body and caused me to hiccup. "I… I… don't know… "

Mama bent and got nose to nose with me. Same black hair, same round face, same full lips set in a solemn line rather than a smile. And that line was aimed at me. "Be strong," she said with the finality of an Army sergeant.

I released another wrenching cry.

Mama hushed me and rocked me back and forth as if I were still a child. I sobbed for the lies, the deceit, the heartache. I tried voicing my next steps, but the words tumbled out in an uncontrollable fit of hysterics.

Mama pushed my hair off my face. "Your makeup is smeared. Your face is blotchy. Your eyes looked like banged-up marshmallows."

Getting lied to by Jake also made me self-conscious about my appearance again. My fingers flew to my face, and I made a beeline for the bathroom for a better look. Splotches, blotchy and angry, colored the skin around my eyes and spread to my temples, covering my face in a puddle of paint. "I look like a circus freak."

"I wouldn't go that far. Splotchy eyes won't make the cut among circus freak hopefuls. But you should clean up, *anak*."

Mama's correction was classic. Even her sarcasm was accurate.

I stepped out of the bathroom and flopped back onto the love seat. "Would you think I was weird if I drank a gallon of coffee?"

"Yes, I would. Four cups is my max before I put someone in the strange and unusual category." She went into my fridge and tossed me a bottle of water. "Drink water instead. It's healthier."

"Water won't help. I need caffeine."

"Water. Then breakfast. Then you're going to tell me your plans."

After some discussion about food choices, we settled on oatmeal, fruit, and a vegetable omelet. I mustered enough domestic talent to help with cracking and beating the eggs while Mama did the heavy cooking. Funny how this tragedy was bringing Mama and me together. Guess we were dysfunctional that way.

An hour later, we sat at the breakfast table like an abnormally unhappy family. After a few bites of food, I started feeling better.

"Maybe we should start our conversation from the beginning," I said, cutting my omelet into tiny little triangular pieces. "This time without all the references to how awful I look."

Mama rested her hands on the table, her posture relaxed and imperturbable. "I wasn't criticizing you. Simply saying you need a plan. When I divorced your father, I was paralyzed for months. Didn't know what to do with myself. How about that modeling? What came of it?"

I tried not to roll my eyes but failed. Instead, I bit into my omelet and recounted what happened at that stupid photo shoot, hiccuping every so often as the hiccupy, sad-depressing-traumatizing parts of the story came up.

"So, you let Jacinta stop you?"

"No. The experience made me slow down. That's all." My voice sounded trembly and tense. "I'll have to earn money on my own now, seeing that I'm definitely getting a divorce from Buttwipe. Liza had referred me to ten agencies, and one was interested. They left a message last week."

"Call them." Mama sipped her coffee, three giant gulps. "Get some work lined up."

Yeah, we were that abnormally sorta-happy family.

"Before, you were talking all this 'I need to be a wife and stay home and have babies.' Now you're talking modeling."

"What's your point?"

I heaved a long, loud sigh. "My point is I'm going to need some consistency of support. I can't have you get wishy-washy on me."

"Watch the attitude. I'm your mother." She pointed her fork at me. "And don't yell."

"I'm not yelling!" I yelled.

"Yeah, you are." She reached over and wiped something off my cheek. Annoying.

"See that?" Mama continued. "Spittle. You were yelling."

Why'd she have to be so frustrating and stuff? "I'll call the agency when I'm ready."

"Anak, you're about to be a divorced woman, and I wouldn't be surprised if Jake tried to pull the plug on financial support, given his son tried to set you on fire. Call them soon. Like yesterday."

Frustration fizzled through me. When I'd first wanted to separate from Jake, it was to gain independence. Now that I was actually separating from him, Mama was dictating how I should do so. A sistah couldn't get a break.

"When are you going to call?"

Ugh. "When I'm ready."

Mama inclined her head and managed to look empathetic. "Okay, when you're ready. But you know the mortgage is due on the first of every month, and there's health insurance to think about."

Okay, so she had a point. "I'll call now."

"Attagirl." She winked and sipped her coffee.

I got up from the table to call, convincing myself this was of my own volition—which it was—well, my own volition, the mortgage company, and Mama to be exact. I had to get up off the couch and get back to living one day. It was simply that the mortgage company and Mama were strong determining factors in changing my "one day" into "today."

I retrieved the cordless, the sticky note with the phone number stuck to the side of the refrigerator and started to dial Liza's agency—Apples and Oranges Models. I stopped dialing. What kind of name was Apples and Oranges Models? Sounded more cheesy than chic. I could picture it now. I'm at a go-see and the photographer's studying my comp card...

339

"Who's your rep?"

"Apples and Oranges Models."

Crickets.

Or worse. The photographer would take one look at my fried-up flesh, take another look at my no-name agency, and show me the door. I hung up the phone.

"Conversation was that quick?" Mama called from the breakfast table.

"No. I um… sort of hung up." I nibbled at the hangnail sitting on my pinky. Hangnails sucked. Better go to the Korean nail shop soon.

"Why'd you hang up?" she asked.

Mama was too nosy. "'Cuz."

"'Cuz what?"

Way too nosy. Tired of her badgering, I returned to my plate. "You want me to call Apples and Oranges Models? I can't go from being represented by Greta to being represented by Apples and Oranges. That name is so corny."

"You speak as if you have a choice. Greta rejected you, and Liza was kind enough to make agent referrals. If you want to stay in the rejection line, go ahead and stay there. It's your life. Otherwise, swallow your pride and get your career moving."

How'd Mama make me sound stupid? Guess that was what mamas did—stupidify their children. Was stupidify a word? It was now.

"All right, Mama, I'll call them this time." This time I actually dialed the number to Apples and Oranges (Apples and Oranges! My goodness.). Someone picked up on the first ring.

"Hi, I'm Hannah Hart, I received a mess—"

"That was me."

"You?"

"Yes, me. Renee Williams. I'm the agent who called you."

The only agent? As in the agent-phone answerer. Greta had a staff of front desk assistants.

"Swallow your pride, Hannah!" Mama's voice bounced in my direction, chastising and quick.

How'd Mama read my mind? That must've come with the parenting job description too. Not like I'd ever find out the answer for myself, seeing I was barren and all.

Barren—the word made it sound like my body carried a biblical judgment, a plague. Perhaps it was. That professor screwed me over. My ovaries malfunctioned and miscarried on the production line—similar to my career. I had to save something: ovaries or modeling. I chose modeling.

"You still there, Hannah?"

"Oh yes. Sorry. I was… thinking." About broken ovaries and shattered careers.

"Your pictures were wow. I did a double-take to see if they were really you. So different. And so brave."

"Brave?"

"Takes a lot of kahunas to allow yourself to be probed by a camera lens, exposing your visible scars."

Visible scars. Wonder if Renee said "visible" on purpose as if she'd already known of the psycho-babble baggage that went along with my newfound "look."

"You've pushed the boundaries of beauty. This is a game changer. In a good way. Yeah, this definitely makes a statement to the modeling world, and it makes a statement about you."

I caught a case of the misty-eyedness. Why'd I get all emotional about my self-image and my character?

"Can you stop by tomorrow at three?"

"Sure." I dabbed at the dumb tear which smeared my already-smeared foundation.

"Great! I'm so thrilled to have a chance to meet you in person. Oh, and don't wear makeup."

I stopped dabbing. "Don't wear makeup?"

"I'd like to see your natural beauty."

My naturally crispy beauty. "Models wear makeup." I jutted my face closer to the kitchen window, evaluating my skin. The pockmarks were settling in and making their home on my face.

"I know. I like to see my models in real life. No hiding behind masks." I heard some tapping on the other end of the phone. "It's a prerequisite for signing with the agency."

Or stay in the rejection line. "Oooh kay. No makeup tomorrow."

"Good. Bring any other pictures of how you currently look. I love the ones where you look like a phoenix, and so I'd like to see more. Digital photos on your phone are fine. Do you have any posted on social media?"

Pictures of the scarred me on social media? "No. I ain't ready."

"Get ready. Because you're on to something here. Try posting a few pictures of yourself online. Your audience needs to get accustomed to the new you."

The new me? She had a point, but I had to wrap my head around her point some more because her point was very— pointy. "I don't know… "

"You emailed me those pictures of you looking like a fire goddess. That's not any different from posting on social media, is it?"

"It's very different. Two words: haters and trolls." I opened the mini-blinds over my kitchen sink. "Three words, but you get the gist. Ain't got no time to respond to haters and trolls."

"Honey, you're gonna get those anyways. Why let them keep you in hiding?"

I nibbled on my hangnail. Forget the Korean nail salon.

By the time I was through with this conversation, I'd chew off the whole nail.

"See you tomorrow?" Renee asked.

Ain't ready for this conversation. "See you then."

I hung up and exhaled. Sheesh. To get out of the rejection line, I had to do a whole bunch of stuff: no makeup, possibly post pix of myself on social media. What was next? Tap dancing?

If tap dancing was the thing, I'd sign up for classes. No way was I standing in this rejection line forever.

~

*N*o rejection lines. No rejection lines. No rejection lines.

Here I sat, at Apples and Oranges Models' headquarters, barefaced with a few pictures of myself on the phone (not on social media), waiting to see if Renee was gonna pluck me from the rejection line. If she didn't, I was prepared to fight. I'd put too much on the line to stay stuck.

A glance to my right revealed yellowed pictures of commercial models lined around her four walls, women of different ages, colors, shapes, and sizes. None of them was scarred. I swallowed the bitter taste in my mouth. What did Renee see in me again?

Regret took hold. My picture wouldn't fit in on this wall at all.

She was finishing up a phone call, one elbow propped on the dented wooden desk while she held the phone in her other hand. Tortoiseshell glasses perched on her nose. Her fingertips tapped the scribbled desk calendar. It was as if I was sitting in an office from the eighties.

Renee had a rotary phone! Prehistoric.

Seconds later, she hung up. "Sorry about the interruption.

An ad agency called about a go-see tomorrow." Her eyebrows lifted a centimeter. "You have the extra pictures?"

"Uh-huh." I stole another glance at the picture of an unscarred model to my right. Her salt-and-pepper hair spoke her age while her ageless skin spoke her perfection. What did that woman look like when she stepped into the office sans makeup?

"Can I look at the new pictures you brought?"

I grasped my cell phone. "Don't think this is such a good idea after all."

"Why?"

"You don't have one scarred model on your wall." My voice sounded like a deflated balloon, but I didn't care. "They're different in other ways, but no one here looks jacked up."

"Neither do you."

My cheeks got all hot, and I focused on my phone, swiping and sliding my fingers across the pictures on the screen. The phone slipped from my hands. Dang it!

I bent to pick it up, but Renee beat me.

Dang it again!

"And it's a good thing you don't look like everyone else."

"It is?"

"You're unique. Unique is good. Unique can't be codified. It stands on its own." Her brown eyes drilled into mine, cemented her words.

My heart went on a roller-coaster ride, dipping to the lowest of lows, rising to outer space highs, and finally leveling to normal. Thank goodness for the normal.

I glanced away. If I kept focusing on Renee's confident assessment, I'd get motion sickness. I came here wanting to get plucked from the rejection line; now I wanted to stay in the rejection line. I wasn't like these folks on the wall.

"Lemme take a look at these photos." She scrolled through my pix, stopped at one, and squinted.

My stomach got all squirmy. Did she change her mind about my pictures on the phone? Did she absolutely hate them now? Told her I was bad. Woman didn't want to listen.

"The lighting looks off here." Renee held up the phone.

"They're selfies." My voice held the burden of a bazillion bad days.

"Ah yes. I know. But you look fab."

Phew. "You serious?"

"Of course I'm serious." Renee smiled. "That's why I called you in. Those pictures you sent me. The ones with the fiery orange backdrop. Were those for a photo shoot?"

"A photographer friend took my pictures as a test shoot for me. He sent them to the fashion editor at Vogue but didn't make any promises." He hadn't called yet to say yea or nay, which meant Jacinta hadn't sabotaged that one either. Phew.

Renee nodded, apparently impressed with the Vogue mention. "Someone else had contacted me concerning you."

Greta the Ruthless? "Oh really?"

"Yes, trying to remember his name." She raked her hands through her hair.

"His name?"

"Yep, it was a guy." She shuffled through the mess of papers on her dull-looking desk. Greta—a minimalist to the core—didn't have a piece of paper anywhere in her office. "Trying to remember who." Renee pushed her hands through her hair again, annoyance scribbled across her features.

Did it even matter? I didn't want this like I thought I'd wanted. "Renee, I should—"

"Jake. His name was Jake."

Yech. "Jake, the asshole?" The words spilled out, and I wasn't gonna mop them up.

"Er. I know his name was Jake. Not quite sure if he's an asshole." Renee tapped her keyboard, clicked the mouse, and tapped some more.

"Believe me, he's an asshole. He's my husband too but more asshole than husband, if you know what I mean."

Blank stare. "I've never been married."

"Trust my word then."

"Not trying to get into your personal business or anything, but he seemed pretty enthusiastic and sincere when he called. He really talked you up."

"I don't trust him." I tucked my hair behind my ear, annoyed that he'd dare try to interfere in my career. His son tried to kill me, and he was concerned about my modeling?

Silence ensued for a minute, and I noted the soft down-turn of her lips, the slight tensing in her jaw.

Shouldn't have badmouthed my husband during a business meeting. That was completely unprofessional.

Hold up. What did I care about being professional? Wasn't like I wanted to be a client at Apples and Oranges. No matter what she'd said about me being unique and standing out, there was nothing left for me. Time to go.

"I'd like to sign you."

My pulse somersaulted. "You would?"

"Yes." Renee smiled just enough to cause a tingling in my sternum. "You sound surprised."

"I am surprised." I touched my neck and rubbed the rough area around my scars. The woman had to be either very crazy or very smart. Who knew?

"Your pictures are amazing, and your beauty tells a story. The world should hear that story."

Hear my story? My story was depressing. Who'd want to hear it? Besides, I was a model. I posed for pictures and collected a check. Ain't no story other than what the fashion editor wanted for a layout. I toyed with the cuff of my sleeve, gulping down the nerves crawling up my throat.

I'd been talking about getting back on track with modeling for so long now, but when I saw those pictures on the wall and when she talked all this stuff about My Story, I didn't know.

"Something the matter?" she asked.

"I don't have a story."

The pity in her eyes caused me to melt into the plastic seat. Not ice cube melt, but cheesy melt... if there was a difference... I never checked.

"You sure?" she asked.

I didn't know. Was I sure?

One second. Two seconds. Three seconds. This woman was waiting for my answer. Anyone else would've changed the subject by now.

Five seconds. Six seconds. Still waiting. The pressure to answer built and built. I'd had so much to deal with these past few days, I didn't want to figure it out.

"My story's complicated." I blurted. "It's so complicated you probably wouldn't believe it if I told you."

"Complicated is fine. As long as you acknowledge your story, you've made a great start."

Acknowledge your story. Had I somehow got hood-winked into an Alcoholics Anonymous meeting covering as a modeling appointment? This was très weird.

"All of our models have a story to tell. It's our trademark, what sets us apart in the industry." She reached over and she took a thin file folder from her shelf and passed it over. "Here's your representation agreement. Take it home, read it over, and sign and email or mail whenever you're ready. Or you can do so now."

I ran my fingers over the document. This was what I'd

been wanting and yet she was asking for more than a pretty face.

She was asking me to add to her collection of stories.

Did my skin speak? Could it tell my story? What would it say?

Too much.

I flipped the contract over so that only the blank side could be seen. "What if they don't like me?"

"They? Who's they?" Renee asked.

"Everyone who liked me when I was perfect. What if they don't like me?"

"Does it matter anymore?"

A warm breeze rustled through the open window. I lost my career. I lost my husband. I lost my chance to be a mother. Why care whether anyone liked me? Today, I had to live.

"You're right," I said. "It doesn't matter. Not at all."

All this time I was worried Renee would reject me when really, I had to stop rejecting myself.

CHAPTER 29

JAKE

I didn't like feeling powerless.

Here I was, sitting in this courtroom two weeks after meeting with the police, and I felt powerless. I'd been feeling powerless since Tim had agreed to the plea bargain because I knew his fate was sealed. I'd decided I'd take control of the situation by making a statement on Tim's behalf. Not to try and get him out of arson, but to give concrete evidence that Tim was getting better since our initial meeting with Grant.

Okay, okay, okay. That wasn't the whole reason. I wanted to save my son from doomsday fate, from his life getting flushed down the toilet.

We'd rehearsed this moment together just as we had rehearsed the moment at the police station. After our lawyer spoke, I'd speak to the judge first and pave the way. Then, Tim would plead guilty. I sat next to Tim and whispered a quick prayer of desperation.

"All rise," the bailiff announced. Everyone stood while the judge, a sixty-something White man took his seat.

Hoo-boy. This would be a tough one. This guy looked like the type to give Tim the maximum seven years.

After the judge motioned for us to be seated, he peered over his bifocals at the computer monitor. "Today we have Tim Ramirez up for arson. All right," the judge said. "We can begin."

Our lawyer mentioned the plea bargain agreement. Afterward, I stood, ready to make my statement. "Your Honor, I'm Jake Hart, Tim's father. I wanted to discuss—"

"I plead guilty, Your Honor," Tim said, voice certain and sure.

My stomach bottomed out, and I quickly turned. "What're you doing?"

"Pleading guilty."

He said it twice. Dammit. "I haven't spoken—"

"Is there a problem?" The judge interrupted our back and forth.

"No, Your Honor. I—"

This time, Tim stood and headed to the bench. "I'm pleading guilty. My father... has nothing to add."

I opened and closed my mouth twice before deciding what to say. Why'd he change his stance? I was supposed to smooth the way.

"You can be seated, Mr. Hart." The judge's dismissal pecked at my resolve, but I sat. Defeated.

"I read your school reports and the testimony you gave at the school. Your report references gang involvement. Is that true?"

"Yes, Your Honor. I'm a member of the Eighth Street Kings."

My legs turned to liquid, but I stood anyway. He'd told me he was trying to get out of gang life. "Your Honor, Tim has been making excellent progress in school. He—"

"Mr. Hart, I appreciate your sentiments, but he's already admitted to guilt. It's in our purview now."

Hurt crawled inside my chest and made its home there. Feeling snuffed by Tim, I walked away from the bench.

The judge resumed his questioning. "Was this a gang initiation thing?"

"Yes, Your Honor."

Each of Tim's "yeses" drew me farther and farther away from him. All I'd sought to accomplish with him was getting flushed down the drain.

"All right. Then my job here is pretty quick. I'll need another week to deliberate and review your case one more time. Then you can return for your official sentence. In the meantime, you will be assigned to the juvenile detention facility until your sentencing hearing. All adjourned."

Tim slumped into his chair, shoulders rounded. "I didn't know they'd take me away today."

My heart crushed. "You pleaded guilty, son. So... your new life begins. Your next court appearance will only seal the deal, and you'll get your official sentence. Why didn't you let me talk before you? I could've—"

"There's nothing you could've done. I made the mess. I have to live with it." His words were showered in defeat.

I couldn't even save my own son. I couldn't help Hannah. I was the one who messed up, not Tim.

The bailiff headed our way, and I felt like telling him to take me to juvie instead. My son deserved a chance to live his life.

"Let's go to the conference room," the bailiff said.

We followed him there and once I arrived, I asked, "When will he go to juvie?"

"Soon as this conversation is over. The juvenile detention center has pretty decent visiting hours. So as long as he

PRESLAYSA WILLIAMS

behaves, he can receive visitors. That's the only announce-
ment I'll make. You two can be alone."

After he left, Tim leaned against the dry erase board.

"Why'd you plead guilty so fast? We had a plan."

He bit his nail and scratched the inside of his thumb,
apparently deep in thought. "Why delay the inevitable? My
future is fixed. I'm ready to serve my time."

I wasn't ready for him to serve his time.

"Hannah must hate me," Tim added.

"That's a true statement. I'm pretty angry with you too."

"If you see her around, can you tell her I'm sorry?"

"If I see her around, I'm pretty sure she'll run in the other
direction."

There was a knock at the door. The bailiff entered and
put handcuffs on Tim. I shredded inside.

"I'll visit you soon, Tim. I'll visit you often. You're not
alone."

They left, and I was alone. No fatherhood. No marriage.
Just me.

Not only just me: me and guilt. I was a sorry sack of dirt.
I'd hoped to be free from the guilt of my mistakes. I'd hoped
to make something better from all this madness and have
some kind of family. Instead, I'd carry guilt.

Now what? If I wanted a family, I'd have to fly out and see
my parents. I couldn't visit them because I wanted to be here
for Tim. I couldn't bring Tim to visit my parents since he'd
be behind bars. The only thing I could do was visit Tim in
prison and encourage him as much as I could, but he'd be
living out those years, however many years the judge would
decide, behind bars and alone.

Grief settled into my marrow. Deep grief. I would never
allow myself to get into another relationship again. I didn't
deserve it.

CHAPTER 30

HANNAH

Sometimes a person had to suck it up and post the real picture of themselves on the internet. (That person being me.)

The more I mulled over Renee's words regarding the matter, the more her words made sense. I was better off sharing them with others.

After leaving Renee's office, I'd decided to go ahead and upload some pictures. I would've uploaded the ones Tim had taken of me when he was snapping photos in my backyard, but since Tim burned me, that wasn't happening. I'd deleted all of those pictures from my email and my hard drive. I didn't want any memory of him.

Instead, I contacted Miguel and asked for permission to post those pictures online. He said no since Vogue was taking an interest in them. His point of contact was going to share them with the executive fashion editor. Yes!! He'd said they'd let him know shortly, which meant I was gonna have to sign with Renee at Apples and Oranges so she could negotiate the deal. Vogue was big time, and so they probably had a complicated contract. Vogue! I kept my fingers crossed.

If it weren't for Liza's connection, Vogue wouldn't be a possibility for me today. She was the bestest friend ever!

Anyhoo, since those photos weren't usable for social media, that left me with my only other option at this point.

Selfies.

Selfies gave me the heebie-jeebies because I couldn't control the lighting or the angle or anything. Yeah, I could put filters on the pictures, but I'd decided to go sans filter. I wanted to be real as Renee had wisely suggested.

After snapping some selfies, I took a deep breath, uploaded a photo, and wrote a cute comment with the image: "Here I am months after the fire, standing strong. #Survivor"

I hit "post" and my heart seized. Oh my gosh. Oh my gosh. Oh my gosh. Did I expose my unfiltered face to the world?

I did. I did. I did. Anxiety flooded through my body, and I stepped away from the computer and turned off my phone, way too nervous about how folks would react. Gah! This was stressful. Why'd I think this would be a good idea? This was a bad idea. Bad. Bad. Bad.

I exhaled and gathered my frazzled nerves. I did it already, and I had to remember why I'd shared that photo. My story. My scars told a story. I wanted to be true to me. Time to look at the reaction on my social media account.

I tiptoed over to the computer as if it would spontaneously combust into flames or something. After pressing the power button, I waited for a few seconds for it to reboot, and then I logged into my account.

"Here goes," I whispered.

The likes and positive comments immediately flooded in.

So beautiful. So gorgeous!

Wow. Look at her skin. She still glows.

I can't believe the fire did that. But you go, girl.

I smiled. This wasn't so bad.

You look like a freak! Followed by the angry emoji.

She looks gorgeous. Stop being such a hater. Can't stand the haters. Did you even read the comment, bozo?

At least the folks out there were sticking up for me. That was kinda nice. Hmm. I wondered if that anonymous commenter was Jacinta disguised. Could be. I wouldn't put it past her to do something underhanded like that to me. I wouldn't put it past her at all. If I ever saw that girl again, I swear...

Know what? I didn't have to see her again. If Vogue offered me the gig, that would be payback in itself.

Then something odd happened. People started sharing the photo. My pulse quickened, fearful that other people who saw my image wouldn't be as kind as those who followed my page.

Then again, who cared? I didn't care what others thought of my appearance. I was free from all that self-conscious fear.

Most of the people on my page liked my stuff, and most of them were transparent with me. I typed out a "thank you," which garnered a bunch of post likes.

My phone rang, and I glanced at the caller ID. I saw an unrecognizable number but answered anyway.

"This is Melinda, Tim's mother."

My body went cold, and I immediately wanted to hang up. The sound of Tim's name coupled with Melinda's voice made me want to upchuck.

"I know it's awkward for me to call you, but I am getting some free days. I wanted to meet you."

"Meet? Meet for what?" The snark in my voice was beyond apparent.

"Could we meet in person to discuss Tim?"

"For what?" Again with the snark.

"Tim needs help, and there aren't that many places where I can turn. My son..."

"Your son tried to kill me."

"I know what he did, and killing you isn't it. I can't even get in touch with Jake. You're the closest person he has... no other family out there."

I didn't say anything. It wasn't my fault she messed up her life and had limited contact with her son.

Finally, I said, "I saw on Facebook that Tim was sentenced. Why don't you visit Tim in juvie yourself since you'll be out and about?"

"I... I don't feel ready to see him now. Look, I'm not asking for your pity. I haven't been the perfect mother. I've tried my best to be good to Tim. It's just... just that when the pressure got tough, I didn't know what to do and so I checked out with the drugs. Only it made things worse for me and my son. I'm trying to do better. I am."

Her words tugged on something invisible inside, something I hadn't known existed. I thought I was alone in my quest to keep on living despite the setbacks, but I wasn't. Melinda and I were trying to live the best we could. Respect. She had my respect.

"Like I said, I'm not perfect."

I looked at my scars. "I'm not perfect either."

"So can we meet?" Melinda asked.

Melinda deserved a chance for me to hear her out. "Yes."

"That's all I ask. Thank you. The rehab center said I could take off two weekends a month to transition back into the real world. This weekend will be my first stint. Will Saturday work?"

I checked the calendar on my phone. "Saturday works. We can meet at Rita's Diner on Main and Fifth. Do you know where it's located?"

"I sure do. Thank you."

After hanging up, I exhaled. Did I do the right thing?

Should I have agreed to meet Melinda? I hoped so because now I was questioning my decision. Was she playing me?

Whatever. I couldn't worry. I'd agreed to meet, and so I'd hear her out. Nothing more.

❧

I must be the most stupidest person in the world for meeting Melinda.

When Jake had mentioned that he visited Melinda in rehab, I was beyond angry. Yet here I was, meeting with the woman too. All of my frustration with Jake over visiting Melinda, coupled with that fire-happy Tim development, must've made me a sucker.

Yet Melinda sounded so sincere. Mix her sincerity with my experiences, and this was what happened: I showed up at Rita's Diner to meet her in person. I swear if Melinda tried to fight me, I'd karate kick her ass.

I sat at a booth in the rear of the diner and ordered myself some pancakes and orange juice. I definitely wasn't ordering her anything. Melinda would have to pick up her own bill.

"Hannah."

A gaunt, thin woman with dull brown skin and hair pulled into a bun stood before me. "Melinda?"

"That's me." She slid in the booth across from me.

Yeah, Jake was gracious enough to pay you a personal visit in rehab earlier. Even my thoughts were snarky. "Nice to see you," I said politely.

"How are you doing?" she asked.

She wanted to make small talk? Oh no, honey. We ain't making small talk today. "Why'd you want to see me?" I pasted on a fake smile.

Melinda paused, and her fingers got all fidgety. This

woman was nervous. "Would you make a statement on behalf of Tim at his sentencing hearing?"

I looked at her as if she'd grown two heads. "Are you serious?"

"Yes. I know that's an odd request."

"It is an odd request. Jake is better for that sort of thing. Me? Well, I'm the victim here, so I couldn't care less."

"I'm sorry about everything." The lines around Melinda's eyes deepened and shame settled into its grooves. "There's no reason for you to do anything for me. None at all. But my son needs someone who will attest to how he's improved recently. When I'd spoken to him on the phone, he mentioned how much he'd enjoyed working with you."

I opened my mouth to protest, but Melinda cut me off.

"Please don't say no—at least consider my request."

"It won't happen," I said. "Sorry."

Now the shame on her face spread and settled into the lines around her mouth. "Haven't you ever done something very wrong and wished you could undo it and start over?"

Oh no, she wasn't trying to have a heart-to-heart with me. We weren't sistah friends. I wasn't gonna spill my heart to her. "No."

Melinda looked away, defeated.

Now her shame was spreading to me. "Okay, okay, perhaps once or twice I've felt that way." Like my decision to marry Jake. I needed to undo that one quick.

"Then we have something in common," she said, her tone lighter, freer.

I looked at the pockmarks on her arms. The memories of Tim's comment about my arms that day when I'd tried on the dress resurfaced, along with the hurt I'd felt. "Don't compare us."

"I wasn't comparing us. I was… forget it. Meeting you

358

ain't getting me anywhere." The sigh she released sounded like she bore a long, heavy burden.

"There's no point in me making a statement," I said. "Arson is serious."

"He had his entire life ahead of him. Now it's wasted because of me. I want to give him more, but I can't. Please help."

I was quiet.

"Tim had told me about the fire," Melinda continued. "He said he'd made a big mistake and a lot of people were hurt. Some gang member dared him to burn part of the community center. In exchange, the gang leader would pay Tim enough money to cover two months of our rent. I was behind on the rent, and in rehab, and the landlord had threatened eviction. Tim was trying to keep up with the rent and bills for when I got out of rehab."

Tim had mentioned his mama was going through some money problems, and that he was the one managing her checking account and bills while she was in rehab. I didn't know how bad the money problems were—not until now.

I was quiet.

In that space, I recalled the sense of helplessness Tim had felt when he came to my house for tutoring after that street fight. I'd recalled the hope in his eyes when he had taken the pictures of those flowers in my backyard. He was a conflicted kid, but a good one too.

"He was trying to help his mama," Melinda continued. "He wasn't trying to harm you or anyone."

"Did you know of his plans to set the community center on fire?" I asked.

"No. If I did, I would've escaped rehab and whooped his butt. Believe me. I would've."

This changed things.

"When's the court date?" I asked.

"I got a letter from the prosecutor's office. Tim already pleaded guilty in exchange for a plea bargain. The formal sentence will be given on March twenty-fourth at two-thirty at the juvenile hall building near the post office. If you said something, perhaps the judge would lessen his sentence."

"Fine; I'll be there, but I'm not promising a thing."

Melinda's eyes shone with tears. "You don't know how much this means to me."

"Like I said, I'm not making any guarantees that I'll do anything. I'll simply… be there."

~

*W*as coming to court today one of the dumbest things I'd ever done? Yeah. It could very well be.

My high heels clacked against the black-and-white checkered floor of the New Brunswick Family Court. I stopped at the security entrance and dumped the contents of my purse —keys, cell phone, lipstick—into the bin and placed it on the conveyor belt. All my belongings whirred through the machine while my insides twisted. The conversation with Melinda, the aimlessness of her eyes, the dejection on her face, lingered. Didn't know what she was expecting me to do here, but after she told me Tim's reasons for committing arson, I was compelled to be present.

He deserved a better chance. Not a second chance, a better chance. Yeah, Tim had done something awful by setting fire to the community center (and me), but this judge needed to hear the whole story. The kid must've felt so desperate when faced with the prospect of losing the apartment he had lived in with Melinda. When I'd spent time with Tim, he had been trying his best to be a better student and get his life moving in the right direction.

Maybe I could say something to the judge that he'd take into consideration. If Tim were given the right encouragement, then he'd be able to make good for himself from here on out.

I don't know. Maybe I was being soft or something.

No. I wasn't being soft. Tim could be rehabilitated. I'd seen it with my own eyes, and I wanted the judge to see Tim's potential too, especially since he was trying to save his mother from homelessness.

If Tim was imprisoned, Jake would be crushed. Oh my goodness. I actually had an empathetic thought toward Jake. Okay, that was a little odd, but seriously, Jake wouldn't take well to seeing his son imprisoned.

I sighed. In some ways, I was like Tim. I needed encouragement to keep moving forward after all of my disappointments. Jake had been my cheerleader.

All right now, Hannah. That's one too many empathetic thoughts about Jake.

The female security guard patted me down, and I walked through the metal detector with no problems. I made my way to the courtroom, all the while thinking about what I was gonna do when I arrived. I would tell the judge Tim's motivation for arson, but how and when? Not so sure.

After making two lefts, I headed inside and sat in the front row right behind where the defendant—Tim—would sit. I glanced around in search of Jake, but he hadn't arrived. Oh, man. I still hadn't figured out how I would deal with Jake. Did I want a future with him? I wasn't sure. We'd had so much... so much history, painful history. There was no way I could simply forgive and move on from all this.

Never mind. I'd get to that later. The only important thing was making sure I put in a good word for Tim.

The place was packed with people, news media with their cameras and audio recorders and steno notebooks, burn victims like me with their warped, yet healing, skin, and police officers, ready to take Tim away for good.

Something within me crimped. There was a very real chance that the kid's life would be tossed down the toilet in the next hour or so.

Didn't matter. I'd do my part and leave. I mentally rehearsed all that I'd planned to say: how I met with Tim's mother and she had explained their financial troubles. I'd mention the gang's financial offer to Tim, and why he must've thought arson was a feasible idea. As I prepped, my pulse went a million miles a minute, turning all my rehearsed words to mush.

Seconds later, I heard the door open, and the familiar smell of Irish Spring grew stronger and stronger. Jake. I turned, and he headed my way, wearing a dark suit. His skin looked more gray than normal, as did his gaze.

"What're you doing here?" he asked, a bit too loudly.

The murmurs in the courtroom fell to a hush at the volume in Jake's voice, and I bit my lower lip, not wanting to answer in front of an audience of one hundred. Jake slid in the empty space next to me.

"You're here to see Tim get his final punishment, I take it... as is everyone else in this room."

Pity arose, but I said nothing. Seeing Jake was hurting me too. How do we fix us? How do we move on from all this wreckage? "Jake, I—"

"All rise." The bailiff's voice bellowed across the space, and everyone, including me, rose to attention. The side doors opened and Tim entered. He wore one of those orange jumpsuits as if he were already guilty. No one here, save me, knew the other side of the story.

The judge, an elderly White man with salt-and-pepper hair, took his seat behind the bench. Shortly thereafter, the prosecution rose and presented their final statement.

"He's a danger to society! He deserves the harshest sentence!" A voice cried from behind me.

I craned my neck to see who it was, but I couldn't decipher. Everyone looked pissed. Everyone looked ready to crucify Tim. Save for Jake, there wasn't an ounce of empathy in this room. Everyone here saw a thugged-out criminal. Another Black kid who'd ended up on the six o'clock news. A menace to good, White society. Would anyone here want to know his story? His pain and his struggle?

"Give him the electric chair!" another voice yelled.

The judge slammed his gavel. "Order in the court."

Tim hung his head, shame coloring his presence, and my heart crimped. The words he'd spoken about his mother bubbled to the surface.

Mama's going to get better. Sooner than y'all think.

The image of Melinda's gaunt face flashed before me. She deserved a second chance too. Drug abuse shouldn't ruin her life. My eyes stung, and my vision turned blurry. This whole thing was so messed up.

Messed up for Melinda—her financial struggles and drug abuse kept her from being a mama. Messed up for Tim—he faced prison trying to help his mama. Messed up for me—his "helping Mama out" left me burned.

"Is there anyone here who would like to make a statement before I give my sentence?" the judge asked.

This was my chance. "I would, Your Honor."

"Please approach the bench." The judge motioned to me.

I stood and made my way to the front while tucking a stray curl behind my ear. "My name is Hannah Hart. I'm one of the burn victims."

Everyone's gaze landed on me and pressure paralyzed my mouth. Most everyone here would be beyond angry with me if I spoke on Tim's behalf, but I had to tell the judge about all sides of the kid, not only the bad side. I had to tell the full truth to everyone who wanted to see this "thug" get punished.

Tim was a son. Tim was a student. Tim was human.

"After the fire, I got to know Tim. At the time, I wasn't aware he'd set fire to the community center," I said.

"How'd you become acquainted with him?" the judge asked.

"He's my husband's son—my stepson."

I said it.

Tim was my stepson.

I looked over at Tim and Jake, their eyes filled with disbelief. "He's my stepson," I repeated.

The air around me thickened and choked. I saw a flicker of "what is happening?" on the judge's face as if to say, "Is this part of some twisted, dysfunctional family drama?" But he said nothing.

"Continue, Mrs. Hart," the judge said.

"When I discovered what Tim had done, I was beyond angry. Because of our tense family history, I thought Tim had targeted me when he set fire to the center. I felt betrayed."

"You're right. You were betrayed," a voice behind me said.

"Order." The judge slammed down his gavel. "If I hear one more outburst from someone, they'll be removed from the court. Continue, Mrs. Hart."

"When I first learned about Tim, I despised the kid. I probably despised him as much as some of you in the room." I scanned the cold, hard, hurting faces in the crowd. No response.

Best to continue. "I'd felt what you all felt toward Tim a million times over. I first felt anger when he was born." My voice trembled, and I fisted my hand to keep from getting teary-eyed. "My husband had cheated on me, and Tim was the result of that relationship. I wanted to be a mother so... so much."

The words caught in my throat. I hadn't realized true rejection until I stood before this unforgiving crowd and bared my unhealed heart to them.

"You don't have to continue, Mrs. Hart," the judge said.

Didn't matter their reaction. What mattered was Tim's story, the whole story. "No. No. I'll speak. When I found out what Tim did at the community center, when I found out what he did to the victims here today, I was done. Completely done. I didn't want to see Tim or his father again."

"Why'd you come here then?" a man in the crowd asked.

Someone else responded. "Hope!"

"Because now I know his full story, and everyone here should too."

I then explained his mother's addiction, and how Melinda would be on the brink of homelessness after her stint in rehab. I explained the gang's offer. I explained how Tim had been making an improvement in school. I explained his need for grace.

All were silent.

A hot numbness swept over my face. Frustration animated my body, bringing up my chin, stiffening my shoulders. No one cared. "I'm not here to justify Tim's actions, Your Honor. But please know he's a person who has been trying to make it despite tough circumstances. He's not some heartless criminal."

When I sat down, my back tingled. A million daggers were pointed straight at me. Man, I'd get backlash, but I didn't care. I'd said the truth.

Jake's eyes settled softly on me, and a sense of comfort warmed my chest. I managed a slight nod. A favorite image of Jake—his face innocent and anxious when we danced our first dance as a husband and wife, the way he threw his arms around me and kissed me on the lips—rose like a pleasant dream.

The image of Jake faded, and I caught sight of my stepson. We stared at each other for a moment. The tense crowd disappeared, leaving the two of us. No matter what happened, I wanted Tim well and happy, like any good step-mother would.

The judge adjourned for five minutes, and the crowd chattered and moved about. Jake shifted his posture and refocused on me. "You didn't have to speak favorably of Tim, but you did."

I nodded. "I know."

"Why?"

"Because of what Melinda had said, and because I realized nothing is perfect. No one is perfect, but we do what we can. Second chances should be fought for." I searched his eyes for understanding. "And so I did what I could."

"I'm so sorry for the pain I've caused you, Hannah. You're a better person than me," Jake said.

I looked into his eyes and for a moment, I felt peace despite this harsh whirlwind. I reached over and grasped his hand. "I forgive you, Jake."

"Thank you." His eyes shone, and then he blinked rapidly, looking away.

Minutes later, the judge returned, and I exhaled, bracing myself for the decision. "Please don't let it be a harsh one," I whispered to the air. "Please."

Jake and Tim's faces were stone.

"After careful review," the judge said, taking off his eyeglasses. "Timothy Ramirez is sentenced to twenty years in prison. He'll be a juvenile detention facility until he turns eighteen. Then he'll be transferred to an adult correctional center. No parole."

Some cheered, some let out cries of outrage, but I sat there stunned. That was his sentence. That was justice?

That was justice.

"What about the plea bargain?" Jake shot up and shouted. "The plea bargain! You promised! My son gave names of the Eighth Street Kings."

"All judgments can be appealed." The judge slammed his gavel. "Court is adjourned."

"That judge on the bench ain't gave my son no kind of break. We agreed to a plea bargain. They must've made a side deal. Some backhanded crooked nonsense."

"I'm sorry, Jake," I said, unable to say more.

"Ain't nothing to be sorry about. It's something to be angry about. Now I gotta appeal this mess."

"Let's see Tim." We weaved through the crowd and stood by Tim's side. He looked as broken as I felt.

"Thanks for what you said, Mrs. Hart," Tim said. "I know you didn't have to do so."

"Any time. You know you have support out here. Me. Your father and your mother." I paused. "I spoke to your mother. She asked me to come here."

Jake and Tim looked stunned.

A wave of emotions had shaded Tim's face: remorse, hope, longing, sadness. "I know she loves me."

"And so do I," I said without hesitation. "So do I."

Tim bit his lower lip, nodded once.

Forget about me calling Jake a jerk. I was a jerk too, holding on to my bitterness and not seeing how a child was suffering as a result.

Man, Melinda had to tell me they were on the brink of homelessness for me to even show up at court today. Now Tim was getting locked up for twenty years, and I couldn't be a stepmom to him. If I would've accepted Tim earlier in his life, then I could've helped out when they were facing eviction. I hugged Tim. "I'm here for you, son. No doubt."

"True dat," Tim said.

I stepped aside, and Jake spoke to Tim for a moment. Father and son. How many moments had I stolen from them because of my anger? Now Jake would be giving fatherly advice to Tim while he was behind bars.

The sheriff took Tim away and my fingers went cold, and a muscle leaped in my jaw. How would I explain to Melinda? Would she relapse when she found out her son would be gone for twenty years?

Her son. My stepson. I could've done better. I could've handled this whole Jake-Tim-Melinda situation better. Been more mature about the whole thing.

When Tim's orange jumpsuit faded out of view, Jake and I left the courtroom in silence.

Outside, the March sunlight blazed down, and I squinted. A crowd of reporters zoomed in on us and tossed out questions like grenades.

"Mr. Hart, can you tell us the sentence?"

"Is he getting the death penalty?"

"Or life in prison?"

Jake grabbed my hand, and we pushed through the reporters, not answering their questions. What could we say? Tim agreed to a plea bargain. He kept his end of the deal, but the prosecutor didn't. Tim would serve twenty years, and it'd be an uphill battle trying to appeal. That's what happened to young Black men in America. The end.

I spotted my sedan. Time to go home. I released my grip from Jake's hand, but he wouldn't let me go.

"Hey, Hannah," Jake said, voice weary.

"Yeah?"

The words from our last argument hovered between us, wrapped us into the quiet and the tense. The rape I'd experienced. The betrayal I'd felt. All of it. Could we still make something of our marriage? Was there hope for us?

"I was wondering if, you know, since we're still technically married and all, if you'd be willing to spend some time with me? We can go to a café, grab some coffee, and talk. I have a lot on my mind. Don't want to be alone," Jake said.

Some things could be salvaged. All wasn't lost. "Coffee would be good."

EPILOGUE

HANNAH, SIX MONTHS LATER

*T*he first time I married Jake, we had this big, fancy shindig. Today, I'm set to meet him at the family courthouse.

The chauffeur pulls the rented black BMW in front of the court's massive stone steps. A mess of paparazzi waits outside to take my pictures. I had landed the *Vogue* assignment, and when the issue came out last month, I'd become more popular.

Popular meant paparazzi.

That's fine with me. I'm ready for the picture-taking, but I'm not fully ready to renew my vows to Jake while my stepson is behind bars. Those folks broke their promise to Tim. He isn't supposed to serve twenty years.

Tim should be here today as Jake's best man, but he isn't. How do I live with this disappointment? With this—injustice? How do I go on?

I do. I just do.

Jake and I had started going back to marriage counseling too. During our sessions, I'd brought up the sexual assault at the college. The counselor had said I had the right to press charges since (ugh!) that asshole was still working at the university, probably assaulting other young women.

Even if nothing comes from it, I'm going to press charges against the professor—not only for my sake, but for the sake of the other women he could've harmed. Or already harmed. The thought pricks.

Through the car window, I see Melinda standing on the sidewalk. She's wearing a gold dress suit. She actually accepted my invitation.

Our eyes meet, and she waves at me. I wave and smile in return. Unspoken sadness travels between us.

I step out of the car. The bulbs flash and the questions from the paparazzi fly.

"What are you doing here today, Hannah?" a reporter asks.

"Getting married to Jake, my husband." I force out a happy-pained smile. Happy because of Jake. Pained because of Tim.

"You looked fab in Vogue," another says.

"Thank you." I twirl around and pose in my white wedding gown, my scars exposed, my smile more happy and less pained this time. My feelings about Tim's predicament arrive in waves, and I don't think that will change anytime soon. Still, I am set on living my life as fully as I can, despite the imperfect.

"So you're reigniting your career?" a photographer asks.

"Yep. I'm modeling. I'm modeling scarred." I twirl again. I smile another smile, the pain over Tim's current situation still pulsing through my heart.

"Congratulations on renewing your vows." A reporter scribbles in a steno pad.

"Thank you."

I look up, and Jake stands at the top of those stone steps, waiting for me. He looks beyond handsome in his black tux, hair slicked back, eyes gleaming. He is movie star handsome. I love him.

Jake winks at me and makes a kissy-face motion with his lips. I laugh, and the quiet grief I've carried over Tim's situation eases. Not disappearing, but easing.

From here on out, Jake and I will get through this together, bearing each other's joys and sorrows and mishaps and laughter. That is love.

This time when I walk down the aisle, I won't hold tightly to photoshopped pictures of fame and fortune and physical perfection. Instead, I'll hold onto this picture of me, the real me, the one retouched by life's aches, disappointments—and injustices.

I breathe into my skin.

My skin: brown, burned, beautiful.

This is me.

ACKNOWLEDGMENTS

Sitting down to write the acknowledgements for my debut
novel has been a long time coming. There were many
moments in my writing journey when I didn't think I'd get to
this point. Yet here I am.

First, I want to thank God, the Author of my life and my
faith. Thank you for making me the way You've made me.

Thank You for placing me where You've placed me, both
in time and in space.

Thank You for gifting me with Your gifts. I hope to
glorify You with them during the time I have on earth.

To my known and unknown ancestors, thank you for
providing me with your DNA, your memories, your medicine, and your magic. I hope to honor you through the words
I write.

Thank you to editor Lindsay Clyde Flanagan for helping
me to make this book the best it can be! Your encouragement
and insight helped this story shine. I am forever grateful for
your insight and your skill.

To my parents, Laysander and Presentacion, the two

people to whom I dedicate this story. Thank you for everything. I have no regrets, only deep love.

To my husband and my love, Daren. Thank you for helping me get to this point. Your wisdom, focus, and steady resolve have become mine as well. I'm glad to share this life with you.

To my firstborn son, Samuel. You were a baby when I started writing fiction. At the time of this writing, you're a smart, talented, and handsome boy. Whenever you see this book, I hope that you're encouraged to always persevere in your own life. I love you, son.

To my sweet daughter, Hannah. I named this book after you. You have such a lovely heart. Always remember that lasting healing and beauty comes from within. I love you, daughter.

To the writing midwives who helped me birth this story, Sandra Byrd, Erin Lindsay McCabe, and Bethany Kaczmareck. I am thankful for your insight and your confidence in me.

To my writing friends and colleagues, Piper Huguley, Vanessa Riley, Laurie Tomlinson, Dorothy Adamek, Loni Crittenden, Briana Smith, and Jen Cilia. Thank you for the conversations, the laughs, the sometimes cries, and the encouragement.

To the Writing Sisters Mentoring Group, thank you for cheering me on and encouraging me as I wrote this story. May we all see our heart-dreams fulfilled.

To Margo Stebbing, your medicine words have helped me dig deeper in my own writing. Your elder wisdom has helped me connect to my own. Thank you.

To the anonymous author who paid for my writing conference in 2017 when I was ready to quit writing altogether, thank you. I left that conference inspired to finish this story.

To Yonni McPherson, you didn't live long enough to see this day, but I am forever grateful for your support and friendship. Thank you and continue to rest in peace.

To Kyonna McPherson, thank you for babysitting my children so that I can write. May all your dreams come true.

To Lee and Maria Hampton, thank you for your confidence in me.

To all of my patrons who have financially supported me. Thank you for taking this journey with me. This is your story too.

To the magic makers and prayer warriors who have moved mountains on my behalf. Thank you. I am forever grateful.

ABOUT THE AUTHOR

Preslaysa Williams is an award-winning author who writes heartwarming romance and women's fiction with an Afro-Filipina twist. Proud of her heritage, she loves sharing her culture with her readers.

She earned a master's degree in public administration from the College of Charleston. Preslaysa then earned a second master's degree in writing popular fiction from Seton Hill University. She also has an undergraduate degree from Columbia University.

Preslaysa is a professional actress, a planner nerd, an avid bookworm, and a homeschool mom who wears mismatched socks. Visit her online at www.preslaysa.com to sign up for her newsletter.